I0589840

THERE CAME A
CONTAGION

DOUG INGOLD

Wolfenden

THERE CAME A CONTAGION

All rights reserved. No part of this book may be reproduced or transmitted in any form or by any means, electronic or mechanical including photocopying, scanning, recording, or by any information storage system without the written permission of the author, except for brief quotations in a review.

Copyright © 2021 by Douglas A. Ingold

ISBN 978-0-9973513-1-6 (print)
ISBN 978-0-9973513-2- (e-book)

Library of Congress Control Number: 2021902892

Published by

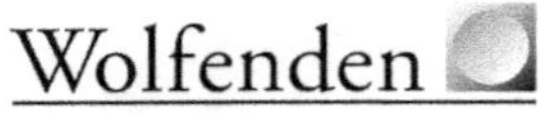

Arcata, California
wlfndn3@gmail.com
wolfendenpublishing.com

Cover, Layout & Design:
Robert Stedman Pte Ltd, Singapore

Printed in the USA

Other novels by
Doug Ingold

Rosyland: A Novel in III Acts

SQUARE

The Henderson Memories

In the Big City

This Novel is dedicated to
Nina Haedrich
(Her memory inspired it, her support and assistance sustained it.)

With additional thanks to
Jan, Steve, Cynthia, Robert and **Gabrielle**

This is a work of fiction. Names, characters, places and incidents are either products of the writer's imagination or used fictitiously. Any resemblance to actual events or locals or persons living or dead is entirely coincidental.

THERE CAME A
CONTAGION

THE FAMILY

ONE

The woman Arved, the wife of Basil Helgen, a farmer in the village, had become pregnant with their second child. The first birth (that of their son Johannes, named after his stern grandfather, who at that time still lived and dominated the home) had nearly cost Arved her life, and Basil had determined to never cause her to become pregnant again.

"I will protect you," he promised. "I will keep you safe." And Arved, wan, the infant Johannes at her breast, had responded, "Yes, Helgen. If that is your wish."

His fear of a second pregnancy combined with the physical demands of their work, the crowded conditions in which they lived and the church's condemnation of all sexually related pleasure kept them apart for several months. The very real problem was that they were profoundly and passionately attracted to one another. As the weeks passed, as the boy grew and their lives returned to their familiar rhythms, looks passed ever more frequently between them. Hands reached out to touch, lips brushed. Every impulse called for their bodies to be entwined.

His wife was capable of a kind of wonderment, it seemed to Basil, a passion that was vaguely frightening, almost blasphemous. And yet, when they were separate from one another, he with the scythe in his hands, she in the house spinning with the other women, there would arise in him a desire—one more powerful than anything he had ever experienced—a desire to bring her again into that state of wild, clinging passion.

"Away," he would mutter aloud, the scythe swinging, the sun hot on his shoulders. "Get away from me, fiend." For how could he explain the all-consuming hunger that rose in him, rose in direct contradiction to his intent, except to attribute it to some outside force?

"I will withdraw myself," Basil whispered one night, his voice husky. "Before the end I will withdraw myself." Blushing slightly, his wife lowered her eyes causing him to add: "Your safety is my desire."

Arved did not lift her eyes; she stroked his neck with delicate fingers, and pulled his face closer to hers.

Then one night, when the child Johannes was almost five, Basil Helgen failed.

§

It was Basil's mother, the widow Marsel, who first suspected a change in Arved. She noticed that her daughter-in-law rarely spoke now in the morning, while before she had often hummed, and late in the evening, Marsel would hear her praying aloud in a singing, chant-like voice. Then one morning she followed Arved outside. She found her holding back her hair with one hand and pushing against the woolen folds of her dress with the other as she retched onto the ground.

Marsel placed her hand on Arved's belly. "My child, have you yet told your husband?" At that point she had to catch the suddenly sobbing young woman to keep her from collapsing entirely.

Basil and Jacob had already left for a day of cutting firewood in the forest. When they returned, smelling of pine resin, their hands and forearms dark and sticky with the substance, Basil entered a room filled with women, all of whom went suddenly silent. In addition to his mother and wife, Jacob's wife Klara was there, holding the baby Irmele; beside her was Sabastian's bride Ursula, and Arved's two sisters: Anna, with her daughter Agnes, and Gisele, the mother of the boy Zacharias.

When Jacob entered the room a moment later, he witnessed a scene he would not soon forget. He saw Basil sit down heavily and call for beer. Then Arved stepped away from the other women; she approached her husband, and with trembling lips, whispered something to him. Jacob saw his brother jump to his feet and call out: "My God, I have killed you and damned my very soul!" Then he turned and ran from the room.

The women were gasping and crossing themselves. They rushed to Arved who had fainted and fallen to the floor. Looking out, Jacob saw his brother half running as he left the property entirely.

It was after dark when Basil returned to the Helgen home. With him was Frau Rachel Mueller, the village midwife. The women in the family were surprised to see the two of them together; Frau Mueller was not normally seen walking about in the company of a man. Gray, short and spiny, it was generally believed she had never married, though there were rumors to the contrary. She could be seen trekking alone over the fallow ground or along the river, a pouch slung over her shoulder. In addition to midwifery, she knew plants and their uses in medicines, and it was said she utilized incantations and charms in her practice. Rachel Mueller was a person whom if you went to see, you went in private and in need, as had Basil with his dark and sticky hands on that fateful evening.

Frau Mueller was made welcome by the women and offered beer, which she declined. She sat across from Arved who was still crying softly, and she studied her for a few moments. Then she asked to meet with the young woman in private. When the two of them returned, she spoke privately with Basil who nodded his head solemnly. Then she insisted that he and the other males leave the room including young Johannes and his cousin Zacharias who were watching wild-eyed from a doorway.

When the men had gone, the midwife spoke: "We must do what we can to help this woman survive her pregnancy and to bring into life a new child." She removed a small packet from her pouch, which she tied around Arved's neck. "We do not want you sneezing, my girl. Sneezing weakens the womb.

Avoid intimacy with your husband. I will speak to him about this. And keep your eyes and thoughts away from ugliness and death. Attend no funerals. If you encounter a body in the street, be it animal or man, turn away. And your workload must be lightened. On the other hand, I don't want you lying about in bed like some lazy duchess who expects her food brought to her and her hair combed by a dutiful servant! I have seen your needlework. This you should keep up. Just avoid lifting sacks of grain or pushing about barrels of beer or kraut. I will come regularly. And when I approach this house, I want to hear your laughter ringing out and your voice singing. Do you understand?"

"I do," Arved answered, wiping her eyes.

"You will bring to us a beautiful child," Rachel Mueller said softly, and she bent down and placed her hands on Arved's shoulders.

TWO

Autumn arrived with its smoky air. The sow had delivered a healthy litter. The cereals had been harvested and safely stored. Where winter rye had been planted, the strips of land showed now blankets of pleasing green. And Advent, that season of cruel nights and bitter days fast approached. Time had come for the Helgen family to deliver its annual rent to the abbey.

The journey would take a full day, and Basil, Jacob and Sebastian were outside before light. They packed the wagon with sacks of grain and hoisted the yoke onto the oxen. The ground was hard with frost. The oxen huffed vapor from their nostrils; the heavy wheels creaked and the men walked alongside wrapped in sheepskin coats.

This would be the brothers' first trip to the abbey without their father. The stern Johannes had died suddenly on the Sunday that commemorates the birth of Saint John the Baptist, and Basil had inherited the land and house. The law did not require that property pass from father to eldest son, but that had been Johannes's will. The brothers had learned the details while seated in the notary's office a short time following their father's death.

The three of them felt muted in the large room with its polished furniture, its cushioned chairs, the table stacked with papers covered with seals and incomprehensible writings. The notary himself was intimidating. An older man, he had a wart at the center of his wide forehead, gray, bristly hairs shooting out from his ears, and what struck Jacob most strongly, on the man's soft fingers jeweled rings that reflected the light entering through the window.

The words read from the will stunned the young men, though the brutal directness of their father's decision struck them as typical of the man under whose dominion they had grown. As a child Johannes had had his right foot crushed beneath the hoof of an ox, and his determined limping stride—as if he were punishing that crushed foot with every step—revealed the character of the man. They could picture him making a decision in mid-stride and turning suddenly into the office of the notary.

He would have demanded that the will be written out then and there. After the text had been slowly read to him, he would have made his mark and watched closely as the mark was witnessed and the document sealed. Then, after setting coins on the table, their father would have abruptly left. Each son could imagine the expression of smug contempt that would have appeared on his face as he returned to the street. It all rang true. Some wave of irritation, some slight, real or imagined, followed by a sudden act that he revealed to no one.

But after the notary had read the will, and after Basil had recovered from the shock, he made a declaration. Yes, he understood that the Helgen holdings, their home, the lands they owned and those they leased, all passed to him, subject to the rights of their mother. And should Basil wish, upon his death his son (the dark-haired five-year-old who stood now at his knee staring with unabashed curiosity at the ugly notary and his finery) would inherit the estate as well. But as to the house and the land itself, both the strips they owned and those they leased from the abbey, it was Basil's promise that the benefits should go equally to himself and his brothers. It was his intent that Jacob, Sebastian and their wives continue to live in the home and farm the land with him, not as hired workers but as partners equal in every way. For all practical purposes, the three of them would be shared owners of the Helgen family inheritance.

The younger brothers looked at each other and then at Basil. The notary, after a moment's pause, and perhaps calculating the additional fee he could charge, proposed that he should reduce the boys' verbal understanding to a formal written agreement that he would date and they would mark and he make binding with his seal. He would draft the document in triplicate, he proposed, three originals each dated, marked and sealed. Having expressed this sound advice there arose on the face of the notary an expression of competence and pleased self-regard.

For a moment the brothers appeared paralyzed. Perhaps each of them was asking himself what he would do with such a document. Where would he put it? How would he keep it safe? And what use could it possibly have, given that none of them could read? Or perhaps it was just that they loved and trusted one another, because Jacob, who was the second oldest son shook his head. Then Sebastian did the same, and Basil said to the notary: "That won't be necessary."

§

"They say horses are faster," Sebastian suggested as the brothers and their oxen left the village in the first light.

"And more expensive," Basil said. "A man would need give two oxen to get himself a decent horse. And what good is one horse?"

"Give me the ox," Jacob agreed. "A temperamental animal, the horse, twitchy. Given to moods. The ones bred for riding even more than your draft animal. They'll kick at you if they don't like the cut of your beard. But a good ox is like a good brother. You can count on him when you need him."

"But a man has two horses," Sebastian persisted. "Two good draft horses trained to the harness, he'd be over this rise and gone by now."

"Our boy's in a hurry," Jacob said, nudging Basil in the ribs.

"A good thing we got all day," Basil said.

When they reached the top of the rise, they could see where the road skirted the lower side of the large forested hill that rose up behind the village. They paused to give the oxen a breather and as they passed a jug of beer among themselves, they watched a solitary crow rise up from the trees in the distance. The bird set out on a flight directly toward them. As they turned and watched, it flew down toward the village and was out of sight in the direction of the pastureland on the other side. Soon there came others, alone or in groups of two or three, each silent, each making deep strokes with its wings. A hundred or more must have passed as they stood watching.

"Your raven will play," Jacob said. "He'll soar and tumble and spin. He'll make more sounds than a clown at a street fair. But these crows look to have a job to do. They got no time to glide, no idea to look around. And you'd think they had no word to say, not for good or ill, not to you, not to me, and not to each other."

"They don't speak good to me," Basil said. "All I see is black, a sky of black."

The three fell silent for a moment. Then Sebastian said, "Your woman will be all right, brother."

"The boy's right," Jacob agreed. "I heard Arved singing sweetly just last night. She's strong, that girl. Bright of spirit. She'll get through this."

Basil did not respond. He watched the last of the crows disappear, then turned and grunted at the oxen to get them moving.

It was noon when they reached the old Roman bridge. A boat stacked with large barrels, its sail up, was being towed upstream by a man riding one horse and snapping his whip at two additional horses in front of him. The towrope stretched from the rear horse back to the hull of the boat and then on to the mast. A man standing in the hull, his hands gripping the rope, was shouting something at the horseman but his words could not be understood from the bridge. In the water flowing below them, Sebastian saw three snow-white swans. When their heads and necks disappeared beneath the surface, their bodies resembled large inanimate mounds of floating feathers.

At the city wall they turned the team south and made their way along the cobbled street toward the abbey. The wheels of the wagon scraped, the oxen snorted, their hooves spreading awkwardly and slipping on the uneven stones. Near the abbey guardhouse, a man stood wrapped in skins. He was moving his legs about and stomping his feet as if cold. Beside him was a horse loaded on either side with finely shaped leather boxes.

As Basil set off for the guardhouse, Sebastian approached the man and began a conversation, sliding his hand along the horse's flank.

"Twitchy, is she?"

"Not even on a Sunday, lad. Her mood's as smooth as cream atop the pail."

Sebastian crouched down and felt along the horse's foreleg. Then he leaned back on his haunches and studied the leg. "God gave them a strange construction when you look at it. Knobs and all, a spindly sense about it, one joint here opposite the one there. And a single toe only, not like the pig, the sheep or the ox." He stood and stepped back a pace. "But they are a handsome creature overall. Where, may I ask, do the problems show up?"

"Problems tend to show up wherever and whenever they are least needed, lad. That is true of man and beast in my experience. But with the horse, I'd say in the leg, the foreleg more than the rear. You have more familiarity with the ox, I take it."

"I do. I hold great admiration for their tolerance and strength. But in their rolling eyes I sometimes see what I fear may be a great hatred."

"Hatred, do you?"

"I do. It's like the coals of a fire that's been bedded down for the night. It smolders below the surface, another burden, I imagine in the journey God has given them, a sullen hatred that they must cart from here to there and beyond."

The man seemed to think about that. He studied the oxen standing thick and stolid before the wagon, the yoke heavy on their necks, their horns glinting in the light. Then he said: "Hatred is a heavy burden indeed, lad. And one born by many with less strength and less patience than the ox."

Jacob had approached and was examining the leather boxes secured on the horse. He ran a hand carefully across the surface of the one near him, and bent close to study its seams and fastenings.

"Now, these announce an excellent craftsman, sir," he said to the man. "An artisan who is skilled in his work. One capable of recognizing the best materials, who has the means to acquire them and the skill to wisely use them."

"Your eye is clear, my friend. I have kept them hidden beneath a covering for much of my journey for fear the packaging would attract thieves as likely as their contents. You might note as well my attire, which resembles that of a picker who ambles about in search of that which has been discarded by others. All of a purpose, I assure you. The countryside is alive with brigands and zealots and I have passed among them without serious notice. But my disguise has proven itself too clever on this frigid morning. That quarrelsome guard at the gate has refused me entrance!"

"And why is that?" Sebastian wanted to know.

"He claims that I am but one of those who, these last days, I have successfully avoided. I removed the covering on arrival to show that sour fellow that I had goods of value to deliver but so far to no avail. He trusts me not and he believes little of what I have to say. Even my naming of the Mother Superior at St. Scholastica did not persuade him. 'A name can be spoken by anyone' was his foul-breathed dismissal. 'A name is not a letter written and signed under seal.' But the Mother Superior did not think to give me such a letter. She naively assumed I would be made welcome, even embraced for the good service I have rendered. Those of good heart are fools, I tell you. She, who would have welcomed one such as me, assumed the same would be true at this dismal place. Yet this man treats me like vermin when I had expected to be made welcome with food and drink, with hay for my horse and a comfortable bed for myself."

"Has he refused you outright?" Sebastian asked, returning from the wagon with the jug of beer and some bread.

"He insists I wait here in the cold until he has had an opportunity to meet with his superior, which he is in no hurry to do. Has he gone to his superior? No, he has not left his post this past hour or more. Has he sent for his superior? That I doubt as well. Certainly no one has come to consult with him, or to examine the materials I have to deliver. The materials I have, I assure you, will speak for themselves. Once they are seen and examined, I will be made welcome. Yet even now he is chatting amiably with that fellow and seems in no hurry to accommodate my needs." He paused to take a bite of bread and a swallow of the beer. "Well now, I thank you, lad. This beer is as fine as any I have tasted in a while."

"That fellow is our brother," Jacob said. "He is well known here. Perhaps he will be able to assist you if the guard remains unwilling to do so."

"If your brother can pry me past that villain, I will be in his debt beyond question. Those with a modicum of power, I tell you, delight in tormenting those with none."

Jacob moved again to the patient horse and stroked the leather box with the tips of his fingers. "These are indeed handsome satchels, friend, and finely made. Can you reveal to us from where you come, and the items you have been transporting in them?"

"From where I come I may speak," the man said. "I began my journey at St. Scholastica, the Benedictine nunnery at Dinklage, far to the east. I have been passing through exposed country for seven days, sleeping in stables and on the floors of churches. Though I stand now at the very gate of safety, until that foul man grants me entrance, I must maintain my silence as to the purpose of my journey. As to the satchels, however, I can inform you that they were fashioned by a master craftsman in the city of Leipzig. A man who goes by the name of Julius. His reputation is well known in that country. Look, your brother has at last freed himself from that devil."

Basil had left the guardhouse. As he walked toward the wagon, he motioned for his brothers to join him.

"We're to proceed to the granary where Elias will meet us."

"Brother," Sebastian asked, "can you help that man? He has been denied entrance by the guard."

Basil chuckled. He grunted at the oxen and slapped the near one on the shoulder. As they passed through the gate, he said, "That fellow will soon have his goods examined, and assuming they are as he says, he will be made welcome."

"But why has he been made to wait all this time? He's been on the road seven days, he tells us, sleeping in stables and on the floors of churches, and is here left to stand and wait."

"He may be a fine fellow, Sebastian, and his purpose may be sound, but as the guard tells it, he has no manners and less patience. He arrived in a sullen state and behaved like a disgruntled noble, demanding to see the abbot himself without delay. Simply put, he does not know how to speak to a man in a guardhouse. This guard kept me there talking, entertaining me with gossip and jokes for the sole purpose, I suspect, of annoying your friend back there. And what did I do? I listened and laughed of course, and told a few stories of my own. I am not a fool. And now we are inside and he is still without."

Visible to them now at the far end of the courtyard was the great arched entrance to the two-spired abbey church. In its underground crypt, encased in stone, were the remains of an apostle, dead and venerated for more than fifteen hundred years. Over the centuries, the Helgen family and thousands of others had made pilgrimage to the site.

Basil was not a man given to sentiment, but he could not set eyes on the church's façade without experiencing again the holy terror he felt first the time he descended into that smoky, torch-lit crypt to stand before the saint's strange cubic encasement. Flickering shadows and wisps of smoke moved over and around it; glints of light reflected off the carved walls of the small cave in which it rested. The object had seemed to him a thing alive.

THREE

About the hour the wagon was making its way through the abbey's gate, Arved and her mother-in-law, the widow Marsel Helgen, were walking home from church; they went daily now to pray for the coming child. Their heads were wrapped in wimples, their arms interlocked. They moved slowly and their heavy skirts brushed against each other; the wooden pattens on their shoes made walking somewhat precarious.

The days of morning sickness had ended for Arved. She was often ravenously hungry and Marsel had become her guardian angel; she prepared soups and stews and served them in a large wooden bowl accompanied by chunks of dark bread that the older woman broke off by the fistful, grunting audibly as she ripped it free from the loaf.

The widow Marsel had borne six children, five of whom had survived to adulthood. In addition to her three sons, she had two daughters, both older than the boys. The daughters had entered the service of the church which had been a source of pride to her. But she had no contact with them, so she extended her maternal impulses toward her three daughters-in-law. And of the three, Arved seemed to her the most precious and the most vulnerable. A shadow of fragility hung about the girl. Marsel fought this idea; she prayed for its removal, but it kept coming back to her.

She had known the young woman since birth. When Marsel first arrived in the village as the young bride of Johannes, Arved's mother, a woman named Hette, had befriended her. Hette had been dead now five years, and that too—the fact that Marsel had lost her closest friend and Arved her mother— strengthened the bond between them.

Marsel hated walking in pattens. She hated it only slightly less than she hated scrubbing filth off her shoes, which is why she wore them. On every walk she complained of them, sometimes vehemently. Each time Arved listened and commiserated, and was never so cruel as to say, "Mother, you have told me that a dozen times!"

The two walked very slowly. Perhaps Marsel even exaggerated her need for caution and the importance of Arved's steadying arm; she wanted to extend this private time as long as possible.

As they neared the house, Marsel asked about Basil, her voice quiet. By outward appearances her son seemed to have accepted the pregnancy. That outburst, when first he learned of it, so uncharacteristic of him, so shocking to everyone, had not been repeated. He was always busy, of course, as were all three of her sons. Much of their work was physical and tiring, and the women accepted that when the men entered the house they needed to be accommodated in subtle ways. Not mothered, not babied, not sympathized with, but given a chair, given food and drink, given a chance to rest; all done at a respectful distance.

In some ways, the women behaved toward the men in the same way the men behaved toward their domestic animals: they provided for their needs without sentimentality or overt affection. Yet, the women's task required greater subtlety. A man knew that the ox was larger and stronger than he; that it could with a sudden move crush him against a stable wall or with a step smash his foot as had happened to the boys' father. Still, they presumed a position of dominance over the ox, the boar, the sow with her litter. The women on the other hand, should they determine that a man needed guidance, had to provide it in a manner that was undetectable to anyone, often to the man himself. In the application of this subtle skill, Marsel was an expert. She had learned these talents by necessity, having lived with and outlived the volatile Johannes.

So Marsel, while her mind may have been slipping, and her steps less steady, remained the unquestioned matriarch of the Helgen family. It was her nature to be attuned to the moods and activities of every family member. She was not comfortable unless she knew where everyone was, what he or she was doing, thinking and worried about. Thus, she asked her daughter-in-law on this morning about her oldest son, and was surprised when Arved suddenly began to sob.

Young women sometimes sobbed in Marsel's experience, especially young women who were pregnant; she said nothing at first but kept walking slowly, her left arm entwined with Arved's right. The morning was cold but not uncomfortably so. A woman approached bearing two buckets hanging from the ends of a pole that was balanced on a pad across her shoulders. She and Marsel greeted one another and Arved too nodded through her tears.

But though she might have appeared outwardly calm, Marsel's mind was roiling. Basil was the block, the foundation stone around which the family was constructed. Without his stability, cracks would soon emerge, and that which appeared solid would begin to crumble.

"You can speak to me, child," she said now. "Tell me what weights so heavily on your heart."

"He..." Arved began, "he is wonderful to me, surely you know. And to little Johannes as well. I am so grateful that he came to me and that you have taken me into your family. I have him because of you and I have my son because of him. So, I owe everything to you. You are my mother now, my only mother..." Arved began to cry again.

"Child..."

"No, Mother, I must tell you. I have caused him such pain!"

"No!" Marsel jerked her arm against Arved's elbow as if trying to wake her.

"Yes! He thinks that he has killed me. In our bed he puts blankets between us. He rolls them up and makes a wall to separate us. He is afraid to touch me!"

They walked a few more steps in silence. When Marsel spoke again it was almost a whisper. "Arved, listen to me carefully. Do you remember what the midwife told you? That you should avoid intimacy with your husband? Did she not say that? Did she not say she would speak to Basil as well? He is trying to protect you, child. He is trying to keep you safe."

But Arved was not convinced. "I'm sorry, Mother, what you say may be true, but you have not seen how he looks when he comes upon me by surprise, when his mind is unprepared. He thinks I am dead, or as good as dead. He believes that he has killed me when the opposite is true. It was my lust, my desire for a second child, that held us together. I wanted him inside of me. I would not let him go! It is I who brought this pain to him." And Arved continued to cry.

§

The oxen stood thick and stoical, absorbed in dreams of their own devising. They were still yoked and on the wagon the bags of grain remained secured and untouched. No progress was going to happen for a while, it seemed, because Brother Elias was being shaved by the novice Daniel. Basil and his brothers sat on barrels watching and laughing because Elias was a talkative fellow who was not about to stop talking just because he was being shaved.

The Helgens watched the long blade enter and leave the pail of hot water and its sharp edge tremble slightly as it slid up along the throat. The throat belonged to Elias but it was the novice Daniel whose fear caused the blade to tremble. Daniel was right to be terrified, it seemed to Basil, because while in his hands was the power to cut or even to kill, it was he who would suffer the most pain should a mishap occur. And it seemed impossible that some mishap not occur because Elias was talking constantly, moving about and taking every opportunity to pinch the boy on his backside. The gesture brought a grimace to Daniel and a leering wink from the monk.

Elias was a heavy man about fifty years of age in a gray tunic. He had a long cloth belt loosely tied around his middle and the belt slid up and down as he moved, seeming now over and now under his heaving belly.

"This boy fucks the pigs, don't you, boy?"

"Oh no, sir," Daniel stammered, seemingly aghast.

"Come now. Don't lie to me. Which do you prefer, the sows or the boars?" And Elias started laughing so hard he had to push Daniel away.

They were clustered near the doorway of the granary, sitting in the sun. On the yard in front of them several ravens pecked in the dirt and hopped about.

"It is the nature of ravens to hop rather than walk, is it not Brother?" Jacob asked the monk a short time later. "I always see them about when I am here."

"They're here because we feed them, Jacob," Elias said. He turned and quizzed the novice, "Tell the gentlemen, boy: why do the ravens hop?"

"God gave them the hop in gratitude, sirs," the boy said. He had successfully finished the shave with little or no blood spilled and was drying the blade with the hem of his tunic.

Elias nodded. "And why did our Lord do that? Can you tell these fine gentlemen?"

"It was the raven who saved the life of Saint Benedict, the founder of our order, sirs." Daniel had turned to face the three men. He recited this information proudly as if he had but recently learned it.

"That's right. And tell us how did the raven do that?"

"Some jealous monks had put poison in the saint's bread, sirs. But before the saint could eat it, a raven flew down. He grabbed the bread and flew off with it."

"That's correct. And what happened to the jealous monks, boy?"

"They are burning in hell, sir."

"Even today?"

"Now and forever, sir."

"Now and forever," Elias repeated meaningfully, winking at the three men.

Finally, the time came in Elias's mind to unload the wagon. The bags were removed and set on the granary floor. The yoke was taken from the oxen and they were given hay. After the grain had been examined, and the bags weighed and safely stored, Basil suggested it was time for them to start back.

Elias, who appeared to have grown quite fond of Sebastian, and who stood now with his arm around the youngest son's waist, pointed a thick finger at Basil and said, "Now, there, gentlemen, is your father's truest son."

"Brother Elias," Jacob replied, "one look at the three of us and it is clear and each is the true son of our father."

"I'm not questioning your mother's virtue, Jacob. I'm sure she is a devout and faithful child of God. I refer to temperament, not lineage. And in that department, Basil is the truest son. Never in my long days did I meet a man less patient, more eager to be off, less willing to enjoy a mug of wine or a pleasant conversation than your father. From the moment he passed the guardhouse he started looking for an excuse to leave, stomping about with that limp of his, twitching that long whip he carried. You'd have thought our abbey was a cage bound on all sides with bars."

"It's true," Basil admitted. "Our father was an impatient man. When I came here with him as a boy, he always wanted to leave while I would have preferred to stay awhile. But now I am a man and I know the long road home and what chores await us when we get there."

"Today you are a lucky fellow, Basil. For I am granting you a brief chance to be a boy again."

Elias laughed over his shoulder as he said this. He had started walking with Sebastian toward the abbey dormitory. The four of them entered the building and descended a flight of stone steps to a cellar where the cool, damp air smelled of fruit and fermentation. A faint amber light entered through thin barred windows. They stood on a floor that was wet in places, the corridor flanked with barrels of various sizes.

On a tall table below one of the windows were several brown ceramic mugs. Elias filled four of them from a wooden spigot and passed them around. They toasted and drank.

"The delicious beer Sebastian offered me earlier, has given me an idea, gentlemen. You are skilled farmers, as was your impatient father before you. More than skillful, you are honest and dependable, as was he. For all his intemperate hurry, we found him and now you to be worthy associates."

As he walked them around the cellar, Elias described the contents of the various barrels, the years of their vintage, the farms where the grapes were grown. Back at the table and still talking, Elias was preparing to pour more wine when Basil interrupted him.

"We appreciate your hospitality, Brother Elias, and your wine is well-flavored. But if you have an idea you wish to discuss I would like to hear it sooner rather than later. Our oxen are steady but they refuse to hurry."

Elias looked at Jacob and Sebastian and shook his head. "Perhaps the two of you should load the oxen on the wagon and yoke your brother to the front. That would get you home in no time."

Jacob and Sebastian laughed, not only at the joke, but at Elias who had found his own remark so hilarious that his laugh turned to coughing and he spilled what remained of his wine.

After he had collected himself, and after he had replenished their mugs, Elias began to talk about some ground that stood adjacent to the two strips of abbey land the Helgens were presently farming.

The brothers looked at one another. "Yes, we know that ground," Basil said. "That is wild ground, never broken to the plow."

Jacob nodded. "I've walked over it. It's rocky."

"And uneven," Sebastian said. "It climbs the hillside."

"According to our records it was farmed," Elias said. "Two hundred years ago, before the Lord sent the black death to purge the people. More souls lived in these parts then, more than now."

"A man would need four or five teams of oxen to pull a plow through that ground," Basil said, shaking his head. "And the ground is not good. It's pale and shaley, given to washing in heavy rains. The rye would be spindly, the barley spare. Lots of work and little return."

"I agree," Jacob said. "You'd have to dig out those rocks before you could touch it with a plow."

"And there are trees that shade the higher ground. They would need be cut down and the trunks removed, the roots dug out…unless…" Sebastian, paused. He looked at his brothers and then at Brother Elias. "Unless you're speaking about vines."

"Vines?" Jacob and Basil stared at Sebastian as if the word was blasphemous.

"God gave the brains to the youngest boy," Elias stammered. And his laugh again caused him to bend over and stagger about.

The brothers continued to stare at one another. They knew about vines. Their father had nothing but contempt for grapes and the people who grew them. And what their father believed he had repeated often and with vehemence. So, they were well-schooled on vines. A man might enjoy a bunch of grapes as a treat, their father conceded. And now and then at the market, he would barter for a few raisins that he passed around among his family. But basically, grapes could only be made into wine, and while wine could get you drunk, it did not feed you. Beer was a food. Yes, you could get drunk on it too but in the process it gave you strength. And that was just the start of it. Vines were a weed, according to Johannes. They grew on bad ground just like any other weed, and Johannes hated both bad ground and weeds. Bad ground grew no grain, while on good ground, weeds and vines took up space where rye and barley could be grown. Moreover, if you planted rye in the fall by the next summer you had fresh bread. You planted barley in the spring and that fall you had fresh beer. With vines, you planted and you waited for years while they took their time growing up and when they finally did, all they gave you were grapes. And lastly, Johannes would tell them, you can store rye and barley for years. If you are a good farmer, if you are diligent and prudent, you will have a storehouse filled with rye and barley. And when crops fail—and there will be years when crops fail—you will still have bread to eat and beer to drink, while the grape farmer will be lucky to possess a handful of raisins to share with his family.

The brothers waited for Elias to regain control of himself, then Basil asked, "What are you proposing Brother?"

"That land lies fallow," Elias said, the emphasis falling on the last word as if he were equating a lack of cultivation with a mortal sin. He rested his gaze on Sebastian. "You're right, boy. Vines. That does not mean you grow less rye or less barley. But you will also grow grapes. Here at the abbey we need more grapes, it's that simple. We ship wine to distant locations. It's in demand. Moreover, we are developing a process. I would show you. I would give you a tour, permit you to taste a sample, but big brother here would object. I note that he is already leaning toward the door."

Basil was tilting toward the doorway, and being so exposed, he balanced his weight on both of his stout legs and said, "I'm prepared to hear you out, Brother Elias, assuming you can complete your explanation prior to the resurrection."

"It's called distillation," Elias continued, ignoring the deadline. "It's like the first of our Lord's miracles. You will remember the wedding party in Canaan, where our Savior turned jugs of water into jugs of wine. Well, with distillation, we turn wine into a drink called brandy. It's complicated, it calls for precision, and it requires a great deal of wine to made a modest amount of brandy. So, simply put, we need more grapes."

"I would enjoy seeing the equipment, learning the process," Sebastian said. Then, after glancing at Basil, "Some other time, of course."

"With vines, you plant and you wait," Basil said. "You do the work and you receive no return for years. I am still waiting to learn our benefit, Brother Elias. You get the grapes, but we…"

"We wouldn't have to plow, brother," Sebastian said. "Not as we do with rye or barley."

Jacob nodded. "Or remove the rocks. Certainly not all of them."

"And the trees at the upper end could wait. We could start near the bottom," Sebastian suggested.

Smiling in the dim light, Elias poured more wine. "We have the young plants here at the abbey, you understand. If you prepared the soil, we would provide the starts."

Basil slammed his fist on the table. "Nobody is answering my question! What do *we* get out of it? When we plant barley on abbey land, Brother Elias, we keep a portion and the remainder goes to you. We plant in the spring and we harvest in the late summer and then sometime in the autumn such as today, we deliver your portion to you. For our labor we get some barley. And the abbey, for allowing our use of its land, receives some barley. But with vines, it's not the same. First, we plant and then we wait. There is no harvest, not for years. And when finally the grapes do come in, then what? We don't want or need grapes. We have prepared the ground, planted the vines, tended the plants for years. And what have we gotten?"

"We pay you," Elias said.

"For the work?" Basil wanted to know.

"No, my friend, for the grapes."

"So, until the grapes are harvested, we receive nothing for our labor?"

"But we pay very well for the grapes. In wine, or in grain, what you prefer."

"In cash?"

"Not in cash," Elias admitted. "And of what use is cash? Cash is the commodity of thieves. A purse is to a thief, what honey is to a fly. Around here you carry a purse you need hide it next to your hairy balls and hope no stranger chooses to play with them while you dine at the tavern. But who is going to steal a wagon filled with grain or with barrels of the delicious wine such as we have been drinking this afternoon?"

Basil was again leaning toward the door. "You're right," he said. "We are good farmers. We will look at the land more carefully. We'll discuss your proposal and advise you of our response."

He nodded toward his brothers and soon they were out of the cellar, Elias following them. In the dormitory they passed a line of young men who were on their knees polishing the lobby floor; their hands were buried in the hides of sheep that they swept from side to side as they slowly proceeded toward a distant wall.

A fresh breeze was coming around from the chapel. The air smelled of animals and hay, and Basil felt himself relax somewhat. He regretted behaving badly toward Elias. His wife's pregnancy had him on edge. Each day was a torment. As he watched her take on flesh he found her increasingly beautiful. She glowed with new life. Alone with her, he could not trust himself. Desire again threatened to overtake him. And the irony was not lost on him that this was the one time they could safely make love without fear of pregnancy. But the midwife had been clear: to couple with Arved while she was pregnant was to threaten both her and the child.

"Brother Elias, the next time we come, I intend to bring my son. I would like him to meet you. I want him to visit this place and come to know it as I have. Like our father, his name too is Johannes. He's only five so it would be a long journey for him. But perhaps next year he will be ready."

Elias wanted to know if this Johannes, was his only child.

"My wife is even now with child," Basil said, the words chilling him slightly.

"So, the loaf's in the oven," Elias said with a laugh. "And rising by the day."

Basil was relieved to see Jacob approach, his hand on the yoke, the oxen plodding beside him, the wheels of the wagon creaking like the joints of an old man.

"Where's our boy?"

"He's chatting with that horseman. Seems he got in and delivered his cargo. He claims it was relics, statuary, venerable objects of various types. The sisters had decided they were not safe at the nunnery."

"Zealots," Elias said. "Marauders. Luther's men. God's children killing each other again. What we call venerable, they call idolatry, that's the nub of it."

With that the three men shook hands and Jacob got the oxen moving toward the gate. The sun was tilting toward the horizon. It would be dark when they got home.

FOUR

In January, 1570, in the late afternoon of Epiphany Sunday, Arved Helgen went into labor, and Agnes, her eight-year-old niece, was sent to fetch the midwife. Breathless with excitement, Agnes pounded on the door shouting, "Frau Mueller, come! And quickly please. Aunt Arved is soon a-borning!"

The birth would prove as difficult and as protracted as had the first. For twenty-four hours the birthing room was crowded with women. The widow Marsel, like Arved and the midwife, had not left the room since labor began. Arved's sisters, Anna and Gisele, were in and out as were her sisters-in-law:

Sebastian's wife Ursula, at nineteen, the youngest of the attending women, and Jacob's wife Klara, who was often nursing Irmele, her six-month-old. The child Agnes, had slipped into the room awhile, thrilling to raw sensations of terror and delight before being sent away to care for Johannes.

At the midwife's instruction, all doors within the room stood open, drawers had been pulled out, Arved's hair unpinned and loosened, bows released of their knots. Over time the room had become ever more cluttered. Heated stones brought in from the hearth cooled forgotten. The chamber pot needed emptying. The band of blue swaddling cloth had fallen to the floor. The air smelled of tallow candles, of oils and herbs, and that familiar scent the human body produces under strain.

Given the number of people and the length of time involved, the process was largely one of waiting, and the women filled the hours with prayer. Aloud or silent, everyone was praying to Saint Margaret or the Virgin Mary. When heard from the outside the room, where Basil waited helpless with misery, the voices combined to form an unintended chant that swelled and receded and swelled again. Painfully clear to his ears was his wife's voice which transformed every spasm into a harshly evoked prayer, half song, half cry.

Early on, Arved had paced the room, praying aloud, grimacing with each contraction, trying to find a comfortable position. Now on the bed, now on the birthing chair, now squatting on her haunches, eased down with helping hands and lifted by them again, the prayers continuous. From time to time, the midwife instructed her to lie flat so she could examine the opening and to rub a stone and oils onto her thighs and lower abdomen. As she performed these practices, Frau Mueller spoke directly to the emerging child, encouraging it to come through the opening door, calling it to enter the world safely without damaging its mother. At other times she spoke to Arved, joining with her in a pattern of breathing, encouraging the opening of every part of her being, urging her to push as the child struggled to emerge.

As anticipation gave way to exhaustion, Arved found herself drifting into slivers of sleep. Images flitted and danced in her mind. So quickly did they enter and depart that she could not identify them, though she thought them potent with meaning. Was that the child she saw? Her own dead mother? An angel's wing, or a shade, sinister and menacing? Only dimly did she hear Frau Mueller report that she could feel the child's head, that it was positioned well for delivery. But the process would be difficult, the pelvis was narrow, the opening slow to dilate. Much labor still was needed.

Basil could remain but briefly within the living quarters of the house. The birthing room was forbidden to him as to every man. He would settle in an exterior room, only to rise again moments later. He paced near the hearth, a chunk of bread in his fist, then fled to the stable, Arved's cries following him out and echoing in his mind. He sharpened tools, some that didn't need sharpening, the grinding stone shooting sparks. He pitched manure from the sow's and the oxen's stalls and lay down beddings of fresh straw; he inspected the wheels of the wagon, applying grease as needed. He oiled every inch of the heavy leather and forged iron that secured the yoke to the wagon's tongue. Nearby, always within hearing, most always within sight, his brothers tried to be available but not intrusive.

Hovering in the midwife Frau Mueller's mind as the hours passed were the stark options she had heard of but never tried, that of crushing the child's skull, thus killing the child to save the mother, or breaking open the mother's pelvis, thus killing the mother to save the child. Had she posed that terrible choice, she knew the mother would choose the latter and the father the former.

Slowly and by minute degrees—the mother's body having abandoned the extravagance of a waking conscious-ness, even that of a separate self, becoming now a perfectly aligned alloy of will and pushing flesh—the child's head crowned and then pushed free. Moments later, she slid whole, wet, red and slippery into the arms of the midwife, trailing cord and placenta, and announced herself with a cry, a new being alive in the world. And still Arved breathed and seemed dimly aware of completion.

Everyone agreed, a miracle had occurred, witnessed by all. Basil, called to in the yard, and told this triple truth: that the ordeal had ended, that he had a living daughter and a living wife, fell to his knees and buried his face in his thick and soiled hands.

The fingers and toes were counted, the cord severed and tied, the child washed and swaddled and placed into the arms of her grandmother. Marsel lay herself and the child on the bed beside Arved, who was breathing comfortably and slowly returning to awareness.

Placentas were much valued by witches, persons in league with devils. They could use them to cast curses and cause injury. Frau Mueller instructed the attending women to carry the placenta and cord out to the family room where they should be carefully incinerated.

When all of this had been accomplished, Rachel Mueller looked down on the sleeping mother, grandmother and child. Feeling suddenly unstable, she eased herself into a chair and allowed her body to relax. She was almost fifty. She had been present at moments of death, the first and most notable the death of her father when she was nine. She had been called to the sides of men who had been injured and were enduring excruciating pain. She had gone on pilgrimage, attended weddings, funerals and baptisms, first communions, festivals and celebrations of multiple kinds. Each of these occasions had its own character and energy.

But for Rachel Mueller, none of them could compare with the birth of a child. Only here were the possibilities of death and new life so richly entwined. Here both the greatest grief and the greatest joy were possible, and yet neither was certain. Each birth followed its own course, and there was no rushing the process. Like a skilled storyteller spinning a tale, every birth kept a tight hold on its secrets until the very end.

But what seemed most remarkable to the midwife about the events that had just occurred, was the character of the child herself. There had been something willful about her emergence from the womb. This child had insisted on entering the world. Turning now toward the bed, she saw that Arved had wakened. She was touching the face of her new child, exploring every visible feature of the bound and sleeping infant.

FIVE

On the morning three days following the birth, Basil decided to castrate the male piglets. Johannes and his cousin Zacharias were summoned to help. Their task was to capture and hold the squealing animals while Basil sliced open the sacks and removed the testicles. It was a noisy, chaotic affair. Structures were hammered together to separate the animals by gender and size. The space confining the young males had to be small enough that the piglets could be caught, and yet large enough that Basil could comfortably perform the surgeries. Zacharias and Johannes were wild with excitement, shouting and laughing, eager to run and catch. In their separate pens the agitated animals grunted and squealed, banging themselves against the wooden partitions that groaned under the strain. All of this was taking place on the ground floor of the family home, just below the living quarters.

The day was cold. There had been a light snow overnight, enough to cover roofs and bare ground and to stretch itself along the level branches of the deciduous trees. As the cacophony raged below, Marsel and Klara prepared a stew with barley, some cabbage and a bit of fatty mutton. The men and boys would be hungry when they came up and Marsel was taking special care to nurture Arved back to health.

The mother had been walking about some, the child always in her arms or sleeping nearby. In the previous two afternoons she had taken a seat in the family room and had greeted the parade of visitors who came by to see her and to admire the new arrival. Marsel allowed this only for an hour or two each day before asking the guests to leave. Arved's appetite had been strong and the child had begun to accept the breast but the mother was clearly weak. She would need extra hours of sleep and days filled with rest to recoup her strength. Marsel had no qualms about clearing the house of guests.

When the stew was ready, she poured some into a bowl and took it to the bedroom where Arved and the infant were lying. The child was awake and agitated but the mother asleep. Marsel reached down to stroke Arved's forehead, but before her fingers had touched skin she felt the heat. The skin flushed and hot, the gown and the bedding moist with sweat. In the moment before Arved's eyes fluttered open, Marsel felt something malevolent enter the room. It came silently and it grew to fill every corner, every crevice and drawer. The prayers had stopped too soon, she realized. There was nothing now to push it back, to keep it at bay. They should have kept praying. They should be praying still, all of them.

"I'm all right," Arved insisted a moment later. "Is the day cold? I'm feeling a little chill."

"Yes, dear, the day is cold." Marsel set the bowl down.

"Oh, and my child is hungry! Come little Elsebett. Did I tell you, mother? I have given her my grandmother's name." She moved so the child could reach her breast.

"Yes, you told me, child. But you too need food. Here, I can feed you as she nurses."

"Not now. I'm not hungry. I'm shivering, and her lips feel cold on me. She too must be cold." Arved's teeth had begun to chatter. "There is such a chill today," she added. "And where is that racket coming from? Is my Basil butchering?"

So quickly did the fever advance, so racked by heat and pain did her weakened body become, that five days later the woman Arved was dead. A beautiful, dark-haired seamstress with an infectious laugh, Arved had been the wife of Basil Helgen, a farmer in the village, and the mother of a boy named Johannes, age five, and a girl named Elsebett, newly born. At the time of her death, she was twenty-seven years of age.

In the village located on a bend of the Mosel River, the infant Elsebett was introduced to one of her aunt Klara's generous breasts while inches away her cousin Irmele made good use of the other. When one of her tears fell on the head of the child, Klara would take a thick finger and brusquely swipe it away.

SIX

Winter had come to Basil Helgen. He was miserable, and the misery inside him seemed to leak out and infect those around him. He sensed caution in most everyone he encountered. They had the wariness of a person in the presence of a large red-eyed dog with sharp fangs and an unstable temperament. He existed in a prison of his own construction. A miserable place it was, and he was miserable inside it. But it was his prison and he preferred it to any other he could imagine.

His lust had caused Arved's death. He had promised to protect her and he had failed to withdraw. Guilt and his memory of her haunted him. Not that she appeared as a ghost. There had been but one such appearance, and that had happened at her internment. His wife's beauty, her virtue, her modesty, her bright laugh and her early death had touched everyone, and the whole village was present first at the funeral and then in the graveyard beside the redbrick parish church.

As Father Severin mumbled above the grave, Basil had pulled his eyes from his wife's shrouded body, and glancing up he saw her standing across from him at the edge of the crowd. The juxtaposition of the body inches away and the clear vision of her dressed as she had been on the day of their wedding, a slight smile on her face, caused him to gasp and call out. For a brief instant he realized that her death had been an illusion, a terrible dream from which he had awakened. The shroud to the extent it was real at all, was empty. He staggered and had to brace himself against the broad shoulder of his brother Jacob, and still he saw her. She did not look at him directly, but seemed intent on the words of the droning priest.

Basil turned toward his mother and started to speak. When he looked back, the vision was gone. He had seen no halo, recognized no heavenly light, but clearly she had been there. Perhaps an angel had delivered his bride that day to assure him that she was at peace. But then the angel took her back, and his raven-haired Arved was lost to him forever.

Overriding that vision in the days following was another, that of the inflamed, vomiting, fever-battered, pain-racked, delirious, putrid-smelling woman, her eyes rolling, her hair wet and matted, moaning on the bed that had been their conjugal bed and had become a birthing-bed and was now becoming her deathbed. So terrible had been her state that it had driven him full-circle like an animal turning a grinding stone, turning him so completely he stopped praying for her recovery and began to pray for her death. Only death could quench the fire raging inside her and end the pain. And so, in the end it had.

In nine days he had gone from the euphoria accompanying the birth (rushing to the church to offer prayers of gratitude, making a substantial donation to the priest) to longing for the death of his wife. He remembered his mother rushing down to fetch him away from the pigs, the first touch of his fingers on Arved's heated forehead, her absurd assurances that she was all right. He had run to find the midwife, half-dragging her back to the house. But all her incantations, her poultices, teas and oils, all the fervent prayers filling the room, had done nothing to stem the raging fire or ease the pain.

Half-mad, he had gone to the high-stepping Father Severin, who was as distant and cold as usual. Severin explained to the desperate husband that Arved was unclean. Birth was a bloody, messy, filthy affair; it had contaminated her as it contaminated every woman. She could not touch holy water; she should not even bake bread; she should not receive the sacraments or attend Mass or come to the church at all. Thirty days would have to pass before she could be purified by a ceremony that would welcome her back into the congregation. And if she does not survive thirty days? Basil wanted to know. If she is dying? Well, if she is dying, the priest could perform the last rites, but it would be wise of Basil, if he cared for his wife's soul, to first purchase an indulgence.

A few days later, Basil held his infant daughter at her baptism, but he had not attended Mass or gone to confession since. This behavior, so unbecoming of him, so violate of the family's values, broke his mother's heart and sent her daily to the church to pray and weep. To protect himself from the despair he was causing her, he boarded himself up at the table. His demeanor was about getting the food eaten, about tasks the family needed to perform.

At night he was out of the house and off to the inn. He sat at a long table with other men, most of whom he had known all his life. They linked arms and sang badly; they bumped their steins together and drank to excess. They told stories and jokes and repeated and revised their shared and personal histories. At times they argued; a couple of times he came home with cuts on his face, his hands bruised and stiff. One night two men who were almost as drunk as he, half-carried him home and dropped him at the front door where he woke with the first ringing of the bells, the ground slick with vomit, his pants soiled with his own piss and shit.

This behavior stood in stark contrast to the young man who had married Arved. Back then he went to the inn and he drank while he was there. But he went to participate in the many meetings required to settle crop rotations, exchange seeds, share equipment and draft animals, to arrange work parties and discuss the status and use of the pastures, the forest, the village green. Back then, the drinking and the socializing had been peripheral to the meetings. Now they stood at the center.

This, too, tortured his mother. She felt intensely the strain his conduct was having on the living web that was her family. She came to feel an unarticulated anger toward her eldest son. Did he imagine himself alone in his grief? Was it not obvious that they all mourned? Had not the young Johannes and the child Elsebett lost a mother? Had she, herself, not lost a beloved daughter? Had Jacob and Sebastian and their two dear wives not lost a sister? But in his high-walled prison, Basil was unreachable, his body thickening, his beard becoming spotted with gray as the months passed.

It was not as though he shirked his obligations. He was up in the morning with the others, quiet, perhaps sullen, but prepared to face the day. He had always been in charge, the one the others looked to. Even when old Johannes had stalked about in full command, it had been Basil who filtered those commands down to specific tasks. It was he who defined the issues, measured out the responsibilities. He wasn't a dictator. "This is what we need to do," he would say, and if Jacob or Sebastian had a different suggestion, he would hear them out.

But over time he was most always right. He had an eye for proportion and an ear alert to change. He seemed to retain in his memory volumes of practical history. He knew their animals intimately. He could tell you the age of each sow, how many litters she had produced, the number of piglets in each, how quickly they had grown and how many had survived. He seemed familiar with each yard of ground under their control. He remembered what had been planted when and where. He knew how a given piece of ground had performed with different crops in different years. He could tell you where water collected and stood, and how best to drain it off. Weather patterns seemed to exist in his mind as much as in the air. Seated at the table he was aware of what was happening outside and he could predict with accuracy, the direction the day would likely take.

All of this had survived the death of his wife. It was his isolation that was new; it grew around him like a thick skin.

In the months following Arved's death, he and his brothers examined the abbey ground where Brother Elias had proposed they plant vines. They visited vineyards and spoke to those who husbanded them. They negotiated with the abbey. Their reputations had value. The abbey would pay them in wine for the work they did to prepare the ground and plant the cuttings. From then until the first harvest, they agreed to tend the young plants without compensation, but when the plants had matured the abbey would purchase their harvest with hard currency that valued both their labor and the abbey's land.

It had been Sebastian who insisted on currency for their payment. In the larger cities, he told them, currency was becoming the more common means of exchange. "And you know, brother, Arved's sewing had brought in some coins, and now that is gone." Basil only nodded, but the remark had caused Jacob to catch his breath. The three of them almost never spoke her name to each other. It was true, though, and each of them realized the obvious. Arved's skill had brought in a few coins, but more than that, she had sewn and maintained the bulk of the family's clothing. Marsel's eyes were no longer strong enough for such fine work. Klara, Jacob's wife, was a wonderful cook. To hear her banging around the hearth meant that good food was on its way. But Klara, a frank and gregarious woman with a taste for beer and bawdy humor, had no skill with a needle. "Give me a needle and I'll soon be bleeding like a stuck pig," she would tell you. And to confront Klara, to insist she do her share of sewing, was something no one was prepared to do.

That left Ursula, Sebastian's young wife. There was a shyness about Ursula that Marsel found charming. Whenever she laughed her hand rushed to cover her mouth and at the same time her eyes widened. It was as if the delight suppressed by the hand found expression in her eyes. The girl had good intent and did her best. She could spin wool well enough. And she had sat with Arved, needle in hand, learning skills her mother had never taught her. She could darn, place a lasting patch on a tunic, repair an apron hem. But she had never fitted or sewn clothing. Ursula was aware of herself as the youngest woman in the family and she feared being caught in error. This shyness slowed her. The young Agnes was more quick with a needle than Ursula. But Agnes's duties were under the command of her mother, and that was another family, one that had its own garments to make and maintain.

As time passed and the period of mourning ended, the solution was for Basil to remarry. Widows, unmarried women were available in the village. Virtuous, honorable women with skills. A match could be made that would benefit everyone. But Basil, that thoroughly practical man, had married Arved for desire. And it was desire, in his mind, that had killed his wife and nearly himself. He could not picture marriage as an economic arrangement; marriage was about desire and desire was deadly. Better to hire someone, a seamstress, a cook, a housecleaner. An older woman, perhaps, one with a landless husband who also lent his labor out for pay. It might mean putting out coins rather than taking them in, but perhaps she would accept grain or pork for her services. If money were required, he would make sure the money was at hand. And it was obvious to Basil that Marsel was the person to find such a woman and oversee her labor.

"But, your father," Marsel began when he spoke to her.

Basil interrupted, anticipating what his mother was starting to say. "Yes, yes, I know. A man should do his own labor. We all heard the homily many times. A man who hires someone to do his work is little better than a lazy noble who expects his leggings brought to him on a hanger. But I'm not going to marry some woman just to get my clothes sewn and my floors scrubbed."

SEVEN

As his son grew, Basil saw in Johannes flashes of Arved. This went beyond a physical resemblance, though the resemblance was there in his dark hair and eyes, his eager laugh. In the boy he also recognized a certain delicacy—he liked to arrange things, to place objects in a specific order or sequence; he could knot a fine thread, loosen a tiny bow; he was quick to find and pick up a pin that had fallen to the floor; he was sensitive to how clothes fit his body, how his hair was cut. All of this made Basil want to hold the child very close, but he resisted the temptation. He wanted the boy away from his grandmother, his aunts, his little sister and the child Irmele, whom it seemed, Johannes would be happy to spend most all the day playing with.

He took Johannes out of doors. He placed him on the wagon and behind the plow. He introduced him to people, gave him objects to carry, animals to feed, plants to watch over. On Saturdays they went together to the communal bathhouse where they bathed and had their hair cut, and Basil his beard trimmed. The attendant—one of the several second and third cousins Basil had scattered about the village—had converted to Luther's gospel. On Sundays, he walked an hour to a neighboring village to attend services. Like most recent converts, the cousin was eager to impart his newly found truth, and like most everyone in the village, he was aware that Basil no longer attended Mass or made confession.

None of that rigmarole was necessary for salvation, he assured Basil. Confessing to a priest got you nowhere. Those tinkling bells and bleeding saints, that stinking incense counted for nothing. Salvation came with faith. Faith alone would save you from the flames of hell. Salvation was a gift from God! Believe this and it will be given to you. He wanted Basil to attend a service with him one Sunday. There, he explained, the pastor read to them from the Bible. Read not in church language but in their own. "And bring this dark-haired boy as well, cousin."

Basil was surprised to hear the man talk so openly, even to his cousin. The religion of the Archbishop-Elector in Trier was the church in Rome, and that was thus the only religion permitted to any subject within his jurisdiction. Basil was not aware of spies running around. Still, the Lutherans must be meeting in secret. He imagined them gathered in a back room, a watchman at the door. Such intrigue held no attraction for him. He was a farmer, and a good one. He had land, a home, possessions under this control. He had a family for which he was responsible.

"I'm not going to sow those seeds, cousin," he told the man as he and the boy rose to go. "I'll stick to the ones I know."

A short time later Basil arranged with the sexton for Johannes to become a bell ringer at the parish church. This was a service he and his brothers had performed in their youth and he had fond memories of it. The bells were a source of pride for the village. Many years before, Basil's grandfather—known in the family as "the old Helgen"—had helped organize a campaign to purchase the bells and have them installed. The village was known for its church with its beautiful window and the sweet sound of its bells.

The ringing of the bells was vital to the orderly operation of the community. There was but one clock and it hung high in the market square across from the church. More than just calling the faithful to Mass, the bells rang to announce births and deaths and to alert men in the fields of coming storms or erupting fires. It was young boys who rang the bells every morning. Whatever the weather, Johannes and another boy would have to rise early and run to the church tower.

On their learning-day the sexton took Johannes and his friend up the rickety ladder to the top of the tower where they stood squeezed together on a tiny platform. So close they could reach out and touch them, the bells appeared massive and latent with power. More astounding to the boys were the vistas available through the arched openings. Here was their world newly discovered: the paths they walked, the roofs of the houses where they lived, the fields, the river, the forested hill, the meadows, even the bell towers of three neighboring villages. "Look! There in the far pasture is old Virgil with the sheep!"

The sexton, who had been through this many times, waited until they settled down. Then he spoke of the village's campaign to acquire the bells, the famous foundry that had cast them, the mechanics required to transport, raise and hang them in the tower. He explained the functions the bells served, from weddings to funerals to the driving out of demons. He showed how the two bells were hung from a common headstock so they moved in unison.

And then—and this was the favored part so far as the sexton was concerned—he tapped each bell with the blade of his knife. He paused. He looked at the boys, and then struck them again. Could they tell the difference in the two tones? A third time the sexton reached out with his knife and slapped the bells. Then he heard it. The grinning Johannes, having inherited his mother's sense of pitch, not only recognized the difference but could match the tones perfectly. The sound of his voice echoed in the tower.

This was the lesson the sexton most wanted to teach. Neither bell alone, he told the boys, was capable. Only together could they produce the pleasing sound for which the village was known. "And the two of you must also work together," he said as he led them back to the base of the tower.

There he pointed to the two long ropes that hung from the headstock. "One of you boys will jump up and grab a rope and your weight will start the bells to moving. Then the other will leap and grab his rope and swing them back. You must time your pulls carefully. But if you do, the two of you working together will send the great bells swinging back and forth and the clappers will strike and the combined tones will peel out across the village and into the fields and woods beyond." Ninety hearty clangs the sexton wanted to hear each and every morning. "That means forty-five strong pulls on the ropes by each of you boys. This will teach you counting and give you strength."

Overjoyed to hear that young Johannes had become a bell ringer, Marsel suggested to her son that perhaps the boy could enter the service of the church, but Basil refused to consider it. "My son will be a man, and a farmer," he told his mother.

EIGHT

As to the child Elsebett, Basil may have been deeply conflicted. Did some shadow of his personality resent her very existence? Did he sense that her life had been stolen from the wife he adored? Of this he revealed nothing, perhaps not even to himself.

Early on he was rarely in her presence. Her aunt Klara had served as the child's wet nurse. And she was often cared for in the homes of Arved's two sisters, Anna, the mother of Agnes, and Gisele, the mother of Zacharias. As the months passed, her grandmother wanted her more and more in their home. She and Irmele were only six months apart, and Marsel delighted to see them together. Johannes, too, treasured his sister's presence.

Elsebett, it turned out, was more naturally robust than her brother. Physically, she was stout and fleshy, resembling more her father's line than her mother's. Even before she could walk she intently pushed objects around a room. Things, it seemed, needed to be other than where they were. Soon walls seemed to confine her. Like her father, she wanted to be in the open air. She liked to touch things. She grabbed up rocks and sticks and lumps of dung. She was attracted to plants and animals, wanting to touch and stroke them.

She climbed, she fell. She was often bruised and scratched. Together, she and Irmele could be terrors. Sometimes they fought and pouted. Other times they snuggled together, whispering and giggling.

Water fascinated the child. If she came upon a pail or a trough filled with the mysterious substance, she tended to plunge a hand in, even on a cold day. It was as if she could not quite believe that it had both surface and depth. Some days she chose to just tickle the surface with a finger, lying down beside a puddle so she could look along its smooth, still surface, a perfection she could destroy with the softest touch. And yet, if she waited, the perfection would magically return. Seeing her one day—lying flat on the ground, repeatedly touching the water and watching it return to a perfect calm—caused Sebastian to pause in his work. What she was thinking? he wondered. Basil soon joined him. Together the two men observed the girl.

"I fear she is slow," Basil said after a moment. This was a fear he had never expressed to anyone.

"Our father thought that of me," Sebastian said, his eyes on the child.

"Father? No, I don't remember that."

"Yes, our father. It is easier for you to have forgotten his remarks, his behavior toward me. This child of yours is not slow."

Basil was surprised by the vehemence in Sebastian's voice. Their father had been harsh with all of them, but had he been more cruel toward Sebastian? The eight years separating them could account for a lot. But he was not prepared to accept his brother's view of the child.

"She was slow to talk," he said, watching her again dip a finger into the puddle.

"And now questions pour from her. She is curious; the world fascinates her. Father tried to beat that out of me. I hope you won't do the same with Elsebett."

"I am not our father," Basil said as the two men turned back to their tasks.

"No, brother," Sebastian said, slapping Basil on the back. "And for that we are all grateful."

All of this the grandmother monitored and marveled at. With the other women busy, and Johannes more and more with his father, it was Marsel who looked after the girls, the two of them so similar and yet so different.

It occurred to Marsel, ever aware of the family and its strands of relationships, that Basil was perhaps disappointed in the child. But the truth was, Basil adored his daughter. He just did not know what to do with her. How to act or what to say. With a boy, he knew, but a girl? Contrary to what his mother imagined, he saw flashes of Arved in the child's movements, in the way she tilted her head, or frowned in concentration. Asleep before the fireplace the child's profile struck him as a living portrait of her mother.

In the village, Elsebett was recognized as the child of the young seamstress who had died so tragically. And certain people, people who gained pleasure from loss and regret, looked on her with pity. They could be seen in the church when she entered hand in hand with her grandmother. Soft clucking sounds escaped their lips and their covered heads tilted toward one another in shared sentiment.

But Elsebett was, in truth, a happy child, brimming with energy, and like her mother was ready to laugh. She sensed her father's shy love. She had a grandmother who watched over her every mood, a brother and two older cousins who took her and Irmele off on adventures. Doting aunts and uncles surrounded her. Perhaps the love they harbored for her mother they showered on her. The rapidly balding

Jacob in particular, his face becoming redder and rounder by the year, could not resist chasing her down, grabbing her up and tossing her into the air. First his Irmele and then her, throwing them high and catching them as they fell, while Sebastian when he finally got a horse, liked to set both girls on Falada's broad back and lead her around the yard, the two of them clinging to mane and each other.

§

One evening when Elsebett was six and Irmele had just turned seven, they were staying over with cousin Agnes, who at that time was nearing the age of sixteen. When it grew dark the older girl led them into the privacy of her room. She placed her candle on the floor, and arranged for the three of them to sit in a circle around it.

"Tonight," she announced, "I am going to tell you about the most beautiful angel in all of heaven. So beautiful was this angel that anyone who looked on him could not look away.

"His name was Lucifer. And of all God's angels he was the most powerful. No angel was so adored, so loved and so feared by the other angels as was he. But Lucifer was not happy because the other angels loved and feared God even more than they did him. And that made Lucifer jealous. He wanted everyone to love and fear him more than they loved and feared God. So, Lucifer decided to start a war against God."

"In heaven?"

"Yes, in heaven itself!" Agnes exclaimed. "Lucifer went from village to village. Heaven has villages, you know, just like we have here. There are angels living in those heavenly villages just like there are people living in our village. So anyway, Lucifer went from village to village recruiting soldiers to fight in his army against God.

"And he found some. It was just like here. You can always find a few grumpy people, or people who want to go fight a war someplace, and the same was true in heaven. Remember, Lucifer was the most beautiful of all angels, so beautiful that if you saw him you could not look away. So, if Lucifer wanted you to do something, it was hard to say no, even if you were an angel living in heaven."

Agnes paused and closed her eyes. As the girls watched, she opened her right hand and passed it slowly palm-down over the candle flame. The act frightened the girls and thrilled Agnes: the attraction, the fear, the pleasure, the pain.

"Think of it," she said when she had pulled her stinging hand away and hidden it behind her back. "You are an angel. You live in your house in heaven and there comes a knock on the door. You open it and before you stands Lucifer, the most beautiful angel in all heaven. Certainly you have heard of him, but maybe you have never seen him up close. He stands now at your door and he is asking you to join him on a great adventure. A war! A war against God himself. Would you join?"

The two little girls shook their heads, looking terrified.

"Are you sure? Think about it. The most beautiful angel in heaven has come to you; he is so beautiful you can't look away. He tells you about all the gold and jewels that God has hidden in the back rooms of his heavenly palace. 'If you join me,' Lucifer says, 'I will give you so much gold and jewelry that you won't be able to carry it all. After we win, you will dress only in silks and satins. Your hands will be covered with rings. From your neck will hang glittering necklaces. You will no longer live in this rude village. You will live with me, Lucifer, in God's palace. We will eat our meat off golden plates and drink our beer from golden goblets. So, will you join me?'"

Irmele looked hesitantly at Elsebett, but Elsebett frowned. After a moment she shook her head vigorously.

"But what if he loses?" she shouted.

"He did lose!" Agnes announced dramatically. "And Lucifer and all the angels who fought with him were thrown from the light of heaven into the darkness of hell."

She leaned forward and blew out the candle. Then, in the perfect darkness she finished her story. "And Lucifer became the Devil, and even today, yes even today in this very village, he is still looking for soldiers to fight his war against God."

§

One day—this was some months later when Elsebett was almost eight—Frau Rachel Mueller, the midwife, came to the house and spoke to Marsel about the child. She knew that Basil had not taken another wife and that the little girl had no mother. She had seen the child on a number of occasions, and had watched her with interest. Frau Mueller told Marsel that she was herself becoming older. She needed someone to assist her around the house and in her work. And she believed the time had come for her to pass on to a younger woman, the skills that she possessed. She was asking that the family consider turning Elsebett over to her for the child's care and upbringing.

NINE

By this time, almost eight years following Arved's death, a certain stability had settled on the family and on the village. While poor years followed better ones, enough rye and barley came in, squealing piglets were born, and the vineyard had begun to produce an annual harvest that the abbey purchased with good cash. Taxes were paid. Sebastian continued to refine and increase his beer production. He sold now a portion to the inn in the village. With the proceeds he purchased the mare and a two-wheeled cart to better transport his product.

Agnes had begun to work at the inn owned by her Aunt Gisele and Uncle Martin, where their son Zacharias also worked. Aunt Gisele was a stern taskmaster and Agnes's days were long and the work hard. She scrubbed, she carried out chamber pots, she fed fires and she assisted in the kitchen where often it was very hot. But the best part was serving food to the inn's guests. Among them were merchants who came from distant cathedral towns, and the ruddy men who plied the river in boats transporting goods and people. Agnes loved to hear their talk and observe their manner and dress. In her mind it was as if the world were coming to show itself to her. Sometimes she even fantasized that among them, disguised as a young merchant perhaps, was a prince who would recognize her virtue, the true nobility of her person. And the money she earned, was set aside for her dowry.

Repeated petitions to the mayor and Archbishop finally resulted in the removal of the high-stepping very unpopular Father Severin. The new priest was a large-eyed, surprisingly young, curly-haired, boy-man named Peter. It was disturbing at first to see in the pulpit a priest who was hardly more than a child. His huge ears and his smooth beardless face rose up from the loose collar and ill-fitting robes like a young plant growing from too large a pot. Husbands grumbled among themselves and to their wives. Were they expected to make confession to this child? They chuckled at the story that Father Peter had been found by the Archbishop in a hole in a meadow, the runt in a litter of baby hares; the Archbishop, it was said, had lifted him up by his ears and sent him off to seminary.

But girls and young women soon found they could indulge in the sly pleasures that came from casting glances and smiles at a young man who was safely unavailable, while the mature women celebrated the opportunity to mother the young father. Parades of them came bearing sweets and samples of their best cakes. They offered to mend his garments while at the same time taking comfort in his blessings. And everyone was happy to have seen the last of Father Severin.

The Helgen family home was, at this point, alive with toddlers. Jacob and Klara now had a second child, a boy given the name Gabriel, and Sebastian and Ursula followed with two sons, David and Thomas, born but a year apart. Irmele and Elsebett were to the little boys, what Agnes and Johannes had been to them.

A woman came regularly to the house to sew and clean and gossip with Marsel. Frau Henn and her husband were cottagers, which is to say they owned no property of their own. For years the husband had worked for the village as the shepherd—he was the "old Virgil" Johannes and his friend had seen from the bell tower—but recently he had been replaced with a younger man.

About this time Basil was drawn back to the church, perhaps more curious about the new priest than devout, but comforted by its rhythms and routines. He still went out most evenings. But he no longer drank to excess, and he skillfully avoided arguments that could lead to violence. Seemingly ever more muscular and stout, his reddish beard sprinkled with gray, he sometimes fell into a story at meal time and could on occasion be heard laughing with his brothers; his laughter brought joy to the aging Marsel.

For several days the grandmother chose to not speak to anyone about the midwife's proposal. Marsel had spent a lifetime baking bread and the principles fundamental to bread baking she applied also to decisions. After her father had been killed during the peasant revolt, she and her mother had moved in with her mother's parents. Marsel's own mother, traumatized by her husband's death, died herself within a year. Fortunately, her grandparents provided a stable home for the child. The family was landless but not without resources. The grandfather was a master ropemaker while the grandmother maintained a good garden and was an excellent cook; she was particularly respected for her baking. It was from her that Marsel learned her skill with bread.

The magic of dough had fascinated Marsel since childhood. She loved its smell. (Even now her knobby hands would at times lift the dough toward her bowing head as if she were performing a sacred ritual.) She delighted in the heft of it. She was fascinated by its texture, by the strange warmth it possessed, by its flex and resistance. Marsel knew dough to be a gift from God, alive in some way. It possessed an intent, a desire to fulfill itself. Dough wanted to become bread, but it demanded respect. It could not be hurried. It required kneading. It needed time to rise. And there was a finality about bread. A loaf cooling on the table could not be undone, could not again become dough.

Like bread, a decision was the end product of a long process. Time had to pass.

And so, for a while Marsel said nothing about Frau Mueller's proposal. When she did speak, she mentioned it first to her two remaining daughters-in-law, to Klara and to Ursula. They talked about it over several days as they spun and cooked.

Ursula worried that the move might make Elsebett less eligible for marriage. Will it condemn her to a life of childless solitude? Happy in her new role as a mother, happy in her marriage to Sebastian, to Ursula a solitary life seemed a cruel fate to wish upon the child. Men, she pointed out, kept their distance from Frau Mueller. Not only was she unmarried and childless herself, her profession frightened them. Physical birth was to men, Ursula suggested, what physical violence was to women: something the mind instinctively shied away from. Would not a girl raised by Frau Mueller seem frightening to a young man? Would he perhaps think of her as vaguely unclean, as tainted by a knowledge of which he knew nothing? Knowledge that was even dangerous in a way. Every woman had heard of the physician who so desired to witness the birth process that he had disguised himself as a woman and had snuck into a birthing room. The poor man caught out by his emerging beard had in the end been tried and executed. The story never ceased to bring a laugh to women, but as Ursula pointed out, it must certainly be heard as a cautionary tale by a young man.

"And that says nothing about the magic," Ursula added with a sudden laugh, her hand covering her mouth, her eyes widening. "Frau Mueller is more than a midwife, she's 'cunning folk.' She knows the white magic. She heals with herbs and incantations. Ask yourself, would you want to marry up with a sorcerer?"

Hearing this, Klara turned from the fowl roasting on the spit and announced, "Well, that would depend on the sorcerer, would it not? Your common sorcerer is little more than a knave, I grant you. But if this sorcerer were a handsome lad who could turn an old cow into a fast horse, or a shock of wheat into spun gold, I would be more than happy to consider his offer."

Klara's remark caused Ursula to gasp, and Marsel to laugh until tears ran down her wrinkled face. As the years had passed she had come to cling ever more to Klara who now swung back toward the fireplace and stood there steady as a boulder in the river. But then, a moment later, Klara too expressed her hesitancy. As she basted the sizzling fowl she said, "It would be a shame would it not? Just when the child is becoming worth her food, we lose her."

Klara was right about that. Elsebett was old enough now that she was regularly assigned tasks around the house, sweeping and scrubbing, and she had recently been introduced to the needle and thread. The child was a willing helper and a quick learner, though she was always looking for an excuse to go outside. It seemed to Marsel that Elsebett preferred helping her father and brother in the field to working with her grandmother and aunts in the kitchen.

But the truth was, Marsel did not know exactly what Klara had intended by her comment. Was she expressing an economic loss, or something more personal? As Marsel pondered a clarifying question, Klara expressed her deeper feelings: "And my Irmele would feel lost without her."

That was true for all of them. They would miss the child who possessed not only her own charms but around whom lingered as well the light of her departed mother. And had not each of them been challenged by the dying woman? They all remembered that Arved's last thoughts had concerned the care and upbringing of the newborn child. Each of them had leaned onto the bed and had looked into the pained eyes of the dying woman and had promised that she would devote herself to the child's wellbeing. "Yes," each of them had promised, "I know that Basil cannot do this alone. Yes, I will do everything I can. I will see that this child is well raised in the sight of God."

The women all felt the weight of the pending decision. They did have an obligation toward Arved, promises had been made. It was true that becoming Frau Mueller's apprentice might indeed frighten off a young man. And the two cousins, Irmele and Elsebett did love one another and each would suffer from the separation. And yes, the family would lose the benefit of her strength, her increasing skill, her presence both in the house and in the field.

"But is it not also possible," the grandmother said now, "that this is a great opportunity for the child? If we reject the offer might we be denying her a benefit her mother would have chosen for her?"

Klara and Ursula nodded, glancing at each other. That was the problem. The child was too young to decide for herself. Her mother was gone and the future was unknowable. And yet they all felt responsible to somehow shape it.

"I will pray on it," Marsel said to conclude. But then she burst out with her deepest fears. "But remember something.

God may not grant me the time or the faculties to see this child into womanhood. That weighs on my mind, I have to tell you."

Her body trembled. Tears began to pour from her eyes and stream down her cheeks. It was embarrassing when Klara and Ursula dropped their tasks and rushed to hug her, one on each side, tears flowing down their faces as well.

"Oh, stop," Marsel kept saying, seeming to push against them and cling to them at the same time. "I am such an old fool!"

TEN

One evening a few days later Marsel approached her oldest son and asked for a few moments of his time. When they had sat down together, and after she had placed her crooked fingers on his thigh, she introduced the proposal the midwife had made. Would he consent to having Elsebett go live with Frau Mueller?

For a long while Basil sat silent and unmoving, though Marsel felt a spasm of energy pass along his leg. In those moments a struggle erupted inside him. His initial impulse was rage. For the first time in eight years he allowed into his conscious mind the possibility that the midwife had caused Arved's death. Something had killed her. The child had been born healthy. While Arved had been exhausted by the birth, she was soon up and walking about, feeding the child, holding it in her arms. She greeted guests, showed good appetite. Then suddenly it all went terribly wrong. Some evil force had clearly intervened. His mother had felt it enter the house. Had he not heard her cry out in her grief? "Too soon! We stopped praying too soon!"

Everyone knew Frau Mueller dealt in magic. She was more than a midwife. She understood herbs and spells. Her magic was said to be white, the kind of magic that does good. She used her powers to heal the sick. But it was said that people also went to her when they sought a change of fortune, something that had nothing to do with physical ailments. They wanted her to tilt events their way. So, while she was respected in the village, an air of caution surrounded her. If a person was capable of white magic, might she not also be versed in the black variety? Did not the good fortune of one sometimes require the bad fortune of another?

Basil himself had run to Frau Mueller immediately upon learning that Arved was pregnant. Everyone assumed that he had sought her services as a midwife, but that was not true. He had wanted her to abort the child and thereby save his wife from the fate that he so feared awaited her. But after her examination, the midwife had told him it was too late. "This child is established. It already has a foot in the world. I will do everything I can to deliver it safely while keeping your woman alive, but there is no turning back."

And she had failed. The child had survived, but the mother had died. And now the midwife wanted the child for herself.

Basil was thrown back again to that time, and the emotions ran confused in his mind. Thoughts of magic black and white swirled about, demons lurked, shadowy plots sprang up. Had she always wanted the child? Could she have plotted this from the beginning? Had she been waiting patiently these eight long years? Had she intentionally caused the death of his beloved Arved?

On the other hand, had he himself not wanted the child dead? The child he had wanted the midwife to kill was his dear Elsebett, she with the unruly hair and ruddy skin, rushing about like a plump doll in her little blue dress and white apron, her heavy shoes slapping the floor, jumping onto his lap, marching beside him behind the plow, shouting out encouragement to the oxen and hurling questions at him: "What are clouds made of?" "Why does manure smell?" And even, "Does it hurt the ground when the plow cuts into it?"

That last question had almost caused Basil to stumble in the furrow. Did the earth hurt when you plowed it? How could anyone even imagine that? Where would such an idea come from? It raised the possibility that she was touched in some way. Touched by a saint, touched by a devil. His Johannes had never asked a question like that. Johannes mostly wanted to know when the food would be ready, or when they could go inside and warm themselves by the fire. Questions any child might ask. Their cousin Irmele who preferred to sit on the floor dressing and undressing her little doll, never asked questions like that.

Maybe Sebastian had been wrong. Maybe the child was slow. No question she was odd. And yet a brightness came from her that warmed him. "That child has hair that defeats the brush," his mother had confided one morning as they were leaving for church. And her cheeks glowed. They glowed the way his brother Jacob's had when he was a boy. As if she had just run the length of a barley field.

Maybe it was just that Elsebett was a girl, a lively, energetic girl. And what did he know about little girls? He thought of Agnes, now the young woman he saw running in and out of the kitchen at the inn. As a child Agnes had annoyed him. She had been flitty, jittery, jumping about like a small nervous bird, and she was always pestering Arved, vying for her attention. And yet, Arved had loved her niece. They had laughed and giggled together as if they were both children.

They were girls: Arved, Agnes, his Elsebett. He knew animals and crops. He could assess the quality of an iron tool by holding it in his hand. He knew weather. He could look at an ox and come close to guessing its age, estimate its strength, analyze its character. He could frame an argument and present it before a room filled with plowmen. But he did not know girls. He did not really understand them. He did not know how to train then or transform them into young women. And now this woman had come, this mysterious spiny woman whose motives he could not decipher. This woman who lived alone in a small house surrounded by unrecognizable plants, who could be seen walking in the pastures and the woods and along the banks of the river picking up objects and slipping them into her pouch. This woman had come and had asked for his child, his Elsebett, the daughter of his Arved.

And so, after a long time, as Marsel sat silently beside him, Basil Helgen said something he had probably never said before in his life: "Mother, what do you think?"

ELEVEN

"Sometimes I call her by the wrong name," Marsel admitted to her son moments later. "I call her Margaret. Do you remember Margaret? That was your oldest sister. My firstborn child."

"Of course, I remember," Basil said. He remembered the name, but only vaguely the sister. Margaret was seven years older than he, and she had been little more than a child when she was given to the church as an oblate.

Marsel giggled. "When I call her Margaret, she laughs at me and says, 'I am Elsebett, Oma, remember?'"

Marsel paused for a moment. She had shed the last of her vanity in the eight years since Arved's death. She no longer covered her head indoors and her thinning hair fluttered around her head and neck as if she wore a covering of delicate white feathers.

"But it's not just confusion. The child does remind me of Margaret. She has the same hair, the same energy. My man feared Margaret's wildness—he called it wildness. She was high spirited, no question about that. She was like him, I guess, poor child. Both choleric, a preponderance of the yellow bile.

"He worried that she would bring shame to the family, that she would be a drain on his resources. He thought he would never find a man to take her. And should he find such a man there would remain the problem of the dowry. If he sent her out to work her worth, she would become a whore, he was sure of it. So, he would have to pay to get her married off. He complained about that over and over. In the end he had to pay to place her in the convent too, but not so much as a dowry would have cost."

"He was a hard man," Basil said.

"He was hard, but he was not all bad," Marsel said. "He took me in you know."

"Yes."

The truth was known in the family, though never mentioned, now that the father was dead. Johannes had impregnated the young Marsel, and rather than abandoning her, he had married her. He could have denounced her and left her shamed. But he had brought her home to his family's village as his bride. It was a generous act. But in Basil's eyes their father had fatally cheapened the gesture by reminding his children of it whenever tensions rose between him and their mother. "I took that woman in when I could have left her pregnant and alone, and now look at her!"

"He beat Margaret, I remember," Basil added a moment later.

"Yes, he beat her mercilessly." Marsel spoke softly, her eyes closed.

This memory, too, brought difficult images into the minds of both of them. If Marsel saw a young girl, Basil saw a big sister who yelled and hurled her small fists against their father's chest. She scratched at his face. He chased her through the house, his heavy limping stride, boots slamming against the floor, his voice raging. He became an animal when enraged. That was Basil's memory of it: a wild man loose with that whip ever-ready in his hand, the same whip he used on the oxen. But with a child he coiled and turned it in his hand. He beat them with the woven leather handle which had blackened from years of sweat and grime. It was thick and possessed a stiff flexibility that only increased its impact when flesh was struck. Basil had felt it himself, and as he sat beside his mother, the smell of that sweat-stained handle came to life and filled his nostrils. No wonder he had only vague memories of the beatings Sebastian claimed to have suffered. Bad as their father's treatment of Sebastian had been, it would have seemed mild compared to what he had witnessed him inflict on Margaret.

"I don't remember how it happened," he said to his mother. "Margaret was just gone one day and father refused to speak her name. I do remember that; he refused to have her name spoken in his presence. But you have always expressed pride that she and Ayla donated their lives to the church. You have even suggested the same for Johannes."

"Only if he should choose. I have made that clear with you, son. Only if he should choose. Ayla chose. Ayla loved everything about the church. And she was older. She was eighteen when she entered. But not Margaret. Margaret was eleven. She was thrown onto the wagon and hauled off to the convent and handed over to the abbess. My man had every right to do that. She was his responsibility and he saw no way out. But that doesn't mean it was easy to bear. To me she will always be my baby, my first born. That child still lives in my heart, and sometimes when I am with Elsebett, I confuse the two."

It occurred to Basil in the silence that followed, that he owed a huge debt to that distant sister who had disappeared from the house one day never to be seen again. He had learned how *not* to relate to their father. He glanced at his mother who appeared lost in reverie. Beneath her eyes, the pale blue shading of her skin seemed at that moment to have been applied with a very fine brush.

"So, mother," he said now, smiling slightly, "You still have not given me your thoughts. About Elsebett and the midwife."

"I have no say in that," Marcel said firmly, opening her eyes. "She is your child. Your responsibility. Even her mother is gone, poor child. No, I cannot advise you. You must decide, Basil. Only you."

"Yes."

But then Marsel added, as if the decision were obvious and had already been made: "I will miss her terribly. We all will. She brings a fine light into a room. In her the humors are better mixed than in Margaret or my man. She is less combative. She has your grace in that way."

"Yes," Basil said again.

"And Frau Mueller has promised me that every Sunday, every holiday, she will bring the child here to the house so that together we can walk to church. So, it won't be like Margaret. She won't be gone. She won't be unseen and unspoken of."

"This will be an apprenticeship, will it not?"

"Yes."

"And a wage set aside for her dowry?"

"Yes, she will be given some coins, but the bulk will be held back for her until she is of age."

"Held by whom?" Basil wanted to know.

Marsel thought about that. "I was assuming by the midwife. That is the custom, is it not?"

"Better that it be held by me, by her father."

"I think Frau Mueller will find that acceptable," Marsel said.

Basil took a deep breath and let it out slowly. "Johannes I can raise. I don't know how to raise a girl."

Marsel's hand squeezed her oldest son's thigh. "So, you have decided."

"Yes," Basil said, "I have decided."

THE MIDWIFE

TWELVE

When the midwife Frau Rachel Mueller was a young girl—she had to have been nine or less because she had been nine when her father died—her father had taken her to the abbey to witness the stoning of the goddess. It was the first and one of the few times she had been to the city and the abbey. Though she had been very young at the time, the experience remained engraved in her memory.

Her father had taken her early that morning before the crowd arrived because he wanted her to see up close the life-size marble statue of Venus. The statue was held captive against a wall in the abbey courtyard, bound there by heavy chains as if it were somehow alive and capable of its own volition. It was a depiction, her father explained, of a pagan goddess that had been carved and worshiped in far-away Roman times.

The statue was very damaged when Rachel saw it. Parts had been broken off and pieces of it lay beside the wall. Much of the body seemed battered as if it had been pounded on repeatedly by small hammers. To Rachel, however, the statue was one of the most beautiful things she had ever seen. On the wall beside it was an inscription. Neither Rachel nor her father could read, but a monk read the words aloud to them, saying something like: "I want you to know that I have been idolized but now I am broken. Saint Eucharius brought me to Trier where I have been shattered. I was honored as a god. Now I stand before the world ruined in this place."

Soon thereafter, a crowd gathered and the people threw stones at the statue. Her father said the stoning was meant to celebrate the victory of Christ over the pagan gods. The people yelled as they threw the stones and they cheered wildly if a piece broke from the statue and clattered to the earth.

Forty years later, Rachel had not forgotten the experience. She could still feel her hand secure in the large hand of her gentle father who threw no stones but who stood with her aside from the crowd. She could still picture the smooth, graceful lines of the least-damaged parts of the statue. She remembered the stone throwers, their loud mixture of rage and glee. And she had never forgotten how the elderly monk had transformed unintelligible markings on the wall into words that he could speak and she could understand.

§

Marsel knew it was clumsy, even brutal, but she could imagine no better way to handle it. One morning she told Elsebett to put on her best dress and pack her things. Elsebett understood what packing meant because now and then she still spent a few days with the families of Arved's two sisters, Anna and Gisele. "I am going to take you to meet someone," Marsel told her. "You are going to live with this woman. You will work for her and learn her ways."

"Forever?" Elsebett asked, tears forming in her eyes.

"Only heaven is forever, child. Now get your dress on and gather your things."

No one knew how to act. Marsel chose a day when the girl's father, her brother and her two uncles were away. Irmele, having been told nothing, was playing with the little boys. Neither Klara nor Ursula looked up from their work when the girl and her grandmother passed through the kitchen. Outside, Elsebett felt her grandmother's hand tremble.

"Are you scared, Oma?"

"No, my child. I am happy for you."

"I'm scared."

"Pshaw! When I was your age, my father was murdered by a rich man on a horse. I was taken to a strange village in the dark of night where my mother died soon after. You are going to another house in the village, that's all. You have nothing to be afraid of. And don't drag your shoes! You will soon be wearing them out and Frau Mueller will think you a lazy child and not want to have you."

A few minutes later as they were walking past the church, Elsebett asked: "Why are you crying, Oma?"

"Because I'm an old fool! You are so full of questions, child, I don't see how you can carry them all. Now come along."

Rachel's house stood at the edge of the village, close to a road that passed out of town toward the river. Elsebett remembered the road. It was the one they had used when Agnes had taken her, Irmele and Johannes to see the fish-birds, the strangest creatures Elsebett had ever seen. Small and gray with a white patch on their breasts, they flew like normal birds except that when they stood on rocks in the rapids, they bounced up and down as if they had to pee really badly. Then they jumped into the rushing water and swam and walked along underneath the surface! She had seen birds that could fly and swim, but never one that flew through the air and walked under the water.

Johannes started to throw rocks at them but Agnes made him stop. She insisted that the four of them sit quietly above the rapids and watch. "They are magic creatures," she whispered. "They have fish fathers and bird mothers, and if you hurt one you will have bad luck for seven years." Glancing at Johannes, she added, "Maybe more. And you can tell they are magic because when they come out of the water, their feathers aren't even wet."

As far as Elsebett could tell that was true, though she could not get close enough to touch the feathers and make sure.

When the river came into sight, she and her grandmother stopped for a moment at a spot just before the road began to descend. Below them, Elsebett saw a house set apart from the others and she asked if that was the house where they were going.

"Yes, my child, that is the house."

Elsebett shuddered and she squeezed her grandmother's hand. "Agnes said a witch lives in that house."

"Oh, that silly girl. She sees devils and witches everywhere she looks. When I see her I'll give her what for! Frau Mueller is not a witch. Witches do bad things. They serve devils. Frau Mueller fixes people who are sick. She helps babies come into the world. She helped you be born. Your dear mother loved Frau Mueller."

"Well, Agnes said she was a witch. She said she could turn a child into a toad if she set her mind to it. And the day we went to the river, she made us walk by very quiet. We could not talk and we had to walk past the house without looking straight at it. If we looked at all it had to be very quick, and only out the corners of our eyes. That's what Agnes said to do."

"When I see that girl I'll give her what for!" Marsel said again, between short breaths. "Frau Mueller is not a witch."

"Well…"

"Now, listen to me! There are some things I need to tell you. You must be a good child, you understand? You must do what Frau Mueller says. No complaints, no arguments. And no talk of witches. She thinks you come from a good home. If you are bad you will bring shame to me and your father and your poor dead mother. You get up when she tells you and go to bed when she says and do all the work she wants you to do. And…" At that moment, tears began to flow again from Marsel's eyes. "And, if you are good, Frau Mueller has promised me that every Sunday she will bring you to the house, and you and I can walk together to church. And you can stay all afternoon and play with Irmele and Gabriel and David and Thomas."

"And have dinner?"

"And even stay for dinner. And see your father and your uncles and Aunt Klara and Aunt Ursula. But only if you are good, you understand?"

"But why are you crying, Oma?"

"Because your Oma is an old fool, child."

THIRTEEN

Rachel Mueller peered through her shutters and saw them standing on the road above the house, the old woman and the little girl in her blue dress and her clean white apron, and she thought maybe she had made a mistake. So many years had passed since she had been a child; it was hard to put herself in the place of that little girl who stood there holding her grandmother's hand, looking so earnest and so afraid.

But there were similarities. Like this child, her mother had died bringing her into the world. That was true—now that she thought about it—of several of the midwives she had known. It was as if, like them, she had devoted her life trying to undue an injustice that she had no memory of, to fix a hurt that she felt—perhaps manufactured—when she saw a happy child with a happy mother. They say if you buy a black horse, you will see black horses wherever you go. In a similar way, Rachel thought, perhaps those of us who have known no mother see happy mothers wherever we go, and are destined to want to keep them alive and able to produce healthy babies.

But there were differences as well. This child's father lived, hers had died. This child had a devoted grandmother; Rachel had had only an angry, perhaps deranged aunt who fortunately, it turned out, packed her off to a convent in a strange town a few weeks after her father's death.

At the convent the child Rachel had been placed in the service of a nun named Gretel who was known for her visions. This skill—she would fall into trances and emerge with divine images, diagnoses and prophecies—drew people to her for guidance regarding their health, their spiritual salvation and their personal fortunes. People came from all levels of society in search of Gretel's guidance, and on the way out, many dropped donations into the welcoming hands of the prioress, a fact that gave Gretel considerable, if undeclared, authority in the convent. It was Gretel who directed Rachel toward the healing arts, though she was not herself a healer. She taught her how to read and sent her to the library to study the writings of Hildegard von Bingen and others. She arranged for her to work in the convent's infirmary and its herbal garden, where she learned the medicinal properties of plants and stones. She introduced Rachel to the wisdom of the four humors and their relation to the elements of earth, water, fire and air.

As Rachel watched the child and her grandmother, she realized how carefully she must create for herself this new role. She had never been a mother herself and she could not now become the mother of this child. The same had been true of Gretel. Gretel had never been a mother, and she did not assume the role of Rachel's substitute mother. No, the role Gretel had fashioned had been different. And how difficult that must have been, because Gretel had truly loved her. Looking now at the child, she recognized how strong the pull must have been, because already she wanted to run out, sweep the child up, kiss her cheeks and squeeze her young body against her own. The longing was unfathomable. It came from some deep well of spirit, from below her thoughts and dreams. And the same must have been true for Gretel.

So, when the knock came at the door, Rachel forced herself to wait a few moments before she greeted Marsel and invited them in. She had prepared some small cakes sweetened with honey, and when they were seated and after she and Marsel had exchanged pleasantries, she passed the plate around. The child refused to taste or even touch one. She sat silent, hands clutched on her lap, eyes cast down, looking neither at her grandmother nor at the midwife.

It was a touchy moment. Who was in charge here: the child, the grandmother or the new guardian? At home, Marsel would have instructed the silly girl to take a cake and eat it, which she had found on her first bite to be delicious. But at that moment Marsel felt close to despair. Something dear, she realized, had been given away. Upon entering this house she had ceded her authority. Her sense of herself as a grandmother did not extend to this darkish room that smelled strangely of spices and herbs. Was the child's refusal the fault of that silly Agnes? Did she believe this woman was a witch and that the cake would actually poison her? Had Agnes been present at that moment, Marsel would have boxed her ears. But who should act? Marsel felt responsible but paralyzed. Was it now Rachel's responsibility to instruct the child?

Then the midwife did a surprising thing. Without a word she rose and stood in front of Elsebett. The girl stiffened pushing herself back in the chair, and for an instant Marsel feared the woman might slap the child. But then she sat down on the hard floor directly in front of the girl, literally at the child's feet, whose shoes dangled a few inches above the floor. The move had not been easy or altogether graceful; Marsel heard joints complain and a solid thump as the woman's bottom hit the floor. She was both amazed at the midwife's behavior, and appalled that she, as the child's grandmother, had caused this bizarre behavior by failing to discipline the child herself.

No one spoke. Her eyes on her lap, Elsebett pulled her legs back as far as she could. She did not want to look at this old woman who was acting so strangely. But she was curious. Big people in her experience did not get down on the floor in front of a child sitting on a chair.

When she finally did look up, the midwife was looking into her eyes and smiling. It was just a quiet smile. The dark eyes seemed to say: take a good look if you want, this is who I am. And what Elsebett saw was a small, skinny woman, well, skinny above but thick below, as was clear from the heavy thighs folded beside her on the floor, and old—not as old as her grandmother, but older than her aunts. The round head was uncovered, which was itself surprising. And the mostly gray hair was very curly and not too long; it had the look of a fuzzy ball you could sink your fingers into. Like the fur of a shaggy dog.

Then, after a long moment, the woman with the head of curls said, "Would you like to see my garden?"

Elsebett nodded and smiled just a little, and the three of them got up, Marsel rushing to assist the midwife who rose with some difficulty. The child started to reach for the plate of cakes, then hesitated. But Frau Mueller nodded, and the girl took a single cake with her as the three of them left the house by the back door and stepped into the garden.

FOURTEEN

Rachel Mueller had not taken vows to become a nun, but she had spent nine impressionable years in the convent, and its rhythms remained integral to her life. Her routine became Elsebett's as well. They were in bed and asleep shortly after dark. In the middle of the night, they woke to pray. Rachel was silent during this hour. Holding a candle, she woke the child with a nudge on her shoulder, and taking her hand led her to a small altar where she knelt on a mat, indicating that Elsebett should kneel beside her.

During the long, dark winter in particular, members of Elsebett's family were often awake and moving about at night.

The fire might be stoked, the chamber pot used, a chair would creak when a body sat on it. Prayer, a devotion that could be performed without disturbing others and without the light required for manual work, was a common nighttime practice for adults in the Helgen family. There was something comforting to the child when half-awake she would hear muffled and yet familiar sounds as the adults moved about the house.

Still, being woken by Frau Mueller that first night had terrified Elsebett. The candlelight was wavering and unstable. The hand on her shoulder, the silent, gray and bony woman poised above her. Agnes's story of Lucifer had been reinforced many times over. Elsebett had an unquestioned understanding that there existed forces, that while not of this world, powerfully influenced it. At the edges of the commonplace, while squealing pigs were fed and peas shelled and shredded cabbage packed into crocks, a great battle was being fought for the soul of each and every person. God, through his church, commanded one side of the battlefield, while the Devil and his minions occupied the other. The Devil wanted to steal your soul, and the church existed to help you save it. Thus, while the fallen Lucifer was unseen, his presence as wavering as the light from the old woman's candle, he was in Elsebett's mind as real as her grandmother was real.

So, the shoulder nudge and the flickering candle not only wakened Elsebett from sleep; they brought back into her awareness the worry she had largely dismissed the night before. Had Agnes been right? Was this strange and powerful woman in whose home she was now confined indeed a witch, a woman who served the Devil himself?

The two of them knelt side by side, and the candle cast its unsteady light on the gruesome crucifix as the woman's lips moved and her fingers slid along a string of beads. Elsebett was fully alert. She held herself very still, her breath shallow. She wanted to pray the way her grandmother had taught her, but her thoughts rushed about, charged and erratic. Then, after what seemed a very long time, the woman set down the rosary and stiffly rose. She took the candle in one hand and the child's hand in the other and the two of them made their way back to Elsebett's new bed. There the woman smiled down on her, and for a brief instant she touched her hair, and then she left.

§

As soon as the light of morning appeared they rose again. After washing themselves they had bread and a cup of weak beer. This was followed by study and work. Their main meal was at noon. In the afternoon they returned to work, and the workday ended with a second hour of prayer, then a light evening meal. As darkness came on they retired to their beds.

When Elsebett returned home for the first time that next Sunday, she proudly announced that she had become a nun and was learning to read. The second part was true. With Gretel's guidance, Rachel had learned to read, and now she started their morning routine teaching the same skill to Elsebett.

Elsebett's news both frightened and exhilarated Marsel. No one in the extended family could read. Sebastian might be able to decipher a few words if handed one of the illustrated broadsheets or pamphlets in common circulation. The same was true of Martin, the father of Zacharias who managed the inn, though he was more capable with written numbers than words. But the ability to actually read and understand the words in a text was rare.

Marsel had never experienced her inability to read as a lack or saw herself as deprived in any practical sense. Stories were told, skills taught and history explained. Even at her present age, when she might forget the bread baking in the oven, or where she had placed their best kitchen knife, her expanded bank of memory was alive with useful information that she frequently called upon to make sense of the world. In the church, and in other public assemblies, written texts were regularly read aloud. Much was also described with visual images. If a person could see, if she could listen and understand, she would not be ignorant of social discourse or news of the day.

Still, that her granddaughter was learning this skill excited Marsel. The idea possessed a charm. It would set her apart from everyone Marsel knew. The ability to read belonged to another class of people entirely. It was as if Elsebett were stealing something and bringing it home to them. Or—and Marsel's rush of enthusiasm was tempered by another thought—it might mean the opposite: that her granddaughter was embarking on a journey from which she would never return.

Rachel had not told Marsel that Elsebett's training would include reading. Marsel had not known that Frau Mueller possessed this skill herself. She realized that first Sunday how casual, even disinterested Frau Mueller had appeared when she introduced the idea of taking Elsebett on as an apprentice. She needed help around the house. She was aging and she wanted to pass her skills on to a younger woman. She liked the child, knew she had no mother. But the offer was presented in an offhand manner. Still, Marsel realized now, she had detected an undercurrent from the beginning. Just any young girl would not do. Frau Mueller was drawn to Elsebett in particular. She wanted this child to be the one. She had been not devious exactly, but careful. She revealed nothing that might concern Marsel, or more importantly the child's father. And the worrisome part now was the father. How would Basil respond to the news Elsebett was so eagerly reporting to everyone?

Age had not diminished Marsel's concern for each strand of her extended family. The day Basil had taken Johannes to the abbey for the first time, she had been alert to their absence until she saw them return. When Klara traveled with Irmele and little Gabriel to visit her parents, a full-day's journey each way that occasioned a two-week visit, Marsel found herself thinking of them constantly.

The strand of the family that concerned her now was Elsebett and her apprenticeship to the midwife. That Frau Mueller had selected Elsebett specifically did not trouble Marsel; it flattered her. That the midwife had proceeded so cautiously, coyly almost, as if she were tantalizing a kitten with a length of yarn, this too only heightened Marsel's commitment. The child had been chosen for important work by a skilled and sly woman who had much to teach.

So, Marsel insisted that Elsebett sit down with her. First, she explained that following a routine at Frau Mueller's house while similar to one followed by women in a convent, did not make her a nun. Frau Mueller, she told the girl, had learned the routine in a convent but she was herself not a nun, and neither was Elsebett. Being a nun was something you chose. And only big girls could make that choice. "So, we don't want to tell your father or anyone else that you are becoming a nun."

"Will he be mad?" Elsebett wanted to know.

"No, not mad because he knows you are not a nun, but he might be confused because Frau Mueller is not a nun. Frau Mueller helps babies be born and sick people to get better. And that is what she is going to teach you. Not how to be a nun."

"Is that why I'm learning to read, to help babies be born?"

"I don't know, child," Marsel admitted. "You will have to ask Frau Mueller that question. But it will be best if I talk about the reading with your father before you do."

"Can you read, Oma?"

The idea caused Marsel to laugh. "Oh no, child, I sure cannot. But maybe when you have learned you will teach me."

And Irmele, a child who seemed to have inherited not a drop of her mother's bluster, made the same request: "Will you teach me too, Elsebett?"

"I will teach you both!" Elsebett shouted. And the idea of it caused her and Irmele to clap their hands together and jump into the air.

FIFTEEN

Certain things went on at Frau Mueller's that did not include Elsebett. People came to the house, they met with her in private and then they left. The midwife established a procedure and instructed the child to follow it. When someone knocked on the door, Elsebett alone would admit them. This was true even if Frau Mueller happened to be standing by the door. The midwife would disappear and only then would Elsebett open the door. She would lead the visitor to the "study," the small sitting room where she and her grandmother had been taken that first day, and then she too would disappear. She should welcome the visitor, but even if she knew them, she should not linger about talking.

"People do not come here to chat," Frau Mueller told her. "You may hear me gossiping with them, even laughing, but never forget this truth: the visitor has come for another purpose. It is my job to discover that purpose. Sometimes it is obvious, other times it is not."

It made no sense to Elsebett that a person would come to the house, knock on the door and not know why they had come, but her teacher insisted that was true.

"The visitor is always experiencing some form of distress," Frau Mueller explained. "The distress has brought them to the door. But what underlies the distress? That is the question. We are mysterious creatures, we souls, mysterious even to ourselves. Our task as healers, is to listen and observe. For now, you need only know this: the distress is always real. It is always valid, however silly it might seem to us. We must never injure the person by mocking or even questioning their distress. That is why I must insist for now that you not chat with the visitors, even if they want to chat with you. You must always and politely leave the room as soon as you have brought them to the study and offered them a chair. As to the reason for the distress, the underlying cause or causes, that we must leave until you are older and know more."

While Elsebett was excluded, it turned out that she was also included, because after a visitor had left, her teacher would always ask her a few questions. How old did she think the visitor was? What was he or she wearing? Had the visitor's knock been urgent or cautious? Did they appear angry or docile? How did they behave? Were they polite, dismissive, insistent, distracted? And Frau Mueller would always end her interrogation with one final question: "Can you tell me one thing about this person that you found surprising or interesting?"

So Elsebett, as she was pulling weeds or washing utensils, had to force herself to remember every detail she could about the person she had just met. The whole experience seemed artificial to her. Why couldn't Frau Mueller answer the door herself? It was almost comical, the way she fled the moment a knock was heard. And since she had just spent an hour or more with the person, why was she interrogating Elsebett about what the woman wore or how she behaved?

As the weeks passed Elsebett's comfort increased and her inclination to ask questions returned. "Why don't you answer the door yourself?" she asked one day after a visitor had left. "Why do you ask me these questions, when you have just been with the visitor?"

They were seated at the table in the kitchen. Frau Mueller appeared pensive and was slow to respond.

"Come," she said after a long pause, "come sit with me." She rose and walked the two of them to the study; it was as if Elsebett were herself a visitor suffering some form of distress. The room had its own small fireplace in which coals still smoldered. The shutters on the window were closed but her teacher opened them partially now, admitting some light and the fresh smell of the garden.

Entering the study with the midwife brought a sense of heightened awareness to Elsebett. The room existed apart from the day-to-day activities in the house. No one slept or ate or prayed there and normally the door was kept closed. As instructed she had not lingered the few times she had delivered guests to the room. On those occasions the space had seemed quite gloomy and forbidding to her. She had not been instructed to bring light or open the shutters, so she would indicate a chair to the visitor and then hurriedly leave. The only time she had sat in the room had been the morning her grandmother brought her. And she had been so apprehensive that she could remember only her own fear. Had there been a fire in the hearth? Had the shutters been open or closed? Was the oil lamp lit? She could not have said.

When they had taken seats, Frau Mueller said, "I am pleased that you have questions. That shows you want to learn. And I am pleased that you feel free to ask them. That suggests you are becoming comfortable in my home."

Elsebett nodded, and looked around. The room was furnished with four chairs and three small tables. On the tables were several stones, some vessels, the lamp and a few candles. Shelving along one wall was cluttered with a dusty jumble of sacks, ceramic containers of various shapes and sizes, a few vases from which protruded dried flowers and grasses.

Watching her, Frau Mueller asked: "How does this room make you feel?"

"I like the big window," Elsebett said. "And it smells good in here."

"Does the room scare you?"

Elsebett caught her breath. She looked at her teacher and then admitted that it did.

"I'm not surprised," Frau Mueller said. "It's not my intent to scare people. But I like that the room appears somewhat mysterious when a visitor first enters. Healing is a mysterious process. It takes place in mystery. It is mysterious both to the healer and to the person healed. If a healer is truly honest, she cannot say why the person has been healed, or if the person does not recover, why her efforts have failed. She might have ideas, thoughts about why a medicine or a technique worked or failed to work. She might be inclined to repeat a technique, or to perform it differently the next time. But in the end the process is mysterious. Always. There are more things I could say to you on this subject, but that will do for now. And the words I have just spoken are my answer to your first question. That is, why I have you answer the door when a visitor knocks. I understand that the meaning might not be obvious to you just yet."

Elsebett nodded somewhat warily. She experienced at that moment, a sensation that in the weeks since she had been with Frau Mueller had become familiar. The sensation was internal, private and somewhat uncomfortable. It involved friction, a slightly abrasive quality as if two objects were rubbing against one another.

Elsebett no longer felt the physical fear that had obsessed her the first day. Frau Mueller was not the witch she had imagined from Agnes's description: a wild-haired hag in a black conical hat with bad teeth and glinting eyes, who offered you a sweet cake while stoking the fire as she prepared to cook and eat you. Rather, she sensed a deep kindness coming from the old woman. She knew now that she could trust Frau Mueller. It would not be inaccurate to suggest that Elsebett was coming to love her teacher.

But, rubbing against that attraction was a sense of caution. It was as if her teacher's affection was a wary animal that showed itself, even approached, but then paused, kept itself at a distance. And that caution in Frau Mueller produced a balancing caution in Elsebett. The other adults in the girl's life: her father, her grandmother, her aunts and four uncles, all had individual characteristics and each varied from the other. But the character of each was familiar and offered itself to her without hesitation. They were what they were, and she loved them without thought or qualification as she knew they loved her. But Frau Mueller was different. She was always alert, somehow wary.

As Elsebett's mind wondered, she stared at her hands clutched tightly on her lap. Realizing now that her teacher had stopped talking, she looked up to see that the woman was watching her in that careful way. She thought she should apologize, but hesitated.

"As to your second question," Frau Mueller said now. "The question, I believe, being—why am I always asking you questions about the visitor after I have just seen the visitor myself? Is that correct?"

"Yes," Elsebett said.

"As to that I will say two things. The first is that I believe you possess the qualities to become a skilled healer. That is why I asked your family to let you come live with me. One requirement of a healer is that she be very aware of the person who requests healing. So, by asking you questions, I am teaching you to pay close attention. Does that make sense?"

"Yes," Elsebett said again.

"The second thing is that help might come to the healer from anywhere. It is a foolish healer who thinks she alone knows the answers. You, in your few minutes with the visitor, may have noticed something that I in the hour I spent with them failed to notice. So, in that way, you are already helping me."

The midwife paused for a long time and then said, "I am going to say one thing more that you will hear from me many times. It is another way of answering your questions, though it may not make sense to you now. Perhaps it never will. But I will repeat it often because it is obvious to me. And that is this: each person, each thing, each plant, each animal, each star, exists separately in this world that God has given us, but none of us is separated. We may think we are, but we are not. We are not separated from each other, not from God and not from the world around us."

Rachel sighed and then quickly stood. "Now, are you as hungry as I am?"

"Yes," Elsebett said a third time.

SIXTEEN

Rachel lay on her bed in the blackened house with the shutters closed, the smell of the extinguished candle fading, the child, she hoped, comfortably asleep in the adjoining room.

The house and the village were truly blackened. On clear nights when the moon was up some glow creeped in around the shutters. But on nights when the moon was down, or the sky was overcast, or as on this night when a dense fog had settled along the river, filling the valley like a thick comforter, it seemed that no light remained in the world. Had God stolen it away, convinced, perhaps, that his flawed creations had not used it wisely the day before? And during the night did he ponder whether to give it back to us?

Rachel liked to imagine God as uncertain, as ever undecided, perhaps even tormented. Was the coming of morning guaranteed? Or was it even now being debated? Could God be multisided? Were different sides engaged in a struggle as the night drew on?

Were she with Gretel on this dark night, she could have expressed these curious ideas to her. She imagined the two of them huddled together in the convent cell. They might have laughed or cried or prayed as they pondered these thoughts. With Gretel nothing needed to be denied or hidden. She lived confined within a convent but well outside of doctrine. Her mind sparkled with images and ideas, her emotions flourished, unstable and unsuppressed.

Rachel thought now of the geese who passed over the village, following the river up or down in their seasonal migrations. You could hear them coming, each gray bird cackling loudly as if complaining about the flock's speed or direction. Chaos reigned—those in front seemed more chased than leading, while those behind rushed to take command— and yet as she watched, fluid patterns formed and dissolved and reformed in ways that seemed somehow orderly. In her mind all life was like that, and God was a name we gave to that creative chaos. If morning comes, she thought, it will have resulted from a similarly riotous conflab.

Best then to keep a candle lit at all times. Rachel knew about fire and had great respect for it. A flame was a thing both dangerous and fragile, a precious possession that sustained life and offered hope. It had the power to transform dark into light, cold into warmth, raw flesh into cooked food. It should be guarded, looked after, protected. While a home with an errant flame could burn to the ground, taking lives and possessions with it, a home without a flame was dark, desolate and cold, hardly a home at all.

She knew from experience that once extinguished, fire became a pouty, stubborn thing—no, not a thing, an absence—a vacancy reluctant to be again inhabited. Fire had to be sought after. It required coaxing, pleading. Embers in the hearth had to be poked through, broken apart and blown upon as the body shivered, as tender knees pressed against the cold stones, as dry ash swirled about clogging her nostrils and darkening her face. And should fire have fled the hearth, taking with it the last of its heat, she would be sent on a clumsy search for metal, stone and precious tinder: a thing dry and flaky and unresistant that could be cupped close and seduced by sparks to smolder; and then being devoutly breathed upon as if by prayer, brought to flame.

And yet knowing the cost, Rachel had on this dark night extinguished the one remaining flame in the house. She felt herself compelled to enter the darkness, to be absorbed by it, even though it would mean frustration, humiliation and pain later on, perhaps for the precious child as well as herself.

She sat up now on her bed and wrapped herself in a wooly skin. The darkness was complete; the silence had become itself a presence, and she a tangle of thoughts, emotions, fleeting images. Energies swirled about. Some compressed themselves like crouching demons in her chest, behind her temples. The words filling her mind in the darkness contradicted those she had offered the child. But I am myself separated, she thought. I am isolated and alone. She felt herself at that moment an incapable guardian of this young life, an inadequate healer, an unworthy teacher.

Her troubled thoughts found their way back to the nun Gretel, and she realized what her teacher would have said to her at that moment. "There is no place to go, Rachel; there is no thing to do; there is no one to cling to, no one to whom you can cry out. You can only sit alone with yourself in the darkness; with the darkness that is within, with the darkness that is without. Be where you are, feel what you feel."

This practice, Gretel had taught her, is the purest form of prayer, unvoiced, undirected.

"When you have gone beyond thought, you will have arrived at the beginning and at the end. You will be where I am," Gretel had said. "You will be where the venerated saints are."

Rachel settled herself in the dark night and pulled the wooly skin tightly around her.

SEVENTEEN

Most days Elsebett was assigned jobs after she had completed her reading study. She drew water and brought it into the house, grasping the pail handle in both hands and carrying it in front of her, taking short, frog-legged steps. Using a short-handled broom, she cleaned ashes from the hearths and carried them out and spread them in the garden. Floors needed to be scrubbed, garments washed and stretched out in the sun. She minded the barley porridge cooking for the noonday meal. Working alone, Elsebett missed her old life. Work was not the problem—as Klara had said, she was beginning to earn her food. But at home she had company as she went about her tasks. Her grandmother and her aunts were always about. Often she and Irmele had worked together, the two of them picking through a mess of lentils, stripping the pods from the plants, the seeds from the pods, tossing the errant stones at the little boys playing on the ground nearby. But now when Frau Mueller was otherwise occupied, Elsebett was alone, and the house seemed to her empty and devoid of life.

Shortly after Elsebett's arrival, Rachel had gone one day to visit a man who was confined to his house. She knew the visit would be unpleasant. The man was elderly. He lived alone in a hovel that smelled of swine and urine and feces, and was looked in upon by neighbors who were themselves infirm. The man refused help from the physician. The problem in his mind was not that he was old or ill or nearing death. The problem was the demons that he imagined surrounded him. They tainted his food, they disturbed his rest, they soiled his bed while he slept. The young priest had come and offered prayers, but according to the man the prayers had been useless: the taunting demons continued their clamor unabated. "Can't you see them?" he had shouted at Rachel the first time she visited. "Can't you smell them?"

Knowing what awaited her, Rachel had assigned home duties to Elsebett and had gone alone. But when she returned to the house a few hours later she discovered a wilted child, her eyes reddened, her mouth downturned. At the table she spilled her food, and apologizing for that and rushing to clean it up, stumbled against a chair leg. None of this was like her. The dejection, so evident on the girl's face, caused Rachel to recognize that the child did not do well alone. And that was a problem for both of them. Rachel had lived alone for years. She treasured aloneness. Focused on her own study, her own work, she could forget the child's existence for hours at a time. She *wanted* to forget the child's existence at times.

Other days were better. One clear October afternoon Rachel decided to bed parts of the garden down for the winter. Near the stretch of backwall beyond the cultivated area was some rotting straw, a large mound of what remained from grain-threshing a year or more before. So happy was Elsebett to be out-of-doors! She ran back and forth between the pile and the garden clutching arms full of the moldy straw, the musty smell filling her nostrils while her teacher spread it in thick layers on the ground. Seeing the woman hunkered down and moving about on her thick haunches as if she were some awkward toad-like creature, required the girl to bite down on her dirty thumb to keep from laughing.

Another morning, Frau Mueller described some hazel trees she knew of. That afternoon they searched them out and filled their sacks and the pockets of their aprons with the nuts. "Here is what I can tell you about this tree and its fruit," she told the girl. "An ill person should not eat the nuts because they will make his chest congested. A healthy person can eat them without damage and I personally enjoy them in the winter. In moderation, of course, and assuming I am in good health. In the spring, a powder can be made by drying the new buds and crushing them. This powder should be applied to the skin of a person suffering from scrofula. There is also a compound I know of. It is made by grinding the nuts and mixing them with parts of some animals and other plants. It is a rather complicated process that I have not personally tried. But the compound is said to help a man produce children. Perhaps for this reason the tree symbolizes lasciviousness." Rachel paused, somewhat embarrassed. "In general terms," she continued, "the tree is more cold than hot and beyond what I have described is not much used for medicine."

On the way home they followed the towpath along the river and Elsebett related Agnes's story about the strange fish-birds that could be seen in the rushing tributary. The story delighted her teacher. She knew the birds; she had watched them.

A few days later the two of them hiked to the village forest. Elsebett knew parts of the forest. Johannes took her and Irmele there at times to gather acorns for the pigs. But on this trip, Rachel introduced her to the forest warden, and the warden—a man who told Elsebett in reverential tones that Frau Mueller had once saved his life—led them to a copse where the shoots had recently been cut from the large stumps and tossed onto piles. The landscape of the copse struck Elsebett as grotesque. The three of them stood among hundreds of short thick stumps with bulbous, almost mushroom-like tops.

"Are these trees never allowed to grow up?" she asked, her voice breaking.

The warden laughed. "No, my dear. Every few years their shoots are cut off so they can never become tall. But by virtue of their service—by giving us their shoots—our Lord has granted these trunks eternal life. If God be willing, the grandchildren of your greatgrandchildren will in this copse gather wood for their hearths as did your grandparents before you."

They were free to gather all they needed, the warden assured them, and they made several trips to the house with bundles strapped on their backs. On prior occasions Rachel had entertained the fantasy that she and the girl were like sisters, but on this day, with her back stiff and her legs aching as they made their final trek from the copse back to the house, Rachel felt that fantasy shatter. The girl seemed to draw vitality from the out-of-doors. Her youth, her strength and endurance stunned and delighted Rachel. It brought the father, the stolid Basil, to mind. In the child, she realized, the father's vitality flourished. But in the girl it had assumed an altered form. It had been tempered, purified by the late mother's innocence and virtue. And this memory of Arved—which in Rachel's mind always led to the image of the young mother dying on the bed and she helpless to alter the course of it, perhaps she was even the cause of it—sent stabs of grief and self-doubt through the older woman.

EIGHTEEN

Rachel was recognized by the local authorities as the village midwife. It was her task, in addition to assisting with deliveries, to present birth information to the village keeper of records. She provided the date of birth, the sex of the child and the names of the parents. She had even been trained by a priest to conduct an emergency baptism should a child be born alive but destined for an early death. It was also her responsibility to properly dispose not only of the placenta and umbilical cord but also the remains of a stillborn child to ensure that they did not come into the possession of a witch.

The house in which she and Elsebett lived was the property of the village. Beyond the use of the house and a small stipend, she was dependent upon donations received from those who used her services. Neither her skills as a healer nor as a midwife gave her status with the medical community: not with the barber-surgeon who ran the bathhouse and performed bloodletting and other minor surgeries, nor with the scholarly and distant physician who lived in a neighboring village. As a woman she could not form or belong to a guild, but her recognition as the community midwife did authorize her to practice her profession. A woman without recognition might have been prosecuted for doing what she did.

Among the women in the village, Rachel was respected by most, revered by some. As a midwife she was experienced, capable and comforting. She was unhurried and she possessed a sense of detached compassion that was free of sentimentality. She had learned early. Short of eleven years of age, she was already assisting in the convent infirmary. Gretel—who never went near the place herself—had insisted on it. Her vision was clear: she saw Rachel there, and the infirmary introduced her to midwifery. Marginalized women from the outside community— prostitutes, the underaged and the unmarried—came in numbers to give birth, often leaving the child behind when they left.

After Gretel had died and after Rachel had decided not to become a nun, a prominent couple—the husband had once been the mayor—persuaded her to move to the village and work with the elderly midwife who lived in the house that Rachel and Elsebett would later occupy. A few months after she arrived, the old woman had died in her sleep, leaving Rachel the lone midwife in a village, that seemed, at least to her, swollen with pregnant women.

The practice of midwifery did not require her to be apart from the girl. The door to the birthing room barred men and all boys weaned and older. But female toddlers crawled about and little girls played with dolls while the mother labored. From the beginning, Elsebett accompanied Rachel when she visited pregnant and birthing women. She was given tasks and encouraged to ask questions. Just coming to a house with the midwife gave her status. Rachel utilized a birthing stool and among other duties, Elsebett was assigned responsibility for the chair. She transported it to the birth, holding it in front of her by two of its three legs. She kept the stool clean and uncluttered and returned it home after the birth. Seeing the girl passing through the village with the stool alerted everyone that a birth had occurred or was about to. Thus, coming and going, Elsebett became a sort of town crier—the stool serving the purpose of a bell—drawing women who questioned her about the pending birth or its outcome.

It was the healing side of her practice that gave Rachel pause. Her calling—and she had long ago accepted that Gretel's vision had been true, this was her calling—took her wherever she could be of use: to the sick, the old, the dying, the insane. She thought again of that man dying in his squalid hovel surrounded by demons. Elsebett hated to be alone, but should she be subjected to that? On the other hand Rachel had survived her father's death when she was only nine. And what she had learned in the sometimes bloody, pain-filled convent infirmary had proven invaluable.

What Rachel lacked was certainty. Unlike Gretel, she did not wake from a trance knowing how to proceed. And while she recognized Elsebett's strengths, she also saw her vulnerabilities. The child had been removed from her home and was now dependent on her alone.

But the real problem, Rachel realized, was her own. The desire to have this child had been so overwhelming that it felt tainted. True, she had needed an assistant. And there would be women in the village who needed a midwife when she could no longer provide the service. But the strength of her yearning troubled her. Elsebett was more than an assistant. Rachel loved her in a way she had not loved anyone since Gretel. She had achieved her goal—the child lived in her home—and now she felt responsible.

Thoughts of the dead mother came to her, the trusting Marsel, the willing Basil, the vulnerable child. They had placed their trust in her, but she did not quite trust herself. Some things Rachel had simply excluded from her life. She had never married. She had never known sexual intimacy. She just did not allow herself to think about these things. She had never had a child to care for, not even a younger sibling. She could have chosen a grown woman as her student but she had chosen Elsebett. She had gone in pursuit of her. Perhaps for the first time in her life, Rachel had opened herself to deep desire. Now she felt the pangs of its pull with each decision she made.

She wanted to protect the child. She loved her innocence and did not want to damage it in any way. But Rachel's calling destroyed innocence. Do women scream when giving birth? Do women come to her who have been beaten by their fathers and drunken husbands? Are young girls violated by family members? Do men cry out in agony when injured or facing death? Do people age alone and insane in smelly shelters beset by devils? She had found all of this and more. So, what to share and what to exclude?

Some aspects of life, it seemed to Rachel, should be avoided by everyone, by young and old alike. Rage did generate rage. Violence did breed violence. Cruelty did give birth to the cruel. Stand apart from these. Do nothing to strengthen them. Was that not the message of Christ?

But the results of these transgressions, and that which was inherent in the human estate—the trials of coming into it, the injuries and illnesses suffered during the course of it, the traumas associated with leaving it—perhaps these could not and should not be hidden from the girl.

Death is as common as birth, Rachel told Elsebett one evening. This was after she had finally taken the girl to visit the demon-obsessed man, alone and mad and clinging to life in his foul hovel. When they were back on the street, Elsebett had almost shouted, tears flowing toward her cheeks: "Can't you fix him?"

The child's cry had been so urgent, so insistent and it had cut through Rachel like a blade. But she felt she had responded well, firmly and without hesitation. "No, I cannot. I cannot fix him. I can only be with him."

"I want you to be able to fix him."

"Yes, I know. But I cannot."

Elsebett looked stunned, perhaps betrayed as they continued their walk home in silence. But Rachel felt a sense of relief, as if she had gone to confession. And it seemed to her that some essential knowledge had passed from her to the child.

So that night in the quiet moments before they retired, she said to the girl, "Death is as common as birth, Elsebett. Both are passages, and both sacred. Not all illnesses lead to death but some do. And the strength of the human spirit, you will learn, is at times astounding."

"But you do heal people," the girl insisted. "People have told me that you have healed them."

Rachel shook her head. "I know, but it's not true. They call people like us healers, but we do not heal. No human has the power to do that. We can only establish the conditions in which a person might heal himself. Or in his grace, God might choose to heal him. Do you understand? You could say we point the person toward an open door, but only he can walk through it. Healings occur. Miracles do happen, but we do not cause them, and we should not expect them. It is our duty, our privilege, to witness these moments close up, to assist as we are able. But it is also our responsibility to not exaggerate what we can do, or be destroyed by what we cannot."

NINETEEN

One afternoon that autumn Rachel handed Elsebett a spring scissors and a large sack made from linen cloth and instructed her to gather the seed heads from the many fennel plants that grew against the wall at the back of the house. The plants' dense green fronds, so dominant in spring were largely gone now, the few that remained being hardened and brown. The petals of the yellow flowers had fallen to the ground and the stalks appeared straggly and spare, as if the long season had made them bitter and somehow foreboding. Some she had to pull down to reach the seeds; others grew no higher than her waist. As she clipped the heads and dropped them into the sack, the licorice smell seemed almost intoxicating.

Back inside, she found her teacher in a room even more mysterious than the study. It was here the midwife stored supplies and prepared medicines. Most interesting to Elsebett were the various vessels lined up along one shelf. In addition to the stone mortars and pestles and several common wooden bowls, ceramic jars and vases, there were other containers made of silver, iron and steel. Each metal and each stone, Frau Mueller had explained to her, had its own character. Silver, for example was cold. Some medicines should be prepared in a silver vessel, and to eat or drink from such a vessel was always beneficial, though the metal itself should never be consumed. Thus silver was unlike gold, which was hot and could properly be added to some medicines and in small quantities beneficially consumed.

Frau Mueller dumped the bag of seed heads onto a long table below a narrow window and the two of them began grinding the heads one by one in their fists, picking out the seeds and placing them in a bowl. "I like to eat the leaves," Elsebett confided as they worked. "But not the ones now."

The midwife smiled. The first memory she had of Elsebett—following her birth, that is—happened one day when she had gone to visit Marsel. Marsel at that time had a complaint about her eyes and Rachel had prepared a powder of rue, sage and chervil that she could apply to her temples at night. Marsel was working in the garden. With her was the girl, who was probably two or three at the time. Rachel was surprised by how connected the child was to the plants around her. As she walked, she extended her hand to brush against leaves and vines. There was nothing grasping or brutal about her behavior, just a casual, almost unconscious caress. At one point she knelt down, and jutting her face forward, brushed her cheek against the delicate leaves of a carrot. The gesture caused both women to chuckle. It reminded them of a grown woman brushing a fine fabric against her face just for the feel of it.

Energy was being exchanged, Rachel realized. The child possessed a natural understanding of how energy flowed between and through objects. Separate but not separated. The little girl knew without knowing.

"Your body knows what it's doing," the midwife told her now. "To eat fennel is to be made happy. It possesses a mild nature, not cold and yet not hot and it sweetens the breath. You were wise to eat the fronds early in the spring. At that time the plant's medicine is in its leaves, but once the flowers begin to form, the medicine flows from the leaves into the flowers and then from the flowers into the seeds. This is true in general of plants that produce flowers, fruits and seeds.

"I dry fennel leaves in the spring and gather its seeds in the fall. The plant is used in many medicines, some eaten, some applied to the skin. It has the capacity to draw out imbalanced humors. What we are doing now though is gathering a supply of seeds that we might use over the winter. We are doing what your father does when he cuts and threshes the barley and rye and stores those seeds so the family can have bread, pottage and beer when the ground is frozen and sterile."

At the mention of her family, Elsebett grew quiet. After a few minutes Rachel said, "On Sunday you will see them again." To this the girl nodded. After another pause, Rachel added, "If we have time, we can prepare some little cakes to take with you. We could flavor them with a few fennel seeds should you like."

"Yes," Elsebett said, suddenly brightening. "Irmele loves cakes more than anything."

§

Every Sunday morning Rachel walked Elsebett to the Helgen home. They put on their best garments, and everyone they met along the way had done the same. Sundays had a festive air. Sunday was the day of the week when Christ had risen from the dead, the day that attending Mass was compulsory and work was forbidden.

To Rachel, delivering the girl back to her father and grandmother both fulfilled a promise and provided satisfaction. Here, she was saying, I am delivering the child back to you. As you can see, she is healthy and happy in my care.

The visit also gave Rachel a chance to connect, however obliquely, with Basil. She had reservations about him, or more accurately she suspected he had reservations about her. And since with each passing day the child became more integral to her life, Rachel's relationship with the father, or the father's with her, became ever more important. He was distant, other-wise occupied, not hostile but not welcoming. She read him for signs and he was reluctant to reveal them. She tried to be courteous but not obsequious, believing he would resent any sign of fawning.

In Rachel's view, Basil was clearly the master of the Helgen house. When he entered a room the tenor of other family members altered slightly. This was true in her experience even of the brothers Jacob and Sebastian. Eye contact shifted. The conversation tilted toward him, or paused in anticipation of what he might say. She saw no sign that anyone feared or resented him. He had assumed a natural position, one rendered vacant years earlier by the death of Johannes, the harsh father. If Marsel was the one tending all strands of the complex family web, Basil was the core toward which energy flowed, and from which it emanated.

One Sunday early on Marsel took Rachel aside to confide that she had spoken to Basil about Elsebett's learning to read.

"Yes?" Rachel felt a momentary alarm. Why had she not anticipated that?

"He was not happy to learn of it," the grandmother told her. "He thinks reading will make her less attractive to the class of young men likely to choose her for a wife. He also worries that the skill might cause her to want more from life than is realistic."

"I see."

"But he did not insist she stop," Marsel added in a half-whisper, as if she feared that expressing the thought too loudly might cause it to turn on itself. "And," adopting now a conspiratorial tone, 'she is even trying to teach me and Irmele, so much does the activity excite her." Adding with a laugh, "The poor child! She has in me a terrible student. I can hardly see the letters, let alone remember them."

Another sticky problem between Rachel and Basil was the dowry. She had accepted that funds be set aside for the girl's dowry as compensation for her services. And Basil had insisted that he, not the midwife, hold them.

On these points they had agreed in principle, but the details were left hanging for several months. Then one day, Rachel found herself sitting across from the father in front of the family's hearth. They were alone, the rest of the family having departed, as if sensing the importance of their negotiations. "What is the girl worth?" he asked her. "That is the underlying question, is it not?"

It was one of the few times Basil had spoken directly with Rachel about his daughter's apprenticeship. He had gone so far as to discuss the subject with Martin, Elsebett's uncle and the owner of the inn. What would be the terms, he had asked Martin, should he take on Elsebett as a servant girl as he had Agnes?

Rachel was reluctant to challenge the man in any way, but the comparison was not fair. "The two situations are not comparable," she said to him. "Agnes is a laborer employing skills she had previously learned at home. Moreover, she still lives at home, I assume. Whereas Elsebett lives with me. I feed and house her. And in my home your daughter is more than a laborer. I am teaching her a trade that will serve her throughout her life."

Basil considered this as Rachel continued. "I understand that you have only your daughter's interest in mind. You are responsible for assuring that she will make a successful match. But I cannot accept that her worth as a laborer is the only issue. The value of my teaching must also be taken into account. More than the dowry, that is the real benefit she is receiving."

"But she will need a dowry."

"Yes, I understand," Rachel said, and the two of them fell silent, not looking at one another.

That she did not have much money to give, was a problem she was reluctant to address. It would sound as though she were appealing to his sympathy. And that might be counterproductive. But the truth was, she could count on little cash income. A pittance came from the village council along with the house. But many of those she served paid her little, and some nothing. And of those who did pay, many gave grain or produce or provided work around the house. One father had plowed her garden three springs after his son was born. Another had repaired her roof. A third family delivered two or three eggs now and then, and had been for years.

But she did receive some cash. Not everyone in the village was cash poor. In good years farmers sold their surplus grain. And there were craftsmen: the cobbler, the smithy, the joiner and mason, the miller, the baker, a woman who wove beautiful baskets. But she had no guarantee of a steady flow of cash, something she felt she needed if she was going to commit to regular payments.

"I can see now that the two situations are not comparable," Basil admitted, ending the long silence.

"Perhaps we could agree on a total," Rachel suggested. "An amount that would come to her at the age of eighteen. Having this total would establish a marker, and I will pay against the total as I am able. As regularly as I can." Saying those words, she realized that she had just admitted what moments before she had been reluctant to reveal.

"As you are able?" the clever Basil asked, glancing at her.

"Yes, as I am able."

Basil slowly nodded his head, and he looked at her with a half-smile. "I understand," he said. "And yes, that will be acceptable."

In that moment, Rachel saw in him something she had not seen in years. In the smile appearing on the ruddy face of the stolid farmer, she recognized the young man who had won the heart of the lovely Arved, the dark-haired girl with the charm-filled laugh. So many years had passed but it all came back to her. Their wedding had brought joy to the entire village.

§

When Elsebett and Rachel arrived at the Helgen home on a Sunday morning, Marsel or one of her daughters-in-law always invited Rachel to join them in the home, and to accompany them to the church. Sometimes Rachel consented; other times she remained only a short while. She had other friends she enjoyed seeing on Sunday.

But it was fun to be part of the Helgen parade to the church. The sexton had the bells ringing in the tall tower. And everyone on the street, from young to old, was dressed in his or her best garments.

The jolly rotund Jacob walked with Klara, his boisterous wife, beside their children, the daughter Irmele and the son Gabriel who was old enough now to walk on his own most of the way. The dark-haired Johannes walked beside his uncle Sebastian, his eyes darting shyly toward the girls they encountered as they neared the square. Sebastian, who was the tallest and leanest of the three brothers, greeted passersby as he walked slowly beside his lovely Ursula with their two small boys David and Thomas, whose hands Ursula kept tightly bound in her own as she fussed over their manners and the arrangements of their hair and clothing.

At the front, the stout Basil walked slowly beside his mother, Marsel's left hand gripping his strong right arm. Attentive to his mother, he was obviously popular among the men they met along the way. His deep voice boomed as he greeted them and his low-pitched laughter rang out.

In Marsel's right hand she squeezed Elsebett's left, and Elsebett, it was clear, reveled in both the pleasure and the responsibility. The girl was mindful of the old woman's instability and insistent that no one rush her slow and careful steps on the uneven paving stones.

On these mornings Rachel often fell in at the rear with Jacob and Klara and their two children. Irmele was always eager to grip Rachel's hand. She looked up with an expression of devotion that was almost embarrassing. The raucous Klara had the ability to evoke uncontrolled laughter from Rachel with her stage-whispered commentary about the passing scene. None of this seemed to fluster the contented Jacob. However outrageous his wife's comments, he just grinned and chuckled and nodded his head in agreement.

Perhaps, it wasn't Klara so much that made Rachel giddy. At no time in her life had she been part of an extended family. With the Helgens, she felt herself in a procession, a large, moving organism making its slow but steady passage through the village. In that sense Elsebett had not just come to her. Elsebett had also brought her to them.

TWENTY

Following the harvest of the cereals, the village held a thanksgiving celebration the first Sunday in October following Michaelmas. The church's altar was decorated with baskets of grain, fruits and vegetables. A group of women constructed a harvest crown from stalks and heads of rye, barley and wheat—a crown so large that it would fit only on the head of a giant. In the morning the people met in front of the church, everyone wearing their best garments. The crown was placed on supports and four tall men, one of them being Sebastian, paraded it around the village and back to the church with the people, young and old alike, following happily behind. The crown was then taken into the church and placed on the altar beside the baskets. Father Peter, the young, large-eared priest, blessed the gifts, and after the Mass there followed an afternoon of feasting and drinking.

Elsebett and Irmele were now thirteen years of age. Elsebett had been with Rachel for almost five years but the two girls saw each other every week and remained close. The day of the thanksgiving celebration was warm and sunny, and the two of them had helped prepare and serve the meal. Now that the men had eaten, the girls could eat themselves. At one of the long tables set up in the market square, they sat across from each other, small cakes before them.

They were talking about stones, a subject that fascinated them.

"Frau Mueller knows all about them," Elsebett explained. "She has a lot of them. She even uses them to heal people. She says that every stone contains fire and moisture and that the Devil detests the precious ones, emeralds, sapphires, stones like that. There is one stone she has, it's called a sard. I've held it. It's kind of reddish and very smooth. She rubs this stone on the mother's legs and stomach to help the baby come out. And she has a belt made from the hide of a deer that has a sack on it. If the mother cannot push the baby out, Frau Mueller places the sard in the sack and puts the belt around the mother and that helps. I've seen her do that."

"The Devil hates them?" Irmele asked, amazed.

"Well, he hates the precious ones, that I know. Topaz is one of the precious ones Frau Mueller told me about. The one she showed me was golden-brown. It is rare and very valuable, so hers is small. But if you are a rich person you should have one, especially if you think someone might want to poison you."

"Poison?"

"Yes! Frau Mueller says that if a topaz stone is placed next to anything that has poison in it, like bread, say, or wine, the stone begins to sweat. So, if you have a ring with a topaz stone, then you should always place the stone close to your bread, and if it begins to sweat you don't eat it. That's an important thing to know. For emperors and princes, you know, people like that."

The cousins grinned; they nodded their heads rapidly up and down. Delighted, they bit into their cakes.

Basil, too, was at the celebration. He had finished his meal but he still sat at the same table a few yards away from the girls, enjoying a beer with some other farmers. Everyone agreed it had been a good harvest, the third in a row. The cereals were in, the storage bins full. But Basil was not the enthusiastic type. A good harvest meant they had taken in five bushels of grain for every bushel planted. From the total, a fifth had to be selected out for the next year's seed stock. There were taxes to pay, the compulsory tithe to the church, rental payments to the abbey, a fee to the miller. Funds would be needed to purchase salt and other necessities they could not produce themselves. The balance was stored to feed the family until the next harvest. One or two bad years they could survive, but more and they would experience hunger.

The young priest came by and sat down. Beer was poured for him and they shared a toast to the good harvest.

"Looks like you'll eat this winter, Father," one of the men said. "The tithes will be rolling in."

"The Good Lord provides," Father Peter agreed, wiping some foam from his upper lip.

Basil noticed that the young priest had been trying to sprout a mustache without much success.

"Truth be told, Father, it is those of us sitting here who are doing the providing." The comment came from a farmer named Dietrich. His father had once come to blows with Basil's father over a damaged wagon wheel, but Basil and Dietrich had never exchanged a harsh word. "It is our land that grew the grain, our labors that brought in the harvest. And the law requires the tithe. One bushel from every ten we harvest, Father. Just like the tax it comes off the top. One in ten of what we harvest, not one in ten of what we keep to feed our families. Better the law was written that way, Father. One in ten of what we what we have left, though that would mean less in your purse and more in mine."

"The law is as it is written," the priest proclaimed. "And the law reflects God's instruction. Let us not forget who brings us the good harvest, who commands the rain to fall, the sun to shine and the grain to ripen as it should."

The men reflected on what the father had said. Then the man Dietrich spoke again: "With all due respect, Father, I've heard that said many times over the years; the Lord brought us the good harvest, and for that we should be grateful, and, of course, we are grateful. But when the harvest is bad, I never hear it said that God failed to make the rain fall, or the sun to shine, or the grain to ripen. Then we're told to be thankful for the little we have received, or that we are said to have caused the failure ourselves, brought it on by our sinful behavior. Tell me Father, is it clear in your mind from your study of the holy teachings that

God alone commands these things? That is, the rain to fall and the sun to shine and the grain to ripen? Or would you say that by our sins we cause the crops to fail? Or do you understand that the Devil himself has a role to play in these events?"

"The ways of God are a mystery, my son," Father Peter said to Dietrich, a man who was twenty years his senior. "His wisdom is far beyond our minds to grasp. This is why faith is required of us, and why at times it is tested. It is true that the Devil seeks to pull souls away from the sanctity of the church, and for this reason the pontiffs and the saints have laid down rules that if followed protect us from the Devil's power. However, I would say these things to you. Yes, all things are as God has commanded. And it is true that we should be grateful for whatever we receive, even if it is less than last year, or less than what we wanted or even less than what we in our arrogance think we deserve. And finally, we do know that in the past God has punished his people for their sins. When Lot's wife disobeyed God's command and looked back toward the sin-filled city of Sodom, he turned her into a pillar of salt. And we know further that he commanded Noah to build the ark and then caused the great flood to drench the earth and destroy everything on it. These are just two examples. What I can assure you is that God is just. That is what our faith tells us."

A silence followed the priest's message. Then Basil spoke. "It is one thing to have faith in God and his wisdom, Father, and another to have faith that he will always provide a good harvest. Some harvests are good, some not so good, and some not good at all. That has been my experience, and the experience of all of us sitting here. Whatever the cause of these fluctuations, be it the sinfulness of man, which we should agree is always present whether the harvest be plentiful or the fields barren, or be it the Devil's hand, or be there some other cause unknown to us, matters little. Bad years follow good, experience dictates that this is our fate."

"Well said, my son," said the young father, "which is why our obedience to the church must be constant."

"And I know," Basil continued, "that in the years of a lean harvest, that the church has used some portion of its wealth to help the poor and those whose storehouse is empty."

"You are correct again, and your words illustrate the benevolence of the church's mission."

"But it is also true, Father, that much of what we pay goes into the coffers of the Bishop and the Archbishop. I have heard it said that a new palace is being planned for the Archbishop-Elector."

"When the Bishop was last here, he spoke of this," Dietrich interjected. "I remember that clearly."

"How wonderful it was to have the Bishop visit our humble parish!" the young father exclaimed. "Who can doubt that we were all blessed by his coming?"

"It is my thinking," Basil went on, "and my respectful suggestion, that the parish construct a common granary here in the village. So, when we have a good harvest and our personal bins are full, that we deposit our surpluses in this granary, and that our deposits be counted as a portion of our tithes. This will assure that our tithes remain in the village and available to you, Father, to assist those who have need of them."

"Now that idea has some weight," Dietrich said. "I for one would help with the construction."

"As it presently stands," Basil continued. "When we have a good harvest and our bins are full, we sell the surplus grain to merchants at a low price. The price being low because the supply is great, and this grain is then hauled away to other markets. Whereas, had we a granary we could keep the grain to provide for our people when the harvest is poor. But to do that, our contributions would need to count against our tithes because we would have lost the gold we would otherwise have made by selling."

Several men at the table nodded their heads in agreement. But when the priest turned toward Basil his look suggested first confusion and then annoyance.

"That instruction would to need come from above. It is not my role to offer advice to the Bishop or to presume that I know how he, or even more arrogantly, the Archbishop-Elector should administer the affairs of the diocese," Father Peter said. "My duties are to the people of this parish. God has called me to this service and I serve humbly in obedience to his dictates."

After a long silence Basil muttered, "Well, winter will come."

"Meaning?" the priest abruptly asked as he stood up.

"Only what we have spoken of, Father. I mean no disrespect. I am a simple farmer. I work the ground and try to provide for my family. However, in my experience bad years follow the good ones. And we had best be prepared."

"Of course," the priest said. "But our first duty is humble obedience, not rabble rousing. You know what God has commanded. On this day, which shines with his benevolence, we have expressed our gratitude for a bountiful harvest and I have offered my blessings on our riches as I am called to do. I have acted with faith in his divine wisdom. I pray that you have participated in the same manner."

"Yes, Father," Basil said to the back of the departing priest.

§

There were men seated at the long table that day who years later would tell their children and grandchildren about that time in the distant past when the village enjoyed bountiful harvests three years in a row. "Imagine it, three years, one after the other. The bins were overflowing, the sows were fat, everybody's stomach was full and our purses were stuffed with coins. Those were the days all right and we thought it would go on forever."

The younger generations probably believed the old men were at best exaggerating, as old men will do, or lying through their decayed teeth, as some old men will also do. The claims were exaggerated, but only in one sense. Some men did not think the good years would go on forever, Basil Helgen among them. The Helgens built themselves additional storage that autumn. When the visiting grain merchants came up the river, they sold at discounted prices only enough rye and barley to purchase the materials needed for the construction. Every spare space in the stable and house was packed with shocks of grain, and the men and boys flailed through the cold winter months until the new storage bins were full. At the time, some in the village thought the Helgens wise, others thought them foolish; then later, several would accuse them of hoarding.

TWENTY-ONE

One morning a few months later, after she had finished her studies, Elsebett was on her hands and knees scrubbing the floor near the front door when she heard a knock, or thought she did. The knock, if it was a knock, was tentative, shy, almost reluctant. Then she heard a voice that she thought she recognized.

"Well, knock, will you?" the voice commanded. "She can't hear that. Knock on the door!"

There followed a louder pounding, an okay-you-want-me-to-knock-I'll-knock, sort of knock. When Elsebett opened the door she found her cousin Agnes and her aunt Anna standing before her. They stood in the fresh snow that had fallen overnight wrapped tightly in sheepskin coats, the tracks of their passage visible behind them.

"You!" her aunt announced, surprised and obviously annoyed to see her niece. Anna was the younger of Elsebett's late mother's two older sisters. Like her daughter, Anna was attuned to drama, but in the mother it revealed a darker more volatile character. In Elsebett's many visits to Agnes's home over the years, the cousins had found it wise to avoid Anna's company when possible, and when that was impossible, to avoid her displeasure as best they could.

"Are you going to allow us in?" Aunt Anna said now, stamping the snow off her feet. "We've come to see Frau Mueller."

Agnes was now a tall pretty woman twenty-two years of age. Elsebett thought her gorgeous, and had always idolized her, an older, wiser, almost mythic creature. But on this day, there was nothing mythic about Agnes. She looked terrible. Her eyes were puffy, teary and red, her expression a bizarre mixture of petulance, terror and despair. And Elsebett was, for the moment, paralyzed by the sight of her.

"Well?" her aunt Anna, said, stomping her feet again, exasperation mounting.

Elsebett apologized, opened the door fully and gave them entrance. She looked at Agnes in wonder and her cousin looked at her as if she were some distant memory. Then suddenly Agnes gasped dramatically. She threw her arms around Elsebett and for a moment clung to her with frightening intensity.

"Well, is she home?" Anna demanded.

"Yes," Elsebett said when Agnes had finally released her. She led the two of them to the study, indicated seats, and, as she had been instructed, left to find the midwife.

Frau Mueller was in the workroom crushing some dried leaves in a mortar. Elsebett recognized sage and thyme.

"It's my cousin Agnes, Frau Mueller, and my aunt Anna. Something must be terribly wrong."

Frau Mueller set the pestle on the table. "I will see them," she said. There were times now when she allowed her student to be in the study during examinations, but this would not be one of them. "Have you finished the floor?"

"Not yet."

"Then return to that. And when you have finished, if I am not back, complete this grinding. I need a fine powder."

§

When she entered the study, Rachel realized that Elsebett had been right. Something obviously was wrong. She knew both mother and child. She had been the first person in the world to see Agnes, having caught her as she emerged from the womb. The child had been one of those newborns who seem surprised on arrival, as if they had opened the wrong door and now found themselves in a world different from the one they had anticipated.

The look of surprise was still there, Rachel thought as she studied Agnes, or was again there, as if asking, what am I doing here?

The answer was quickly provided by the mother: "She is with child!" Anna sputtered, throwing her large hands up to cover her face. "This one! Mine!" And she began to sob, a heavy heart-rending explosion of grief.

Agnes's hands were knotted on her lap, palms opposed, fingers clutching fingers; her eyes dropped now to study them.

"Are we certain of this?" Rachel asked quietly.

"Certain enough," the mother said, recovering herself. "The blood does not come. The act causing it has been performed she tells me. Is that not right? Tell the woman!"

Agnes nodded, not raising her eyes.

"Speak, child! Tell the woman!"

"Yes."

"My sister Gisele knows the rascal. Ten years this girl's elder. And always in pursuit of the young ones. Hides trifles on his person. Sweets and spangles, he offers them in the quiet of the hallways, luring them to his room."

"Seven," Agnes said softly.

"Oh, seven is it?" the mother bellowed. "And you believe him do you? And what matter is that, seven, ten? A married man, he is, you can be sure of it."

"He swears he is not."

"And you believe him?" Anna exploded again. "A wine merchant, no less! A river rat from far Nuremburg. I should never have allowed this fanciful child near that inn. It is rife with the untethered. And Gisele promised she would watch over her. Oh, for the love of God, my child's life is ruined and mine as well!" And the sobs returned.

After they had subsided, Rachel asked: "What would you like to say to me, Agnes?"

The young woman slowly shook her head but she neither spoke nor looked up. The mother started to speak but Rachel raised a hand, stopping her. The three of them sat without speaking for some time, Anna's heavy breathing being the only sound in the room.

"Have you spoken with him?" Rachel asked finally. "The gentleman, that is."

"The gentleman!" the mother cried, unable to contain herself. "She spoke to me of this only this morning. She swears she has told no one. Not a soul knows, not but the three of us and Gisele. I have not yet spoken to my man, this girl's father, under whose dominion she resides. The very thought of doing so terrifies me."

"He will kill me," Agnes said now.

"Who is that who will kill you?" Rachel asked.

"My father. He will have to," Agnes said, looking up at last. "I have sinned and as my father, he is responsible. I have brought shame to him, as well as to my mother and myself."

Rachel saw that Agnes was serious. And what she said was true. She had sinned, both in the eyes of the church and in the eyes of the law. And until she was handed over to a husband, she remained under the dominion of her father, irrespective of her age. He was her legal and spiritual guardian and she had violated his most central instruction. Better she were revealed a common thief than this. Rachel knew the girl's father. That he might inflict violence on his daughter was likely.

Still, she needed to have a clear answer to her question, so she asked again, "Just so I can be certain I understand, Agnes, can you assure me that you have not as yet spoken of your condition to the gentleman?"

"I have not. He comes only every couple of months."

Rachel allowed this information to settle in the room. Then she asked a question more probing: "Have you and he spoken of this possibility?"

Agnes gave a slight shake of her head.

"I see. I assume you know him to some degree. Were you to speak to him, how do you think he would answer?"

Agnes did not respond, though an answer was suggested by the way her eyes dropped back to her clutched hands, which were visibly trembling now.

"Well, I can tell you his response," the mother said. "He will accuse her of seducing him. This is the way of men and the standard practice. We are the seductresses, they the victims. And if he hauls her before a court, he will prevail and she will lose. She will be banished from the village, cast out alone in the world with an unwanted child, her family disgraced while he goes on to his next victim. That is the truth of the matter."

"I guess I could speak to him, when he comes," Agnes said, her voice tentative. "Maybe he will offer to marry me. It is possible, I guess."

"And the risk in that?" Anna shouted, exasperation overcoming her.

"I'm afraid your mother is correct," Rachel said to the young woman. "If you tell him, and he does offer to marry you, everything will be as it should. You will become his wife, and he your husband and the father of your child. But should he respond as your mother predicts, the results would likely be as she says. So, speaking to him is not without risk. It will in fact be very risky. That is why I must insist, if I am able to help you, you must address my question to your heart and answer it most honestly. Were you to speak to him, Agnes, do you have any confidence in how he will respond?"

The long silence that followed Rachel's question may have contained the moment when the child Agnes, she with the bright dreams and the rich fantasies, became a grown woman.

"No," she said at last, her lips trembling, "I cannot promise he will respond responsibly or with a good heart."

And with those words, Agnes rose from her chair. She fell to the floor before her mother's knees, and burying her face in her lap, began to sob.

TWENTY-TWO

Frau Rachel Mueller sat quietly as mother and daughter passed from sobs to whimpers and then to an extended silent embrace. Finally, the young woman returned to her chair and offered a sniffled apology to the midwife.

"We have come to you in desperation," Anna said, using her apron to dry her face. "We have nowhere to turn."

"Yes…I never thought…," Agnes said, worrying her own apron in her hands, her voice trailing off as if it had lost its way.

Rachel smiled at her. "I am pleased you have come to see me," she said. "And I will try to help you as best I can. But first we must discuss some difficult things. Forgive me for being bold, but frankness is needed at this moment. And I have to insist on your complete honesty, Agnes. Is that clear?"

"Yes."

"So tell me, have you coupled with any man other than this gentleman, this wine merchant?"

"No!" Agnes said, seemingly appalled at the thought of it.

"All right. And how many times have you had congress with this man?"

"Well…three," Agnes admitted, after glancing at her mother. "Three times."

"Three!" Anna shouted, and jumping to her feet, slapped her daughter's face. "Not two hours ago you told me, once! One time, you swore, squealing like a pig and falling to your knees."

Agnes closed her eyes, pushing up her cheeks as tightly as she could.

"So, three? Is three the number?" Rachel insisted quietly, after Anna had returned to her seat.

"Yes, I'm sorry, mother. But, yes, three times. The first was near the Feast of the Holy Cross, I think. Before the harvest feast."

"All right. And the second?"

"The second and third happened at the same time. Well, the night he arrived and then the next afternoon, just before he left."

"Oh, Mother of God!" the mother gasped.

"And when was that, Agnes?"

"Around the beginning of Advent, I think."

"Saint Andrew's Day?"

"Around then, yes."

"And not since?"

"No, I have not seen him since that time," Agnes said, her voice wistful.

Rachel then asked when her blood had last flowed and Agnes surprised her by saying she did not remember. "I have tried to not think about it," she said.

"I see. Have you felt a quickening?"

"Yes! Well, something. This morning, last night. I didn't want to think about that either. But it's there, I know it's there!"

"All right. I will ask now that you remove your clothing and allow me to examine you. I will not hurt you but it is necessary."

When the examination had been completed, Rachel watched in silence as Agnes clothed herself. The midwife felt very tired as she watched the young woman. Not so much physically tired as weary. This child, and Agnes did still look like a child to her, born so fresh in the world only a few years ago—she remembered the birth clearly—was now deeply immersed in its trials. How quickly time moved; how insistently events took hold of us.

"So, let me summarize," she said when Agnes was again seated. "And forgive me, but I must be brutally frank. Yes, you have within you the beginnings of a child. And based on what you have told me, the gentleman you described is the child's father. You have choices, none of them, I am sorry to say, are painless or without risk or consequence. You can hide your condition for a time by binding yourself, but you will continue to swell and take on weight, and eventually, come summer, the child will insist on entering the world.

"Your mother has vividly and correctly described the risk you take should you confront the gentleman. He may deny having any congress with you, boldly accusing you of slander. Or he may claim that he has been but one of many who have made use of you."

Rachel paused for a moment, seeing how violently the young woman shuddered, and then continued. "You must recognize that it will be in his interest to wrongly accuse you. And we cannot discount the possibility that he will employ others to verify his false claims, thus further damaging your reputation. But all that aside, if he simply does not want to take responsibility, he does not have to. You will be seen as Eve, the seductress, and he the victim. That is the way of the church and the way of the law."

Agnes had fallen again into her mother's arms. The two of them were crying, but Rachel felt she must continue.

"If you remain in your home in this village, and allow the child to come to term…"

"My father will kill me!" Agnes blurted out, breaking away from her mother, her voice angry. "He will!"

"I leave that assessment to the two of you," Rachel said. "But irrespective of your father, the people of the village will not allow you to remain here with your child. You would have to leave."

"Banished!" the mother said, shouting the word as if it were a weapon.

"Yes," Rachel said softly. "So, as I see it, there are two choices. I can arrange for a convent to take you. You will be safe there. You can have the child and people will be available to help you. You may leave the infant in the convent or take it with you, though of course you could not return here with the child. If you keep the child, your life will need to be somewhere else, probably in a city."

"In a city?"

"Yes. And your prospects, I have to say, would not be good. If you leave the child with the sisters, you might return here. Assuming, of course that you can devise some explanation for your absence. It can be done. This is not so infrequent an occurrence as you may think."

"And the other?"

"I could prepare a substance that you would take," Rachel said slowly.

"Is there magic in it?" Anna asked, suddenly revived.

"Magic? Well, a very harsh magic, and I am reluctant to recommend it. The medicine is cold and noxious. Its nature is to destroy, and it wounds even a healthy person. It should cause you to abort the fetus but you will react with nausea, diarrhea and vomiting, as if you had eaten poisoned food. And since its will is to destroy that which it finds, it could render you infertile, or…it could even end your life."

Fortunately, Rachel was watching closely as she finished the explanation, and she saw Agnes's eyes roll back in her head. By moving quickly, she caught the young woman as she fainted and before she crashed to the floor.

TWENTY-THREE

It had started to snow again, and a strong wind had come up blowing the accumulation into drifts. As Agnes and her mother trudged back toward their house, everyone they met was hunched over, bent by the wind. Winter had stripped the scattered trees of leaves. Their trunks, their exposed limbs and twisted branches looked black and tormented against the gray sky.

There was much to think about and Frau Mueller had insisted that no decision be made before the remainder of the day and night had passed. But Agnes recognized one thing. She was trapped like an animal. No, it was worse than that; even a trapped animal could hunker down and cower before its captors, while she, however much she cowered, the fetus would continue to grow.

The bells in their tower rang news of the midday. Hearing them, her mother insisted they go straight to the church. They would find the priest, she said, and Agnes would make confession. "It is not just your life, but your soul, child, that is in danger!"

Her mother's sudden demand destroyed the fantasy Agnes had been concocting, a fantasy somewhat delicious in its horror, in which she would find a precipice along the river's edge from which to fling herself. She imagined the pain her death would inflict on her severe father. Her insistent mother. Even on the cold midwife and the village itself with its shaking heads and wagging tongues.

But, no, her mother was right. There was no escape. Even her own dramatic death would fail to provide it. The Devil would delight in her suicide. As her crushed and broken body was dropped into a grave unmarked and outside of sanctified ground, her soul would be flung from heaven's gate and into the waiting arms of Lucifer, the Devil himself.

The priest was not available, the sexton informed them. He had gone to a neighboring village, and given the weather, who knew when he would return. As the sexton departed, Anna pulled her daughter toward the altar. The church was empty and the lumps of snow they stomped loose from their pattens followed them a few feet into the sanctuary, having no cause to melt. To the young woman, the church felt hollowed out, devoid of promise. It was shivering cold within and without, the bricks, the air, the cruel judgment hanging over her. What had been a place of solace became now one of condemnation; even the cross-hung Jesus glared down on her. Her mother was sobbing audibly as the two of them knelt on the cold stone.

Her mother being occupied with prayer, Agnes was forced again to face her predicament. Crying now herself, she experienced an explosion of extraordinary thoughts and emotions. Her life was ruined, that was certain. Not one good option was open to her. The idea of entering a convent appalled her. Besides, how could that be accomplished without alerting her father? And more than anything she feared his condemnation. Frau Mueller's vivid description of how the medicine would attack her body had terrified her. She detested all forms of illness, always had. She had a healthy body and a bright disposition; all sicknesses seemed insulting to her. To voluntarily ingest something knowing it would cause such horrors—her imagination now was insisting that it would disfigure her, leave her marked for life if it did not kill her outright—well, it was simply too ghastly to contemplate.

That left Heinrich, the wine merchant. They were all wrong about him: her mother, Aunt Gisele, Frau Mueller. Her aunt Gisele, the only one who had actually met him, had no understanding. Trifles in the hallways? How silly. He brought her honied delights from Lucca, stories from other worlds, a small blue-colored stone that he swore had come from across the sea, that she had secreted into her hope chest. He was funny, charming, attentive, patient, but steady, forceful, and he was endowed with the eyes of a forest stag that looked out at you from beneath sweeping lashes.

Heinrich! In the past six months Agnes had thought of little else. Their love was over now, as was her life. But if there was one consolation in all of this, she could honestly say that in the last half year, she had lived life as she had always imagined it was supposed to be lived.

So, how old was he really? Seven years, ten? He was certainly older than she was, but not old, young but not immature. Had he lied to her? Possibly. It made sense that he would, and she saw now how that could be. Was he married? Though he swore not, his very attractiveness suggested otherwise. Even assuming, as he claimed, he was but seven years older, it was difficult to imagine that some attractive woman with means and designs had not previously captured his heart. Surely, every woman he had ever met desired him. In Agnes's imagination, it was clear that he loved her more than that scheming other woman who had become his wife. He had lied because he had to. Because he loved her so, wanted her so. To be true to their love, he had been obliged to speak falsely to her.

But should she now confront him with her situation, what would happen? How then would he react? How could he? There were children probably as well. Yes, he would have no choice. Circumstances would require that he denounce her in the terrible ways that her mother and Frau Mueller had described. And then, that denunciation would destroy him as well. Having betrayed their love, he would by honor be required to end his own life.

And this recognition fit with her deepest understanding. She had somehow betrayed him by becoming pregnant. Her body had betrayed her, causing her to betray their love. Thus it was obvious; if she truly loved him—and she did—then she could not burden him with this news. There was truly no escape.

Shivering with cold and dread, Agnes reached out and gripped her mother's arm. "Mother, let's go home. I have made a decision."

TWENTY-FOUR

The storm was the worst in years. The snow lasted three days and the wind hurled to the ground what shocks of grain remained in the fields and flattened a few of the bins hastily built to shelter the abundant harvest. When the sky cleared, the air turned bitterly cold. Dogs froze to death in the street, a poor family's house burned to the ground; the old man finally died in his ill-heated hovel after which his demons, having no one to torment, at last departed.

"Mother," Agnes confided later that night, "I will make confession in the morning and do the penance the priest prescribes. Then I will take Frau Mueller's medicine, and it will surely kill me."

The first impulse Anna had when her daughter spoke those words was to mutter what Father Severin had always said: "The wages of sin is death." In her memory there was scarcely a homily of his that did not include that phrase.

But hearing those words, Agnes looked at her mother in abject horror. Anna gasped at her blunder, threw her arms around her daughter and the two of them sobbed as quietly as they could, knowing the father was in the adjoining room drinking beer with his brother.

§

Elsebett had not been able to avoid it. Her aunt's explosions, the sobs and cries coming from the study could be heard whether she was scrubbing the entrance floor or in the cold workroom grinding the dried herbs into powder. She did not know what had happened to her cousin, but she was desperate with worry when at last the outside door closed and she heard Frau Mueller walking toward her.

Nothing in her teacher's countenance comforted the girl. Frau Mueller did not acknowledge her presence when she entered, but went straight to the shelves of sacks and containers. Picking through them, she selected a large, covered, ceramic bowl. Taking it down with both hands she placed it carefully on the counter, her hands cupping it as if she held a Eucharist chalice. In Elsebett's memory, that bowl had never been removed from its shelf.

After several minutes, during which the midwife seemed lost in contemplation, Frau Mueller said, "I have spoken with you often about the different plants and their properties. I have talked about their nature, be they hot or cold, moist or dry, about their usefulness for this or that ailment, about the dangers they may or may not pose, about their application as an unguent or a poultice or as a substance to be consumed. We know that some are used singularly while others serve best in combination, that there are favorable seasons to collect a plant's leaves or flowers, its roots or seeds. And of course, we must always be careful with our harvesting, our grinding and our blending so that the medicine in the plant is available to provide optimal benefit.

"We must also be aware that each person who comes to us is a unique blend of the humors and the elements, and that this blending is in flux, that some draw the airy spirits while others repel them. We must always acknowledge the person as she is, and honor the distress she is experiencing, whatever its cause. Thus, the unguent I prepare for one person may be somewhat different than for another, even though they both seem to be suffering from the same affliction. Is that clear?"

"Yes," Elsebett said, feeling no comfort about her cousin, but grateful that Frau Mueller, who continued to press her hands against the ceramic bowl, had at least acknowledged her presence.

"Normally, if a treatment fails, we may alter the combination somewhat to see if we can improve the results. But sometimes, in some circumstances, that is not possible. That is why, today, I need to speak to you of another serious subject, and that is dosage. When we prepare a poultice which will be applied to the skin, we try to prepare enough, but should we make too much, there is only waste. The plants are precious and the gathering and preparing of the medicines are laborious, so we abhor all waste and try to avoid it. But when we are preparing a medicine that will be taken into the mouth, chewed and swallowed, or perhaps mixed with wine and drunk, then we must use special care. Too small a dose may well be ineffective, while one that is too large could be harmful, even fatal to the person, depending on the plant or plants used."

Frau Mueller then turned and looked at Elsebett for the first time. "Before Agnes and her mother left, I told them I was going to speak to you about the situation in which they find themselves. Not surprisingly, they were opposed to this. The matter is one requiring the upmost confidence and you being eight years younger than Agnes, and a member of her family, they did not want me to reveal anything to you. But I told them that you were my apprentice, that I needed your help and you needed my instruction. I also told them that in these matters I knew you better than they did."

"Better?" Elsebett asked, surprised.

Frau Mueller nodded. "I told them that you have been in my home for more than five years. I have watched you closely and I know you well. I told them that I trust you to not share what I tell you, not even with your grandmother, or your father, your brother, Irmele, or, for that matter, with anyone. So, Elsebett, I must ask you: Was I wise to make this prediction, or was I a fool who will come to regret her words?"

Elsebett did not respond immediately. She wanted to promise anything, so eager was she to learn the news. But she realized that Frau Mueller was about to hand her a burden. Perhaps it was a burden that Frau Mueller herself wanted to lighten by sharing. But certainly, it would become a burden for her. In her young life she had never known anything she could not share with her grandmother or Irmele, with Agnes herself.

"It scares me," she said now.

"Yes," Frau Mueller agreed, "as it should. It is the nature of our work. People come to us with secrets and we are compelled to hold them tightly in our hearts. I suggest you not answer immediately. That you recognize the question as difficult encourages me. Perhaps we might both benefit from a period of reflection while we have our meal."

§

It was cold everywhere in the house. They built up the fire. They broke some of the dark bread they had purchased from the baker and heated the pottage. Their work was done in silence.

Elsebett wished she did not know even the little she already did. Had she been away when Agnes and her aunt came she would not be experiencing this torment now. Knowing some things and yet so few of them, enlivened her imagination, causing it to shower her with possible horrors. Was a mass growing on some hidden part of her cousin's body? (She remembered the woman who had come to the door recently with a huge growth bulging from the base of her throat. How frightening that had been.) Had Agnes found signs of leprosy on her person or even the dreaded plague? But why then would Aunt Anna be so angry? And why the upmost secrecy? It sounded as though even her uncle, Agnes's father, had not been told. And how was she expected to behave when she greeted her grandmother this next Sunday? To know something so important about Agnes and not be able to share it felt like torture. Even with the best of intentions, might she not burst out the news? Or be more reticent? Her grandmother, she knew, was alert to every nuance.

But Elsebett did know already. She knew both too much and not enough. She was desperate to learn the answers and equally desperate to not be burdened by the answers she longed to know.

Rachel, for her part, was also uncomfortable. As she watched the girl shovel pottage into her mouth—regardless of the circumstances Elsebett's appetite never seemed to fail her—Rachel recognized a strange irony. Had she done for Arved what Basil had wanted, and what she was proposing now for Agnes, this girl would not be sharing a meal with her. Elsebett would not exist. Both Arved and Agnes were similarly advanced in their pregnancies. If Agnes could be induced to miscarry now, Arved could have as well. That had been an occasion of great delicacy. She had held Basil's desire for an abortion secret from Arved, and Arved's eagerness to have the child secret from Basil. No, she had told him, it was too late, the child was too advanced. Though it had not been too late, or if it had, then perhaps it was too late for Agnes as well.

That realization brought other problems to Rachel's mind. Her deepest impulse was to heal, to lessen discomfort. People normally came to her with something wrong that needed to be fixed. But there was nothing wrong with Agnes, she was simply pregnant. In that sense she did not need to be fixed. The problem was the inverse of normal. That which was natural and functioning, needed to be arrested and expelled. She could think of it as a purge, and she was not unfamiliar with purging. When something unwholesome was present in a person she might induce a purge to remove it. Her formula contained ginger and other herbs that were taken to correct the malady. Those ingredients possessed an innocent nature, it seemed to Rachel. They came to cleanse. They might sicken as they cleansed but they did not kill. But a fetus was not an unwholesome presence, and the dried roots in the ceramic bowl were not innocent. They came not to cleanse, but to destroy. How to release their power while still restraining them, that was the challenge facing her.

When they had finished their meal, Elsebett said to her teacher: "I can only hope that I will be worthy of your trust, Frau Mueller. I know I will be as trustworthy as I am able. Please tell me why my cousin suffers so."

When the truth was told to her, the girl instantly crossed herself.

TWENTY-FIVE

The four of them met in the study two mornings later. Elsebett had started a fire in the hearth; the shutters were tightly closed against the cold and the oil lamp glowed on a table. When Elsebett greeted them at the door, she and Agnes had fallen into each other's arms. Now they sat side by side holding hands. Both of them felt somewhat odd about the transformation occurring in their relationship.

Agnes had seen her young cousin infrequently during the past year, and in spite of her distracted state she noticed that Elsebett had changed. Though she remained buoyant and well-fleshed, she was as tall as her teacher, only a couple of inches shorter now than Agnes herself. The change was most pronounced in her hands. Not only were the fingers elongated, honed to practical work, but the hand, the one she now gripped, had lost the dimpled pudginess that Agnes had associated with childhood, the presence of which had confirmed her own maturity, her generous, caring, superiority over her younger cousin.

For Elsebett's part, the changes in Agnes were equally profound, and it seemed to her they involved a disconnection. Something had come loose, releasing an instability; one moment her cousin was in tears, the next in laughter. Surprisingly, Agnes appeared in the peak of health. Warming now and lit by the fire, her color was high, her cheeks had taken on some flesh, her movements were quick and lively. Perhaps the presence of

Elsebett brought forth an urge to perform, because she confessed flippantly to the midwife that her pregnancy had caused her not a moment of discomfort. The only change was that she was always hungry. "I could be a natural at this!" she exclaimed, as if her condition were a terrible joke.

The comment caused Rachel to again raise the convent as an option. "I do not want to oversell it. Your life would not be that of a lady. But they would feed you, shelter you, watch over you, assist with the birth."

"My man makes that impossible," Anna insisted. "How could I explain her absence for a month or two? He is a suspicious one. And possessed of a violent temper. When first we married, he watched me like a hungry wolf. And he keeps his eye on this daughter too, you can bet on that. Oh, and he was right and I was wrong! He wanted no life for Agnes at the inn. But I swore Gisele would keep her bound to the right. And look now how she has fallen into temptation."

The hand that gripped Elsebett's squeezed so tightly it hurt. And the pain reaffirmed her astonishment that her cousin actually was pregnant. What did that mean? How had that come to pass? Elsebett's understanding was very limited. What little she knew came from animals, dogs mostly and the breeding of sows. And she assumed it was connected somehow with the rustlings in the night when Uncle Jacob and Aunt Klara were "getting friendly," which was the way she once heard Klara describe the activity.

One recent Tuesday morning Elsebett had experienced her first period. Terrified, and fearing she might bleed to death before she could speak to her grandmother, she had gone to Rachel. Rachel gave her cloths and some practical advice regarding her new status, but nothing about getting pregnant. The conversation she was now listening to further confused her. Something was missing. Did there not have to be a man? She had heard no mention of a man. She would love to talk to Agnes, but the present moment was clearly not the occasion. For now, she was fully occupied in a new and surprising role, that of comforting her distressed older cousin.

Anna's words about her husband struck Rachel, momentarily stunning her. They exposed the fantasy that had lingered in her mind; that in the end the young woman would choose the convent. She would have so preferred to make those arrangements to what now confronted her.

"Well, all right then," Rachel said, recovering herself, "we must lay out a plan. Where and when to do this. And how you should prepare yourself, Agnes, so you will be as comfortable and as safe as possible."

"And it has to be done so her father never knows," Anna interjected. "I cannot say how he will act should he learn of her folly."

"He will kill me," Agnes asserted. "That's how he will act. And most violently."

"But is there not a man who is cause of this?" Elsebett suddenly blurted out, unable to restrain herself. Then mortified by her transgression she raised her free hand to cover her mouth. The one rule Frau Mueller had insisted on when she permitted Elsebett to attend consultations, was that she should never speak, never disrupt, never interfere. "You are there to observe," her teacher had told her, to learn. "If you have questions, you must save them until the visitor has left."

The three other women shared a look of stunned silence but then Agnes began to laugh. "You, cousin, are as red as a cardinal's hat!"

"I'm sorry," Elsebett stammered, glancing toward her teacher, and growing even more colored. "Should I leave?"

The look on her aunt's face suggested that her leaving was an excellent idea, and Frau Mueller herself appeared momentarily paralyzed. But Agnes would hear none of it.

"No, no, cousin. You must stay with me, always at my side. And when we have time I will tell you the story from its beginning to its tragic end." She turned then and placed a kiss on Elsebett's flaming cheek.

TWENTY-SIX

And so the plan was laid. Agnes and her mother would return to their home where Agnes would go straight to bed. Anna would put the word out that her daughter had gotten into some bad air and had a fever, that she was quite sick and should not be disturbed. Meanwhile Frau Mueller and Elsebett would prepare the medicines and the following morning they would bring them to the house.

"The medicine in this pouch will protect you from demonic invocations, magic formulas and other such enchantments," Rachel told Agnes as she tied an amulet around her neck. It was the same small sack, filled now with freshly dried leaves, that many years before she had placed around the throat of Arved at the time of her pregnancy.

"You may take this evening's meal in bed, but after that you must begin a fast," she continued. "Take no food or drink in the morning until we arrive. I will then give you medicine that will quiet your humors, and God willing, ease the disruptions brought on by the second medicine. A short time later, I will give you the medicine that will cause the miscarriage. You should prepare the room, Anna, as for a birth, with water, towels, a pan and so forth. But, unlike a birth, no one can be allowed into the room beyond the four of us. There will be heavy bleeding that may last a couple of days or more, and this will reveal much if seen. There will be clots in the blood, perhaps the fetus and placenta will be visible, so you must find ways to dispose of these substances without raising suspicions."

"May Elsebett spend the night with me? It would be a great comfort to have her there."

"I will need Elsebett with me," Frau Mueller insisted. "She is to help in preparation of the medicines. It will be a very important learning experience for her. Besides, you must be well rested come morning. I fear the two of you would spend the night talking."

The two young women smiled, confirming what Frau Mueller had forecast.

"I will come with my teacher in the morning, and I will stay with you. I will stay until you are well…if my teacher agrees."

"Of course," Frau Mueller said. "Your role will be as friend and comforter."

"I dread this night as much as the morning that follows it," Anna said as she stood up. "It will be a long night filled with airy spirits. Child, if I can spend it near your bedside, I would be helped by it. My prayers will be silent ones as I watch over your sleep."

Agnes rose then and threw her arms around her mother.

"This night will be long for all of us, I fear," Frau Mueller admitted. But when the words had come out, she regretted them. She was getting too involved. Honor the person's distress but add nothing to strengthen it; that was the role of the healer.

§

Rachel and Elsebett needed to have their work finished before the light failed, so they rushed through their meal and went straight to the very cold back room. The purgative medicine, the first that would be given, was a complex compound containing a number of dried substances including licorice, cinnamon, some flour and a pungent gray dust that Rachel said came from a mushroom. As Elsebett pulverized and mixed these ingredients, Rachel loosened a heavily wrapped bundle revealing several plants' stems she had cut in the late summer. From one of the stems she managed to extract a bit of sap which she mixed with the dry powders to form two small bean-sized pills.

The second medicine, the one that would cause the miscarriage, was both very simple and very complex. "The medicine comes from a single forest plant which when mature can grow taller than our heads. Its feathery white flowers are quite beautiful, but its nature is cold and harsh. You will find it near water, in a moist forest. I found what I collected along the shaded edge of a meadow. Because of its harsh power, you must treat the plant with great respect and restraint."

Frau Mueller turned to the covered ceramic bowl that she had taken down from the shelf two days before. She removed the lid and the two of them looked at the contents. What Elsebett saw was an ugly mass of knobby, reddish objects with hairs curling off them. "This plant is ashamed of its harsh nature," her teacher said. "It tries to atone by producing beautiful flowers, but its true nature, and thus its power, shuns the light and remains hidden beneath the earth. This is why we collect not the leaves or the flowers but the roots. In its root, is found the true nature of the plant."

Rachel reached into the bowl. She lifted out one of the roots and set it on the shelf. "Earlier I spoke to you about dosage. The problem before us is what I was thinking about.

The medicine from this root will make your cousin ill. Thus, it is very important that the amount we give her works the first time. We must give her enough medicine to cause the miscarriage, but not so much that it injures or even kills her."

Elsebett studied the ugly root. It stretched about the length of her hand and was at its center as thick as two or three of her fingers. The prospect terrified her. She had no idea. Would the whole root be required? Or several? Or—and this was a measurement she had seen Frau Mueller use once before—would the amount that fits into the slit in a scribe's quill be enough?

Rachel watched her student closely, seeing her fear. Only when the girl looked at her, did she speak.

"When I first came to the village an old woman lived in this house. She was a midwife and a wise woman. A kind and generous couple brought me here from the convent so I could live and study with her as you now live and study with me. She was a strange woman, I never felt truly comfortable around her. Also, she died too soon, before I had learned all she could have taught me. But while I was with her, she did teach me much. What I want to explain to you now, is that there exists a living wisdom, Elsebett. It is a wisdom that that old woman had herself learned as a girl from an old woman, and that she passed on to me as I now pass it on to you. This wisdom has come to us through the ages, but it is alive still. It is carried in the hearts and minds, in the hands of people like us, and it changes somewhat whenever a new woman learns it. It exists in convents, in the great monasteries and in tiny houses in small villages like our own. What I am saying is that you and I are not alone on this cold afternoon. We are separate, but we are not separated."

"Did the woman who lived here teach you about this plant?" Elsebett asked.

"She introduced me to the plant. She spoke to me of its qualities but she did not use it while I was her student." After a pause, Rachel added, "And before now, I have not used it myself."

It was an admission that Rachel had warned herself not to make. That she had, made her realize that Elsebett was no longer just a student. She had become a colleague. From a student, you hid your fears. With a colleague, you shared them.

"So, you don't know how much to give her?" her colleague wanted to know.

"I have some ideas, but no certainty," Rachel admitted. What she thought but restrained herself from saying was: Your cousin's lust has put all of us in this place of turmoil and danger.

The words she did speak were more practical: "I want you to cut this root in half. Put one half back in the bowl and place the covering on it. Then chop the remaining half into many tiny pieces. When you have finished, you must place the pieces in the mortar and thoroughly crush them. From that crushed material, I will select the amount we will give to Agnes."

Elsebett nodded, but when she reached for the knife, Frau Mueller gripped her elbow. "Now, remember what I have told you. This plant is very powerful. It must be treated with respect. When you have finished the work, thoroughly clean the workbench, then carefully wash and dry the pestle, the knife and your hands. We want all of the medicine to be in the mortar, and none on the knife or the pestle, or on you. Is that clear?"

It was.

TWENTY-SEVEN

Morning arrived, cold, clear and windless. As they were preparing to leave the house, a knock came at the door. When she opened it, Elsebett found her aunt Anna wrapped in her heavy coat.

"My child is already sick," she told the midwife, stomping her feet. "She complains of nausea, and in the night she vomited on the floor. I fear the airy spirits have already laid claim to her."

"Has she shown any sign of bleeding?" Rachel asked.

"Not to my knowledge. She has not spoken of it. But she is most troubled."

"Thoughts of this day have roiled her humors. And your husband? Is he within or without?"

"He knows of her illness and is eager to avoid her, as is true to his nature. An illness in anyone sickens him," Anna said bitterly.

This report brought some comfort to Rachel. She knew the husband to be an unstable spirit, best avoided when possible. From the first visit of Anna and Agnes, she had been alert to the danger the husband posed. Deception would be necessary.

And should the truth of their deception become known to him, any or all of them could be at risk.

Several years earlier Anna's husband had come to Rachel complaining of terrible pain in his back and leg. The man was walking most cautiously, grimacing with every move he made, and enraged that this mishap had befallen him at a time when his labor was required in the fields. Rachel had felt an instant sympathy, knowing that the man was in pain, and that his family's wellbeing did indeed depend on his labor. But she also thought that rest was the best and quickest cure for his problem. So she had suggested that he return home and confine himself to his bed for several days.

To this prescription the man had responded angrily, complaining that she was a fraud who knew nothing. He was the victim of black magic, he insisted. A curse had been laid against him, probably by a certain jealous neighbor. Then he turned suspicious. Was Frau Mueller, herself, in the pay of this neighbor? Had she laid the curse on him? The moment had been a frightening one for Rachel. She was alone in her house with a suspicious, angry, pain-filled man who had come in search of some enchantment that might release the curse, realign the light and shadows tormenting him. He did not deserve to be treated like a child and told to go to bed.

So, she had prepared a compound that smelled terrible and would taste worse. "You must take all of this," she warned him. "But do not consume it until you are at home and seated on your bed." Then before he left, she had placed her hands on his lower back, and holding them there had intoned several Latin phrases. He had never told her if the cure had worked, and she had never asked.

§

They found Agnes seated on her bed with a bowl on her lap. She was repeating the name Heinrich, almost as if it were a chant. She wished he were here now to hold her hand. Elsebett thought her cousin must be delirious. She had no idea who this Heinrich was.

"Have you eaten?" Rachel wanted to know.

Agnes swore she had not. The bowl was to catch what came out, not to hold what might go in.

"He is such a fine young man. He must never know," Agnes said with a solemn tone. "Only if I die should he be told."

Rachel wanted to know if there had been any sign of bleeding.

Agnes did not think so. "But yes, if I die he should be told. It will break his heart but he must be told."

Rachel insisted on an examination. In the night she had fantasized that perhaps Agnes's fear of the medicine might itself cause the miscarriage, but it was not to be. There was no sign of discharge.

Frau Mueller then asked Elsebett for the two small pills they had prepared the day before. Giving them to Agnes, she instructed her to chew and swallow them with a bit of watered-down wine. A few minutes later the young woman rushed to the chamber pot and emptied her bowels.

"I feel better," Agnes said.

"This is as it should be," Frau Mueller said. She sent Elsebett to empty the chamber pot and instructed Anna to bring some heated stones from the hearth and place them beneath the covers.

"The medicine is cold. You must be warm when it enters you."

"I am frightened," Agnes said, pacing about.

"Yes, I understand. But get beneath the covers, Agnes, and warm yourself."

"This does have to happen, does it not?" the young woman pleaded when she was in the bed. She grabbed Elsebett's hand and squeezed it tightly.

"It does," Frau Mueller said. From her pouch she removed a small packet made from a square of linen cloth and tied with a bit of thread. She loosened the thread and opened the cloth to reveal a quantity of the pulverized root. This was the first time Elsebett had seen the amount her teacher had selected, and she studied it closely. It could, she thought, if packed tightly, be fitted within a half of a walnut shell.

"Will you pray for me?"

"We will all pray for you," Elsebett assured her.

"I am going to put this in your mouth, Agnes. I will place it on your tongue and I will give you more of the watered-down wine to help you wash it down. You must consume all of it. I want you to wash the liquid around in your mouth to make sure you take every bit of the medicine."

Anna knelt now beside her daughter's bed, crying and praying aloud.

"For my soul?" Agnes asked, looking at Elsebett, her eyes terror struck.

"Yes, I will pray for your soul," Elsebett promised.

Agnes opened her mouth very wide. Frau Mueller said, "Hold God in your heart, dear Agnes." Making the sign of the cross, she placed the medicine on the young woman's tongue and handed her the vessel with the wine.

TWENTY-EIGHT

The next Sunday her grandmother wanted Elsebett always at her side. The winter had been hard on the elderly woman. Her eyesight had continued to deteriorate and she was less stable on her feet. "When I wake in the night, I am like a jester on stilts," she complained.

Walking through ice and snow to the church would not be possible for her. Perhaps in the spring, she told her granddaughter, "if the Lord lets me stay in this world."

Elsebett agreed to remain in the house and be her company. They sat themselves near the hearth and Elsebett took up some needlework she had brought with her from Frau Mueller's home.

"Your mother was a very skilled seamstress," her grandmother said. "She did not only our family's work, but she sewed for others in the village. Have you been told of her skills?"

Elsebett had been told of her mother's sewing so often, and with such enthusiasm, that for a long while she was wary of the needle, fearing her every wayward stitch would be compared to her mother's skilled handiwork. But she did it now, slowly and carefully, though not particularly well.

"Yes, Oma. I know my mother was very skilled as a seamstress. But please, since we have this morning together, if you would, tell me everything you can remember of her."

"I was afraid for my Basil at first," Marsel said, staring into the fire.

"For father?" Elsebett was surprised.

"You see, I knew your grandmother very well—Hette, that is, your other grandmother. She was my best friend. When my man brought me to this village, I was a stranger and Hette welcomed me. I adored Hette because she was so different from me. There was something exciting about her. I mean no disrespect. She was a proper married woman, virtuous and true. But Hette loved everything about festivals, about markets, about dancing and celebrating. She lived from one feast day to the next, planning and dreaming. That woman loved to dance! And her husband too. He could dance for hours, while my man would have none of that. Of course, with his limp, dancing would not have been easy, had he had any interest in it. Which I can tell you, he did not."

"Could Hette sing?" Elsebett wanted to know. "I know my mother could sing. They say that."

"Gifted with it, both of them one and the same, daughter like mother. I possessed none of those skills, which is why I admired her so."

Elsebett shook her head. "I'm like you, Oma. When I sing, people wince."

"Now, let me see," Marsel continued as if she had not heard, "Hette's Gisele and my Margaret were born about the same time. And then my Ayla came into the world… no, that's wrong. Before Ayla, Anna was born. That's right. Then came Ayla, and then Basil followed by my little Jacob. About the time your uncle Sebastian entered the world, your mother was born to Hette."

"So, if my mother was alive today, she would be my uncle Sebastian's age?"

"Very near, child, very near as I remember. Now, the thing about Arved was how she resembled her mother. Both were dark of course. Dark hair, dark eyes. This is not so true of your aunts Gisele and Anna, as you know. Your brother carries that darkness, though you do not, and your cousin Agnes is possessed of it. All coming from Hette. It has to do with how the humors are blended, I suppose."

"Yes," Elsebett said cautiously.

"And speaking of Agnes," Marsel said, suddenly turning "she has been sick I understand."

They had arrived at the subject Elsebett most feared: the first time her promise to Frau Mueller would be tested.

"Yes, Oma, she was quite ill, but the medicine Frau Mueller prepared seems to have worked. She is recovering now, I believe."

"That fanciful child! I am happy to hear of it. When she was small she was most every day in this house, you know. Always by her aunt Arved's side. You would have thought she had no mother of her own. Then when your brother was born, she idolized that baby, holding him, carrying him around the house, watching him while he slept. She was very sick, I understand."

"For a few hours she was," Elsebett said. Then hoping to change the subject, she added, "I wish I could have heard my mother laugh."

"Her laugh was given her by an angel," Marsel said. "She almost died, you know."

Elsebett had heard the story many times, but she encouraged her grandmother to continue.

"Yes, she sure did. As a small child, a year, not older. Poor little girl. She was very sick, feverish with a terrible cough, and so weak. For weeks she lay only in bed. But Hette was loved of God. And she was so tortured with fear of losing her. Her prayers were so pleading and heartfelt that God decided to give the child back. And when he did, he directed an angel to make for her a special laugh. It was given as a sign of the miracle, you see, and to cheer her mother's heart. That is what we have always believed. But now I know God gave Arved back to us for another reason too."

"What is that, Oma?"

"God gave Arved back so she could bring you into the world to comfort me, Elsebett. That is why."

TWENTY-NINE

Later that afternoon, after she had enjoyed the Sunday meal with her family, Elsebett went to see Agnes. It was now the third day since she had taken the medicine and Elsebett had been with her all of every day and night, except for the visit to her grandmother's that morning. The harsh root had done its hard service. Agnes had begun to bleed a few hours after taking it. Soon the blood became clotted and Frau Mueller determined that the fetus and placenta had vacated the body. Minutes after taking the medicine, Agnes had become nauseous and had retched uncontrollably for a long time, crouched on the floor before the chamber pot. Tears flowed, her nose ran, she felt the need to urinate. Though her bowels had been emptied by the purging, they insisted on discharging whatever they could. The bleeding, when it began, was accompanied by severe cramps in her abdomen and lower back.

By that Sunday afternoon Agnes was through the worst of it. The nausea and retching had diminished when the cramping began and the blood began to flow. It was as if the body could not do everything at once, and so it focused on particular tasks. The bleeding had largely ended by Saturday but the cramps continued. Now, they too had largely given way to a state of battered exhaustion.

Agnes had eaten no food since Wednesday, the evening before she took the medicine, though on Friday and Saturday she had managed to keep down a few swallows of weak beer. Now when Elsebett arrived she found her aunt Anna feeding broth to her daughter with a spoon.

Seeing Elsebett enter, Agnes became embarrassed. She pushed herself up in the bed and complained, "I can feed myself, mother."

"Let me baby you one last time, child. You do look miserable, do you know that?"

"Knowing how I feel, mother, I need not see how I look. And you, cousin, tell your Frau Mueller that the penances she imposed were much worse than those assigned me by Father Peter."

"You well deserved them both, Agnes," Aunt Anna said as she dipped the spoon into the bowl.

The comment caused Agnes to roll her eyes. But Elsebett could see that this ordeal had brought them closer. Anna had not, as tradition would have dictated, reported Agnes's sin to her father. She had taken responsibility for protecting her, and finding help. Anna had become party to the conspiracy in a way that endangered even herself. And Agnes, it was clear, understood and was grateful.

"My Oma sends greetings to you both," Elsebett said, taking a chair. "I assured her you were getting better, so I am happy to see you like this. And she told me, Aunt Anna, that when you were a little girl, you and my aunt Margaret, whom I have never met, that you and she were endless trouble. Each of you was trouble alone, she said, but together you were more than twice as bad."

"Mother!" Agnes erupted in mock horror. "I never knew."

"If there is any truth to it, you can put it at the feet of Margaret. She was older than me by a year and a half and if there was ever no good to be up to, she was up to it. Truth be told, I pray for the convent that took her in, though I loved her, I have to say. Your look reminds me of her, Elsebett. She was about the age you are now when her father grabbed her up and hauled her off. You have been nothing but a blessing to us in this ordeal, and I will be forever grateful for what you and your teacher have done. So, it's not your manner that reminds me of Margaret, thanks be to God, but the look of you."

"I have her hair, Oma tells me. So, that gives me sympathy for her."

When Agnes had eaten what she could, Anna departed with the bowl and spoon, leaving the cousins to themselves.

"You should rest," Elsebett said. "And I need to get back to Frau Mueller's. She will be happy to learn that you are improved."

Agnes had closed her eyes and allowed her head to fall back against the pillow. But now she opened them again and pushed herself more erect.

"Please wait, cousin. Let me rest for just a moment, and then I must talk to you. It is very important."

During Agnes's nap Elsebett straightened the room a bit, then feeling exhausted herself, she returned to the chair, closed her eyes and fell quickly to sleep. Since Wednesday, what sleep she had gotten had come in snatches, and she had eaten little more than chunks of bread. But at home that noon—Elsebett still thought of the Helgen family home as her home—her aunt Klara had served the family a hot pottage containing chunks of a well-smoked ham taken from the chimney. Her body, having enjoyed the hot meal with a generous pouring of her uncle Sebastian's beer, and recognizing now Agnes's improved state, insisted on sleep for itself.

When she finally opened her eyes, Agnes was looking at her.

"Do you remember my hope chest?" she asked with a mysterious smile.

Elsebett did remember, particularly the two little caps, one of them sewn by her mother.

"Would you fetch it?" her cousin asked. "It hides still beneath my bed."

Elsebett got belly-down on the floor, and reaching in the dark, found the box and pulled it out. It was smaller than she remembered, but just as finely made.

Agnes held the box on her lap, hands on the lid. "There is something I want to show you." She opened the box and pulled out a cloth packet that, though smaller, was very similar to the one that Frau Mueller had used to transport the harsh medicine. Agnes loosened the tie and opened the cloth to reveal a small smooth stone that had an intense bluish color. The stone seemed to have been polished but had not been faceted and was irregular in shape.

"You should see it in the light of the sun," she said. "Were the day not so cold and I not so weak, I would have you open the shutter." She held the stone near the candle flame and its light intensified the blue color. "My Heinrich said it came from across the sea."

She placed the stone in Elsebett's palm. To the younger girl it felt magical.

"I will speak to Frau Mueller," she said handing it back. "She knows many stones, their characters and their uses in healing. Perhaps she has knowledge of this one."

Agnes placed the stone carefully in the center of the cloth. She gathered the corners and having neatly retied the bow, returned the packet to the box. Elsebett watched the work closely. Her cousin had a precision in her movements that she had always admired. Perhaps her mother had possessed the same. Agnes, too, was skilled with needle and thread. As she watched her cousin tie the bow, she thought she might be seeing how her mother's hands had looked and moved.

"Yes, do," Agnes said. "Ask her what it means when a man gives such a stone to a girl. Must it not mean that he loves her? I am sure Heinrich loved me as he swore he did. No, loves me still. And now I am imprisoned here by weak health and condemnation! And should he come to the inn, what shall he learn of me? Will he be told that I am ill or dead? Or gone on pilgrimage? Or married off to a plowman? Or taken in service of the church? What stories my aunt Gisele might tell of me I cannot foresee, so my imagination is made ripe with speculation. You all think—yes, even you, dear cousin—that I have sinned and made foolish error. Well, I have sinned, and I have made foolish error. But it does not follow that my love was false, or his, or that I wantonly seduced him, or he me. I have done my penance, and against all my fears I have survived. Am I to languish here the rest of my days, dead in all ways but one, a victim of my father's fears and rages? He is my master until I marry, of that I can do nothing. And the man I love? Who can say what he will think when he finds me absent from the inn?"

Elsebett took the hope chest from Agnes and returned it to its hiding place.

"Well, cousin," she said, when she had regained her chair, "first you must recover your strength. Without your strength you can do nothing. And strength my teacher tells me, comes from a quiet mind as well as from rest, good food and healthy drink. So, do not trouble yourself unduly. Rather, seek for peace within. When your strength has returned and your mind is quiet, you will see what choices are open to you. Of your stone I know nothing, only that it is important. Precious stones, I have been taught, have great power and are hated by the Devil, so the gift given you was a powerful one. And its existence connects you to the giver. Perhaps, from time to time as you are healing, you should take it in your hand, or hold it in your mouth. I trust it will give you strength, and perhaps guidance."

THIRTY

On the walk to Rachel's home, Elsebett was shocked that she had taken such an authoritarian tone with her older cousin. Had she been presumptuous to advise Agnes, a grown woman she had always idolized? But her thoughts and words had come so naturally and Agnes had listened, grateful, it seemed, for the guidance. The sensation she felt as she hurried through the cold afternoon was both embarrassing and thrilling.

Frau Mueller, she found, was eager to hear about Agnes.

"I am encouraged by her recovery," Rachel said when she had questioned her student carefully. "Though the root abused her terribly—and we can only hope it did not render her infertile—it did cause the miscarriage and she is recovering. So, we can say that the dosage appears to have been correct. I noticed that you studied the amount closely. We must both remember it should the need again arise.

"But I am saddened by the further message in your report. It seems that your cousin has suffered much but learned little from this ordeal. That she continues to harbor desire for this man is most unfortunate.

"The stone you describe is probably a sapphire though I cannot be certain without seeing it. The sapphire is hot, composed more of fire than air. It has great power. It can quiet wrath and ward off unwanted lust. It has this power because the Devil abhors it. Both rage and lust spring from the Devil. He uses them to pull the person into dark and unwanted places. Thus, I find it strange that this man would choose a sapphire to give her. Perhaps he was ignorant of its meaning and its powers. Perhaps he too was blinded by the stone's beauty.

"As a symbol, the sapphire represents the love of wisdom. Unfortunately, badly needed wisdom is lacking in Agnes. In answer to the question she asked that you present to me—and I answer for your benefit as much as for hers because you are reaching the age when you will encounter these temptations—I have to say that, yes, a man certainly can give a precious stone to a girl and not truly care for her. Giving such a stone speaks more to the man's wealth and lust than his respect and love. It also reveals, I have to tell you, something disturbing about your cousin.

"That he should give her such an expensive gift suggests strongly that he saw a weakness in her, a flaw in her character that he felt he could exploit. Had she been innocent of tempting him, she would, of course, have refused the gift he offered. Thus, it seems that both were blinded by lust, and the precious stone passed between them, its true meaning unrecognized, its benefits ignored, its powers transformed to serve the Devil rather than repel him.

"We can see in this episode two important lessons, Elsebett. The first is a basic truth: that which is powerful is also dangerous. In this case, the sapphire could have been used by either Agnes or this man to quell their own lust or that of the other. Perhaps, had the lust been quieted, the two of them might have developed a loving and respectful relationship. But in this case, the stone's power strengthened their lust rather than quelling it. Their blindness allowed the Devil to use the beauty of a stone he abhors to serve his desires. In the end, the stone became a tool of blindness rather than wisdom, and it caused damage rather than benefit.

"The second lesson is a humbling one for both of us. It shows the weakness of our power to heal and the limited strength of any medicine we might employ. If people do not want to be healed, Elsebett, they will not be healed. Or, if healed of one malady they will soon acquire another. In this case, the malady was their lust. If the person is unwilling to be helped, even a medicine so potent as a sapphire is useless, and in fact dangerous. Thus, I am called back to that which I have always told you, and you are probably tired of hearing: As healers we go where needed and we offer what skills we have, but the healing itself is magical and out of our hands. We must not take credit for the successes or be destroyed by the failures.

"It is good that your dear cousin has survived. She is a young and charming woman with much to learn. The dreaded root has given her a second chance to do that."

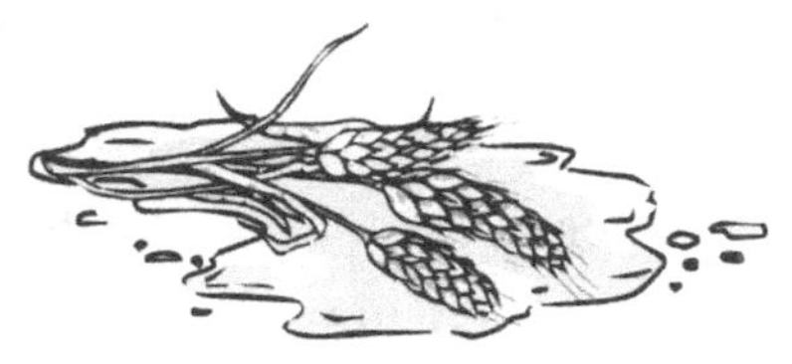

STERILITY

THIRTY-ONE

The bitter winter was followed by a cold and rainy spring. The rye that had survived the hard freeze struggled to regain its vitality, and the planting of the barley was delayed, the ground being too sodden to turn. Markets cruelly twisted. Future supplies appearing now to be threatened, prices began to rise. Those who had to purchase their bread—the landless and the imprudent—had to pay more while with the fields wet and idle, they had less opportunity to sell their labor and earn the money needed to feed their families.

The resulting tension spread through the village, touching every person to one degree or another. The Helgen family had ample grain for now, but could only worry about the future. After the long winter the brothers hungered for activity and were frustrated by their inability to get into the fields. The women were as eager to have them gone as they were to go, glancing at each other as the men paced back and forth in the house like penned animals.

Frau Henn, the woman the family had hired to help with the housework, complained that she needed more pay. Given the rising prices and the village council having replaced her husband with a younger man, they could hardly feed themselves. Basil, feeling pinched himself, was unwilling to part with more cash; he authorized her to take some rye flour, while suspecting that she was stealing beyond what he had authorized. His father's adage came back to him: the hired always hate their masters. Resentment drives them. They begrudge giving their labor and feel cheated by their pay. Leave them alone and they will think themselves justified to sit beneath the shade of a tree. Admit them to the storehouse and they will fill their pockets. Hire a worker and you have purchased an enemy; Johannes had believed that a law forged with good iron.

Some afternoons Basil would bust free of the house and go wandering among the young rye, dragging his son Johannes with him. The sky was low and gray, the earth dark, the tender shoots fragile and uncertain. A soft and slippery mud lined the fields, pools of water stood where water should not be standing. There would be barren, weed-filled patches come harvest. He and the boy cut channels to release the captive water, but with more rain coming and the mud slick and mobile, their lasting success would be minimal. The son stood back, hiding his impatience, while his father hovered over the young plants like a concerned mother, bending down to straighten water-weighted stalks as rain water dripped from his hat.

Later, they would go to the inn and drink beer with other frustrated plowmen. The lot of them smelled of wet wool and frustration. They complained about the weather, about empty fields, thieves prowling in the night, creeping mold and exploding rodent populations. There was no end to it. You got your crop in, got it threshed and winnowed and stored only to have it attacked by mold and rodents—who, if they were not gnawing a way into your bins, were busy reproducing.

During the long winter these men had cursed the dark, but spring's longer days, rain-soaked and raw, seemed now just as cruel because their sap was running and they could find no productive use to make of it. Added to the frustration was the late Easter which caused Lent to linger endlessly. Only one meal a day was allowed, and that in the evening. Everyone was tired of eating salted fish, the only flesh permitted. One afternoon a man explained to Basil how the Pope's new calendar was truer to the seasons, but sprinkled as it was with saints' days, the Protestant jurisdictions refused to accept it. So the dates might change when you traveled from one city to another. You could now leave one place on a Friday, the man said, and arrive at your destination the weekend before you left. "I would travel the other way," Basil replied. "Maybe there the rain has stopped and the sun has come out."

Johannes broke free of his father's table and went in search of his cousin Zacharias. At this time, Johannes was eighteen and his cousin twenty-one. Zacharias was being groomed in all aspects of the inn's management. He had committed to a woman who was a year younger than he, a daughter of the man who managed the village's mill near the river. Johannes found his cousin hauling firewood into the kitchen where his uncle Martin was barking orders at the staff.

"We're busy," Zacharias told him. "Weather that empties the fields fills the inn."

"So, what is bad for the plowman is good for the innkeeper?"

"In the short term, but when the money runs out, they will want to eat and drink on credit. And credit is easily forgotten, soon resented, and paid reluctantly. Better, they were in the fields growing their crops than in here borrowing against them. And with the rains comes the fever. Serving girls complain of it and want to stay home. Some of them are less than sick but more than eager to not work. Some you trust, others you learn not to. Our cousin Agnes was gone for almost a month a while back, and I'm not convinced she was sick at all. Such is the life of the innkeeper."

"My sister says Agnes was very sick for a few days. She was one of those helping to treat her."

"She may have been sick, if Elsebett says. But her recovery was unhurried in my view."

Marsel had been through wet springs before. The advice she gave her daughters-in-law was simple: feed them and stay out of their way. The rain will stop, the sun will soon burn them red and they will complain of the heat and their sore backs.

THIRTY-TWO

The rash of fevers spreading through the village kept Rachel and her apprentice busy. People came to their door, calling them out to bedsides. "The important thing," Rachel said one windy morning as they made their way through a light rain, "is to do our work while keeping rested ourselves. Better a healer with a quiet mind and a rested body than an anxious, exhausted one who soon needs help herself."

True to her own advice, Rachel cheated on the Lenten fast and had them early to bed. And it seemed to Elsebett that the advice worked. Though they were frequently with the sick, they did not become sick themselves. The aging midwife was always capable and attentive to those in distress.

Frau Mueller had other thoughts brought on by the rash of illnesses, thoughts more darkly shaded, that she tried to explain to her student. The concept of a contagion fascinated her, and it seemed to Elsebett, that it also frightened her. She saw them everywhere and it was a mistake to limit them to physical illness. "Take a thunderstorm," she proposed one day. "We see a few clouds gather. They grow thicker, darker. A bolt of lightning streaks across the sky followed by an explosion of thunder. Soon the wind is up and rain is pouring down. After an hour or two, the lightning has stopped, the air is calm, the rain has ended and the clouds have cleared. What we are experiencing now—this rash of fevers—is like a storm."

For Rachel, storms, outbreaks of disease, foul moods that spread through the village, mob cruelties (she related the story of the stoning of the Venus she had witnessed as a child) were forms of the same phenomenon. She had seen even joyous celebrations turn abruptly vulgar or even violent (a wedding one time where one brother had attacked another and the party had descended into a family brawl). They were all examples of a common phenomenon, it seemed to her. And contagion was the word she used for it. In a village such as theirs, life was so compressed, the shared mind so fertile, that a strong emotion could escape an individual and take on an existence of its own. A word passing from one pair of lips to another's ear, might transform into a rumor. Rumors grew and flourished. They spread quickly, rooting themselves in most every mind before fading like a flower in winter. A rumor was a form of contagion according to Frau Mueller.

"Why is it," she suddenly asked her student, "that we now have all these people bedded down with fevers? Not one or two but twenty or more?"

"Bad air?" Elsebett suggested tentatively, expressing the prevalent view.

"Or is it fashion?" her teacher surprised her by responding. "Could it be fashion? Fashion is a form of contagion, is it not? A young woman appears at church one Sunday with a purse different from everyone else's and soon more young women are trying to make or purchase the new purse. Why? Is that not a contagion of a different sort? Could the rash of fevers be no less an expression of fashion? By this I do not mean to suggest that those calling for us are not ill. They are ill. Some of them might even die of what afflicts them. The question is why? Why now? Why so many?"

"But the young women you speak of choose to make or buy the new purse," Elsebett countered. "Our patients do not choose to get the fever. I'm sorry, Frau Mueller, but I do not see how they are the same."

"You are quite right, Elsebett. They are not the same in that new purse is chosen while the fever is not. But I am suggesting they may be the same, or at least similar, in the way they spread. It is true that fevers seem to come from bad air; that is the commonly held belief and I have no reason to doubt it. But truly, is the air any different now than it was before the fevers began? And has everyone not walked through the same air while some have succumbed to the fever and others have not? And will the air be less odorous after the fevers have left than it is now? All of this I wonder about."

Bad air was but one of many possible sources, according to Frau Mueller. Contagions were born as well in the dark recesses of the human mind. Not all were negative. As a young woman she had made a pilgrimage to the city of Maastricht, and the mood among her fellow pilgrims seemed to her now to have been a contagion, one of homage and adventure. But more common were petty jealousies, festering envies, grating grudges that sought revenge. A nightmare might linger after the dreamer woke, it seemed to her. It sought to be more than a remembered dream. It desired to know itself believed, and being believed, proclaimed as fact in the village square. All contagions were potent, some dangerous, Frau Mueller said. They needed to be treated with respect even if born of fantasy and delusion.

"So, contagions *want* to happen?" Elsebett felt compelled to ask. "They have a life of their own?"

"It is a way of looking at them," her teacher responded. "Thinking of them in that way is helpful, it seems to me."

The conversation troubled Elsebett. Her teacher made the world sound treacherous, fluidly sinister. There were already devils to contend with, sin-filled urges capable of bringing disaster in their wake. Thoughts of Agnes were seldom absent from the young woman's mind. What had led her playful cousin to tumble into such torment in the face of all she had been taught? Had she not experienced the truth of it up close—seen firsthand the bloody clots of unformed child splashing into the pail—she would have denied such a thing could occur to any young woman, especially her dear cousin. Did she now have to suspect that someone's bad dream might rise up to infest the countryside? Bring ruin to crops? Cause the able to fall ill? Could one maintain a quiet spirit in the face of all her teacher had just described?

Frau Mueller did not relent. "It is our job to be awake," she told her student. "You are here to learn. We are both learning. And a quiet spirit is the only bulwark we have against the forces that are out there."

§

Among the people falling ill with the fever that spring was the widow Marsel Helgen. At first she denied her cough was anything to be concerned about. One Sunday with the snow gone and the morning bright with unaccustomed sun, she even joined the family trek to church. But inside the building she felt hot and clammy one minute, chilled the next. The harsh winter, it felt to her, had not yet left the church's stone floor, its brick walls, its enclosed stale air. It was almost as if winter had hidden itself there to await her arrival. Following the service, Jacob and Basil had to half carry their shivering, leg-weak mother back to the house where she was promptly placed in bed.

And there she lingered for several days, apologizing to anyone who entered the room to deliver a bowl of soup or a cheerful word. For Marsel, the experience of being waited on was so undeserved, so inappropriate that she could not help making it unpleasant for anyone who sought to assist her. Had anyone actually waited on Marsel since she had been weaned? Now she lay in bed, a bother to all and of use to no one.

"Oh," she would say, "you have so much to do yourself and now you have to wait on me!"

Irmele admitted to Elsebett that she was almost afraid to enter their grandmother's room. Any benefit resulting from the drink or crust of bread she delivered, was more than offset by the strain on their grandmother caused by her insistent stream of apologies.

One morning the old woman came tottering into the kitchen insisting that she was better, compelled to help with the breadmaking. Ursula stood alone kneading dough. The sight of Marsel crossing the floor on unsteady legs and then grasping the edge of the table to steady herself made Ursula speechless for a moment.

The sturdy worktable where the dough was kneaded had been a central feature of the room for decades. The husband Johannes had built it for his young wife shortly after the birth of Margaret, their first child. Typical of the man who relished the occasional dramatic gesture, the table had been constructed in secret without consulting the woman who would spend count-less hours using it, and then presented with a dramatic flourish. It was a tall table; the kneading was done standing before it. Sometimes where would be three women gathered together, each working her own loaf-sized mound of dough. The work was a pleasant, shared task, but time consuming and physically active. The ritual was also as central to the family's survival as the harvesting of grain, and it was Marsel who had super-vised the operation for years; she was baking bread long before anyone else in the family had even been born.

"You sweet child, working here alone," she said as she grasped the dough from Ursula's hands, her fingers clutching it almost as if it were a source of strength. But then Ursula saw Marsel waver. For an instant she was not certain if it was her mother-in-law, or herself, or the very earth that had suddenly gone unsteady. Marsel teetered; she lost consciousness and fell to the floor, making a thick sound when she landed, as if a sack of grain had fallen from a shelf. There was blood as well. Her head must have banged against the table's edge on the way down because a gash had opened on her forehead.

Marsel was appalled at her blunder. Her effort to help had only brought more work for everyone, and she apologized profusely as Ursula assisted by Irmele—who had heard the crash and come running—carried her back to her bed and then pressed a cloth against the cut.

"The dough! Did I ruin the dough?" Marsel stammered among her stream of apologies.

Ursula assured her that the dough was fine. She was surprised at her boldness; she was actually pressing against the old woman's shoulders to prevent her from trying to rise.

"Yes, Oma. Please lie back now," Irmele said. "The bread is fine. I will run and find Elsebett."

She glanced toward her aunt. Both were alarmed that this woman who had been their source of strength appeared now so fragile, so confused and in need of help.

Irmele's suggestion that Elsebett be called brought a new wave of protest from Marsel. "No, no, child. Do not bother Elsebett. Frau Mueller needs her. There are many people in the village who are *really* sick and need their help far more than I do."

THIRTY-THREE

Frau Mueller had taken down a sack and opened it so Elsebett and Irmele could see the dried leaves inside. A strong, bitter smell rose from the bag as it was opened.

"This plant is beautifully balanced," the teacher said. "It is moderately hot and more dry than wet. Its flowers possess a bright gayety, but it is the leaves we use. Dried now, the coloring is subdued; but seen fresh, the green is softened by yellow so the effect is more gentle than the dark green of many leaves. I gather them in the spring, but they are not developed enough yet this year so I have been using dried ones. Two or three leaves taken once a day, fresh or dried is what I recommend to help your grandmother. The leaves should be crushed. The taste is bitter so we sweeten it with a bit of honey. It will do her no harm and should help still the fever and reduce the amount of phlegm that fills her head. Too much phlegm can disturb a person's balance, and that may have contributed to her fall."

Irmele's dimples were pronounced as she glanced at her cousin. She was excited to be in the company of the wise woman and her student. She had been in the house before but never in the work room. She could not resist looking at the dark and mysterious shelves and the profusion of containers. And she wondered about the precious stones, whether Frau Mueller really had some, and if she did, where they were hidden. Could it be that there actually was a stone, a topaz like Elsebett had said, that would protect you against poison? The idea of it! It was almost like having a guard dog that you wore on your finger.

"Perhaps we should crush enough leaves for several days, Frau Mueller, if that is all right," Elsebett suggested, looking into the sack.

Her teacher agreed. "But only add the honey to the dosage as you give it to her. And the two of you should stay with her until she is better, by turns or together."

Frau Mueller also believed in fluids. She wanted the sick to be drinking. Weak beer was preferred. The village water was as likely as bad air to make people sick. But she knew a spring that delivered good water. It was inaccessible in winter, but now it was flowing again and she and Elsebett had recently been there to collect some. So she gave the cousins a jug of spring water to take with them.

Elsebett felt torn between Frau Mueller and her grandmother. Often her work involved sitting with the sick to make sure the medicines were administered properly. She wanted to be with her grandmother, but she knew her teacher needed her as well.

"Will you be all right?" she felt brave enough to ask.

"For now, yes," Frau Mueller said. "Go and stay. I will stop by myself tomorrow. But in the meantime, stay with your grandmother. She needs you."

§

Marsel was angry at her sense of exhaustion, at the weight she felt pressing down on her chest, at the incessant cough that took command of her body. The troubled looks on the faces of her sons and daughters-in-law confused and frightened her. She had the sense of herself as misunderstood. All this kind attention, but no one quite believed her. If she could just get up and start moving about, her strength would come back. But she was trapped. It was as if she had become a heavy-bodied beetle that had fallen onto its back and lay helpless, waving its many useless legs. She really must get up. But then after thinking these thoughts, and quite against her will, she fell back into sleep.

She woke coughing to find Elsebett and Irmele leaning over her; the two girls lifting her into a sitting position so she could swallow some powder and wash it down with water. Then it was Frau Mueller seated beside her bed, asking questions in a voice so quiet that Marsel had to strain to hear. Had she always been there? Or had she just arrived? All of this fuss being made over her. It was embarrassing.

Her oldest grandchild, the young Johannes, whom she loved deeply—had he been in the world at the same time as her husband, his namesake?

"Yes, Oma. I remember him." The young man sat in the chair where Frau Mueller had sat. Was she gone? And when had he come in? He took her hand in his own rough hand, lifted it up and held it. That was so like him. A sweet boy he was. The two of them had always had a secret compact. "I remember the whip he carried everywhere," the boy said now, tears in his eyes.

Marsel misread her grandson's tears; she thought the boy still grieved for his grandfather. She too remembered the whip. It had been an extension of her husband and she had hated the sight of it. Her man was not a drunken man, just a dominant one who used rage to extend his dominion throughout the family. He rarely beat her, perhaps because of the pathways she had devised around and through him, subtle influences, passive controls, or maybe he actually recognized his need of her and restrained himself. But on the children, he used it regularly. Respect, self-control, honesty, politeness, obedience, diligence, attention to detail, all were taught with the whip.

Ayla, her second child, became a saint in the face of that whip, learning quickly to close her eyes and fall into prayer whenever his anger rose. Marsel had always suspected that Ayla's tactic began as a trick. She was a clever girl, and the trick a clever one because her husband had a surprising fear and respect for priests, nuns and all aspects of church authority. But what may have begun as a trick grew into a feature of Ayla's character, one that she eventually inhabited and chose to there remain.

Margaret, by contrast, had resisted and hated and suffered, and had resisted again, hated again and again suffered. Nothing in Marsel's long life had brought her such pain as those epic asymmetrical wars between her husband and her firstborn child—not the violent death of her father, not even the despondent death of her mother, the death that had left her in the care of her grandparents. How conflicted she had felt as she witnessed that drawn out struggle between father and daughter, how inadequate, how shamed, how paralyzed, how ridden with guilt.

Her boys' upbringing, it seemed to her now, had been relatively easy. Basil, like herself, was a skilled tactician. He had learned to maneuver carefully in close quarters, seeming to serve, but with an eye always toward shaping, influencing. And Jacob, her dear, jolly, Jacob, he too learned a trick. His trick was to follow a step behind Basil, moving in strict obedience. Both were beaten and both suffered. But Basil devised tactics from the pain while Jacob learned to hide in the shadow of his more adroit older brother.

It was Sebastian, the youngest of her children, who—except for Margaret—had suffered the most. But his pain brought less agony to Marsel. Maybe she was just older and somewhat numbed by the time Sebastian came along, but she had never really understood Sebastian, how bright, how curious, how inventive he was. She had accepted her husband's reading of the child: he was impractical, inattentive, given to fancy, easily distracted. Not a bad boy, not hostile or combative, but he was scattered, perhaps defective in some way. He did need to be disciplined, his wavering energies channeled, brought under control. She had always given him the same advice after the whip handle had reduced him to sobs. "Be like Jacob," she would tell him. "Listen to Basil, Sebastian. Do what Basil says, do it the way he does."

When Marsel's thoughts had returned to the room, she found Johannes still there holding her hand. "And Elsebett?" she asked him. "Was she born then?"

"No, Oma," Johannes replied. "Opa died before Elsebett was born. She was born when my mother died."

Privately, and not surprisingly, Johannes had always linked his sister's birth and his mother's death. It was not blame he felt exactly, but the two were associated in a disturbing way. Of this he had spoken to no one, not even to his grandmother. But she knew. She understood and accepted. That was the thing about his grandmother: she understood. She scolded, she swatted, but never did she not understand. Without his grandmother, the world would make less sense, seem less fair to Johannes.

When Marsel woke again she found the wild boys gathered around her bed: Gabriel, David and Thomas, her youngest grandchildren, ten, nine and eight now. The grandbabies, she fancied them in her mind when they were tiny, the wild boys now. Wild because they ran in a cluster; they had the ability to disappear and when they returned they brought with them the wildness of the out-of-doors. Outside air clung to their clothing, they moved in a rush of it. That and the sense she had that they shared a secret that was both private and funny. She had never needed to learn what the secret was. It was enough to see it in their glances, their shared smiles to know it was there.

She had known the wild boys to be different than Johannes. He had been struck a blow by his mother's terrible death, and Basil, his father, had had to shape him into a man, sometimes forcibly with great will and determination. No such thing had happened to them so they had less need of her. Their mothers fussed over them, their fathers and uncles ordered them around, cuffing them now and then. They tolerated, they obeyed, but the force of it bounced off harmlessly, protected as they were by their shared conspiracy. They were like her own sons, Basil, Jacob and Sebastian in some ways, only closer in age and temperament and without the shadow of a limping man overseeing them with a whip. How odd it seemed to her suddenly that five of her six grandchildren—all of them save Johannes—such vital parts of the family, Helgens through and through, had no personal knowledge of the man she had married, the thundering Johannes. Just as surprising, no memory in them of the sweet Arved, who in Marsel's mind, seemed even now a bright presence forever young.

Sometime after the three grandsons had left, Marsel had a troubling experience: she looked out at the world and saw that she was not there. Was it a dream? A vision? A message from God? Something she actually saw? Opening her eyes she recognized Elsebett who sat now in the chair holding her hand. When had she come? How long had she been sitting there?

"I looked out and I am not there, child."

"You are here, Oma. And I am here with you."

"No, out there! I have looked out and I am not there. I see all of you. I see Margaret and Ayla, they sit alone in their cells without me. I see my sons, they trouble themselves with worry and I cannot help them. I see Klara and dear Ursula bewildered by the hearth. I see Irmele, sweet-fleshed Irmele, so innocent! She will need a kind-hearted man and where is the one who will recognize the good in her? And you, dear child, you are the heart. You must never let yourself be distanced from your brother. He has such need of you."

Elsebett thought for a moment about the many things her grandmother had said, and she felt the weight of them settle on her. Most surprising was that she would speak now of Johannes. Her own feelings for him were confused. Could Oma be right that he had need of her? He was the older, stronger one, the one who had run when she could only crawl. Who had lifted her onto chairs, bending his knees and grunting to get her up; he had liked to give sudden tugs on her ever-tangled hair, sneaking up behind, stealthy as a cat, his quick grin showing it for a tease. As a small child she had idolized him for this, and for his size and his dark-eyed beauty.

But in the last few years they had seen less of one another. Their father had taken hold of Johannes and like some master craftsman had shaped her teasing brother into a sturdy plowman while she had become the student of the midwife. Now he ran with other boys his age. He seemed to have a particular friendship with a boy named Abraham who had come from a neighboring village and was an apprentice of the joiner. If she saw her brother at all it was only on Sundays or by a chance encounter on a village street.

She sensed a distance in both Johannes and Abraham. One Sunday, Johannes had questioned her about Frau Mueller in a suspicious way. He wanted to know if she really trusted her teacher. He asked if the midwife was a practitioner of dark magic. Elsebett would have been astonished to hear these words come from anyone, but her brother? Without thinking she had laughed in his face. Then half joking, she asked: Tell me, dear brother, do you still believe that silly fantasy that Agnes told us years ago? The one about the witch's house? No, of course not, he had said. But then he told her what his friend had told him, that the joiner's wife suspected Rachel of witchery.

"That is absurd," she said, feeling angry. "A witch is a person in league with the Devil. Frau Mueller loves God. She is a great healer. This village is full of people she has helped."

"She did not help my mother… our mother," Johannes said darkly.

"Our mother? What do you mean?"

"She was the midwife when you were born. Surely you know that. And you know what happened to our mother. She gave birth to you. She held you in her arms, and then she died a horrible death."

Elsebett was speechless for a moment. She had never associated Frau Mueller with her own birth or her mother's death. But of course she would have been there. She was the village midwife.

"Birth is dangerous to women," she stammered after a moment, quoting her teacher. "Dangerous to the child and dangerous to the mother."

"I see she has never spoken to you about it," Johannes had said, and his tone insinuated that that in itself was suspicious.

Elsebett looked now at her grandmother. She had closed her eyes again and seemed to be sleeping. Elsebett took a deep breath and released a slow sigh. She had a lot to think about. The full import of her grandmother's words had just struck her for the first time: my grandmother believes she is dying. She looked out at the world and she was not there. Is that not what she said? Can that not be what she means? And Elsebett began to cry.

THIRTY-FOUR

The death of Marsel Helgen took a fortnight. Compared with the last two deaths in the family—the abrupt, almost violent taking of her husband Johannes and the heartrending cruel passing of Arved —Marsel's was a good death. Good in the sense that she and the family had time to prepare for it. It did not seem particularly painful for Marsel, though her breathing became labored, loud and irregular near the end. And she found terrifying those moments when she could not complete a breath. Rather than a physician or a healer, Father Peter was called to her bedside.

The father had been in the parish for several years now and he was growing into his job. As a young man he had had a pronounced fear of death. In its presence he could smell the sulfur given off by devils and feel the heat coming from the flames of hell surrounding them. At his first death as a priest, the wife and soon-to-be widow, a squat, no-nonsense peasant woman, had pushed the babbling, terrified young man into the bedroom where her dying husband lay, crying "Father, Father," before closing the door behind him. That story, complete with the refrain "Father, Father," had spread through the village like one of Rachel's contagions. "Father, Father, the Reluctant Priest," was on the lips of most everyone for a while. In the tavern, it took the crueler form of "Father, Father, the Reluctant Rabbit," since at that time he was still known principally for his thin neck and elongated ears. But Father Peter rarely trembled now when he came into the presence of the dying, and normally he even managed to control his stammer.

In the village certain understandings were accepted by everyone. Humans, it was understood, possessed both a body and a soul. At death, the soul survived though the body did not. While the body decayed it had to be carefully buried because in the future, at the time of the final judgment, it would be physically resurrected and the soul would be reunited with it in heaven. For the soul there were three possibilities. Prior to the resurrection, it would most likely find itself for at least some period in purgatory. Purgatory was a physical location, as real as the graveyard and located very near to it. Only those few persons with the purity of saints passed directly from physical death into heaven. While those who died, having committed mortal sins for which they had not confessed and done penance, would proceed directly to eternal damnation.

To be in purgatory was to exist in a state of instability and torment because the soul had acquired flaws during its lifetime, the results of impure thoughts and desires, temptations succumbed to, venal acts committed, and thus it had to be purified before it could enter into the presence of God. Purgatory was a form of smelting in which the impurities adhering to the soul were burned away; it involved heat, perhaps flames, and the less time spent there the better.

Father Peter told Marsel that purgatory awaited her unless the Devil succeeded in pulling her away at the last minute. She could be sure that he was lurking nearby, looking for an opportunity to tempt her. The deathbed was fertile ground, the priest insisted, the site of a great battle. But the church was there to guide her, and to keep her safe. He whispered these words to her prior to anointing her with oil that had been blessed by the Bishop and offering various prayers over her, these acts done in the presence of her family.

It was not clear exactly what Marsel was thinking. At first she had much to say, though the organization of her thoughts and their expression were compromised by her deteriorating physical condition. She appeared possessed by a sense of urgency. Does bread need to be baked? Had those garments she had hung to dry by the hearth been put away? Were the wild boys getting fed properly? They were so self-contained that even their mothers sometimes neglected to look after them. At least it seemed so to her, now that she could no longer watch over them.

In time the scope of her concerns widened and grew more general. When Agnes and her mother appeared at her bedside she made them promise to look after Elsebett. "I worry that heavy responsibilities will fall on her. She is so able that we take her for granted. And she is little more than a child. I regret that I have not done all I could for her. The poor girl has no mother, you know."

It took several minutes for Marsel to express these simple thoughts. Following them she entered a long pause during which the mother and daughter thought the old woman had fallen to sleep. "And don't forget our Johannes, Anna," she said reviving herself. "He is your kin as much as mine. Oh, I wish your dear sister could have lived to see him now. How proud she would be. Mother to such a strapping, handsome boy! But he is troubled, Anna. He needs looking after. He must meet and marry a virtuous girl. I worry that his looks will tempt the wrong kind of girl to pursue him. Beauty is dangerous. This you should know as well, Agnes. You and Johannes both have Hette's beauty in you."

Marsel's remarks caused mother and daughter to glance at one another, the one's glance confirming the warning, the other's deflecting it. Again the old woman closed her eyes and appeared to be sleeping only to speak further a few moments later. "I wish Margaret was at my side, Anna. I would love to see her one more time." Later, very close to death, Marsel was granted this wish in a manner of speaking, seeing Margaret in Elsebett, confusing the two, thanking "Margaret" for the kind attentions Elsebett was providing her.

As her death approached, the widow Marsel was pressured by her family to finally turn her attention away from those most dear to her, and to direct her attention toward her own salvation. It would be a busy time for her and the family because steps could be taken now that would lessen her time in the torment of purgatory.

That gift had been denied her husband, as everyone knew, even those born long after the fact. His dramatic collapse walking home from church on the Sunday of St. John the Baptist—so typical of the man's life was his sudden death!—had virtually assured him of a long stretch in purgatory, though the family, and indeed the community, had participated in rituals, purchased indulgences and masses and had spent hours in prayer following his dying. Johannes, the father, had sequestered a small stash of coins over the years as a reserve against disaster. As acts of penance and almsgiving, his three sons had walked through the village, handing out his carefully preserved treasure to the poor in hopes that their efforts would shorten the torment of the man who in life they had feared and had at times hated.

Of the three, the young Sebastian had been most affected by the father's death. Their relationship had been so troubled, full of gaps and jagged edges, moments that snarled and bit when remembered. As he came of age, Sebastian had secured for himself a certain distant stability with his father, but the stability involved an avoidance that would later have to be addressed. For Sebastian, his father's sudden death had represented a final cruelty; it had stolen away that which to the estranged is most precious: the possibility of reconciliation.

So, in the last hours of Marsel's passing, family and friends gathered in the room where she lay, filling the space with prayers. Father Peter returned to hear her final confession and to administer a last communion. And Sebastian, so tormented, so eager to avoid anymore the agony of separation, fell prostrate before his mother. He threw himself on the edge of her bed, begged the pale, shrunken figure to forgive him for wrongs, real and imagined, remembered and forgotten.

"Be like Basil," she was heard to whisper to her youngest son. "Be like him."

THIRTY-FIVE

The village church was a simple rectangular structure made of red brick with three stone steps leading to the front doors. It had a steeply-sloping roof overseen by the bell tower housing the famous sweet-sounding bells, and was the second Christian church to have been constructed on the site. The earlier village with its wooden church had been virtually abandoned during the period of profound bewilderment following the plague years. Occupied from time to time by transients, squatters and domestic animals, the old church had eventually burned to the ground. The site, however, including the burial grounds on the river side of the building, remained sanctified ground, no record being found to the contrary; though to be safe a bishop had performed the necessary rituals when the new church was completed nearly a century before the day of Marsel Helgen's burial.

Buried in the cemetery and awaiting their resurrection were the bones of several Helgens and hers would now lie among them. The people saw themselves as a community consisting of both the living and those who had proceeded them in death. Thus, the burial grounds were not fenced off from the church or from the square in front of it, but were an accessible part of the village. Children played in the graveyard, animals grazed, meetings were held, celebrations happened; stalls were set up on market day and goods sold between the crosses. It felt comfortable to be in the presence of those who were loved but now deceased.

Marsel breathed her last in the late afternoon of a Thursday, the Thursday after Easter. At the moment of her death, her grandson Johannes ran to the church, tears flowing, and tolled the bells to announce her passing and to deter the Devil who was ever present in his mind. Candles were lit and set up around her bed. The women washed her body and dressed it for burial as friends gathered to pray for her quick release from purgatory. During the night a watch was kept over the body. In the morning it was displayed in front of the house and then as the church's bells continually tolled, the body wrapped in a burial cloth was carried to the church as part of a procession. Leading the way was Father Peter, holding aloft a large crucifix followed by the men bearing the body and then the Helgen family and after them most everyone in the village who could walk. Behind the family, the procession constituted a ragged sort of social ordering from prominent to common, while trailing at the back came the beggars and the drunks, in hopes that alms would be given them.

Along the route from the Helgen home to the church, prayers were chanted and songs sung. At the church a Requiem Mass was celebrated. The procession then reorganized as the priest and the body left the church for the short walk to the burial site where more words were spoken, rituals performed and prayers fervently offered for the salvation of Marsel Helgen's soul, a widow, the daughter of a murdered peasant, the mother of five and the grandmother of six.

The crowd gathered beside the open grave and the mound of wet, freshly dug earth. And as the shrouded corpse, showing itself still flexible, was lowered into the gaping hole, death itself became almost overwhelmingly present. What had first been experienced as the death of an old woman named Marsel Helgen, became now the personal death of each person present. It was felt by the wealthy and the poor, by the old and the young, by the dead woman's sons and by a stranger passing through the village, who seeing the crowd, had paused on his way from the inn to the river's dock. Some sensed its cold touch, others could smell it in the air. For a few the very soil of the graveyard seemed soaked with it. Death was everywhere: unpredictable, unknowable, unavoidable.

Father Peter maintained the appearance of calm by clutching his prayer book and focusing on the ritualistic duties assigned him. The granddaughter Irmele tried desperately to stifle her own fears and direct her prayers back to her grandmother's salvation. The boy Abraham, the friend of Johannes's, looked up from the grave. He raised his eyes first to glance shyly at the two young women, the pretty granddaughters of the deceased who were bending now to take up fistfuls of earth. Then ashamed of himself, he turned his gaze toward the other crosses tilting at diverse angles around the graveyard, and it seemed that the already dead were mocking him. They laughed, an unpleasant laugh. Were they laughing because death was not so terrible as he feared, or because it was far worse than he could imagine? They knew, they understood and they refused to say.

§

All of this had to be paid for. The continual tolling of the bells, the special mass, the distributed alms, the gravesite itself. It all cost money. At the burial Basil had found himself studying the mound of earth, judging the content of its moisture, his thoughts ever on the fields, the struggling rye, the delayed barley. But now he thought about money, and the strange sense he had of weariness, of age, the futility of every effort. What was the point, really? It was all just about bread to eat and beer to drink, and the amassing of a few coins to get yourself buried in the proper way. Each year he and his brothers mounted an enormous production full of drama and tension and exhausting physical effort to what purpose? To eat and drink so they could keep working and do it again another year.

The death of his father had stunned and frightened Basil, calling him to new responsibilities. The death of his beloved Arved had cheated and enraged him. The death of his mother had defeated him. At least he felt defeated late that night back at the house, the three brothers seated at the table drinking Sebastian's beer, the candle burning down, a cold rain falling again outside their door. Sebastian said it well in his own odd way: "It feels we are broken apart, brothers, a scattering of separate parts. The glue is missing."

That Sebastian had had problems with their mother, they all knew. Granted, she was on her deathbed so it may have been too much to ask. But all she could whisper was that he should obey Basil. In saying those words, she had reconfirmed what he had always believed; in her eyes, as in the eyes of their father, being Sebastian had never been acceptable. He should be like Basil. He should copy Basil. Jacob, they liked to say, did that. He copied Basil. But in Sebastian's eyes, Jacob was not like Basil at all. Jacob was just Jacob.

He did not hate his brothers, or begrudge them for whom they were. But neither was he like them. One of the great triumphs of Sebastian's life, in his mind, was that he had managed to grow to adulthood and still have in his personality some elements that felt authentic. He was still Sebastian. He gave credit for that miracle to Ursula, his lovely wife, the mother of their two boys. Ursula valued him not as some poor reflection of Basil, but as the very Sebastian that his parents had never accepted, every absent-minded blunder, every quirky idea, every inspired insight. Ursula was hesitant to speak and reluctant to be noticed. Embarrassment was probably her most public emotion. But in private she loved to laugh and she found delight in her husband's spontaneous insights and odd actions. "Tell me something," she would whisper into his ear when they were in bed. "Tell me what you saw today, tell me something you thought about."

When the brothers had their father to fear and avoid and work around, it had served to focus their intent. After he died, it was their mother's absolute clarity of vision that permitted no doubt. They were a family; family was the point, the reason for it all. Feed the family, guard the family's possessions, look out for each of its members, protect the family. She never said those words. She just knew her truth. She expressed it in her every act, lived it from the marrow of her bones out into the world.

So when Sebastian said to his brothers, that with their mother's death, the glue had gone missing, Basil felt a sense of relief. His youngest brother was right. But more importantly, the way the words were spoken suggested that Sebastian was still in the family. Basil knew that if the family were to come apart now, it would be Sebastian who left.

As they looked at each other across the table, it became obvious to each of them that they could remain a family, but they did not have to. They could share and coordinate, or they could fight and fly apart. Previously, these possibilities had not been recognized, or at least not verbalized. Now the possibility appeared as a gaping hole, as real, as frightening as a grave. With their mother gone, they would have to do intentionally what before they had done habitually.

As to Jacob, well Jacob had his own way of saying things. He spoke his words slowly, his thoughts meandered, he preferred to travel the long way to his intended conclusion. That night he reminded his brothers how in autumn when they were children, their mother used to send them into the woods to find nuts. Every year they did this, setting off, each with his own sack. Most years when they shelled the nuts, their mother would throw the shells to the hogs. But one year she had saved the shells as well as the nuts. During that long winter, as they well remembered, she had crushed the shells and added them as filler to the bread dough. Of money that hard year there was none, of flour there was fearfully little.

"We were born not to nobility nor to wealth, brothers," Jacob said. "Our status is humble and our lives hard. And we live a great distance from God, whatever the reluctant priest may say to us." As to Basil's lament that there seemed to be no point to it all, Jacob had a simple answer. "Perhaps our labor may serve no purpose other than to produce bread for us to eat and beer to drink so that we might have the strength to keep laboring. Perhaps it is just a circle without greater meaning that we tread until we die. But having plentiful bread to eat and good beer to drink is far better than having little or no bread to eat and little or no beer to drink. And our doing this labor together is far better than each of us trying to do it alone."

THIRTY-SIX

Later it would seem to Basil Helgen that the death of his mother marked the end of one era and the beginning of another. For one thing, a few months after her death—and fifteen years following the death of Arved—Basil took a new wife. Katharina was a widow, safely beyond childbearing years, with two grown children of her own: a daughter who had married a plowman in a neighboring village, and an able son about the same age as Johannes.

The brief courtship came as a surprise to everyone, perhaps even to Basil. At the Feast of All Saints, Katharina served him a delicious cake and they enjoyed a pleasant conversation. A short time later—so short that he was still seated on the same bench in the market square—Father Peter approached him. The priest seated himself, accepted some beer and began to speak of the woman in a favorable way. Yes, Basil said, he was acquainted with the woman. Yes, he knew her to be a widow. Indeed, he had known her late husband.

A few weeks later, after some financial wrangling, he made an offer of marriage and Katharina accepted. Their pact was presented to the village council and quickly approved. The policy that marriages required secular approval had been adopted by ordinance between Basil's first and second marriage. The village fathers had decided it was in the best interest of the community that couples demonstrate financial security before they married. The conduct of the lower classes needed to be improved. The poor, the unestablished, were easy prey for the Devil. And the Devil relished chaos and always sought to instigate mischief. They drank to excess, they gambled, they were lax about piety. They had too many children, and their children became drains on society. To delay marriage by insisting that a couple demonstrate financial stability would frustrate the Devil and benefit everyone else. Though when it came to a mature, well-established couple such as Basil and Katharina, the requirement was a mere formality.

The second feature of the era that began with his mother's death was that harvests became irregular or poor. For three successive years following Marsel's death the harvests were marginal. During those years it seemed to Basil that the ground itself was reluctant to do its work. Seeds did not want to sprout. The stalks of those that did sprout failed to produce large heads of grain. Growing things required a certain predictability, and what had been stable was now erratic. As before, some months were cold, others warm, some years wet, others dry. But the variations were more extreme—the cold colder, the hot hotter, the wet wetter and the dry drier; the winds blew longer and with greater ferocity. Basil, having grown up in the shadow of an angry father, recognized the signs. A fragile sense of control had been lost. A kind of fury was being set loose on the land. God was angry. In the face of anger you hunkered down, you worked harder, you became more devout. You prayed more frequently and with greater fervor. And still you worried.

He was not alone in his thinking. At the inn, the grumbling plowmen used the term "sterility" to explain the phenomenon. The earth was becoming sterile. It was not just the plants. Animals, too, it seemed were less fertile. Pig litters were smaller and the number of piglets born dead or deformed was greater. The Helgens had not found this among their own swine. Basil's careful record keeping, all preserved in his orderly mind and available for recitation upon request, revealed no abnormal patterns. But at the inn's long table, he was but one of a group of uncomfortable men. And he was cautious by nature.

"We have not noticed great change ourselves," he said, "but it does seem with this last litter, that the piglets are smaller than earlier years and are growing to size more slowly."

That the smaller piglets resulted from the sow being less well fed, occurred to him. Supplies were low, storehouses near empty. Everyone was being stingy with what they had. The animals like the humans had less to eat. And smaller litters, too, could result when sows received less feed. All of this crossed his mind but he did not argue the point. It was a time to be quiet and diligent.

"It's not just here," a man said. A member of his family, farming in a village a day or more away, had reported the same poor results.

"And it's not just plants and animals," a third man announced. His wife's sister, a virtuous woman married to a good family less than half a day's distance from the inn where they sat, had given birth to a malformed child just the spring before.

"Call it what you want," a fourth man added, "weather, weariness, sterility. But it is as clear to me as the nose on your face that a wickedness has been set loose on this land. I am not going to name the cause of it, but what we are seeing is not natural. When you cannot give your child all the bread he wants, something is wrong."

Basil said his goodbyes a few minutes later. When he rose from the table, a couple of the plowmen looked at each other and grinned. They were grinning because it was well known that Katharina did not tolerate a husband of hers hanging about the inn. This was old news, but old news lingered a long while and reawakened periodically, as if gossip itself were a restless sleeper.

Basil, the consensus went, had more liberty than Katharina's first husband, a solemn, early-to-bald fellow named Jeremias, who had fallen from a roof to his death some years before. Jeremias had not been allowed to set foot in the inn except to attend meetings and then only while business was being conducted. As a young married couple, Katharina and Jeremias had been known for their arguments. Many involved his frequenting the inn; conflicts that at times became as loud as cat fights, as public as weddings.

It was believed in those days, by both men and women, that Katharina was dominating her husband. This was an unacceptable violation of village custom, especially when conducted in such a public manner. Her conduct led to murmurings of a public shaming. Nothing came of it, though the spectacle may have been averted because someone spoke to her of the possibility. For whatever reason she mellowed, and perhaps her husband's tragic fall a few years later imbedded in her mind a new thought: life was ultimately not under her control, or the control of any mortal for that matter. The sudden death certainly pushed her deeper into the arms of the church.

THIRTY-SEVEN

The new marriage, it was agreed, benefited the Helgen family. Katharina was an experienced and skilled homemaker. She could sew and cook. She knew her way around a garden. Physically she was stronger in her forties than Arved had been in her twenties, and she brought a modest dowry when she arrived. The marriage allowed Basil to dismiss Frau Henn, the woman who had worked with the family for fifteen years. That relationship had deteriorated over time—the hired woman had been close to Marsel, but only tolerated by Klara and, when possible, avoided by Ursula, who thought her sloppy and unpleasant smelling.

Frau Henn complained loudly about being dismissed. She told Basil to his face that his decision brought shame to the memory of his dear mother who would never have permitted such a travesty to occur. He was throwing her and her husband into dire poverty at a time when work was almost impossible to find. Furthermore, she knew Katharina; her own husband was a cousin of the late Jeremias. She knew her to be a deceitful, calculating woman who would make his life miserable and had probably instigated the firing herself. "If you do not recognize that you are being played for a fool, Herr Helgen, then you certainly are one," Frau Henn had shouted in her fury.

The conversation—though "conversation" was hardly an adequate characterization of the encounter—took place in private, but it easily escaped to the ears of Irmele, who was spinning in an adjoining room. The altercation caused Irmele's eyes to widen and her tongue itch to wag. How exciting to have this gossip to report, first to Elsebett, then to her aunt Ursula and to her mother, who conveyed it to Katharina, who quickly passed it on to the broader community.

And how had the stolid Basil responded? That was the question everyone asked.

"With dignity," Irmele announced, proudly. Though she admitted, she could not actually *see* his response, she had *heard* no sign of violence, not even a raised voice coming from her uncle.

The dismissal was a fine thing to have happened so far as the Helgen women were concerned. Frau Henn was recognized now as an ungrateful hag who had been generously paid for fifteen years while doing barely adequate work and had probably been filching a bit whenever the opportunity arose. And so the adage, old even then, that the enemy of my enemy is my friend, helped to welcome Katharina into the Helgen circle.

But, personally, Basil took no pleasure from the exchange. He was sensitive to hardship, aware of it hovering always at the edge of things. He knew his decision would bring hunger to the woman and her husband. The Henns were childless cottagers, a landless couple who survived by their labor. Given the poor harvests, the supply of laborers was far greater than the village could employ. Furthermore, as this couple aged their value as laborers diminished.

The termination of Frau Henn benefited Basil's family and his wife wanted it, so he did not regret what he had done. Perhaps he even appreciated that Katharina had first suggested it—and she had in fact proposed it even before they married. But when she brought news of the gossip back to him—relaying it smugly to confirm how right she had been about this woman—he had dismissed her with a sharp comment: "They will suffer as the result of it and I am sorry for that."

Basil recognized early on that this second marriage was unlike his first. The first had been ruled by desire, this one by practicality. With Arved he had had to control his lust—a task he had failed with fatal results. With Katharina he felt a need to protect himself in a way that at first he could not quite articulate. Their relationship was in the economic interest of both, but it was not platonic. Sex was part of the bargain and they enjoyed it frequently. It was not so passionate as it had been with Arved, but it brought pleasure and satisfaction to them both.

But he was wary. Katharina had an astute instinct for economic opportunity but the instinct favored not just herself. It extended as well her family, that is her *prior* family: her son, her married daughter and her daughter's husband and their children, perhaps even to her two sisters and their families. Katharina had left none of them behind when she entered the Helgen home, and now they inhabited her talk ever more frequently.

She worried first about her daughter's husband. He had a weakness for games of chance and Katharina hated all forms of gambling. That had been the problem with her own father—his gambling had devastated the family's financial stability. That was why she had been so insistent that her first husband not spend idle hours at the inn. It was not the drinking so much as the lure of chance which she recognized as Devil-induced, a way the Evil One could bring ruin to an otherwise stable and devout family. Early on, before she committed herself to marry, she had asked Basil directly, "Do you gamble?" To which he had given a response that pleased her: "Every seed I put in the ground is both a gamble and a prayer. That is more than enough for me."

But now Katharina wanted Basil to concern himself with her daughter's family. The daughter had started to raise chickens. "Beyond all her other responsibilities, now she has to worry about the varmints who come at night to devour them." Maybe the Helgens could purchase eggs from the daughter. Perhaps Basil could examine the shelter the daughter's husband had constructed and make it more secure. She also worried about her son. The son knew oxen and was an excellent man with a plow. He worked a bit of land leased from the abbey, but perhaps Basil could hire him in the spring. Katharina was in that sense very like Basil. Both were loyal to their families, but their deepest loyalties were not to the same families.

As time passed Katharina's economic instincts grew ever sharper. In the privacy of their room she began to distinguish *their* family from the other Helgen families. After all, he was the eldest son. His father had given the house and farmland to him. Of course he had been very generous to share the benefits equally with his brothers; the entire village knew of his actions and admired them. She herself applauded them; but when it came to his will, to making provision for the next generation, would it not be reasonable, more natural, to look favorably on their sons…?

"*Our* sons?"

"Well, Johannes, of course. But why not some provision for my Samuel as well? He is your stepson, and a fine young man."

The thought made Basil's head hurt. His death? The next generation? Slighting his brothers and their sons, while favoring her boy? He had enough to worry about with the present crop of barley, with the security of the stored rye. "That will have to wait," was the most he would say on the subject.

THIRTY-EIGHT

Jacob and Sebastian were happy that their brother had taken a new wife, though it seemed to happen very quickly. The three of them were still mourning their mother when Basil announced his intent to marry. Jacob in particular had been surprised by the depth of grief he felt. He knew his mother had lived a long life. It was not surprising she should be gone. But her death shocked him in a profound way that seemed to grow over the weeks and was slow to ebb. It contained a sense of exposure, a vulnerability added to the many other vulnerabilities, and Jacob's normal equanimity faltered. Hard ground he was plowing now. Even Klara's full-throated presence, normally a joy to him, grated. Her boisterous surface hid a tender interior, and he tried to temper his behavior to forestall the distemper that rose when she felt crossed. When he failed, his daughter looked at him with dismay, knowing she would have to absorb the bulk of her mother's irritability.

Elsebett was back and forth between Rachel's and her Helgen home. She found Frau Mueller increasingly distracted. She had been hearing news from beyond the village that troubled her. A new man had been named the Archbishop-Elector of the territory. This man had been strongly influenced by the Jesuits, an order recently recognized. The order was a militant opponent of the reformation, and fiercely loyal to the pope. The new Archbishop was already moving to "purify" the territory. The few enclaves of Jews, located in towns and distant villages, had been forced to leave. There was talk as well that anyone following Luther's teachings would be expelled. These actions were supported by laws of the empire—the religion of a territory's elector was the religion of everyone residing within it—but until now they had been enforced only against those who were otherwise troublesome.

When Elsebett related this news to her brother, he confirmed it. A friend had shown him a silver spoon he had purchased from a family of Jews who were passing through the village on their way out of the territory. And their father's cousin—the Luther's man who managed the bathhouse and who had washed Johannes's hair every week for years—Johannes understood that he was packing his possessions and preparing to leave. But, unlike Frau Mueller, Johannes was not overly troubled by these developments. "There is a sterility, sister, that is spreading everywhere. The sun shines poorly. Trees bear less fruit. Last autumn our vines gave only small and shrunken grapes. The barley is off, the rye suffers. Animals are born weak or even deformed. Perhaps God is displeased with us for allowing these heresies in our midst. By removing those of false belief, his blessings may be returned to us in full measure."

"Does our father believe this as well?" Elsebett wanted to know.

"He is saddened about his cousin. Though in error, he is a good man, no question of that. But you know our father, his heart is in the soil. He is more troubled by the sparsely sprouted rye than his cousin's banishment. When the crop is not bountiful, when the storage bins are not full, when an ox comes up lame, he holds himself responsible. I support anything that might ease his burden. If God is angry, he needs to be appeased. Our father does not argue with that."

"I have prayed that his new wife will bring some comfort to him," Elsebett said. "Is this not true?"

"It happened very fast."

Elsebett nodded, watching her brother for some clue as to his deeper thoughts. When he did not elaborate, she said, "Well, we know he is not a reckless man, brother. The courtship may have seemed quick to us. But fifteen years passed between our mother's death and his second marriage." She started to laugh. "No one can accuse our father of being rash, brother. Not after fifteen years."

Johannes found nothing humorous about her observation. "This woman is not our mother, Elsebett. You would do well to remember that. She is nothing like our mother. She has her own children. It is they who reside in her thoughts, not us."

Elsebett knew both of Katharina's children, the married daughter less well than the son. Samuel was often at the house on Sundays. He was shorter than Johannes, but strongly built and vaguely handsome, square-jawed, with bushy eyebrows over blue eyes. His curly sand-colored hair was nearly as thick as her own. But she located a discomfort in his manner that made her cautious. He was a brother, but then he was not really a brother. She found herself presenting her demure mask to him, eyes downcast, lips closed, hands quiet. This was the pose she adopted in public places, or in the presence of males outside her family, an artifice she wore as needed.

By this time Elsebett was seventeen. Her father had been married almost two years and she had been with Frau Mueller for nearly ten. They were friends as well as teacher-student, sharing pretty much whatever came into their minds. And she loved to joust with her aunt Klara, and to joke with Uncle

Sebastian and to exchange whispered secrets with Irmele. To draw out the wild boys she asked no questions; questions she had learned made them shy. Rather, she told stories from her own childhood, tales involving Agnes, Zacharias or Johannes, and these led them to stumble all over each other to share what adventures they had had.

Whether it was her reticence, or in spite of it, she did not know, but Katharina's son seemed quite attracted to her. Samuel looked at her frequently, addressed comments toward her, fell in beside her on walks to and from church. She found this attention very pleasing. There was something alluring, she discovered, about how reticence drew the attention of boys. Abraham, Johannes's best friend, was another who wanted to be at her side or Irmele's. He came to the house on Sunday afternoons with a deck of cards in his pocket and a whistle he had made from wood and on which he could play simple tunes.

It was clear to Elsebett that Katharina would have preferred to not have Abraham around. While she tolerated his presence—he was, after all, her step-son's best friend— she insisted that his deck of cards be banned from the house. Johannes thought this unfair. The dispute ended up before Basil who ruled that Abraham was always welcome and that the cards could stay but nothing of value could be wagered in the games. The decision left Johannes gloating and Katharina muttering that cards were dealt by the Devil's hand and no good purpose could derive from them.

Like Johannes, Elsebett thought often about their father. Living in different houses perhaps gave her a clearer perspective of him. Though aging, he still gave the appearance of strength. There was more girth to him (this was true as well of her uncle Jacob), though his size gave no hint of weakness. He simply took up more space. His skin, too, seemed to have thickened. The backs of his hands, his neck, the un-bearded portions of his face had grown a ruddy, almost buckeye-like husk that seemed unaffected by the seasons. He lowered himself with caution into a chair and when he rose he used his heavy arms to push himself back to his feet. His voice had deepened and he spoke more slowly. He seemed less inclined to laugh.

It was clear, however, that Katharina gave him pleasure. He listened to her with care and addressed her with respect. Elsebett had never seen her father with a wife before or with any woman he cared about in that way, so she found it fascinating to watch them. She remembered how her grandmother used to speak of the way her parents had laughed, teased and joked. Even danced, Oma had claimed. Her father did not behave in that way with Katharina. There was respect, there was appreciation, but she saw no signs of frivolity or joy. Whether it had to do with his age, the nature of his second wife, or the failing harvests, she could not say.

Such thoughts evoked in Elsebett a strong yearning to be physically close to her grandmother. The yearning had an "almost" quality about it, a barely missed opportunity. It was as if her grandmother was here and not here, intimately here and forever not here.

THIRTY-NINE

Elsebett's life was unusual compared to those of other young women in the village. Because of her work she was often in the streets, making her way to some house or out on the fallow ground gathering plants. Usually her outings were in the company of her teacher, but as the years passed she went more often alone. Everyone knew she was the midwife's associate. It gave her license to be outside unaccompanied. Irmele's life was more typical; she was mostly house-bound except for trips to the market with her mother or to church or to the occasional celebration or feast day with the family.

Katharina, Elsebett came to understand, thought her life should more resemble Irmele's. She had spoken to her husband about it, apparently. "That girl," she had said to him, "is under your control. She is your responsibility. And yet look at her."

It was the old argument. By studying to become a midwife, Elsebett was making herself less attractive to young men. And her frequent sightings in the village—she had even been seen walking alone out along the river—put her reputation at risk. There was no control over her. Katharina thought this behavior caused the people of the village to wonder what she was about. She could become the subject of gossip, perhaps she already was, and that would damage, possibly fatally, her chances as a young woman.

"Look at Frau Mueller," the stepmother argued. "Has a man ever offered to marry her? Has she not lived a life of isolation in that strange house at the edge of the village?" The midwife existed outside the domain of any man, that was the problem. She was not a wife or mother, not a widow or a spinster living in the home of a brother and his family. No, she was just a woman alone. There was something unnatural about that, it seemed to Katharina. She might be respected by some for her skills, but she was feared by others, and not truly accepted by anyone. She lived within the village but she was not fully a part of it. "A crone such as Frau Mueller, might get away with such a life. But a young, unmarried woman?" Would Elsebett's future not be affected by this? And was her father not obligated to exercise some control?

Basil said nothing to Elsebett about his wife's concerns. She learned of them through Irmele. Among the other women, Katharina spoke freely. She had reason to be proud. She had lost her first husband, but she had raised a daughter and had seen her successfully married. Yes, she might have some reservations about the young husband, what mother does not? Still her daughter was married, and her status in the neighboring village was secure. The women there accepted her. She was invited to spinning bees, pea shellings and other events. During holidays and celebrations she was at the center of things. "When I go to visit, I feel myself a part of everything. I am accepted, welcomed in, because my daughter has successfully married into that village. The husband comes from a good family, you know. I made sure of that."

Katharina had been through one of the great challenges of a parent's life—the successful marrying off of a daughter—and she had succeeded. She knew the difficulties; that is why she was concerned about Elsebett's future and Basil's responsibilities to secure it. "About dear Irmele here," she confided, touching the girl's shoulder, "we have nothing to fear. Her modesty, her piety and virtue are obvious to all who know her. When the time comes, when she has 'seasoned' as the saying goes, she will be a prize for any young man. After all, she is a Helgen. And to marry into the Helgen family is an honor, as I well know."

Klara and Ursula tried to defend the decision that had led to Elsebett becoming Frau Mueller's apprentice. Like everyone else, they had seen her walking alone through the village. Even beyond its borders. But they knew Elsebett to be a young woman with admirable skills and unassailable virtue. They were proud of her and they believed she was held in high regard by the community at large. She could read. She knew things most people, even most men did not. They looked to her for advice. She had taken charge of her grandmother's care—it seemed most natural that she should—and she had handled it with gentleness and understanding. To question the decision that had placed Elsebett with Frau Mueller was to question not just Elsebett, but Basil and Marsel as well. There was something unseemly about that, almost vulgar.

"I suggest no criticism of the child's character itself," Katharina responded. "She gives every appearance of being devout, and of good intent. It is her reputation in the village that concerns me. I am the girl's step-mother. I have a responsibility to speak my mind on these matters." Katharina lifted her face and jutted out her jaw. "To be perfectly frank, I believe the midwife has been lax with the child. She could be teaching her all she needs to know without sending her willy-nilly through the village and into the fields beyond. The place for an unmarried girl is in the church and by the hearth. That is God's way. And that is what young men expect. We all know that."

"Have you spoken to your husband of this?" the shy Ursula cautiously asked.

"I most certainly have, as my duty requires. And I can tell you that he is not fully happy with the midwife. Quite aside from her loose control, there is the ongoing question of the dowry. As you may or may not know, the girl's compensation, excepting pocket change, was to establish a dowry for her. As Basil wisely insisted from the beginning, the funds were to be paid to him as they were earned, rather than at the end."

"And have they been?" Klara wanted to know. "I have seen Frau Mueller meet with him many times over the years."

"My husband is tightlipped on these matters, as he has every right to be. But I suspect it has been a challenge for him to hold the midwife to her commitment. I heard him mention recently, quite as an aside, that he could have placed his daughter in service at the inn with her uncle Martin and aunt Gisele.

There, of course, she would have earned a decent dowry and not have soiled her reputation."

"What are you suggesting?" Klara exploded. "Her reputation soiled?"

"I am not saying, dear Klara, that her reputation has been soiled. Though I worry that it is threatened."

Irmele, who had a fine mind and an excellent memory, whose life was confined to home and altar, and who adored her cousin and envied her freedom, relayed this conversation to Elsebett breathlessly and almost verbatim, relishing in the delicious pleasure that comes when one has a secret to share that is flavored even mildly with malice.

Elsebett did not know what to think. Her feelings, though, were more accessible. She felt dismayed and guilty at the same time. She loved being out of doors. She loved the river and the meadow and the woods. She loved to visit pregnant women and new mothers and sick old people. She was always offering to run this or that errand in the village or to gather firewood or roots outside of it. And Frau Mueller welcomed her offers. She had become less strong over the years, a painful stiffness had become visible in her movements, and her enthusiasm for the long hike or the steep climb had diminished.

As she made her way back to Frau Mueller's house, Irmele's revelation caused Elsebett to experience the village in a new way. She had the sense now that people were watching her. Not the men so much but the women. Before, she had only seen those who smiled and greeted her, but now she was aware as well of those who did not smile or speak, who stopped talking and watched as she passed, who looked at her over walls or from doorways.

That evening as they were sharing a simple meal in the late light of spring, she spoke to her teacher about what Irmele had told her. Rachel listened carefully.

"Has your stepmother spoken to you of this?" Frau Mueller wanted to know.

"Not directly, Frau Mueller. 'I saw you here,' she says. 'I saw you there.' I did not think about it before, but these are the words she says to me. 'Did my son not see you alone one day in the meadow?' She asked me that a week ago. She wants me to sit more straight at the table. She insists that every strand of my hair be covered. If I am slow to help she urges me to start."

"And your father? Has he spoken to you of these matters?"

Elsebett assured her teacher that he had not. He remained unchanged so far as she could tell. They still walked together to church every Sunday, only now instead of her grandmother walking between them, he walked in the middle with his daughter on one side and his wife on the other. He had not uttered a word to reproach her.

Frau Mueller thought for a long time before she continued.

"When I was your age," she finally said, "I was confined within the walls of the convent. You know of this. But have I told you that for me the convent was a prison? I loved some of the people there, but the convent itself, well, yes, it is not unfair to say it felt like a prison. The building was very old even then and the walls were thicker than I was long. In Gretel's cell there was what we called a 'squint,' a tiny opening, tall but very narrow. I used to lie on the flat stones and look out the squint to the trees, the clouds, the birds. How I loved the birds! That was where I wanted to be. I wanted to be outside with the birds. And except for the garden, I never was. I fear, dear Elsebett, that your stepmother may be correct. I have been lax. More than that, I have been a fool. I have tried to give you the life I never had myself. In doing so I have damaged your chances and ill-served your father who placed you in my care."

When she heard those words, Elsebett jumped from her chair and threw her arms around her teacher.

"No, it is my fault! Entirely mine. I have looked for every excuse. I have lingered by the river. I have taken the long way around. I have petted every dog. I have talked with every-one I see. I am so sorry! I have betrayed your love and trust."

"No!" Frau Mueller insisted. "You have done nothing of the kind."

"I have! I have behaved just like a boy!"

FORTY

Frau Rachel Mueller had great respect for Basil Helgen. In that way she was no different than most people in the village. But it was also true that mention of his name gave her apprehension. There may have been men who joked with him, slapped him on the back. But that was not true so far as she knew of any woman, and it was certainly not true of her. They had known each other for years and they met regularly. He was always courteous, correct and to the point. He anticipated regular contributions toward his daughter's dowry and kept a careful account. Not once had he criticized her management of the girl's training, not to her at least. But as he made no criticisms, he also gave no compliments. The one compliment had been very simple and that had happened several years before.

"My daughter seems happy," he had said one afternoon after they had counted out the money.

"Yes, I think so," Rachel had responded quietly. She had never forgotten his words. They were among the most precious she had ever heard.

So, on the morning following Elsebett's revelations, Rachel Mueller gathered all the money she could spare and set off alone to find Basil Helgen.

She encountered him in the village, walking behind his team of oxen; he was loaning them that day to his wife's son. When Rachel suggested she could come later to the house, he said, "No, I will come to your house. I will come this evening."

She returned home to find Elsebett in the garden pulling weeds. Her cousin Agnes stood beside her talking.

It was a day of unusual encounters, it seemed to Rachel. So far as she could remember, the last time Basil Helgen had come to her house was that afternoon many years before when he had first learned of his wife's pregnancy. He had come anxious and out-of-breath, smelling of wood pitch. She had never told Elsebett of that visit, and swore she never would. Now, by strange coincidence here stood Agnes, party to another troubled pregnancy. When had it been? Three years ago? Four?

Agnes was to marry. She announced this eagerly, hardly bothering to greet Frau Mueller. "In Cologne! To a wine merchant!"

"In Cologne? To a wine merchant? *The* wine merchant?"

No, no, another wine merchant, Agnes explained. One far more handsome, and more successful than that Heinrich; he had never given her another glance once she resisted his advances.

"My Salomon is a certified journeyman, and soon he will become a master merchant in his father's firm," Agnes continued, half shouting. "Both families approve. It's all been negotiated, signed and settled. Can you believe it? I am going to live in Cologne! One of the greatest cities in the Empire!"

Agnes might have continued indefinitely, scarcely bothering to breathe, had Elsebett not jumped to her feet and embraced her. The two of them were crying and hugging and jumping up and down. Rachel, too, had tears in her eyes as she embraced Agnes, but there was something bittersweet in the emotions she felt. So wonderful it was for Agnes. And what a relief it must be for her mother after the trials her daughter had put her through. But the contrast between her good fortune and the suspicion hanging over Elsebett was stark. And Rachel felt responsible for the difference. She had failed this wonderful child.

§

Basil Helgen arrived late that evening. He was greeted at the door by his daughter and ushered into the study as if he were a visitor come to seek healing. Frau Mueller had explained that he was coming and had instructed her to do as she was now doing. But she had not told Elsebett what to do next. How odd it felt to perform the standard protocol with this man who was her father. He seemed to fill the room with a presence that was at once familiar and very strange.

She felt no physical fear of him. He had never struck her; not a whipping, not even a slap. She had seen Johannes whipped more than once, and Irmele swatted about by her father, her mother and even by their grandmother. But Elsebett could not remember ever being touched in anger by anyone. How odd that she had never before realized this. Certainly, she had not been less troublesome than Irmele, less subject to pouts or fits of annoyance. But for some reason, she seemed to have been allotted a measure of forgiveness just by coming into the world. And yet now, because of her reckless wandering far and free, she had brought worry, perhaps shame to him. That, at least, was the message she had taken from Irmele's revelations.

She showed her father to a seat. "I will tell Frau Mueller you are here," she said and turned to leave.

"Stay a moment." He was still standing. Now he sat carefully and motioned for her to sit as well. As she did, she noticed that he was looking around the room.

"I have been here before," he said, still studying the shelves with interest. "Has Frau Mueller spoken to you of my previous visit?"

"No, sir."

"It was a long time ago. Before you were born. I came the hour I learned that your mother was pregnant with you."

"I see."

"Perhaps you do not," her father said vaguely. He seemed poised to say more, but then hesitated. "Well, I want you to know that I am proud of you. I would not have expected so much from a girl, especially one your age."

"Thank you, father," Elsebett said, her eyes brimming.

Basil Helgen looked away. "And I am grateful to Frau Mueller. She helped to bring you safely into the world, and by all accounts she has trained you well. You should tell her now that I am here."

"I will get her."

"Yes," her father said as he continued to study the shelves.

FORTY-ONE

Rachel Mueller was troubled when she arrived to meet Basil Helgen. Elsebett had been wiping her eyes when she summoned her. When Rachel suggested they return together to the study, the girl had declined, shaking her head and suddenly embracing her teacher before stepping away.

"I have some money to give you," Rachel said to the girl's father. "For the dowry."

She took a pouch from her waist and the two of them counted the money on the table. They agreed on the amount and on the total that had been paid over the years. He took possession of the money and she took down a piece of paper on which she maintained a running account. She dipped her quill in some ink and wrote down the figures.

When she had finished Basil asked to see the paper.

"My father did not believe in writing or reading," he said, looking at the document. "He held that they ruined the eyes and softened the mind. 'What you put to paper you soon forget,' that was his way of thinking. And then when the paper is lost, so too is the memory." He handed the paper back to her. "I have followed his instruction and I believe my memory is very good. People say that of me."

"Yes." Rachel said. She thought of her own illiterate father and of the monk who had read the words to them written on the abbey wall those many years ago.

"She could decipher this?" Basil said, pointing to the paper. "My daughter?"

"Yes, she does quite well, both with numbers and with words."

"Sebastian, my youngest brother, he could read the writing as well, though he tells me she is the better reader. With words she is better than he is, with numbers I could not say. I would not have thought that of a girl. But of the other things you have taught her, what now is the state of her understanding?"

Rachel thought about that. "Were it permitted women to establish a guild in this profession, I would certify her as a skilled journeyman. I trust her to work at all levels, but my trust comes from knowing that she would come to me or to some other master with any question she had. That is the true mark of a master, in my opinion. She knows her own skills thoroughly, but also the boundaries of those skills. That is my assessment. Your daughter is quite capable, as I assume you know."

Basil Helgen nodded. "Yes, I have come to realize that, though when she was a child, I thought she had been touched in some way. She went about things differently. I had worries about her."

Rachel Mueller leaned toward her guest. "But, if you will, Herr Helgen, give me your thoughts on something that troubles me greatly. I have heard it said that there are those in the village who believe that our Elsebett, by the very skills she has learned, has frightened off the young men. I have also heard that her activities in and around the village, as she runs errands and makes visits to the sick, as she gathers herbs and other medicines—all done at my request and under my guidance, I assure you—have placed her reputation in doubt. I have learned this information only recently, and I must tell you how much it distresses me. If I have done anything to injure this most virtuous child's advantages in life…then I am very sorry, and I offer you my deepest apologies."

When she had finished speaking, Rachel Mueller turned away and placed her hands over her eyes. Basil Helgen had himself turned toward the window, where outside it was growing dark. For a long time neither of them spoke.

Finally, the father said, "I am proud of my daughter, Frau Mueller, and all she has accomplished. I have no reason to believe she has done anything that is inappropriate or wrong. So no apology is required; indeed I am grateful for the service you have provided her. You know, my own mother tried to discourage me from seeking the hand of the first Frau Helgen, this child's mother. She believed that Arved was so full of life and song, that she would not find me acceptable and I would gain only disappointment. But I persevered and to my credit I won her heart. Into this village there will come a young man with the courage and the wisdom to see our Elsebett for what she is. And if he can convince me that he deserves her, then he will obtain my consent and the dowry you and I have established for her."

Rachel removed her hands from her face, grateful that the room had darkened. "From the bottom of my heart, Herr Helgen, I thank you for these kind words. I would like to suggest, with your permission of course, that until Elsebett does marry, that she remain here with me, not as a student, but as a partner, as my junior partner. If you approve, I will take this proposal to the council. As the village midwife, I should be free to name a partner."

Basil Helgen rose from the chair and stood legs apart, his large body dominating the room. "I will support your proposal before the council. And I will speak with the present Frau Helgen about the rumors you have described. I have been too tolerant. I will hear nothing further from her that detracts from my daughter's reputation."

As they were walking toward the door, Rachel asked him about the status of the crops. He reported that the barley was late and the rye sparse. This year would likely be no better than the previous two.

"There are many now," Basil Helgen said when they had reached the doorway, "who put the blame on witches. I have heard just today of this. The Archbishop-Elector has made witchcraft a major concern of his. He has assembled a body of men: judges, notaries, bailiffs, constables, executioners, and such other functionaries as will be needed, who will travel from village to village to search out and remove all those found to be in consort with the Devil. Witches have the power, they tell me, to ruin crops, to cause floods, droughts or vicious storms. They can render sterile that which is by nature fertile, be it plant or animal, woman or man. It is also said that God cannot be pleased with those of us who tolerate such Devil worshipers in our midst."

"Do you find this credible, Herr Helgen?" Frau Mueller asked. "What you speak of troubles me greatly. I fear the Archbishop's decision could cause a most horrible contagion.

His proposed cure for our troubles could be far worse than the troubles themselves."

"We will see what comes of it, Frau Mueller. Removing the Jews and the Protestants has had little effect. But something unnatural is occurring. Something must be done to return us to better times. May God hold you in his grace, Frau Mueller."

"And you as well, Herr Helgen."

CONTAGION

FORTY-TWO

The contagion that Rachel Mueller so accurately predicted and so rightfully feared actually began almost two years before Basil Helgen heard and spoke of it. In a distant hamlet, an elderly woman—a crone with a tainted reputation who used charts and curious symbols to prophesize future events—was accused by a neighbor of being a witch. The woman had entered into a pact with the Devil. And, in exchange for her soul, the Devil had granted her supernatural powers that allowed her to inflict harm on her enemies. The accusation was made by a neighbor whose husband's sow, a mature animal that had produced several large and healthy litters, had recently given birth to only three piglets, two of which were born malformed and soon died. The births were unnatural and perverse and something abnormal must have caused it. Besides, the two women had hated each other for years.

The accusing neighbor did not address her complaint to a court of law. She spoke it over the back fence and in the market square to anyone who would listen. Everyone knew the Devil existed and was active in human affairs. A person who lived at the margins of village society, who had largely failed at life but who carried malice in her heart, might align herself with the Evil One; the sweet possibility of revenge having overwhelmed the distant horror of eternal damnation.

In normal times, the lifespan of such an accusation was brief and limited to the neighborhood where it arose. Such things tended to dilute as they spread: a harsh accusation became gossip that faded to rumor that ended a sarcastic joke told over mugs of beer. But these were not normal times. The weather had become unpredictable, the harvests less abundant. Storehouses were near empty. Not every face in the village was familiar anymore. People moved from place to place; they entered in search of work, some lingered, some left. Storage bins needed to be secured, not just against mold and the ever-reproducing rodents, but against the slouching men who could be spotted in the shadows, and who soon disappeared.

So, the accusation about the malformed piglets did not weaken. It spread from cottage to cottage, eventually reaching the sharp ears of the village priest. The priest communicated the claim to his bishop and in time the accusation—now a vibrant story involving a crop-destroying hailstorm as well as the malformed piglets—reached the city and duly arrived at the palace of the Archbishop-Elector where it was received with enthusiasm.

The office of the Archbishop was the nerve center of the territory. It stood at the pinnacle of both spiritual and secular power. It oversaw the sphere of prayers and saints on one hand and of village councils and courts of law on the other. It was a heady place to be employed because large sums of money were being allocated to purge the territory of heretics and the ungodly. The Jews had been banished as had the followers of Luther and Calvin. Now, it appeared, the territory was also infested with witches; they too would need to be exposed and eradicated. Funds were made available and many men were eager to lend their training and expertise in furtherance of this noble goal while at the same time benefiting themselves economically. In ornate chapels divine guidance was sought. In the treasury, chests were opened, coins counted out and distributed.

However, it was a tricky business to ferret out a witch. While a Jew was a Jew, and a Protestant a Protestant, witches were not obviously witches. A witch did not wear a particular style of clothing or worship at a particular church or synagogue; a witch did not announce herself publicly or readily admit her allegiance to the Devil. By definition, he or she (a witch could be either) had the Devil's help, and the Devil was slippery and devious.

The problem was real, but nobody from the Archbishop down wanted mob rule. Crowds of angry plowmen were not going to march on a woman's house and drag her to the stake just because of a hailstorm. No, the prosecutions had to be done with the force of law. Fortunately, for those whose job it was to prosecute such cases, there existed both legal and spiritual precedence. A papal bull published a hundred years before had confirmed the existence of witches and empowered their prosecution. The wildly popular text *Malleus Maleficarum*, written by a Dominican monk, had declared that witchcraft was a form of heresy. The Emperor, himself, had signed a decree that elevated witchcraft to a capital crime. Before that, a person proven to be a witch would have been banished. Now the offense was punishable by death. Also, before the decree, the crime of witchcraft required two separate proofs. The prosecutor had to prove first that the accused was a witch, that is working in consort with the Devil, and second that her curses had actually caused the sow to produce the malformed piglets, or the hailstorm to erupt. After the decree, that second step, the almost impossible proof of injury, would no longer be required. If a person was shown to be a witch, that alone proved the crime of witchcraft and authorized the penalty of death regardless of whether it could be proven that the accused had brought harm to anyone.

Still, the challenge was formidable. How did one prove in a court of law that a person was a witch? Witches might fly through the air on brooms, but not in the sight of witnesses. The sexual relations they were alleged to have with devils were not performed openly. Though witches were believed to gather in large conclaves to worship the Devil, these meetings were not held in the market square at midday.

A few prosecutors argued that there existed an objective proof: a person who was a witch would have one or more suspicious marks on her body resulting from her relations with the Devil, a so-called devil's mark. If a mark was truly a devil's mark, the area of the mark would not be subject to pain. Thus, these prosecutors argued, a woman's body could be exposed and examined before the judges to see if there were suspicious markings. If there were, a needle could be inserted into the mark and the judges could observe how the accused responded. The problem with this proof was that witches lied. They lied even in the face of death. Thus, a witch might act as though she was feeling pain when the needle was inserted, when, in fact, she was not.

The most effective method for proving witchcraft, it turned out, was the confession. A person who confessed that she was a witch, was without doubt a witch. A second proof was the "denunciation." A denunciation was different from a simple accusation. Anyone could make an accusation, but if a person who was herself a confessed witch, "denounced" another person as a witch, that was strong evidence against the accused. The problem with this approach was that people were not about to confess that they were witches. And if no one confessed to witchcraft, no one would denounce another.

On the Archbishop's staff was an influential bishop who finally solved the problem of proof. The bishop was considered a moderate on the subject of witchcraft because he did not believe in the devil's mark; nor did he believe that girls under the age of twelve could be guilty of witchcraft. But the bishop did believe strongly in both the confession and the denunciation. Furthermore, he was convinced and he argued persuasively that confessions and denunciations obtained through torture were valid and could be presented to judges as proof of the alleged crime. Here, at last, were the means of finding and eliminating those women and men who were working in consort with the Devil and against the common good of the people.

And so, after the accusation had been made in the hamlet and word had traveled to the city and into the offices of the Archbishop-Elector, and after money had been appropriated and prayers offered and skilled men recruited and hired, and after legal theories and procedures had been discussed and formulated, the time had come for concerted and lawful action.

FORTY-THREE

The villages of the territory were isolated and distant from one another; the roads connecting them were poor; the means of communication informal and wildly undependable; still the territory was eventually alive with talk of witches. The entire territory, it seemed, was infested with them, and there were men of high status and learning, men from the office of the Archbishop himself who were leaving the city and venturing out to investigate these accusations and bring the guilty to justice.

It was an exciting time. "Excitement" was the word that kept coming into Frau Rachel Mueller's head when she thought about what was happening. Excitement was the energy, the propellent, it seemed to her, that was causing the contagion to spread. "Perhaps we humans are born with a love of excitement," she said to Elsebett one evening. "Perhaps we crave it."

Her words amounted to a self-accusation; she hated her inability to resist the latest rumor, the gossiped tale. The story fascinated and horrified her. She wanted to turn away but could not. All aspects of her life seemed to tingle with news of the distant contagion.

"My brother is feverish over it," Elsebett admitted. "He talks of little else. Last week he caught a ride on a cargo boat and went to the city. He saw the Archbishop's men pass down the street. Learned men, he told me, noble men dressed in the finest fabric. Some were in carriages; others rode on fine horses. 'They are men of purpose,' he said. 'One look at them and you could not doubt that they take their responsibility seriously. If there are witches lurking about, these men will find and exterminate them.' That is what he told me."

Rachel pondered these words, eyes downcast, her gray curls shaking with disapproval.

"Let's hope they are indeed learned men of noble character," she said finally. "Their tasks are multiple and complex. We have all seen how inconstant weather can bring hardship and destabilize the common good. If the Devil is behind these fearful trends, that must be dealt with. And if there are people working actively with the Evil One, they must, of course be rooted out and exposed. Who would suggest otherwise?

"But is it the Devil? And is he working through witches? Who can speak with certainty? Some say that God has caused the erratic weather, not the Devil, and that God's ways are a mystery. Others say the problem was the Jews, though the Jews have been with us since before the time of Christ. Others contend that the troubles came to pass because of Luther's heresies. But both the Jews and the Protestants have been removed from the territory, and nothing has improved. Now some say it is God who shapes the weather, as he shapes all things, but that he has brought on this period of want because we have tolerated witches in our midst. Burn the witches, this school of thought contends, and God will be appeased and the tired earth will return to fruitfulness.

"I sense only uncertainty in all of this. Uncertainty conjoined with desperation. I have to say that I fear for all women, for women and men. Contagions have lives of their own, Elsebett. Of that I have no doubt. They seek to fulfill themselves. Before—back when the harvests were good—there was rarely talk of witches. Now the air is full of it. But the people we now accuse of witchery—were they not alive back then? And were there not clusters of Jews in the territory? And Protestants? And if these people are witches now, were they not witches back then? Or have they suddenly all become witches? It seems to me a treacherous muddle. Where it will end, I have no idea, but I fear the worst."

"People seem to have become more devout," Elsebett suggested, hoping to lighten her teacher's mood. "That might be a good thing, don't you think? The church is filled with people praying."

"Yes," her teacher said without enthusiasm. "Who would suggest that more people at prayer is a bad thing? What harm, after all, can increased piety bring us? Better that the men are on their knees in the church, than slapping their mugs together at the tavern, though I would feel more secure were they in the fields walking behind their plows. To question any of this, hints at madness. I fully admit that, and yet I cannot help myself. I am sorry to burden you, dear Elsebett, but I have no one else. Am I alone in questioning this? I am coming to doubt myself. I have begun to doubt even my own sanity, but I cannot believe any good will come of this. That's all, I just cannot."

"You said it yourself, Frau Mueller. Excitement. We all crave it. Excitement and suspense." An idea struck Elsebett at that moment and she started to laugh. "Do you know what this is like, Frau Mueller? This is like we, all of us, are living inside the head of my cousin Agnes, where everything is excitement, drama and suspense."

"Then heaven help us!" Frau Mueller sputtered, throwing her arms around her student.

FORTY-FOUR

In most ways life went on as before. Women continued to get pregnant and need the services of the two midwives. People suffered ailments and came to the house in search of healing. Plants, wild and domestic, still sprouted in the spring. Their leaves and flowers, their seeds and roots had to be harvested at the right time, dried carefully and stored in a manner that preserved their potency. In the copse the old forest warden had retired to the home of his daughter and son-in-law, replaced by a young man who in his free time set traps for birds. Frau Mueller had caught this young man when he emerged from his mother's womb but he was more interested now in demonstrating the ingenuity of his traps to "the pretty young lady" than to her. On the trek back to the house, Rachel carried fewer shoots, and Elsebett carried more.

In the Helgen home, Ursula had become the primary baker following Marsel's passing, though Irmele and Katharina also worked the dough. Klara remained her own monument, uncontested at the fiery hearth, smoking meats, cooking stews, roasting flesh. Though she spun, she did not trouble herself with the needle; though she devoured bread and possessed a reckless affection for cakes, she never touched the dough until it had emerged from the oven and was cool enough to grasp.

Ursula had quietly managed the baking during the weeks of Marsel's decline and death, and when Katharina arrived, she did not step aside, though Katharina had a fuller voice, a verbal confidence and an ease of expression that Ursula lacked. Katharina had baked during her first marriage, and—as she was never hesitant to report—she had taught her daughter to do the same.

When Katharina grumbled to her husband Basil said, "You stand in the position of my first wife." To which Katharina responded, "But, Helgen, I am the older woman and the more experienced baker, the wife of the eldest son. Your first wife was but a child back then and your mother was alive."

It was a tricky moment for Basil. Favors came his way when his wife was content, but he had an instinct for preserving the family. "Sebastian's wife is now the senior baker in the Helgen family," he said, concluding the discussion.

The family had an adequate supply of flour but only because of determination, skill and efficiency. All steps of the process were performed with care and deliberation—the planting, the harvesting, the threshing, the winnowing, the storage and the milling. At the mill the young Johannes, the younger Gabriel, David and Thomas—stood always close at hand. It became their responsibility to oversee the milling process. The miller was known as a sharp dealer, quick to charge, quick to dismiss. He was of the third generation in his family to operate the mill. His ancestors had cut the original millrace and had constructed the mill. Generation after generation they had all been the same: abrupt, inflexible, hard dealing. Any trace of flour uncollected by the farmer, the miller was eager to secure for himself. Basil and Jacob taught the boys the necessary skills.

"The miller wants to rush you, that is his device. What remains scattered on the millstones after the grinding he wants for himself. So, you must sweep carefully, and sweep again. Do not forget the underside of the upper stone, the one that turns. Much remains there, caught in its imperfections and the crevices that channel the flour. Start with the upper and then brush the lower. He will tell you he needs you to finish. He has another job waiting; he wants to do this or he wants to do that. Do not defer to him. Insist on your right to sweep and sweep again. The flour caught on the stones is ours, not his. Collect it all, bag it carefully. Every particle is needed."

Around the storage bins, the men devised traps and warning systems: obstacles to trip over, objects that clanged when bumped in the dark. The four boys had shifts now. Except on the coldest of nights, two of them slept in the pitch black of the stable where rodents scurried and bats flitted in and out over their heads. Johannes and Thomas one night, Gabriel and David the next.

FORTY-FIVE

Johannes was now twenty-two years of age. He was a handsome, dark-haired young man in the prime of physical health, one accustomed to coy smiles and shy glances coming his way from the young women in the village. With his grandmother gone, there was little beyond work, food and shelter tying him to the Helgen home. He had great respect for his father and uncles but he wanted to experience himself outside of their shadows. He preferred to spend his free time at the inn, the tavern or in the dense activity of the market square. A man of the world, that was how Johannes imagined himself. He wanted to banter with the lingo of rivermen, share the scuttlebutt of horse handlers, sit with the hard-drinking men whose work brought them into the village and sent them beyond: men who told coarse jokes and whispered wild tales from the outside world.

And they liked him, these men. He was handsome and quick, and his grandmother and father had raised him well. He talked less than he listened. He did not brag or humiliate himself in their company. Neither cruelty nor rage rose in him when he drank. There existed a precarious tension among men that it pleased Johannes to navigate. He came to recognize the boundary between the tease and the insult, and how that border-line might shift from person to person, from night to night, from moment to moment. A thrown fist, while not common, was ever possible. Knives hung from waists and he had been threatened by one early on. That night he learned how alcohol could bring a demon to life in what had seemed a quiet spirit. He saw that multiple levels of respect and dismissal existed among these men and he sought to find his place. He honed what he possessed of his father's cunning and his grandmother's wisdom.

The intrigues of the witch hunts fascinated everyone, but these traveling men were particularly charged with rumor and speculation. They brought news from diverse locations, having heard from someone who had heard from someone who had been present at the very place where it happened. From an old boatman overnighting at the inn—a man well known to Zacharias and recognized for his sober voracity—Johannes learned that the woman in the hamlet who had been accused of causing the neighbor's sow to produce the malformed piglets was now a confessed witch. She had openly admitted to having hexed the sow. It had been proven, the boatman assured him. "The confession spoken before the court and documented in writing and announced by proclamation. Moreover, and to the surprise of everyone, the accusing woman—the wife of the farmer with the hexed sow—having been denounced by the confessed witch, did herself confess to being a witch. She had herself, she fully acknowledged in a confession marked by her and read aloud in the courtroom, attended a sabbath of witches, and did there at this gathering and in the full view of the other evil doers fornicate with a devil."

"Fornicate with a devil? How can this be?" Johannes was stunned. "And who could have seen such a thing? Are devils now so plentiful and possessed of such power as to be visible to the human eye?"

The boatman raised a finger to calm the young man. "Visible to the other evil doers, you see. Visible to the witch denouncing her. Not visible to you or me."

Johannes looked around, astounded at the world being revealed to him. "Both of them witches? Both having confessed?"

"Openly and officially," the boatman assured him. "The accused and the accuser, traitorous creatures the two of them, each turning on the other. Neighbors to each other, think of it. This is what happens when you become handmaiden to the Devil. All virtues disappear, all thoughts of decency, of loyalty and respect are tossed aside. A neighbor's sow is hexed, and the two women turn on each other like vipers, fangs exposed. A witch, you see, serves but one master. His will is supreme."

"I am astonished," Johannes admitted. "If there be two in that small hamlet, could there not be more?"

"Likely, indeed likely," the older man said.

"And what will become of them now?"

"A witch is same as a heretic, and heretics are burned alive, that is the established law. The punishment you see, lad, is in that way a double punishment, both a present and a future punishment."

Johannes did not understand.

"Death being the present punishment. But with a burning, you see, there is nothing left to bury. Thus, at the time of the resurrection, there will be no grave opening and nothing to rise from it to greet the coming Christ. A punishment most harsh, both present and future," the boatman concluded.

"That is harsh indeed," Johannes said quietly.

FORTY-SIX

That Sunday, at the table crowded with Helgens, Johannes was the center of attention. Irmele felt vaguely nauseous as she listened to her cousin's words. She was not sure she should be listening at all. The thoughts that rose in her, the images that filled her mind, were so sickening, and yet so captivating, so horrible and yet so horribly seductive, that once they entered her head she feared she could never get them to leave. Could a girl scrub bowls or knead dough while her mind roiled with acts of such incredible malice, betrayal and sordid lust?

How could these women have arrived at such a state? That was the thing Irmele could not stop thinking about. Were they really human at all? Had they ever been human? Or had they been born of swine? Had they nursed on the milk of long-tailed demons? Had their mothers been debased beyond anyone's ability to imagine? Or—and this was the most terrifying thought for Irmele—were these two women once normal girls like herself and Elsebett, girls who had grown up to become normal women, but who had, somehow, someway, been turned by the Devil? Turned against their will, perhaps even without their knowledge? Was the Evil One that cunning? Could he lure a girl such as herself, a female of good faith and good intent, into schemes and plots so devious and debased? All women, she had been taught, were sensual beings, vulnerable to passions and flights of fantasy. Had these women been powerless to resist? Was she?

Irmele dropped her spoon to the table and crossed herself. What she wanted most at that moment, was to jump up and run to the church where she could prostrate herself before the statue of the blue-robed Virgin. But she had just been to the church.

"Where is this place, Johannes?" Irmele's mother asked. "The village where all of this happened. Is it far from here?"

My God, Irmele thought, I pray that it is far. I pray it is very far.

Johannes did not know exactly where it was. It was not on the river, he told them. It was some distance from their village and far from the city. He had inquired about its location because he thought it might be possible to attend the burning, but the distance was such that the journey was impractical.

As Johannes expressed his desire to attend the burning, Ursula gasped and Irmele crossed herself again.

"Also, getting food, drink and lodging would be difficult," Johannes continued. "The place is very small, no more than twenty cottages, maybe less. That is what I understand. And of course, huge crowds are expected."

"So, these women, they have not yet been executed?" Elsebett asked her brother. "And when they are, it will be done in public? Is that what you're saying?"

"They have not. And of course it must be done in a very public way," Johannes explained. "That is the point, is it not? At least one of the points. If the authorities are going to deter others, the penalty for this crime must be seen and understood by all. Besides, the people will clamor for it. I doubt the authorities could keep them away even if they wanted to. Once the court's findings are fully known, there will be talk of nothing else at the inns, in the churches and in the market squares throughout the territory. And there is more; the executions will be carried out with the full accordance of secular law and ecclesiastical authority. There will be many officials present of high rank and great distinction."

There was a long pause, then Elsebett said to her brother: "So, the killing of these two women, the burning of them alive, it will be a kind of pageant? That is what you're saying, is it not?"

"A festival!" Klara exploded. "A festival of death. Sounds about right."

Irmele winced. She did not know what her mother was saying. "A festival of death, that sounds about right?" Was that a good thing or a terrible one? This was her mother, through and through, Irmele thought. She had a way of expressing herself forcefully and loudly but sometimes her daughter had no idea what she meant. And it seemed to poor Irmele that the problem was hers alone. Not her father, her brother, her aunts or her uncles ever questioned these outbursts, so it seemed that every-one else understood them.

"Well, if some witch had hexed our sow, I would want to see her dead," Basil said. "I have no problem with that. You cannot have that kind of thing happening, not if you want to feed your family. It's bad enough with storms and rats and thieves in the night. With rain bringing mold, and winds and hail and floods that wash away your seedlings, and droughts that turn them brown before they've had a chance to mature. God gives us enough to deal with. The last thing we need is some woman putting a hex on the sow."

"That's right," Katharina agreed. "'The wages of sin is death,' that is what Father Severin always said. Making a pact with the Devil is about as much of a sin as a person can imagine and death is what comes of it. That's God's way, and the way it should be. And I think, for myself, it would be good to see the burning. It might be difficult, but everyone should witness a thing such as that. It would be like seeing God in action. Not a miracle, maybe, but something just as powerful. It might even be cleansing to see such a thing first hand."

Johannes smiled smugly across the table at his sister, and Elsebett smiled just as smugly back at him. While she had not forgotten her grandmother's admonition to look after her brother, still she loved to tease him.

"So, tell me, brother," she said now, "you suggested two reasons for attending this spectacle. First, there is the pageantry of it all, the rich and noble men of the law and the church decked out in their finery. Second, there is the moral lesson, as you said, and as our stepmother has described. To see a woman who is said to be a witch burned to death, will keep us from becoming witches ourselves. Is that not the idea?"

"Not 'said to be witches,' sister, confessed to be! These witches have confessed before the court."

"So tell me, brother," Elsebett persisted, "for which of these reasons do you want to go? It is for the pageantry, or for the moral lesson? Are you really afraid that you might yourself become a witch? Or already be a witch and not know it? Except, you being a man we would call you a sorcerer, I believe. So, come now, brother, let us hear the truth of it. Are you already a sorcerer? Do you have a magic broom hidden in the stable that allows you to fly from here to there and beyond?"

Elsebett and Irmele looked at each other, and the two of them fell into fits of laughter. Except that Irmele, seeing the expression on Katharina's face, soon stopped.

As soon as Elsebett's laugher had died down, Johannes responded with assurance. "I like to think I am a man of my time, sister. It is my desire to participate in the important events of my lifetime. Had I been twenty years old during the uprising of '25, I would have stood beside our brave great-grandfather, swinging a flail for the rights of the common man. But these are different times. Today, the great event is the ferreting out of witches and I wish to witness what I can."

"There is none of us, dear Elsebett," the scowling Katharina inserted, "who would not benefit from a moral lessen such as this. Not even one so superior as you, one who reads and writes and who wanders alone willy-nilly through the village as if she were the Archbishop himself."

In the stunned silence that followed Katharina's stinging words, Elsebett felt herself grimacing. She looked toward her father, hoping he would speak on her behalf. But Basil was still talking with Jacob about the hexing of pigs and preoccupied with pouring himself more beer.

"My dear stepmother," Elsebett finally said, "I apologize if you misunderstood."

"I did not misunderstand. What you said was clear to all." Katharina pushed out her bosom, and looking up, she jutted out her jaw, exposing the tendons in her neck.

"Well, I meant no disrespect. And I do not consider myself superior to anyone. Johannes and I love to tease each other, that's all. We always have. Is that not true, brother?"

But her brother also failed to support her. "I love you, my sister. But this time you went too far. I am not a sorcerer, and it was reckless of you to so accuse me. Reckless, even in jest."

"But…" Elsebett felt betrayed.

"We live in treacherous times," Johannes continued. "Are you aware of how sporadic the weather has become? How challenging it is for our father to put food on the table? Do you have any idea what he has endured so that we might enjoy this meal today? And it seems that witches are the cause of our problems. They do the Devil's bidding, that we know."

Elsebett's eyes filled with tears. "I am sorry. Father, please…" She paused, but her father said nothing to comfort her. "I am truly sorry, but this whole thing just sounds absurd to me. Some woman fornicating with a devil! That cannot have happened. That has to be the blathering of a mad woman. These women must have lost their senses, if ever they had any."

Their uncle Sebastian had been quietly sipping his beer. Now he spoke for the first time: "Or it was the torture that brought it on."

"What do you mean, Uncle?" Johannes asked. "These women have confessed to everything. There is no doubting what they say. And just because you and I have not seen a devil, Elsebett, does not mean that they are invisible to all. They do appear before the witches who serve them. That is the trade they have made, you see. By abandoning all hope of heavenly salvation, these women have received special powers from the Devil. Among them it seems, the Devil's minions become visible to them. And, according to the sworn testimony of both women, one of them did fornicate with a devil in a market square."

But Elsebett was more interested in what her uncle had said. "Please, tell us more of your thinking, Uncle."

"Well, I am told the women were tortured. That they confessed to these crimes only after great pain had been inflicted on them. Before being tortured both had denied everything."

"Tortured?" Elsebett asked, astonished. "What kind of torture? What was done to them?"

"We do not know," Sebastian said quietly. "These things are done in secret. Much of this is done in secret."

"Is Uncle correct, Johannes? Is that your understanding as well? After denying any wrongdoing, torture was inflicted on these women in some secret place, and they then confessed? And that confession will cause them to be burned to death? Can that be true?"

"Absolutely true," Johannes said. "That is very clear in the law. To expose a witch it is perfectly legal and appropriate to submit them to torture. Where Uncle Sebastian is in error, if I may be so bold as to say, Uncle, is suggesting that torture somehow taints their testimony. Witches lie, we know that. They have no qualms about lying. They have already given their souls to the Devil; thus they have no fear of breaking God's rules, and they are free to lie as they wish. So, how then is one to bring them to the truth? Torture is the only means. On the other hand, would an innocent woman even if she were being tortured, falsely confess to being a witch? I think not.

An innocent person remains subject to God's commandments. To make a false statement sworn under oath, would condemn the witness to damnation. So, ask yourself this question: Would you ever confess falsely to anything, knowing that your confession will result in your being burned alive in front of everyone in the village, following which your soul would be cast into hell for lying? Of course not. Knowing the penalty, no one would confess to such a thing were it not true."

FORTY-SEVEN

In January, Elsebett celebrated her eighteenth birthday. She was now a partner in the midwifery practice, though in her mind, certainly, a junior partner. The village council had accepted Frau Mueller's proposal naming her to this position and had granted her a small stipend. The appointment recognized that as part of her work she would frequently be seen walking alone in and about the village. Her father had attended the meeting and spoke in support of the appointment. At times now she helped facilitate the birth of a child without her teacher being present or having any direct involvement.

As to the healing side of Frau Mueller's profession, Elsebett knew herself to be less accomplished. Here her role was subordinate and basically unchanged. She gathered and dried plants. She pulverized leaves and roots; she prepared compounds in accordance with her teacher's instructions. She delivered medicines to the ill and saw to their proper administration.

It remained Frau Mueller's preference that Elsebett welcome visitors and deliver them to the study. Now though, she accompanied her teacher back to the study and remained there as a matter of course. Often Frau Mueller would elicit her advice as to the course of the patient's treatment, sometimes in front of the patient. But it was clear to Elsebett that her teacher was instructing more than consulting her.

§

Elsebett still went every Sunday to the Helgen home. Sometimes Rachel accompanied her but only rarely now did she join the family procession to the church or return for the mid-day meal. Marsel was gone, and in Katharina, Rachel sensed a reserve, an implied, if unexpressed, judgment. She had known the woman for decades, had suggested remedies for reoccurring headaches, had delivered her two children, had rushed to her husband's side when he fell from that sloping roof to his death. They had never been emotionally connected, but they had always been civil. And they were civil now, but their encounters were more comfortable in public than in the Helgen home. Rachel no longer felt as welcomed there as she had before.

The same was becoming true for Elsebett. Irmele remained her closest friend. She felt welcomed by her uncles and aunts, and by the fast-growing Gabriel, David and Thomas. She continued to walk to and from church with her father. But Abraham, who had been Johannes's closest friend—the boy who formerly came every Sunday with his deck of cards and his wooden whistle—had completed his apprenticeship and was now a journeyman working in a town some hours away. And Samuel, Katharina's son, was spending more time in the village where his sister and her husband lived. There was talk that he had met a girl there who interested him.

With her brother, Elsebett had a complex, and not entirely comfortable relationship. That they loved each other, neither had any doubt. Spotting the other on a village street brought a grin, a lightening of the spirit to each of them. They teased, they joked; they worried if the other seemed distant. And yet, they saw the world in different ways. What interested one did not excite the other. Johannes avoided any thoughts about the birth of children, a subject that Elsebett, it seemed to him, could ramble on about for hours. Her fascination with precious stones left him cold. Johannes had come to share their father's, and their uncle Sebastian's, interest in things mechanical: wagons, harnesses, maintenance of the family plow that his grandfather and namesake had designed and had constructed. Of these subjects, Elsebett could muster no more than a polite curiosity.

Johannes's new tendency to explore the wider world, however, intrigued her greatly. As a person who frequently walked the village and entered the homes of others, Elsebett witnessed more of its life than most women. But she had no access to the tavern, the inn, or to the gossip of men. Unlike Johannes, she had been to the city only once, and had never visited the abbey where the Helgens delivered their grapes and bags of grain. She hungered for news of the outside world and Johannes acted as her messenger.

Neither sibling felt comfortable around their stepmother. The woman had an opinion about everything and was never hesitant to express it. And she seemed to enjoy playing one of them against the other. So adept was she at this, that when the siblings finally talked about it, they learned they held diametrically opposed opinions. Johannes was certain that Katharina preferred Elsebett to him, and Elsebett was equally certain the opposite was true.

At least their father seemed content and that was a comfort to both of them. Elsebett never saw her father and stepmother argue, but it saddened her to realize that Katharina's growing influence coincided with their father's decline. In matters of farming his dominance remained unchanged. But as to the inevitable minor tensions that arose within the extended family, he was now almost completely silent. "You women need to work it out," was the most he could be made to say. It did not mean that Katharina's preference was always adopted; Klara defended her territory fiercely, and both Ursula and Irmele would resist if unreasonably pressured. But because Basil had abrogated as ruler, unresolved squabbles could linger at or near the surface.

Frau Mueller suggested to Elsebett one evening that perhaps the tensions in the Helgen home are but another element of the larger contagion, a side eddy, if you will, in the great stream flowing through the territory. "The uncertainty in the fields has infected your father and his brothers, you see. They bring it into the house where it aggravates everyone in ways both subtle and obvious. Moreover, being weakened himself, your father is less willing to confront the powerful will of his wife."

Frau Mueller smiled, pleased with her analysis. "What a contagion calls for is a cause, someone or something to blame. We might think of it as a trick. The contagion produces a sleight-of-hand to draw attention away from itself. So, it has brought into the awareness of each of us, the possibility of witches. Witches are the cause of all that ails us. Find and kill the witches and the pain will end, the tension we are feeling will subside."

Elsebett could find nothing in her teacher's words to argue with. Her analysis made sense, but it did not satisfy.

"But that is madness!" she found herself saying. "That is pure madness."

"It may be madness, Elsebett, but that does not mean it's not real. It is, I'm afraid, very real."

FORTY-EIGHT

One Sunday, Johannes brought a new guest to the Helgen home. It was a proud moment for Johannes, but a surprising and apprehensive one for everyone else because this young man—his name was Frans—was obviously not of the peasant class. He was tall and gangly—"colt-like" Sebastian would later say of him. The cut and fabric of his clothing, the soft leather of his tall boots, the elegant leather pouch he carried, all set him apart from the Helgen men and women.

Johannes had met Frans at the inn the night before and they had encountered each other again that morning at church. Frans was passing through the village on a journey up river, but he was not leaving until the following day and so he accepted Johannes's invitation to join the family at their Sunday meal.

"Frans can tell us much about the trials taking place against the pestilence of witches," Johannes announced as they approached the table, "because he is directly involved."

Elsebett shivered slightly as she and Irmele exchanged glances, eyes gleaming. Jacob hurriedly secured the best chair in the house. He placed it near the head of the table and instructed the young man to sit down. Sebastian brought him beer. Basil stood aside as he studied the guest with a cool and appraising eye while Klara fumbled and banged at the hearth and Ursula fussed to cover her hair and struggled to make the wild boys settle themselves. Katharina brought out bowls and fresh loaves of bread and readied her husband's seat at the head of the table.

"It will be a simple peasant fare, sir," Klara boomed after the men were seated. "Not what you are used to, I suppose, but a sturdy stew for the working man. And the bread is a peasant's bread, you can be sure. But I trust you will find it as good as any in the village."

"And my uncle's beer, Frans," Johannes added proudly, "is the same beer he provides to the inn that we enjoyed last night."

If the young man heard the words of Klara or Johannes it could not be known because he did not respond to any of them. His attention seemed focused solely on one thing.

"Who is she?" he whispered to Johannes after they were seated. "I noticed her this morning in church, and now I see her again."

"That's my sister, Elsebett. She visits us on Sundays."

"And her husband? Is he…?"

"No, no, she's not married." Then laughing and in a strong voice Johannes said: "Sister, you're not married, are you? Frans here wants to know."

Elsebett blushed, but managed to not drop or spill the bowl of stew she was delivering to the table.

"That is true, brother," she stammered as she placed the bowl safely before their guest. "Had I married, you can be sure I would have told you."

The young man, too, was embarrassed. "I apologize for seeming so bold," he said glancing up at her. "I should have asked in confidence, not in your presence."

"This girl is my husband's daughter," Katharina said firmly. "And you, sir. Have you taken a wife?"

"I have not yet had that honor, madam. I am twenty-one years of age and a student. Or, I was until this pestilence broke out. Now, I work under the direction of the Archbishop, not directly, of course. But under his command. My role is humble, but worthy I believe."

"Yes, do tell them," Johannes said.

"I am sent to a village. There I find lodging and make contact with the priest and the village authorities. Word is then spread that I am available to hear accusations. If a man or a woman in the village suspects that another person is involved in witchery, they are encouraged to provide me with what information they have in support of their accusation. My responsibility is to faithfully and accurately record their statement, which I then read to them. If my work truly expresses their intent, I have them sign the document or make their mark, as the case may be. Then I make three additional copies of the statement and have the witness sign them as well. Finally, I deliver all the signed statements to my superiors."

"So, you are not involved with the trials themselves?" Sebastian wanted to know.

"I am not. I was present at one day of a trial, but only as a spectator. Normally, by the time the prosecutors and judges arrive in a village, I will already have been sent elsewhere."

"Are the statements given to you, made under oath?"

"They are not, sir. What I hear are stories, complaints: poisoned dogs, stillborn children, storms that destroy one man's crop, but not the crop on the neighboring strip, precious items gone missing in the night, sows that become suddenly barren, a group of lambs that seemed to run madly off a cliff and fell to their deaths in the river, a young ox that collapsed for no apparent reason.

"My job is to encourage people to talk, to express what they know and believe. I explain that later, after their statements have been evaluated, they may be asked to make a sworn statement or even to testify before the court. But to me, they simply need to tell their stories. I want them to feel free to do that.

Sometimes the statements of several accusers will implicate the same person. Other times accusers will implicate each other. It is not my task to determine who is lying and who's telling the truth. That is the role of others higher up. My job is simply to faithfully record what the people want to say."

"If everyone keeps asking this young man questions," Klara shouted from the hearth, "his stew will become cold and remain uneaten."

"Yes, yes," everyone agreed as if scolding themselves. The young man did need to address his attention to the meal. But after he had taken a few bites, and as Elsebett was delivering more bread to the table, it was he who broke the silence.

"If I may, young lady…"

"Elsebett. You may call me Elsebett."

"Yes…sorry…thank you…yes." Frans ran a hand across his sparsely bearded chin. "Johannes said that you visit here on Sundays, and yet you are not married. So, pardon me, but I was curious. Are you then in the service, perhaps, of another family? My parents are in service, which is why I ask. They serve in the manor house of a noble family and it was there that I was raised."

"My daughter is a skilled midwife," Basil explained to the young man, "certified by the village council. She lives in the home of her teacher."

"And she knows letters," Sebastian added. "Numbers as well, is that not right, Elsebett?"

"And precious stones and medicinal plants!" Irmele shouted from across the room. "If you become afflicted with scrofula, or some other ailment, you would be wise to seek her counsel, is that not right, Elsebett?"

"Scrofula!" Gabriel shouted with glee. "Scrofula! Scrofula!" And this outburst was echoed in unison by David and Thomas: "Scrofula, scrofula, scrofula!"

Elsebett still stood beside the table, a loaf of bread in either hand. She was blushing again and her eyes were brimming with tears, but she knew not what to do. She felt herself frozen in place.

"Well then," Frans said quietly, smiling at her. "If all this is true, it seems that it is I who should be serving you." And he reached up and took the loaves of bread from her hands and placed them on the table.

FORTY-NINE

When the table had been cleared and the bowls and utensils cleaned and put away, the women joined the men for a few bites of Katharina's cakes. That the cakes were Katharina's cakes and not the traditional "Helgen" cakes—that is cakes made under Ursula's instructions following the lessons she had learned from Marsel—demonstrated how Katharina's influence had continued to grow in the family. Irmele resented this development more than Ursula because Irmele loved cakes, and she knew that "Helgen" cakes were more moist and flavorful than Katharina's cakes.

"When I marry,"—Irmele had often whispered to Elsebett— "the cakes I bake for my husband and our children will be Helgen cakes. Of that, dear cousin, you can be certain."

When the women entered the men's presence, Katharina balancing her cakes on a large board and Ursula brushing away the flies, they found the men admiring the leather pouch that Frans kept always close at hand. Everyone felt more relaxed now. Frans might be a member of the Archbishop's staff, and a capable and educated young fellow, but he came from the servant class, and was not himself a noble or a man of inherited wealth.

"This, young man, is an item I admire greatly," Jacob said as he examined the pouch, turning it in his large hands. "It is of the finest quality and most skillfully fashioned. The style and the craftsmanship remind me of some satchels I saw many years ago. Sebastian, you might remember this. We were outside the abbey, as I recall, and the satchels were on the back of a gelding under the control of a rather agitated traveler—you remember him? This fellow had been denied entrance through the gate. He was a most complaining fellow, but the satchels were of the finest workmanship I had ever seen."

Sebastian nodded, taking the pouch into his own hands. "Yes, Jacob, I remember the gentleman and the satchels, though the horse was a mare, I believe, not a gelding. Later that day, once he had gained entrance and after both he and his horse had been fed, he appeared a more pleasant fellow."

"That may well be true, though I have no memory of it. I do remember that he told us the name of the master craftsman, the man who had constructed the satchels, but I cannot spring the truth of it free from the folds of my memory. The traveler, himself, had come from the east, I believe, on a journey of some length."

"Yes," Sebastian agreed.

"So, young Frans," Jacob asked, "do you know the history of this possession of yours? It would be curious, would it not, were the craftsman one and the same man? Should you should know a name, a place of origin, it might waken my memory."

"Yes, I can speak to this, sir, to a degree."

Seeing the approaching women, Frans hesitated, his eyes meeting Elsebett's. He waited until the older women had seated themselves and the cakes had been placed in the center of the table.

"But first I must bore you with some history, if I may. As I mentioned, my parents are in the service of a noble family. I, and my two sisters, were raised on the grounds of the manor house, a day's good walking from the city, though downriver, on the other side from your village. My mother attends to the needs of the lady, who has become quite frail in recent years, while my sisters work in the kitchen—they are both younger than I. And my father…well, when I was small, my father maintained the horses and the two coaches. But in recent years he has become the overseer of the lord's lands. Back when I was twelve or so, the lord was thrown from a horse, you see. While not confined by his injuries, he finds that walking a distance or even riding in a coach an ordeal to be avoided."

"They are elderly, this couple?" Sebastian asked.

"They are, sir. Indeed."

"And childless?" Basil asked. "Given the lord's infirmity, I would assume that a son, or a son-in-law would be overseeing the lands, not a groomsman, meaning no disrespect toward your father."

"I recognize none, sir. Your observation is reasonable, and it leads me back to the point of my story. The lord and his lady had two children, a daughter followed by a son. Both were considerably older than myself. The son, who was the younger of the two, was only a couple of years younger than my father. So you are quite correct, sir. Had misfortune not befallen them, the son, or in his absence, a son-in-law would now be overseeing the estate."

"It does sound unfortunate," Ursula said. "The lady frail and the lord infirm, and both of them elderly."

"Yes, my lady. The daughter died from a fever at the age of nine, long before I was born. All I know of her are stories told to me, and I have heard many of them both from my mother, who knew the girl when she was herself a child, and from the lady herself. The lady has always loved to speak of her daughter. To this day she regularly visits the grave and the small chapel nearby. I have often driven her and my mother to the graveyard for this purpose."

"There remains then the son," Sebastian said. "Of him you have yet to speak."

"Or the confounded pouch. That is where this all began, if memory serves," Johannes said, eager to turn the conversation back to the witch trials.

"Yes, yes. I must apologize for being overly long. It is a failing of mine, one of many I assure you. My father has often said that I am like a well-greased wheel. That once I begin to turn I just keep spinning." Looking then at Elsebett, who stood with Irmele behind the older women, he laughed happily.

"So, do continue, my friend," Johannes insisted. "Days do have ends and the cakes are cooling."

"I will, and I do promise that the two strands of my story, that is the son and this leather pouch, are connected. By the way, the son bore the name Jacob, the same, I believe, as you, sir," he added, nodding toward the uncle. "So, the son, as I said, was about the same age as my father. I have been told that the two were very close, to the extent permitted by the disparity of classes. As children, they played together daily, and often slept in the same bed. But the son received a formal education while my father learned only the practical skills needed for the care of horses and carriages.

"Now this Jacob possessed a great hunger for adventure. When he had completed his training in the law, he returned to the estate to help with its management, with an eye, of course, toward eventually inheriting it. But the son was restless. He had heard tales of the new world, the one far across the ocean, and more than anything he wanted to visit those exotic lands with their strange peoples, plants and animals. My father tells me that when the son returned from university he spoke of little else.

"Jacob understood his responsibilities toward his parents. He knew that as their sole surviving child, he meant everything to them. He knew they expected him to marry and to produce for them a covey of grandchildren. He understood these expectations, and he accepted them, my father says. And he has always said of Jacob that a more honorable and honest man could not be found on this earth.

"I must tell you that my poor father has never forgiven himself for a decision he made at that time. You see, after some months Jacob came to an understanding with his father. He would take leave from the family for three years. He would travel to the Americas, and then return, at which time he would assume management of the estate, marry one of the local girls of good birth and raise a family. The father agreed to this with great reluctance, though the mother, that is the lady of the lord, resisted the decision with all the strength she had. To this day she still rues over it, though there was nothing she could have done to prevent it."

"And your father?" Irmele asked. "You say he had a role in this?"

"Yes, young lady, a subservient role, you could say. Jacob wanted my father to accompany him on the journey. He would be his man, his accomplice in all matters large and small. But my father had no hunger for foreign adventures. He was in love with the girl who would become my mother. So he declined to go. He would marry, he insisted. He would stay on the estate and manage the horses. The lord and the lady both wanted him to accompany their son. They knew Jacob to be somewhat rash and volatile, while my father is a man of more balanced humors. But my father was not a serf, though we descend from serfs; the lord could not order him to accompany his son on this journey."

Everyone thought about that for a moment. Then Elsebett said: "Being a freed man, your father could not be ordered to make the journey, this I understand. But still he lived on the lord's estate, and under his grace and protection. Thus the lord did have great power over him, I would think. Could he not have threatened to banish him from the estate had he refused to honor this command?"

"Or cast out the girl!" Klara exploded. "Order her off the property. That would have persuaded him to go."

"What you are suggesting is correct," Frans said. "All of these things the lord could have done. And had he made threats such as these, my father might have consented to the journey. Then he, like Jacob, might never have returned. But if you knew this lord and his lady, if you knew the love they have for my father and mother, you would understand why such harsh threats could not have been uttered."

"And the poor Jacob?" Irmele asked. "Can you say what became of him?"

"Less is known, young lady, than we would like, and more, I am sorry to say, than any parent would want to know.

I have personally seen and read the two letters that came from him. The first was written from the port of Genoa shortly before he sailed. It tells of his journey across the mountains to that place and the arrangements he was making for the ocean voyage that lay ahead. The second letter arrived, I believe, a year or more later. It was composed shortly after he arrived in the land that he called the New World. It told of the difficulties of the voyage—he did not tolerate well the rolling of the ship on the waters. But he spoke of friends he had made aboard ship, of the native people seen in that land, and something of the exotic smells, plants and animals he had already witnessed.

"When I read that letter now as a man, I find in it a certain wistfulness. Notwithstanding all the opportunities that lay ahead of him, I suspect he had already come to question his decision. Of course he says nothing that would alarm his parents, but I find regret between the lines. I have read the letter to my father and he agrees. The letter hints at a wildness, an almost brutal ambition, not in the land itself, but in the people surrounding him that he found perhaps alarming."

As Frans was describing the letters, the three wild boys had entered the room from outside. They stood in a line now near the door, their eyes on the cakes. Quite naturally the three of them assumed almost identical positions, legs apart, their hands clasped before them. Seeing the boys, Ursula jumped from her seat. Crossing the room she pulled Thomas, her youngest child, into her arms.

"And nothing more? No word of him?" she asked, clutching the child and turning back toward their guest.

"Not for a long time, my lady. Years passed. I remember, as a child even at the age of these boys, that a doom-like uncertainty hung over the family. Then one day a stranger arrived at the house. This man had in his possession certain items that had belonged to the son. Among them was a ring that had been given to him by his mother before he left…"

"And that confounded leather pouch?" Johannes shouted, pointing at it. "Have we finally arrived at the pouch? I pray you, tell me that the pouch was among the possessions."

"I am sorry, my impatient friend, but the pouch was not among them," Frans admitted, laughing. Then holding out his hand for all to see, he added, "But here on my finger is the ring. The ring that has been to the New World and back. It was presented to me by the lord's lady the day the lord sent me to university."

After the ladies had admired the gold ring with its yellow stone, Ursula asked: "And this Jacob? Did the stranger know his fate in detail?"

"He did, my lady, and his fate is difficult to describe. He was murdered, you see. Viciously so. It had to do with a cave lined with the ore of silver, and who had a rightful claim to it."

"Do you stand now in the place of this Jacob?" Katharina asked. "In the eyes of his parents, that is? You have his ring, as you say."

"No, madam. No one can stand in the place of their son. Nothing has removed from them the shadow of his loss, though they know at least not to expect his return. That his body lies buried in an unmarked grave in some wild and foreign land haunts them both, and my father as well. In his mind dwells the possibility that had he gone, he and Jacob might have returned joyfully together. But, in gratitude for my parents' service, and my own, they have given me some opportunities afforded a son, including a formal education, which leads me at last to…" Frans paused, seeing that both Jacob and Basil had fallen asleep in their chairs, their beards resting on their chests.

"Uncle, the pouch!" Johannes exclaimed. Jumping up, he nudged his uncle Jacob's shoulder. "It's the pouch, Uncle. Our long-aired friend has wound his way to the pouch."

"Will you then inherit the lord's estate?" Katharina persisted, glancing at the two young women, and scowling toward Johannes.

"No, madam. That is not possible. The estate has been in the family for generations. The lord has a younger brother. It will pass to the brother, or to his heirs upon the lord's death."

"The pouch, you say?" Jacob mumbled, rousting himself.

"Yes, Uncle, the pouch."

"Yes," Frans agreed, "the pouch." He took it in his hands and held it up so Jacob could see it again. "When I left for university, the lord's lady gave me the ring, and the lord himself gave me this pouch for carrying my books and papers. Here is what I can tell you about it. It had belonged to the son,

Jacob. He had acquired it while he was a student and he had intended to take it with him on the journey. But in the confusion and turmoil of his departure, it was left behind."

"So, he acquired it while he was a student at a university?" Jacob asked.

"That is my understanding, sir."

"And where, so far as you know, did he do his studies?"

"The gentleman studied at the university in the city of Leipzig," Frans said.

"Then it is one and the same!" Jacob exclaimed, slapping his thigh. "That is exactly where the unpleasant fellow said his satchels were made. Is that not right, Sebastian? The very place."

"I have no memory of it, brother, not one way or the other."

"Well, it is clear to me," Jacob said, giving his thigh another slap. "The craftsman's name still eludes me. But I am certain now of the city. It was the nap that brought it back to me. Nothing serves a man's mind and body better than a little nap, have I not told you, wife?"

"If anyone should know the truth of this, Helgen, it is you," Klara said, rolling her eyes and glancing toward her daughter.

FIFTY

One evening, a few months later, Elsebett and her teacher heard a knock at the door. Following their custom, Frau Mueller disappeared and Elsebett went to welcome the visitor. Standing outside was her brother. Johannes had never been to Frau Mueller's house, so far as Elsebett could remember, so his appearance gave her pause. Was something wrong at home? she wondered, forgetting at first to welcome him.

"I have a terrible aching in the head, sister," Johannes mumbled, looking down at his shoes.

"Your head? Well, I'm sorry. Come in, please. Perhaps Frau Mueller can help you."

Johannes shook his aching head. He seemed determined to keep staring down at his shoes. He moved them about now, stirring up the dust.

"I know the cause of it, sister, and only you can help." His right hand was now covering his mouth.

"But…"

"The cause of it is here. Come." He led her to the corner of the house, and standing there among the cabbages was the lanky Frans, holding his pouch and grinning broadly.

So often had she thought of him that Elsebett's first impulse was to rush up and throw her arms around him. She managed to control herself, perhaps because Johannes was staggering about choking with laughter. Embarrassed, she curtsied awkwardly, and extended her hand to briefly touch his. After a few moments of exchanged words, grins and blushes, she led them into the study and hurried to find her teacher.

"It is the young man," she whispered excitedly. "The student I told you about."

"The student? The one in the employ of the Archbishop? That young man?"

Elsebett nodded, somewhat disappointed by Frau Mueller's characterization. In her mind she had worked to make Frans as much like herself as possible in class and interests. She thought of him as a servant boy who had the good fortune to become a student. But her teacher was correct. He was not a student now. He was one of the Archbishop's men.

As she followed her teacher toward the study she felt uncomfortable. Frau Mueller had become increasing preoccupied with the witch trials. The contagion, as she called it, was never far from her mind. In casual conversation, her words kept circling back to the subject. But so far as Elsebett was aware, her teacher had never met someone directly involved.

But Elsebett soon realized that she need not have worried. Frau Mueller was a professional. In the study her demeanor rarely waivered. She was polite, somewhat reserved, a careful listener. When she probed, she probed carefully.

"I have gone now to four villages," Frans explained in response to her questions. "In all of them I have heard reports of witches."

"In every village, you say?"

"Yes, Frau Mueller, in every one."

"I am surprised. Before, there was rarely talk of witches, and now, it seems, they infest every village."

"Yes, every one. And the people come to me eager to talk. No one is coercing them. They make no profit by speaking to me. I believe the Archbishop and his staff have recognized and are exposing a foulness that before had festered beneath the surface. Surely, exposing Devil worshipers to the light of day can only help the long-term health of the people."

"Well," Frau Mueller said, nodding her gray head. "I, of course, agree with you. If there are people who worship the Devil and do his bidding they must be exposed and dealt with. But is it not possible, that this has nothing to do with the Devil or with witches?"

Frans seemed taken aback. "I don't understand, Frau Mueller. Nothing to do with witches? How can that be? That is all the people want to talk about. Witches in every village, as I said. And what is a witch, but a person in league with the Devil?"

"I wish to raise with you, as an intelligent young man—both of you, intelligent young men," she added, with a nod toward Johannes. "I want to raise the possibility that the people who come to you with talk of witches, really wish to vent their own malice. To settle scores, to seek revenge. Perhaps to burnish their pride. I am sorry to speak so bluntly, and I have no desire to disparage your work, but I worry that every dispute, every festering grievance has now become an accusation of witchcraft. Even the three of you are old enough to remember that we did not enjoy heaven in this territory before there was talk of witches. Crops failed, people had complaints, animosities, hatreds. I worry that the Archbishop by mustering this campaign has made available to every angry person, a means of extracting revenge on his enemies by accusing them of witchcraft."

Johannes adjusted his position. He frowned and looked toward Frans.

But it appeared to Elsebett that Frans had listened carefully to Frau Mueller, and he pondered his thoughts momentarily before responding. "I would not deny, Frau Mueller, that among the people I have spoken with, there can be found an element of malice. I have even witnessed a certain glee in some of those who have come to me, something of the spicy relish that often accompanies gossip. And there are times when the charges they make sound so outlandish that it is hard to give them credence. My responsibility, of course, is not to judge the accuracy of what is said but to faithfully record it. And that, by the grace of God is what I attempt to do.

"I can give an example. There was a case, early on. A man came to me who seemed almost to be babbling, so incoherent was he at times. I wrote down his words as faithfully as I could, but when I delivered his statement to my superior, I apologized for the man's foolishness, saying that I should not have troubled him with it. But my superior disagreed. 'You have behaved correctly,' he told me. 'We are battling a very sly and devious enemy. Even the words of a fool might help expose a witch. On the other hand, the healthy and the comfortable may be those most oblivious to the problem, or even covering their own foul deeds.' The Archbishop and those closest to him, he told me, now recognize that this evil extends well beyond those marginal people everyone first suspected, the purveyors of dark magic, the palm reader, the fortune teller and such."

"The healthy and the comfortable," Frau Mueller repeated quietly. "Even they may be covering their own foul deeds?"

"Yes, Frau Mueller. Those were his words and they strike me now as prophetic. I have in this pouch a statement given to me in private by a parish priest who accuses the local mayor of his village, a man of noble birth, of being a witch."

"A priest accusing a mayor of witchcraft!" Johannes exclaimed. "Now that is rich, that is rich indeed." It seemed to Elsebett that her brother was delighted by this news.

"I cannot, of course, tell you more," Frans cautioned. "Not the names of the individuals nor the village where they reside. But that was the statement given to me in confidence just yesterday. The priest claimed that the mayor was a carouser, an abuser of heavy drink, a man who avoids the Mass and never makes confession. He believes the Devil has led the mayor astray from God's church and now uses him for his own ends."

"Everything the priest has told you about this mayor may be true," Frau Mueller said thoughtfully. "I have no reason to assume that the Devil is content to seduce only the tormented hag who has suffered a life of abuse and hardship. If a man of noble birth, and a mayor at that, is vulnerable, the Devil might well attempt to beguile him into doing his bidding. On the other hand, hearing only your words and knowing neither the priest nor the mayor, it does strike me as a perfect example of what I have described. That is, that the priest holds a grudge against this mayor; perhaps, he resents his disregard for the church; perhaps he even envies the man's decadent way of life. I have known priests who harbored a great deal of envy. Before this time, the priest would have complained about the mayor to his friends, perhaps he would have even despised him and wished him ill. But now, given the current of the time, he accuses the man of witchcraft, the penalty for which is death."

"There is more, Frau Mueller," Frans said. "According to the priest, the mayor has said publicly and often that the Archbishop's campaign is a sham. His words set me to thinking. Would the Devil not want it broadcast that the campaign against him is a sham? Is that not some evidence that the mayor is doing the Devil's work?"

"I find what you report frightening," Frau Mueller admitted. "Are the authorities saying now that anyone who questions the rightness of their campaign, is by virtue of this questioning, himself a witch? Surely, you cannot believe that, young man, not as a person trained in the law."

"I can believe it," Johannes interjected. "Clearly a person who seeks to discredit the campaign is doing work that aids the Devil and his minions."

"No, Johannes," Frans said firmly. "Frau Mueller is correct. To question the campaign would not alone be proof of witchery. But to repeat it publicly and often is some evidence, it seems to me. According to the priest, the mayor believes the Archbishop is a fool, an unwitting tool being used by devious men for their own profit. I know this is not true. I have had the honor to meet the Archbishop. My lord knows him well. He has dined at the estate. His beliefs are strong and clear, and he is far from being a fool, of that I can assure you."

Frau Mueller took a long and careful breath, and then glanced at Elsebett. When they were in consultation with a patient, such a glance would have indicated that her teacher had detected something significant in the patient's words or actions, and wanted to alert her. In this instance, Elsebett could not determine what the glance had been intended to convey. Finally, her teacher spoke:

"I have not had the honor to meet the Archbishop but I am confident that what you say of him is true. To reach the position he has, an archbishop and one of the Emperor's electors, confirms your assessment. It is also obvious that the Archbishop's campaign is not a sham. People are dying as a result of it. Dying a most horrible death."

Frau Mueller paused. She seemed shaken in a way Elsebett had never seen before. Her teacher gathered herself before continuing.

"We must acknowledge that," she added. "Whatever we may think of it, people are being put to death in a most horrible way."

"They are not people!" Johannes blurted out. "Witches are being put to the flames. Such creatures are not people. They are handmaidens of the Devil."

"Brother, witches or not, they are also people," Elsebett said, surprised at her brother's vehemence.

"I don't consider them so," Johannes insisted. "Is the Devil a person? Of course not. Nor are those who have sworn to serve him."

Elsebett looked toward Frans. This young man, who seemed to her so intelligent and gentle, he would caution her rash and eager brother. But Frans did not respond. He seemed focused on the pouch in his lap and did not look at her.

FIFTY-ONE

Rachel and Elsebett helped with the harvest that year. The grain harvest was relatively successful and all able villagers were in the fields. Basil and Jacob both remained cautious, however. Compared to good years, the amount and quality of the grain was well below average. "Though the sun shines and the rain falls, the earth remains tired," Jacob lamented.

One day, early that winter, a knock was heard at Frau Mueller's door. It was late morning with a cold wind; flurries of snow swirled about as if restless and hesitant to land. Opening the door, Elsebett found her cousin, Zacharias, smiling at her. Flakes of snow had caught in his cap and mustache and clung to his woolen tunic. From a protected fold he removed a packet and handed it to her.

"This was given me by a man who arrived at the inn. He spoke your name and said it was intended for you. He had been instructed to deliver it to me, knowing I could be trusted to complete its journey."

Elsebett took the packet and glanced at it. She realized it contained a letter, though she had never before seen a letter, much less received one. But yes, that was her name written there. Nothing in the world could have pleased her more than to open the packet, but she knew she had first to admit her cousin into the house.

In the study she and Frau Mueller welcomed Zacharias with honey cakes and drink, the unopened packet resting expectantly on the table. He was eight years older than his cousin, a married man now and the father of two small children, both of whom the midwives had helped deliver. Zacharias had become a prominent young man in the village. He was a member of the council and possessed of a quick mind through which streamed the endless details required to manage a successful inn.

"Yes, yes, very busy," he told them, his speech pattern abrupt. "The more business, the more the work; the more staff, the more the problems. But we strive to keep our guests comfortable and well fed; that is the idea behind it."

"I am pleasantly surprised to learn that the inn is so busy," Frau Mueller said. "While the harvest was a little better, the plowmen have struggled in recent years, and in my experience, when the plowman struggles, so does the cooper, the seamstress and the market vender."

"That has been true of the innkeeper as well, Frau Mueller. But there is a new passion now that sends men along the roads and up and down the river. Before it was the wine and grain merchants that comprised the bulk of our guests, but added to them now are the Archbishop's eager men: notaries, copyists, special accusers, constables. These men have money to throw at you. They demand the best and are willing to pay for it."

"The Archbishop sees to that, I suppose," Frau Mueller said quietly.

"Of course, Frau Mueller, he has opened the treasury. But the law itself lends a hand. They tell me that a person convicted of witchcraft has his property confiscated. His children are sent into exile and his assets sold to help pay for his arrest, trial and execution. It is a thriving business in combination: a furious populous and an eager prosecution that generates its own wealth. I have no idea where it will end, but in the meantime, we innkeepers and those who supply us benefit by it. Thus, the prosperity spreads through the village. As you know, Elsebett, I buy as much beer from your uncle as he is able to spare." Zacharias chuckled and added: "Sebastian produces a fine wine as well, but he is more stingy with that. I am treated to a cup when I pay him a visit, but he keeps the better part for himself and the family."

"Pardon, me, Zacharias, but we know where this business ends," Frau Mueller said, her voice sober. "It ends in death. It ends in people burning at the stake."

"Forgive me, Frau Mueller. You're quite right. I did not intend to make light of it. You asked if the inn was busy and I was just explaining…"

"No, please," Rachel interrupted. "It is I who am sorry. I who needs ask for forgiveness. You are absolutely correct.

You were simply answering my question. Please do accept my apology. This whole business has me beside myself. I cannot help thinking that one day it will come to our village. Then we will all see for ourselves."

"Indeed. Then we will." Zacharias rose and pulled his hat down over his head. "Meanwhile, I need to get back to the inn. The problems are endless and when I turn my back they rise up on their hind legs and stand ready to bite me as soon as I return."

Elsebett jumped to her feet with delight, clasping her hands before her chest. She remembered her cousin Zacharias most fondly from when she was a child of four or five. In those days he and Agnes would take her and Johannes into the heart of the village for a festival or fair. And now fondly as well for bringing her the letter.

"And my uncle and aunt? May God bless them, and your wife and little ones as well."

"All are well, thanks be to God, cousin. Mother and father are still active in the business to a degree, though both are failing in their eyes. Their experience picks me up when I falter."

"And our cousin Agnes? Have you word of her?"

"None of recent telling. She is in Cologne, as you know, and caring for her little boy. Her husband is a merchant: wine, fabrics, but other things as well. Cheeses from the north, fruits. On one visit he brought us several nicely-ripened quinces. He does on occasion stay with us at the inn and he relates word of her when he comes. She is, of course, much devoted to the child who seems prone to illness, but at last report was doing better. Cologne is well outside this territory with a different prince-elector. It has not experienced the fury of the witch trials, so far as I am aware."

When they had closed the door, Rachel smiled at Elsebett and said, "And now, I will return to my work and allow you the pleasure of your letter."

"No…"

"But of course." And she turned and walked away.

In the study Elsebett took the packet to the window and opened it carefully. The letter had a date at the top followed by the name of a town which was located on the other side of the city, some distance from the village. It had been in transit for three weeks.

My Dear Elsebett: Forgive me first for being so bold as to address you so, and indeed to write to you at all, but I must confess that thoughts of you and the brief times we have spent together, are seldom far from my mind. I trust that by the grace of God you, Frau Mueller and all members of the Helgen family are in good health and well supplied for the coming winter. Cold weather stands here on the doorstep, and I assume the same holds true for you.

My parents and sisters were well when last I saw them, thanks be to God. I spoke to them most favorably—and at length as you might suspect of me—of you and your family. My father enjoyed particularly your uncle Jacob's enquiry into the origins of the leather pouch that is my treasure, but that was formerly owned by the lord's son. As a man who himself sneaks the occasional nap, my father appreciated your uncle's respect for the same. He confirmed that the pouch was indeed fashioned in the city of Leipzig. He asked that I convey to your uncle that the craftsman was a master called Julius, who was famous and most respected in those parts. One day, God willing, you will meet my family in person.

I am sorry to report that both my lord and his lady are doing poorly. When the days shorten and the weather becomes colder, the lord suffers more from his old injuries. More severe is the lady of the manor. She is confined to bed and under the constant care of my mother and sisters. Of late, blood has begun to flow from her mouth and she has become so weak that my mother fears she might not long survive.

I deeply lament that my work has not taken me near your village in recent weeks. Be assured that had the opportunity arisen I would have justified a stay at Zacharias's inn and taken full advantage to visit with you and your family. I will soon be traveling to the city to meet again with my superiors, where I will carefully stroke the tail of the fox, as they say. May God grant that my journey is uneventful and that I arrive in good health.

The activities in which I am engaged show no sign of abating. People in every village continue to report unfathomable events, suspicions and accusations. In the last few days I received a letter from a colleague. He works under the chief prosecutor helping to administer the trials and has of late been located in a village I know. You may recall as well my speaking of this place. It is the village where the priest had accused the mayor of being aligned with the Evil One. My colleague writes that when the prosecutors had completed their work, not only the mayor, but several other men of stature and breeding, and every woman in the village save one, had been consigned to the flames.

Such devouring seems hardly possible to me. I remember the village with fondness. It was set in a pleasant valley, and the day I arrived the market was open and the streets were crowded with villagers and animals transporting goods to and from the main square. It had an attractive, well-maintained church and a new village clock, which had been acquired at great expense, and of which the people were justifiably proud. During my stay a troop of players arrived and entertained the villagers. The players, both men and women, performed over three nights. You would have marveled at their skill and erudition. Without doubt they had been well taught and had studied many storybooks. During my stay, I housed at the inn where I found the food was of good quality and plentiful and the wine adequate. So pleasant was my time there, that it seemed to me a place where, by God's grace, any decent soul could happily live out his days.

Thus, it is not within my power to imagine how the village must now appear, so complete was the devastation my colleague described. I quote here directly from a paragraph of his letter: "Our work is difficult and demanding, but the cause is noble and the renumeration excellent. Surely God's favor has led me to this high position and good fortune has guided my path. I am reminded of the Psalmist's words: 'Yea though I walk through the valley of the shadow of death, I shall fear no evil.' For this I am both humble and grateful."

I must confess to you, my dear Elsebett, that when I read my colleague's letter I was moved beyond words. Like everyone else, when speaking of our work he talks only of good fortune, of high position and excellent renumeration. But I hear in his words as well the heavy burden that I feel and dare express to no one but you. He has truly journeyed through the 'valley of the shadow of death,' but it was I who led him there. It was I with the statements I duly delivered to our superiors, that have made his journey possible, indeed inevitable. Were he present in this room where I now sit, would I dare convey my doubts to him? I fear not. Everyone with whom I associate speaks as he does only of the "nobility" of our cause. Even my sisters, my father and mother talk solely of the great opportunities afforded me and the importance of the crusade that I am a part of.

In all this time, only one voice has spoken differently, and that was your teacher, Frau Mueller. I remember fondly the comfort of her study and the frank discourse we enjoyed there. I have pondered often the distinction she tried to explain as we were leaving and the four of us stood in the doorway. Do you remember? The distinction between the "pestilence" and the "contagion." As Johannes and I were walking back to the inn, we decided that there was no distinction, that she was simply using two words to describe the same thing. I understand now how wrong we were. The "pestilence" she referred to is the nearly universally-recognized infestation of witches, while the "contagion," as I understand her usage, refers to our ever-more rabid obsession to search them out and eradicate them. Where before I thought only of the pestilence, now my thoughts dwell ever more on the contagion. She seemed to believe that the contagion is more real than the pestilence, that the former created the latter. I am not prepared to go that far, but for her insights, I am most grateful. Please, convey this to her.

But I beg of you, share the contents of this letter with no one but her. And certainly speak not of it to my good friend, your brother. I apologize for laying these burdens upon you, burdens that I have willingly taken on and should be content to carry myself.

Finally, if I may dare to advise you, I would caution both you and Frau Mueller to be very careful with the words you speak and the ears to whom you direct them. When I left the pleasant village I described above, I had collected but three statements: the one in which the priest accused the mayor, plus those of two women, one accusing a midwife of selling a placenta to a suspected witch, and the other given by the suspected witch herself accusing a third woman of having killed and eaten the suspected witch's cat. Now, based on my colleague's letter, other men of stature besides the mayor have been given to the flames, and but one woman in the entire village remains alive. Such is the savage and unpredictable energy of this contagion!

Though I would treasure a word from you, I believe it best that you not attempt to write me. My work allows for no fixed abode and I will not be back with my family for some time.

Furthermore, I dare not risk having your letter arrive at the office of my superiors where it might be opened and viewed. Know that I am otherwise quite well, and that my thoughts are often of you. I send you many hundred thousand friendly and sincere greetings! And I commend you in trust to the grace of the loving God. Yours, Frans.

FIFTY-TWO

The winter that followed was brutal, but its strength had the benefit of weakening the contagion. The long nights, the cold and stormy days, discouraged travel and lessened the flow of gossip. The Archbishop's men retreated to their comfortable homes, and confined fire to their domestic hearths. Two children came to term in the village that winter; the boy born to a family of cottagers was small and weak and survived only a few days. The other was a girl born healthy to the sexton's daughter. This child was given the name of the sexton's late wife and her christening brought joy not just to the sexton and his family, but to the community at large because it felt normal and right, and because the sexton's wife had been well-loved and was fondly remembered. In addition to the short-lived boy, two men of advanced age died that winter and were buried in the hard ground of the graveyard. These burials, though made brief by the bitter cold, provided rituals that were familiar and comforting.

Finally came the lengthening light of early spring, and with it joy to everyone. Along the streets and paths, the bright, clear days had people greeting one another with smiles, as if saying: "Would you look at how God is blessing us?" Yokes were set on oxen and plows hauled from strip to strip; seeds were sown in the fresh-smelling earth and the good weather continued. It continued for weeks until what had been good became bad: high, clear skies, still air, no rain. It seemed that the prayers offered up in the dark of winter had been granted with a cruel vengeance. "Only a foolish seed would sprout in this dust," Sebastian said to his brothers, his boots raising a powdery cloud. Basil and Jacob looked at one another, recognizing once again how truly odd their younger brother was.

When their prayers for rain were at last answered, they received first sprinkles and then torrents accompanied by winds that snapped tree branches and disassembled roofs. The Helgen residence consisted of one long building extending back from the street. The living quarters stood in a line beginning at the front (one flight up with swine below), while in the rear was the stable with oxen and the mare below and hay and grain storage above. The kitchen was located between the two ends with a "mud room" between it and the stable. The building had been cobbled together over many years by different Helgens; the roof sheeting varied from sleek tiles at the stable end, to thatching over the kitchen area, to decaying wooden shingles held down by rotting boards secured by lines of stones above the bedrooms. It was at the front that most of the storm damage occurred, and where rainwater now made its way with intermittent drips and splashes onto beds and tables.

"No thing tells a man what next to do so clearly as does the weather," Jacob philosophized to Basil as they stood outside staring up at the roof. "Even more when it is rain water landing upon the head of a man's wife. That, I think, is the most clear instruction. My Klara did during this long night so persuade me."

Katharina was not happy about having rainwater falling on her head either, but having lost one husband to a storm-damaged roof, she did not intend to lose another. Fortunately, Johannes jumped to the project. He was a graceful lad with a well-tuned sense of balance. New materials were acquired and with the help of Sebastian, the roof was soon repaired. The two men performed their work carefully so to not damage the nests of the resident barn swallows. "Never kill a split-tail," the father Johannes used to admonish his sons. "Kill a split-tail and as surely as our Lord attacked the Devil, lightning will strike your stable."

With the coming of spring, the contagion woke and stretched itself. In Elsebett's young heart, it had always seemed that the Archbishop's men would never turn their attention toward the village. This was a difference between herself and her teacher, who believed their arrival was inevitable, a difference they respected but did not belabor. In Elsebett's mind, the men would pass through; they might stay the night, but they would not remain to do their deadly work.

It was obvious to her that no witches lived in the village she knew so well. Perhaps because she knew no other village, it was possible for her to imagine that the villages where the Archbishop's men were finding and burning witches were different from "our village." Maybe in other villages there were witches who with the Devil's help did cause terrible things to happen. But nothing like that was going on here.

Unfortunate things happened in Elsebett's village too, of course. Tools slipped and gashed arms. Mothers died in childbirth. Children and old people grew ill and died, men and animals went lame, crops failed, women lost their sight. During the fierce storm that everyone was still talking about, a bolt of lightning had struck a large deciduous tree near the house where she and Rachel lived, burning a jagged gash along the length of its trunk. People came to look at it. They stood about talking. Some could not resist running their fingers along the blackened scar, touching it cautiously at first as if it were, or just might be, capable of burning them.

But Elsebett found no evidence of witchcraft in any of this. These were just things that happened. In her mind, the strange events that occurred in those other villages must have been tainted in some way that caused them to stand out from the normal course of things. If a calamity had resulted from a witch's curse, you would know it. Something would say: this is the Devil's handiwork. In her mind, that was the skill the Archbishop's men must possess: they could tell a toad from a frog, a goat from a lamb, God's work from that of the crafty Devil.

So one Sunday early that summer when Father Peter introduced a young man to the congregation, announcing that he had come to the village to hear stories of malicious acts, the work of devils and witches, Elsebett felt disappointment more than alarm. Disappointed to see that the short squat fellow standing beside the long-eared priest looking somehow both frightened and frightening, was not "her" Frans, but a fellow who bore the name Braun, Herr Braun.

Father Peter in his elevated pulpit appeared somewhat apprehensive as he introduced the young man. He began by speaking in general terms about the witch trials, almost as if he thought his congregation was not familiar with the phe-nomenon, which for several years had been on the minds of everyone. He praised the Archbishop-Elector for initiating such important work, for devoting his precious time and treasure to the effort and for recruiting skilled men such as Herr Braun to undertake the task. He spoke favorably of the secular courts which had assumed responsibility for the rigorous prosecution of these sorry cases. He encouraged everyone to cooperate fully with all aspects of the investigation.

Such was the tenor of Father Peter's introductory remarks, but soon he warmed to his task. Spiritually, the young priest had traveled a great distance in the years since he first arrived as a shy, long-eared young man, who had been, as he now admitted, hardly more than a boy. Along with a growing confidence, he had developed a profound distaste for what he called "superstitious practices." The so-called dark arts may at first seem harmless, he told the congregation, since they do not directly invoke the Evil One. But over time they did cause a "secret hidden trust" to be placed in the evil enemy. And thus their practice invariably distanced the practitioner from the church "which is the sole means to salvation." By "practitioner," Father Peter made clear, he meant not just "she who reads the palm, but just as surely he who offers his palm to be read."

"And by superstitious practices, I do not limit my meaning solely to soothsaying or the presumptuous revelation of future events, which only God Almighty is rightfully entitled to know, but also to those who would interpret dreams or draw up horoscopes, or utilize divination to locate stolen objects, or who would invoke incantations, be they 'white' such as for the healing of livestock or 'black' done for the purpose of injuring the same. All of these practices and others of a similarly diabolical, forbidden or hidden nature are but steps on the path leading to the deliberate invocation of the Evil One, or even to the worship of him. Such superstitions are not slight or venial sins, as some may assume, but are the invention of the damned Devil, may God graciously protect us from him, who from the beginning of the world has incited men to idolatry."

Standing in the crowd before the pulpit, Elsebett felt her hand squeezed by Irmele. From childhood, her cousin had possessed a hunger for knowing the future. She loved having her fortune told by the old women who frequented the village market.

And Elsebett heard now as well her father move uneasily behind her. From the time she was a small child, she could remember how when a sow was ailing, an old woman would come to the house to stand over the stricken animal and chant rhyming incantations in some incomprehensible sing-song language. It had seemed so natural to Elsebett, so much the order of the day.

"The Devil's kingdom was destroyed," Father Peter shouted now, "through the bitter suffering and death of our dear Lord Jesus Christ, but the Evil One still lives. And under the pretense of benevolence, the Devil has now introduced hidden appeals for his help through these superstitious practices. His goal is to secretly and deceitfully regain possession of those poor souls lost to him upon the death of our Savior on the Holy Cross. Assume, therefore no false comfort, nor allow your diligence to slacken. Know that the Evil One lurks even now outside the doors of this holy church whose sanctity alone protects us from his grasp."

He urged the people to report fully all conduct that was in any way suspicious or that might suggest the handiwork of the Evil One himself. "It is not just word of witchery—the foul worship of the damned Devil, or the invocation of his aid—that I would have you report to this esteemed servant of the Archbishop, but also any evidence of the suspicious practices I have described, which are surely precursors to idolatry and the worship of the Devil himself.

"Because we know that if the suspension of witchcraft and these dark arts are not undertaken with fitting and thoroughgoing diligence, that God Almighty will be moved to righteous anger against us and may punish us and our village with pestilence, war, crop failures and other plagues."

In spite of Father Peter's exhortation, it still seemed to Elsebett that nobody would actually go to see Herr Braun. The young man had been assigned to the storage room at the rear of the church, a room where the tables, benches and utensils were stored between feast days, a room she knew to be dark, musty, and crawling with orb-weaving spiders. She felt a certain sympathy for this Herr Braun, who would be sitting there alone with his quill, his ink and his paper, a single candle burning beside him, while the life of the village continued on outside, oblivious to his presence.

FIFTY-THREE

How very wrong Elsebett was. How quickly and thoroughly the arrival of the mysterious, almost never-seen Herr Braun, changed everything. His name passed across every lip. His presence wormed its way into most every sentence. The windowless, rude and clumsy shed where he sat—in its eighty rickety years no one had given it a second glance—seemed now to have taken on a glow. Elsebett could not walk past without asking herself if the man was in there, and if so, if he was alone, or was he at that moment listening to some fantastical tale such as Frans had described hearing in the villages where he had been.

The setup was a clever one. On the wall of the shed was a large double-door which on the occasion of feast days was opened so the benches and tables could be taken out and returned. Elsebett had assumed that one would pass through the double door to see Herr Baun. But this door remained closed. A second door gained entrance to the shed: a door located in Father Peter's study. A person who wished to speak with Herr Braun would first enter the church and then pass through the door located near the confessional which gave entrance to the study. Thus, a curious observer in the sanctuary could not know if the villager entering the study was there to seek counsel from Father Peter, or had passed through to speak with Herr Braun.

The number of curious observers was large, and the number of villagers entering Father Peter's study was also large, with the result that speculation was rampant.

"I went to see him," Katharina admitted the following Sunday, though her tone of voice conveyed assertion more than admission. "I went to introduce myself, and I thought to deliver him a fresh cake as a gift from our family. I considered it only appropriate as your father's wife that I do my small part to make him welcome. Here is a young man who has come from the Archbishop to provide a service to our village. Should we allow him to sit there alone and ignored in that musty room? I think not. The last young man, you will recall, we actually had to dinner. I offered the same to Herr Braun, though he felt obligated to decline."

"He declined?" Elsebett asked, somewhat surprised.

"He did, which as he carefully explained to me, was only proper. He does not want to be seen as taking sides. He dines alone or with the priest, they tell me. He sleeps in the parsonage, a guest of the father. Nor would he accept so much as the cake, though I did persuade him to allow me to present the cake to Father Peter with the understanding that he and the father would share it; so firm are his principles in this matter."

"Are there sides?" Elsebett asked, looking at her brother. "I did not know that there were sides."

"He is very strict about this," Johannes acknowledged. "I too went to see him. I thought to invite him to the inn for an evening to enjoy a mug and meet some of the men. He declined. And for the same reasons as our mother has described. I had the impression he wants to maintain a clear distance from all of us." To Elsebett her brother looked somewhat downcast as he spoke these words.

"Such objectivity is absolutely necessary," Katharina confirmed, "if he is, by the grace of God, to do his job properly."

"I don't understand," Elsebett said. "This Herr Braun is not a judge who must make a ruling, or a prosecutor whose job it is to interrogate. He's simply a young man who is doing what Frans does. He has come to see if anyone wishes to make an accusation of witchcraft, to tell a story in private that he will copy down and have the person acknowledge. Why does this require him to remain aloof? To make himself cold and distant? I thought that no one would go see him, and now I learn that two members of my family have already seen him, and moreover that he has refused their offers of kindness."

"It is obvious that you are right, Elsebett: You do not understand," Katharina said, thrusting out her jaw in the manner that had become so familiar to her stepdaughter.

Johannes looked at his sister sympathetically. "I, too, am disappointed," he admitted. "I do understand that he cannot talk about his work in *this* village. That would be inappropriate, but I was eager to learn of his exploits elsewhere. Why he cannot be sociable to anyone in the village, is beyond me. I spoke to him of my friendship with Frans. He acknowledged that he knew Frans but would not speak more on the subject. What he said to me, quite bluntly, is this: 'If you have an accusation to make, I am here to be of service. But if not, then I ask that you depart so others may enter if they wish.'"

"That was cold," Elsebett said. "That was cold indeed."

"Cold, yes, but necessarily so, Elsebett," Katharina said.

"Why mother, why is it necessary that he be so cold?" Elsebett asked.

"Because we are all suspects," her uncle Sebastian interjected with a sudden harshness that did not seem natural in him.

"All...?" Everyone looked stunned.

Sebastian nodded. "Yes, each one of us. Any man, woman or child in the village may go to Herr Braun and make an accusation against anyone. He does not know Katharina or Johannes, you or me. He is not acquainted with we plowmen, or with the baker, the miller, or the miller's wife, the mayor or the mayor's daughter. Nor does he want to be, because he has no idea who will come next to tell him a tale. Or who the tale will be told about."

"Well," Katharina said after a pause, "it is not that *we* are actually suspects, brother. It is…"

"We could be, sister," Sebastian insisted. "We do not know. Furthermore, what we learned from the young Frans is that Herr Braun will not judge or evaluate the stories told to him. It doesn't matter how unlikely or fantastical the story might be. Or how obviously false it is to those of us who know the people involved. No, Herr Braun will simply write the story down and deliver it to his superiors."

"But the superiors will know," Elsebett stammered. "They will know, will they not?" She turned to her brother. "Have you not told us, over and over, how knowledgeable these men are? How expert? How rich and well-appointed? They must be able to tell the truth from a fabrication?"

"Well…" Johannes muttered vaguely, "…of course."

Poor Irmele realized that her fingers were wrinkling her good apron terribly. The outfit was her best. The one she wore every Sunday to church, to every procession and feast day. Her hands were sweaty and she could not keep them still. They insisted on clutching the apron and squeezing it over and over. She carefully released the apron and smoothed it out. Then she opened her hands and set them palms up on her thighs. But the moment her attention was pulled back to the frightening words flying like demons around the table, the hands flipped again. And there they were, grabbing and balling up hands-full of apron.

"I had my palm read," she confessed to the family. "More than once. And my horoscope prepared, well that was only one time, and I did not understand all those lines and dots. It was very confusing. Another time, an old woman explained a dream I had. She said the shocks of rye were my children. That I would have three of them, but the two that had blown over would die."

"That is who needs be told about!" her mother Klara shouted now. "That woman, and those like her."

"Be born alive, the children, that is," Irmele continued. "That is what she told me. Which is why they were standing at the beginning. But then die, because they blew over. In my dream I kept standing them up and they kept falling over."

"That is who needs be told about!" Klara shouted again, banging the table. "That woman, and those like her. The Devil's work, for certain, saying that to a child!"

So powerful was Klara's voice and manner that both Jacob and Basil stopped snoring. They lifted their bearded chins from their chests, shook their heads and looked around. But then, a moment later the heads began to droop again and soon the snoring resumed.

"Do you think I should go to this man and confess these things?" Irmele asked Elsebett, her voice pleading.

"Confess to the priest, child," Katherina advised. "That is where you make your confession. Not to this man. He has no power to absolve. That is not his function."

"My father's wife is right, Irmele," Elsebett said. "If you feel you should confess, do so to the priest, not to Herr Braun."

"I worry that someone will make an accusation against me. But if I have already told him. If he already knows that I meant no harm, that I truly regret my error, then maybe he will not take it so seriously."

Irmele was soon sobbing uncontrollably. She lifted her wrinkled apron and buried her face in it, but her muffled sobs continued.

FIFTY-FOUR

At night now Rachel Mueller spent long hours in prayer. She sought the purity of prayer that Gretel had described to her. The place where: "When you are there, you will be where I am. You will be where the venerated saints are."

Rachel tried to go there. She wanted to find Gretel. But Gretel was not there. Or Rachel was at the wrong place. Or Gretel had left. She was alone.

Of course, she had never actually found Gretel there before. It was not a place where you met and hugged and shared recipes. She had always been alone in prayer, but before "alone" had meant something more like "present." To be alone in pure prayer was to be present, and this presence had a universal quality. It had an every where, every time, wavery energy about it. It was rich, full, comforting, a recognition that you were separate but not separated. But now she felt a desperation in the aloneness, a frightening isolation. She was separated indeed.

Nor was it just her prayers that were betraying her, or she betraying them, or she betraying herself. When Elsebett was away, their home now imprisoned her as well, cut her off. Its walls became barriers that energized her fears. "Out there" was going on. "Out there" was dangerous, or it could be. It involved her, or it could involve her. Stories were being told to that young man, or they could be. She was a character in them, or she could be. Or her dear Elsebett was, or she could be. Agitation, aggravation.

Rachel found herself walking through the village, looking at people, appraising their expressions, their greetings or failures to greet, their smiles or their averted eyes. With every face past encounters flashed through her mind, pleasant, unpleasant, stable, unstable, a storehouse of gratitude or festering grudges. Every mistake she had ever made now came forward to announce itself.

Again and again she walked past the church. She entered the sanctuary, looking about. She dipped her fingers in the water; she crossed herself; she lit a candle. She knelt before the impaled Savior. But everything had changed. No comfort could be found there. People entered and left, lingered about. People slipped into the priest's study, the door shutting quickly behind them. There was a furtiveness about it. A sidelong glance. Or was it just her? She felt pushed to enter the study herself, to introduce herself, explain herself, but she resisted.

Do you speak or do you remain silent? Is to enquire, to suggest guilt? Is to show an interest, to implicate? Do you accuse another so to direct attention away from yourself? She was resolved not to do that—having no belief that anyone she knew was actually in league with the Devil, she could not make such an accusation—though some probably thought it the best course to take. To accuse not from honest belief, but for self-protection.

An attitude had come to the village, it seemed to her; something or someone had to be sacrificed. An element of local pride may be involved. In every other village, the Archbishop's men were finding witches. Surely, we too must have witches in our midst. Do we not have the church with the sweetest bells? Are we going to be exposed as the only village in the territory that could not produce a single witch? Look at the calamities that have befallen us. Does the graveyard not have fresh mounds? Are the storerooms not half empty? Does thunder not boom off the great hill above us? Did lightning not gash a jagged scar in that tree? Was that not a sign saying that evil is at work in our midst?

"Local pride?" she caught herself thinking. This was madness. Her mind had become the mind of a horse trapped in a burning barn. She simply had to stop thinking about it.

But then at the baker's shop, buying small loaves for the next morning, she felt again her distance from those indigenous to the village. Though she had lived in the village for decades, she was still an outsider. An outsider because she had entered the world elsewhere, a fact that could not be erased. The bones of her ancestors were not sprinkled through the graveyard. Her grandmother had not been a sister of the baker's grandfather.

Also, there existed a dialect native to the river, one that varied slightly as it passed along its course from village to village, from town to city. This dialect, thick at the bottom, became diluted as you moved up in class. Words had flowed from Gretel in a way that suggested her noble birth and her inflections had infected Rachel's speech in subtle ways. Rachel's tongue formed familiar words somewhat differently than did those native to the village.

The baker's wife was chatting in dense dialect with a customer, and, even after all these years Rachel had to concentrate to catch the meaning. Perhaps, she thought now, her attitude had been condescending. When she first arrived, the dialect had tormented her. She was not adept at the musical subtlety of it, its mashed consonants, its oddly stretched vowels. She had found it irritating, at some level erroneous, and she had absorbed it reluctantly. Her job was to deliver children. What had been important was to understand and be understood. She did understand, she could be understood, but now she recognized again that the sounds she made were not their sounds, not exactly. The very way she spoke probably grated on their ears.

As she listened to the two women, Rachel felt that the interwoven, interrelated village was shrinking into itself, drawing itself tighter. The contagion had arrived in the presence of a young man who sat now in a room adjoining the priest's study, and the village was contracting to protect itself. Perhaps it would feel compelled to cast someone out, to sacrifice one with the hope of saving those remaining.

As these thoughts passed through the mind of Rachel Mueller, she repeatedly admonished herself to stop thinking about it. "Do your shopping," she would mutter. "Go see poor old Frau Imhoff who is alone and who always brightens when you come through the door."

FIFTY-FIVE

Two weeks later the young Herr Braun finally departed and all that remained of his visit were rumors of accusation and betrayal. Even Basil Helgen, who wanted nothing to do with the subject, was caught in its web. His wife was quite happy to speak of little else. Who had gone to see Herr Braun and what had been said? She had more answers than questions, but her answers were speculative, air-borne, unsubstantiated. She was, it seemed to him, quite delighted by the excitement of it all.

By contrast, the men he encountered were on edge. The broken plow, the damaged roof, the ever-unpromising weather, the wife's complaints all seemed tied now not so much to the witches themselves as to the agitation surrounding them. That things had been better before, of this there was universal agreement. What was needed was some resolution, some action that brought life back to normal.

Whatever was wrong, "fix it," the men were saying. "If it's witches causing this, dammit, then find and burn them and get it over with."

§

When a knock came next to Frau Mueller's door, Elsebett found Zacharias again offering her an envelope with her name written below a red wax seal. In the study he told her and Frau Mueller that an Archbishop's man had approached him about renting most of the inn.

"It's for the trials," he explained. "They will need rooms to house the people involved. The trials themselves will be held in the dining room, which we can have the use of at other times. So, we will still be able to prepare and serve food and drink. I was worried about that, because if we are to have so many guests, we will need a space to serve them."

"So, there will be trials, cousin?"

"Oh yes. He was certain of that. There will be trials. And the prosecutors, the judges and assessors are finicky. They have strict requirements about their rooms. They insist on privacy, of course, and security. The executioner, this gentleman told me, the man in charge of the actual burning, he has his own demands, not simply for himself but for his man as well. He insists that their rooms be located as far as possible from the kitchen. And, strangely, he eats no meat, but insists always on a supply of fruit at his table. And his wife always accompanies him, I understand, and she, too, must be paid the highest regard. So too the woman who waits on her. And, oh yes, I heard more than once, that the executioner is most demanding about the care and feeding of his horse. A white stallion of unstable temperament, I am told. He has a man who guards it day and night. That is my understanding."

"My!" Elsebett exclaimed with a sigh.

"Yes." The steady Zacharias looked unusually perturbed. "The gentleman who approached me was quite uneasy about the arrangements. I gathered that at the last place, the accommodations did not satisfy, and he was held responsible. So, it is going to involve a lot of work for us, preparation, worry and expense. But I could not in good conscience turn him down. There is no other place in the village and the remuneration will be substantial. The Archbishop does not argue about bills presented him, and pays them promptly. That has been my experience."

Rachel glanced at Elsebett and then said to their guest: "Of course they want the trials to be held here."

"Absolutely. Where the crimes occurred. The idea is not simply to punish the guilty but to instruct the people by example. I thought of that myself, Frau Mueller, and I asked the question you may yourself have pondered. If a person has been accused of witchcraft, why not transport her to the city along with any witnesses and hold the trial there? Why send the whole judicial system on the road as if it were some traveling theater troop? But no, it is as I have just described to you. They want to assure maximum impact on the people."

Elsebett's throat tightened and she thought she might faint. Until that moment she had never believed such a thing would happen in the village. It had never felt real to her that it had ever *really* happened anywhere else, either. But now her cousin Zacharias was discussing a witch trial as if it were a business transaction. Not just possible, but inevitable.

What will it smell like when a person is burned to death? The question was unavoidable, and so embarrassing, so disgusting, that she had always pushed it away. A person was being put to death most horribly, and foremost in her mind was the possibility of an unpleasant smell. The shame she felt at that moment caused her to forget the envelope resting on the table.

Frau Rachel Mueller had other thoughts. "Tell me, Zacharias, this gentleman who came to see you, did he reserve the inn for a specific time? Did he already know when the trials will happen?"

"No, he could not provide a specific date. And that is a problem for us. It will be a few months away. Maybe not until next year, there are other villages, other trials. He promised I would receive a month's notice. But I worry that he is but a minor functionary, and that his promise, while sincere, may be easily ignored. When the time comes, I fear we could have no more than a week to prepare."

"And the same, I assume, is true of the duration. Once they do come, did he indicate how long they will stay?"

"I, of course, asked the same question," Zacharias said. "And again he was uncertain. That will depend on the number of accused, and that number is unknowable. I should count on two months, but it could take much longer. The accusations multiply as the accused are interrogated. That has been the pattern, according to him."

"Interrogated." Frau Mueller repeated the word solemnly.

"Yes." Zacharias paused a moment. "And he promised me that the interrogations would not take place at the inn. The trials will happen at the inn and the judges, prosecutors and staff will be housed there, but the interrogations themselves will happen elsewhere, probably in the village offices near the church. The accused will be held and interrogated there. That was another mistake he admitted to. At the first village where he made these arrangements, he had scheduled the interrogations to take place at the same inn where the court personnel were staying. The judges were not happy."

"No, I suppose not."

Zacharias nodded. "They can be difficult to bear, apparently. Even if you are outside and see nothing. And the burning itself will also not happen at the inn. I insisted, and he promised me that. The market square will be the place. Before the church, near the stocks, you know, in the center of the village."

Elsebett jumped from her seat. She ran outside to the privy, both hands covering her mouth.

FIFTY-SIX

An hour would pass before Elsebett finally opened the envelope and read the letter from Frans:

My dear Elsebett: I apologize for my delay in writing to you and for my failure to visit you and your family in the village with its sweet-sounding bells. Please do not interpret my silence as evidence that my thoughts are not often of you. I hope you do not think it inappropriate of me to confess that I think of you most every hour of every day. Indeed, I marvel at the strangeness of this. How can it be that the few moments we have spent together shine out from my dark and dreary thoughts like precious jewels? I would think that memory of those moments should have faded by now, and that you, so busy with your own work, would find your thoughts of me distant as well. But somehow, and forgive me for being so bold, I dare to venture that you, too, hold dear those few moments we have shared.

I am writing from the home of my parents where much has happened. As I believe I advised you earlier, the lady of the manor was in ill health and very weak. It is my duty to inform you of the blessed departure from this life of that pious lady now three days previous. I was summoned home and, and by God's grace, arrived in time to spend the final days with her and the lord. As you might imagine, the lord is bereft and has at this moment little interest in anything beyond his own grief. It was good that I have been here to assist my family with the arrangements necessary for the funeral and to accommodate the large number of visitors who have come to pay their respects. By the grace of God, the lady now lies next to her beloved daughter, where together they await the final resurrection.

Prior to being summoned here, I was called to a new service by the Archbishop. Please understand that what I am about to describe is and must remain confidential. You may, of course, share these words with Frau Mueller. I encourage you to do so, but I ask that my report not go beyond the two of you. The hard truth is that developments related to my new service have instructed me that even so seemingly harmless a practice as sharing one's thoughts in a letter, can be dangerous indeed.

One morning when I was in the city to deliver the statements from my latest assignment, my superior directed me to accompany him to the Imperial Monastery of St. Maximin, which as you may know, is located a short distance outside the city's walls. He provided me with no information as to the purpose of our journey. He simply ordered me to bring writing materials and then he set off for the front gate. The day was wet, blowing a cold wind. I had already made my way by foot from the inn where I had spent the night, and I was ill disposed to return to the elements. So, I was grateful that he had a carriage waiting. My superior is a brusque and formidable figure, well positioned in the Archbishop's inner circle, and not accustomed to sharing information with a lessor person such as myself.

Thus, the two of us sat silently as the horses led us through the city and out to the monastery. I, of course, was somewhat apprehensive, having no idea as to the purpose of this outing.

At the monastery my superior was greeted with great deference, as you might expect. We were offered food and drink which he abruptly declined on behalf of both of us, though, the truth be known, I was both famished and thirsty, having not enjoyed a taste of food since the night previous. But, my superior had no thoughts for leisure. He instructed the brother to take us immediately to what he called "the inner chamber," and directed that "the prisoner" be brought to us without delay. He then set off directly after the monk using that intense walk for which he is known.

I must write that never in my experience have I witnessed a sight more pitiful than the one which would soon be presented to me. I am further ashamed to expose you to these horrific details, but I must share them with someone I trust, who will, I hope, understand my distress.

We were admitted to a small room that was bare but for a table and three chairs. Fortunately, two candles were burning on the table, for the light entering through the one narrow window would not alone have allowed me to do the work I would soon be asked to perform. My superior and I were still standing when a guard led—or I should say—half-dragged, a man into the room. This man was a portrait of dread and dejection. His clothing hung in tatters, his dark hair was matted, his body oddly distorted. He seemed incapable of walking on his own or of moving his arms freely. It was as if his shoulders and elbows, his hips and knees had been somehow separated one part from another. Each move the guard forced on him brought forth a moan from his swollen lips.

The guard dragged this pitiful creature across the room and deposited him in one of the chairs as if he were but the carcass of a boar delivered in the course of butchering. My superior remained standing but motioned me to take one of the chairs opposite the fellow. You cannot imagine the shock I experienced a moment later when I realized that the shamble of a being slumped across the table from me was a man I knew and highly respected. It was good that I was seated; otherwise I might have fallen to the floor, so great was my astonishment.

As you know, prior to the "contagion," as your teacher so rightly calls it, I was a student at the university in the city. One of my teachers was a priest who was a professor of theology and a writer on subjects related to that field of study. I knew and admired the man and his writings. I knew him to be a thoughtful scholar, a fine writer and an eloquent orator with a slight accent derived from his birth in the city of Gouda in Holland. He was a strong believer in the church and had written forcefully against the reformation.

What I did not know at the time, is that he was, with equal strength, opposed to the witch trials. My understanding now is that he questioned whether there are such things as witches as we presently define them (that is persons who have made pacts with the Devil), and he particularly dismissed the validity of confessions obtained under torture. I now know that while he did not reveal these thoughts to his students, he did express them in letters that he sent clandestinely to various church and secular leaders.

It also appears that he was preparing a book-length treatise on the subject which he had shown to colleagues and which he hoped to have published outside the territory of the Archbishop. That, at least, is my surmise because my superior pulled what looked to be a manuscript from his papers and proceeded to read parts of it to the prisoner. This went on for an hour or more. My superior read not just from the manuscript but from the letters I referred to above, which he claimed the prisoner had written and sent without the knowledge or permission of his superiors. These acts my superior characterized as seditious, heretical and quite possibly treasonous. He claimed that the allegations made in the letters and manuscript were contrary to established church doctrine, scandalous, erroneous and foolhardy.

At the conclusion of this long and disturbing discourse during which the prisoner slumped silently and dejectedly never once looking in my direction, my superior then commenced to dictate a lengthy statement that I was obliged to write out. The document had the character of both a confession and a recantation in that the prisoner was confessing to having written certain statements and then recanting the truth of them. This was a difficult, very apprehensive moment for me. My superior is an impatient, though an educated and articulate man, and I knew I must get onto the paper every word he uttered both correctly and with a clear hand. Fortunately, my previous work of listening to and copying accusations served me well in this instance.

Once he had finished dictating and I copying, my superior took the statement and silently read it through. When he was satisfied with my work, he instructed me to read the document aloud to the prisoner. He had me read it twice, slowly and clearly. At the conclusion of my second reading, a surprising and heart-rending moment occurred. The prisoner moved. He slowly lifted his head and looked directly into my eyes. I was certain that he had recognized the sound of my voice. Our eyes met and then he quickly looked away. What passed between us in that instant haunts me still. Did he look away so as to not reveal that he knew me? Was he trying to protect me? Or did he look away in shame? Or, was it disgust he felt seeing me in this position, believing that I had become one of the enemies who now surrounded him? Could he have even thought that I was among those who had betrayed him? The answers to these questions, I will likely never know.

There is more to tell, but I want to get this letter off to you. However, before I close, I must insert some light into this tragic story. One must always have an eye out for that which brings comfort and joy, especially in these dark and frightening times. Thus, I want to tell you what the lord arranged for his lady in the final days of her life.

To know the lord's lady was to know that she loved music and dance. When I was a child she used to organize large parties at the manor filled with food, music and dancing, to which many people in the area were invited. The parties would require long hours and hard work for my parents, of course, but they were also times of great excitement for all of us. After the lady became frail, the parties ceased, though occasionally the lord would arrange for a musician or two to visit and perform. And this is what he did now. A group of four musicians, a lute player and three players, each with a different-sized viol, came and stayed at the house for the final week of the lady's life. Every day they would set themselves up in her bedchamber, carefully tune their instruments and then perform pavanes and galliards periodically throughout the day.

How beautiful this was! So melancholy, so sweet. To just pass the room was to have one's heart lifted. My mother, who was often in the room holding the lady's hand, was convinced that the music brought great comfort to her in her final hours. I hope, dear Elsebett, that you can hear the sweet sound of a lute in your ears as you read these words. Certainly nothing on this earth so closely expresses the celestial realm as a pavane, well performed on a well-tuned lute.

And so until I again see you, I send many thousand friendly and sincere greetings, and I commend you in trust to the grace of our living God. Your Frans.

FIFTY-SEVEN

Two weeks later Frans arrived in the village. At some risk he had fled the office at midday when his superiors were in a meeting. Outside the gate, he had found a boat headed upriver, having taken off a load of fabric at the crane. By late evening he was knocking on the door of Frau Rachel Mueller. He came luggage in hand, somewhat out of breath, his words tumbling over themselves as he spoke. He and Elsebett greeted one another joyfully but somewhat shyly, both embarrassed by the intensity of emotion that welled up in them when their eyes met and their hands touched.

In the hour that followed it became clear to Elsebett that Frans had come as much to see Frau Mueller as herself. He came the way she had seen so many come, in search of a comfort they could not quite provide for themselves. Of course, all of this lay beneath the surface. A fire was lighted in the study. Pleasantries were exchanged; seats taken; drink and cakes shared; the cool, still, evening air acknowledged and appreciated; the journey from the city recounted.

It also occurred to Elsebett that this visit differed from most in that her teacher was as eager to learn from their guest as their guest was to learn from her. Indeed it was Frau Mueller who first broke through the formalities to expose the deeper issues.

"Your recent letter, that Elsebett was so kind to share with me…about your experience at St. Maximin's?"

"Yes?"

"A beautifully composed letter. But there was something missing, young man," Frau Mueller said. "You never told us if the prisoner signed the confession. I am curious. If you may say, did he sign? And further, if you may, what exactly did he confess to and recant?"

Frans laughed. "Yes, well I see I have left you in suspense, and for that I offer my apologies. No, the prisoner did not sign at that time, though he certainly has signed by now. My superior went over the document line by line with him, confirming that the prisoner acknowledged the truth of each and every statement and would willingly sign it. He then had me add an attestation clause stating that the signing would take place in the abbot's private chamber and listing the names and positions of four eminent men who, in addition to the abbot, would witness the signing and affix their signatures attesting to it. Thus the signing was to take place as soon as these men could make themselves available. My superior insisted that the confession be a very public and open exposure. I assume it will be posted throughout the university and the city. As I said, the prisoner was a highly-respected professor, who, as my superior declared, had betrayed everyone from the Supreme Pontiff down."

"Yes," Frau Mueller said thoughtfully.

"You might be interested to know that he—my superior, that is—was disappointed by our work that day. On the return carriage ride he grumbled about it. Apparently, my professor is well acquainted with the Archbishop and while the Archbishop is furious and feels betrayed by him, he decided to spare the man's life if he fully confessed his heresy and recanted. My superior would have had him confess, recant, and still be given to the flames. Such was the anger he expressed in the carriage."

"I see. And the thoughts your professor expressed in the letters and the manuscript? Are you at liberty to divulge them?"

Frans nodded slowly. "They are etched in my memory, Frau Mueller, at least the basic positions he took in his writings." Frans then closed his eyes and it seemed to Elsebett that he was reading the document in his mind. "First, as to witches themselves, he claimed that it was pure superstition that witches can transport themselves in any way different than other humans. Witches do not fly and anyone who claims to have seen this is doing so only because of torture. Second, there can be no contract between a devil and a human being. Third, devils do not assume human bodies. Fourth, there are no sexual acts between devils and human beings. Fifth, neither devils nor human beings can raise tempests, rain or hailstorms. Sixth, that spirit and form apart from matter cannot be seen by human beings. Seventh, it is rash to assume that what devils can do, witches can also do by the aid of devils. And finally, the idea that a superior demon can cast out an inferior demon is, my professor wrote, contrary to the teachings of Christ."

Frau Mueller released an audible sigh of relief. "I am heartened that there exists in this territory another human who believes such things," she said, "though the circumstances that caused it to be revealed to me are appalling. For this poor man I can feel nothing but the deepest pity."

"Yes." Frans nodded. "He also made several assertions regarding church authority and behavior. He said that the popes through their bulls have not said that witches can do the things such as I have listed above."

"Have *not* said?" Rachel asked.

"Yes, Frau Mueller. My professor held that it was a mis-interpretation of the bulls to suggest the popes had made such claims. He also asserted that those pontiffs who have granted the power to proceed against witches have done so only because they feared that if they did not, they would be unjustly accused of magic themselves."

"That is surprising."

"Yes. He also wrote that those persons who today confess to witchcraft have been compelled to do so only by severe torture. They are confessing falsely, according to him, and thus innocent blood is being shed. And finally, and perhaps most harshly, he claimed that there exists an economic purpose behind this contagion, if I may use your terminology, Frau Mueller. The witch trials are a form of alchemy, he wrote, in which gold and silver are being coined from innocent human blood. My superior read that paragraph from the treatise aloud to him several times and had me insert that exact language into the confession."

"But all of this he has now recanted, is that not true?" Elsebett exclaimed. "I am confused. Can we know what your professor really does believe and what he does not?"

Frans looked so miserable at that moment that Elsebett thought he might burst into tears.

FIFTY-EIGHT

"Forgive me," Frans stammered. Then slowly he brought his hands up and covered his face. For what seemed a long time no one in Frau Mueller's study moved or said a word. The quiet evening had become night. The only light now shone from the two candles, one at either end of the table, their yellow spires still and straight.

Perhaps Elsebett felt the most discomfort, convinced that her words had somehow brought Frans this sudden wave of grief. The wise Rachel felt a degree of comfort. At least she was not alone in her understanding. For the first time since the contagion had arrived, she was able to sit for a few moments as Gretel had taught her, silent and in the full presence of her emotions and those of her young companions.

It was Frans who ended the silence. "We know, my dear Elsebett," he said finally, lowering his hands, his eyes red. "I am sorry to tell you this, because it shows my life and myself to be a lie, but we know. We know exactly what my professor believes at this moment. He believes what he wrote. He believes it with all his heart. It is his recanting, and my life, that are false."

"But…"

"Not from fear of death," Frans continued more forcefully, as if Elsebett had not spoken. "I do not believe he has recanted for fear of dying. He recanted because death has failed to come to him. The torture devices refuse to kill, that is the brilliance of them. And the torturers have grown most skillful in their slow application. The pain they inflict is endless and death does not arrive to end it. This morning I gathered the courage to speak with a colleague, a man who has been present when confessions were torn from the accused. Everyone confesses, he told me. In the end, everyone confesses. Only a fool does not confess early because surely he will confess in the end."

Frans shook his head, as if to clarify his thinking. "That fellow—the man I spoke with this morning—he has become so hardened by what he has witnessed, that he was laughing as he spoke thus to me. 'Confess early, young man,' he announced as if it were a joke. 'When your time comes, confess early, for surely you will confess in the end.'"

Elsebett felt herself shiver. She placed some sticks on the fire, stirring the coals with a metal rod, then kneeling to blow the flame back to life.

"In the convent where I lived as a child," Frau Mueller said, "there were records kept of most everything, of births and deaths, of the changing seasons, of storms and other calamities. That is one thing the sisters were accomplished at: the keeping of good records over time. Thus it could be known by people living now, something of what had occurred before the birth of anyone now alive. The records went back hundreds of years, back before the terrible scourge of the black death, a time when the convent served not as a refuge, it seemed, but as a cabinet, sealed and locked away. Wars, plagues, storms, uprisings along with the humble mention of births and deaths, all this was noted in careful script by different hands over many generations.

"For a year, when I was seventeen, I entered the records under the instruction of the prioress. The records fascinated me; through them I could read back into time. That was the direction, I preferred, moving from today to yesterday to the day before, and beyond. In those moments I imagined myself an explorer, a solitary torchbearer moving deeper and deeper into a cave."

Embarrassed now, Frau Mueller giggled. "I was such a silly, romantic child. But there was something very important I learned that year. I learned that on this earth God grants all things a span of life. A child might be given a day or a hundred years, but there is always a span that begins and comes to an end. The same is true of wars, storms, droughts, floods and plagues. They begin, they gather strength and finally they fade away. In the midst of a contagion it sometimes seems as though it will go on forever, that it will continue to gather strength until the entire world is consumed in its fiery madness. The present contagion is like that. Every report sounds more alarming than the one previous. Those infected become ever more powerful, rabid and demanding. The threat grows ever larger, ever more close at hand.

"But this contagion, too, has a span of life. It is not given us to know its length or the breadth of its destruction, or even if we shall survive to the end of it. But I can promise you that one day it will end. Someday, a young girl in the convent will leaf through the lines of script. She will find our time noted there, and she will marvel that such madness could have happened."

A short time later they prepared themselves a meal. This should have been one of the happiest meals of her young life, but Elsebett could find no joy at the table. Her normally vivacious Frans was in despair and unable to shake free of it. He felt himself in a kind of purgatory, he told them, his dreams twisted and turned against him. Everyone he knew, from the grieving lord who had funded his education, to his parents, his sisters, his colleagues from work and school, everyone celebrated his accomplishments, the course his life had taken. Only he and these two women knew the truth: He had awakened to find himself in the service of a mad master from which no escape could be safely made. He felt trapped. The more he advanced, the more would be asked of him, and the worse he would become. But to leave, to show the slightest inclination to withdraw was to place himself at risk. Not only himself, but his family. The fate of his professor was proof of it, it seemed to him.

"I fled today and came running to you," he confessed. "I ran, and gave no explanation. I felt furtive, illicit, myself a criminal. At the cathedral where I knelt a moment to pray, the Archbishop himself came through with an entourage talking loudly about some construction or other. I cowered, covering my face. At the city's gate a man was beating unmercifully on his horse; a woman was screaming at him; the child in her arms wailed with every ounce of strength its tiny body could muster. A foul-smelling beggar brushed against me, pointing at them and cackling with delight. The world was going mad, or was it? That was the question hanging before me unresolved: either I was mad, or the world was. I could think of nothing but the two of you."

They finished their meal, and when the table had been cleared away, the two women prepared a bed for Frans in the study. It was too late for him to leave, Rachel told him. The inn would be closed and barred for the night, and he would not be admitted. Frans accepted her thinking with simple gratitude, his docility suggesting that he had lost all desire to consider such choices for himself.

After the three of them had knelt briefly in prayer, the two women left the room, closing the door behind them. In the darkened hallway, a single candle wavering between them, Frau Mueller lifted her curly gray head and gave an instruction to her student. "Go back," she whispered. "Go back and comfort him. Comfort him and yourself." Then she extinguished the candle, and in the perfect darkness, walked away.

AGNUS DEI

FIFTY-NINE

he Archbishop's men did come to the village but not until the following year. They came not as soon as Zacharias had been led to expect, and the advance notice he did receive was brief, causing him, his parents and staff to rush about preparing as best they could.

The men began to arrive the week following the Feast of the Ascension—the holiday commemorating the resurrected Christ's departure from earth for heaven. It felt an odd coincidence to Rachel that as the risen Christ was departing, the Archbishop's men were arriving.

There must have been twenty or more of them. Most came by boat but some arrived on horseback, others by carriage. The village was abuzz and whenever a new group entered, the sexton had the sweet bells peal out so the curious could come witness the spectacle.

When he heard the bells clanging, Johannes dropped whatever he was doing and rushed with the others to watch.

Judges came, bailiffs, prosecutors and notaries with their crews of assistants scurrying about. Father Peter, the mayor and members of the village council stepped forward to welcome them. A few notables were recognized by the more knowledgeable in the crowd who pointed them out to others. Among the new arrivals was a man known to most every adult in the village, and a surprise it was to see their former priest, the sour, high-stepping Father Severin prominent among them.

Rachel had not joined the crowd—she had purposely kept herself away—but she was in the market square the day Severin stalked through, moving like a gray heron in shallow waters, and the sight of him caused her to shudder. So different, the man looked now. Older, of course, as was she. But it was not the priest's graying hair that struck her. During his last years in the village, the father had reminded her of a molting bird: his dark and disheveled garments faded and dirty, the upper reaches speckled with stains of food and drink, the lower with dust and smears of mud. But now the man passed in clerical glory: his black robe, new and spotless, over it a mantle lined with shimmering crimson. His curious stride resembled a prance.

The people were awed by how elaborately, not just the priest, but most of the men were attired. Their clothing had been sewn from beautiful fabric, finely woven, brightly colored, and present in such abundance that it hung in folds and drapes about them. Each man, it seemed, was covered in enough cloth to fully dress two common men. Jewels glinted in the sun, silver and gold flashed from chests. Billowing hats topped the heads.

Everyone recognized that here were eminent men. And imperious they were; they had grown accustomed to curious crowds and had learned to ignore them. As the murmuring, pointing peasants clustered a few feet away, the elegant luggage was loaded onto carts, and with scarcely a glance at the crowd, the dignitaries proceeded straight to the inn.

One afternoon a long wagon pulled by a pair of oxen arrived in the market square and was parked below the clock tower in the shadow of the village hall. On the wagon were two brawny men and resting in the wagon's bed was the torture ladder, an object that seemed potent with paradox and power. Johannes came running when he heard of its arrival. Jacob and Sebastian, too, were in the crowd that pushed against the wagon's tall wheels to examine it.

The wooden construction was simple, almost crude, Jacob realized, a ladder-like object about three feet across and ten feet long with flat rungs. Near both ends wooden rollers had been fitted, secured by iron bands. Through one end of each roller, a hole had been bored so a rod could be inserted to turn the roller, thus making it into a winch that could shorten or lengthen the rope tied to it.

"Our father assembled a winch something like that to raise the roof beams when he was building the stable," Jacob said.

Sebastian remembered "Only here it's not rafters but wrists and ankles, I assume, that are bound and pulled. Like the one father constructed, this device has ratchet teeth, I see." He pointed them out to his brother. "So they can stretch the poor wretch and then by engaging the teeth hold her in that uncomfortable position."

Jacob nodded, grimacing slightly.

One of the men on the wagon leaned forward. "I built this rack myself, along with my colleague here. Some prefer the strappado, but I hold with the rack. The pain can be more finely tuned, I would say."

"And when we hold them stretched there, friend," the second man said, "what you hear are popping sounds. Sounds the body makes when its parts are separating. Sounds you would not soon forget were you to hear them. It is loud, I tell you. I dare say it would bring a shudder to the bravest of men. The cries of the witch and the popping of her body as it is pulled loose from itself."

"She's a truth maker all right," the first man agreed. He gave the ladder an affectionate nudge with his boot. "Many are the confessions we've heard come from the mouths of witches brought in to watch. Rack one, you see, and the others rush to confess even before their own ankles and wrists have the ropes knotted around them. It's the sounds that do it."

Jacob looked across the wagon and saw Johannes. The gaze of his handsome nephew was moving back and forth between the two men and the device lying in the wagon, the ropes coiled there, the metal rods, the rough-hewn supports used to hold the ladder at an angle. Johannes looked slightly ill, it seemed to Jacob.

But then the young man looked up and spoke. "We've seen no sign as yet, gentlemen, of the most famous among you, the executioner himself. The man who it is said rides a snow-white stallion and dresses like a noble lord. Perhaps no witches will be found in our village for you to rack or him to put to the flames. Is that why he has yet to appear?"

From the first man came a snorting sound, something between a laugh and a cough.

"Oh, there are witches about, lad, you can be sure of that. Your village will prove itself no different from the others. They may be of good family or poor. They may be old and wizened or as young and innocent-looking as a freshly picked peach. Your witch may be as obvious as the wart on the tip of a drunkard's nose, or she may pass among you unnoticed, seemingly both virtuous and pious. But they are here, and we will find them. It is what we are employed to do."

"As to the one you speak of, lad," the second man said. "We call him the Showman."

"The executioner?"

"That's right. That's the name we have for him, the Showman. Did you know he was a blacksmith before this started? A valued profession to be sure, but hardly one meriting the splendid animal he rides or the garments he now cloaks himself in. And his wife dresses as richly as he."

"He keeps to himself, that one does," said the first man. "He makes a mockery of nothing and speaks only to the purpose. He arrives just when needed and he leaves nothing more than smoldering ash behind. But the man does put on the best of shows, as you will see."

The second man spoke again, nodding toward Johannes. "We have been told he drinks not a drop and feeds himself solely on fruit and bread. It is further rumored that he believes himself condemned to an endless purgatory. That every fire he ignites beneath a witch is another flame he must endure in the afterlife."

"But why then does he do it?" Johannes looked crestfallen, as if he had just witnessed an angel crash to earth.

"Each must strike his own bargain," the second man explained in a grave voice. "As he has struck his, so too have you, lad. As have I and every man."

SIXTY

There came then a few days of disquieting pause. The Archbishop's men huddled at the inn—they had taken command of the facility such that the normal evening drinkers were diverted to the rough tavern where now plowmen and journeymen shouldered up beside the village's true drunks, its opportunistic thieves and those women who rented their bodies out for bread and drink: people they normally noticed only when they were displayed in the stocks. In the week or so of quiet, sows were bred, weeds pulled, a wall constructed, garments sewn and a child was born blind. Under Basil's watchful eye here and there among the rye a few grain heads began to fade from green toward tan.

Unlike most villagers, Basil was not preoccupied with the new arrivals. Unless a meeting had been called, he rarely went to the inn anymore. He was fifty-four now and under his second wife's steady pressure he preferred a quiet night at home with Sebastian's beer to the jostling, shoulder-slapping camaraderie of the inn. But he could not help being informed. Among the ladies of the house, speculation regarding the investigation was nearly constant, whether they were spinning yarn, kneading dough, scrubbing a floor or directing a bedtime monologue toward their husbands.

Quite beyond the failing harvests and the frightening prospect of unpredictable arrests and denunciations, it was generally agreed that the arrival of Father Severin had profound implications for the community. Here was a man they had forced from the village fifteen years before. Public meetings had been held, more than one petition signed and delivered to the former archbishop; a delegation of notables had traveled to the city to meet with his senior staff. The priest's eventual removal had seemed a triumph at the time. It was the kind of thing the peasants revolting in 1525 had given their lives for: the right of a community to control its destiny, including the choice of its spiritual leader. But now the banished priest was back and supporting him was the full authority of the church and the law. Why was he here and what did he want to accomplish?

"You supported those petitions," Katharina declared to Basil. "You spoke at the meetings. I hardly knew you then but I remember you standing and speaking."

"That does not make me a witch, wife. This is about witches, they tell me. Devilish women who hex sows and bring storms of hail and wind."

"As a priest I found the man acceptable," Katharina continued, puffing her pillow. "An odd fellow, no question. They said he wore out the spigots on wine barrels, so much did he drink. But as a priest he was acceptable. The penances he assigned were reasonable. His homilies were stern but blessedly brief. Both of my children were christened by the man. But he is not here to christen babies or deliver homilies. His purpose has to be revenge. Why else would he be here?"

No one knew but most everyone was eager to speculate.

The first person taken into custody was the woman known as Frau Grede, a widow of advanced age who for years had told fortunes for a modest fee. An explorer she was, of palms and planetary movements, of cards and the tumbling of dice, any gimmick that might provide an insight into the character of the person seated across from her. On market days, in a corner of the graveyard, she set herself up on a thick carpet beneath an awning and behind a drape. The carpet smelled strongly of the two lean dogs who curled themselves in the corner; one of the two seemed always asleep while the other watched the visitor with brown, attentive eyes. "I want my people to have their privacy," she said of her enclosure.

Frau Grede's brilliance had little to do with divining the future or even her ability to learn what her customers most feared and desired. As she watched the cards fall or studied the crevices in a palm, the seed of an idea would rise in her and from that seed would sprout an elaborate tale. It was the purpose of her life, she understood, and a blessing from God, to give voice to the stories that came to her.

A short time before the Archbishop's men arrived in the village, Irmele had entered Frau Grede's enclosure, her precious coins snug in an apron pocket. After Father Peter's admonitions against all forms of superstition and magic, Irmele had resisted fortunetellers. Still, she was fascinated by the unknown, the mystical. It seemed to Irmele that knowledge existed just beyond her reach, wisdom that promised insight and power. Some magic potion was available, some incantation could be intoned, a glimpse of the future revealed. To receive such insight might change her life forever. And so, one Saturday morning, Irmele had slipped into Frau Grede's enclosure.

Irmele had grown to become a large-boned young woman with an open innocent face. She possessed two ever-growing braids of blond hair, that since the onset of puberty she had had to wrap around her head and enclose beneath a wimple whenever she appeared in public. She placed her knees on the carpet and offered her open palms to the ancient woman, her heart beating wildly.

"Tell me who you are, child, and from whence you come that I might know the inner workings of your heart," Frau Grede said studying the palms. She spoke in a husky voice that seemed to Irmele both near and far away.

The girl stammered a few phrases, though later she swore to Elsebett that she could remember not a single word she had said. For a long time the old woman neither spoke nor moved, though her thick, stained hands with their broken nails felt surprisingly warm to the girl as they probed and traced the lines of her palms.

"In the deep forest, high on the great hill behind our village," the old woman finally began, still staring into Irmele's palms, "there lives a man who talks to wolves. He speaks to them and they to him. When he approaches their lair, he calls out a special word known only to them. Because he knows and speaks this word they give him safe entry into their cave."

Glancing up, the old woman said, "Did you know that wolves are very wise?" She paused and returned her gaze to the palms. "Very dangerous, but very wise."

The story continued until the bells had announced the hour of midday and Irmele's knees ached and her feet were badly cramped from crouching so long on the carpet. "One day," the old woman finally concluded, "this man's son will spy you as you gather wood in the copse. Perhaps, he already has, though that I cannot say for certain. You will not see him at first, but he will see you. And you may feel his presence though you see him not. This boy will want you for his bride. But he is very shy, you see, very shy."

Irmele had felt the boy's presence, she realized. She was sure of it. "Will I marry him?" she asked, unable to restrain herself.

"Ahh." Frau Grede released the girl's hands and leaned back, a motion that caused several of her vertebrae to pop so loudly that Irmele could hear them. "The future reveals itself slowly and reluctantly, girl. What you want to know must await a later day."

§

Frau Grede denied vehemently to the Archbishop's men that she was a witch or had any contact with the Devil or any of his minions. She denied she had ever cursed anyone's animal, or husband, or made lame a child. At that point the torture ladder, which for days had remained more or less on display in the wagon bed, was moved inside to a back room of the village hall; a room with exposed beams, high barred windows and an arched doorway that could be closed and bolted.

A short time later, her face lit by torches, Frau Grede described a witches' sabbath she had attended. She told of prancing pipers and squealing pigs. She described horned devils with erect penises and bat-like wings and tails that switched about when they moved. She talked of rancid smoke and sulfuric smells, of witches riding on goats and flying on brooms with black cats hunched on their backs. She described a woman who pressed her face against the ass end of a male goat, and another howling as she was sodomized by a devil. She described eating the brain of a cat and seeing writhing snakes and leering skulls, and a large caldron that contained a mysterious substance that was thick and bubbling and from which emerged a twisted human hand. The caldron, Frau Grede claimed was suspended over hot, orange flames, and the flames, it seemed to her, required no fuel but burned with an eternal and eager rage.

At an elevated table sat a judge wearing a red robe. To one side of him sat the prosecutor and on the other side a young man who wrote a record of everything that occurred. They heard Frau Grede's joints moan and pop as they stretched and they smelled the urine soaking into her clothing. Everyone, even the hardened men tightening the ropes, was impressed by the elaborate tale the old woman provided. But the men at the elevated table were not satisfied. They wanted names. Whom had she recognized among those flying witches and prancing pipers?

It was then that Frau Grede's imagination failed her. The poor woman had no enemies and her heart was burdened with no malice. She was a woman possessed of a shy nature whose personality flowered only in her stories.

"All were strangers," she told the men. "Among them was not one I knew."

The men looked at one another. Then the prosecutor nodded toward the two men standing on the floor and they pushed against the rods tightening the ropes, tightening them a notch each. The woman cried and moaned and yet she could not think of a single name to give them. Not one.

"I went alone," she cried. "I flew a great distance over the mountain to a clearing in a forest. It was there the sabbath was held. I saw no one I knew."

"Bring in the special accuser," said the judge.

SIXTY-ONE

The prosecutor left the room and returned a short time later with the high-stepping Father Severin, elegant in his crimson-lined mantle.

The judge addressed the priest: "Father, you know this village. You served as pastor here for several years. It was you who suggested this woman and you were wise to do so. She has confessed to attending a witches' sabbath."

"Her confession does not surprise me," Father Severin responded. "The future is known only to God, but yet this woman has been selling it for years. Where could she get her fabrications but from the Devil himself? I have seen the damage her stories have done. Instead of coming to me, the one appointed by God, those who were troubled in the spirit turned to her. And she led them away from the church. Her behavior pleased the Evil One. Of that I had no doubt."

"And yet, Father, the woman claims that at the sabbath she saw no one from this village. No one she knew. I find that hard to believe. Perhaps you can assist her memory. You knew well the people here. Who might she have seen and failed to recognize?"

Father Severin suggested several names, and the rods were pushed and the ropes tightened and the sounds of Frau Grede's body being stretched could be heard by everyone in the room.

§

The first thought Irmele had when she learned that Frau Grede had been taken into custody was that now she would never learn more about the shy young man who had spied on her while she gathered firewood in the copse. Then she realized how selfish her thoughts were and she ran to find Elsebett so she could tell her the story in full.

She found the two midwives side by side in the work-room pulverizing leaves in stone mortars. Irmele recognized mint, but other aromas rose to her as well.

"That poor woman," Frau Mueller said after hearing Irmele's breathless report. "Never in her long life has she harmed a soul."

"Well, if she has done no harm, then perhaps she will soon be released," Elsebett said, smiling toward her cousin. "And certainly you have done no harm by going to her."

"You think not?' Irmele asked, looking wildly at the two of them. "But Father Peter has denounced all such superstitions."

"No, Irmele. You were right to see her if you were curious," Frau Mueller said. "Even Father Peter would under-stand a young woman being curious."

As she spoke those words, Frau Mueller truly believed her assessment accurate. Of course, the priest would not openly approve of Irmele's visit to Frau Grede. Learning of it, he would frown, sternly rebuke and assign penance. But Rachel had always sensed a generous heart in the young priest. Beneath the words he used to scold the girl would hide a genuine sympathy that would lessen the harshness of the rebuke. Compared to Severin, Peter was a more contented spirit, his humors more stable and better balanced. She imagined that his impulse, upon hearing the girl's confession, would be to question whether he, himself, was doing all he could to guide his flock. But her assessment of the young priest, she now realized, was based on observations that predated the contagion's arrival. Everything had changed now. Nuance, ambiguity, ambivalence, tolerance: qualities such as these were being squeezed out, leaving as residue only a brutal certainty.

"And if she is released," Elsebett gushed, "you will learn further news about your shy young man. And maybe next time I will go with you. Do you think she might speak to me of Frans?"

As Rachel watched the giggling young women fall into each other's arms, she felt a wave of despair wash over her. She did see no harm in Irmele's curiosity, though personally, she had never been a person who had a particular interest in knowing the future. "Attend well to the present," Gretel had advised her. "This is what faith means. See well to the present, and God will see to the future."

But the future seemed to be gathering a shape and an intensity that Rachel found herself unable to ignore. The arrival of Father Severin had dashed any hopes she had that the contagion would pass harmlessly over their village, or would at the very least, not involve her or Elsebett. Even the sweet Irmele seemed now caught up in it.

Rachel and Severin were of a similar age. They had known each other a long time, and perhaps as young people they were actually attracted to one another in ways neither was prepared to acknowledge. As a bitter young priest banished from the corridors of power, Severin had arrived in the village determined to prove himself by expanding the church's influence and dominion. That which was in error he would correct, such was his mission. And in Severin's mind—or so it had seemed to Rachel at the time—women, in general, were in error. While he acknowledged the necessity of midwives, he found everything having to do with conception and birth to be gross and repugnant. That alone had placed her in the priest's disfavor.

Further, Severin set great store in physicians and the medical arts. He personally had himself bled by the bathhouse surgeon on a monthly basis, and he swore that the practice contributed to his health and wellbeing. When he suspected there was bad air about, he hung an apple around his neck spiked with cloves. To purge himself, he would annually retreat to a hot spring; there he bathed and drank vast amounts of mineral water, believing that its passage through his body removed the many impurities that had collected there.

All of these practices he insisted on describing with great enthusiasm to the young Rachel. It had seemed to her that he sought her out for this purpose, as if he were an exuberant priest not only for the church but also for the medical arts. It was not surprising that he addressed his medical sermonettes to her. He deplored the so called "wise women" who utilized herbs and incantations to heal, and he saw, correctly, that she was becoming one. His practices were based on science, he told her, hers on superstition, on the dark arts. And in his mind such practices invariably involved the shadowy hand of the Devil.

Rachel, for her part, soon found him as unpleasant as he apparently found her. The fluid, mystical religiosity that she had absorbed from Gretel clashed with the priest's hierarchical, rule-bound regimen of obedience and empty ritual. She sought sunlight in his homilies but found there only stern correction. Every Sunday his words poked at her like barbs, and her frowns of disapproval were visible from the pulpit. Once, when they were both still young, he confronted her about her behavior in church.

"My behavior?" she asked, astounded.

"You obviously hate everything I say, everything the church teaches, and you make no effort to hide your displeasure."

The man looked sincerely devastated, and Rachel could not imagine why. A parish priest troubled by one frowning parishioner, and a woman at that? The passing of time improved nothing. If she frowned, he noticed. If she stayed away, he confronted her about her absence. His annoyance became anger.

"You draw women away from me, and like sheep the men follow their women. They turn to you for solace and not the church. You place their souls in danger. God is righteous in his anger, but his anger is great."

"Father, I do not understand. I deliver children. I treat fevers. I ease what pain I can. I knowingly do nothing to anger God, or you."

It was true that she did not understand. Surely other women had frowned in his presence, and had avoided Mass. That she possessed some strange power over people in the village, a power that drew them away from the church, struck her as absurd. His disapproval of her seemed personal and inexplicable.

Over the years as the priest's status in the community fell, he became more distant, more disgruntled; a figure both comic and tragic as he stalked through the market mocked by snickering boys. When the people met to urge his removal, she was present but did not speak. When petitions were proposed, she did not sign. She was happy to see him go, but was not among those who journeyed to the Archbishop's palace to present the petition. And yet, the priest hated her. She realized this truth once again when he spotted her in the crowd as he made his triumphant return. Their eyes met and she could feel it to her core.

"Frau Grede will not be released," she said firmly now to the surprised Irmele and Elsebett. "I am sorry to tell you this, but to find her innocent would suggest error. And these men prefer to not be in error." Then Frau Mueller handed her pestle to Irmele. "Would you mind crushing a few leaves, dear girl? My wrist is troubling me."

SIXTY-TWO

They burned the witch Grede at a stake placed in the center of the market square between the church and the village hall in the month of August two days before the Feast of the Assumption of Mary. There had been hangings and beheadings in the square previously, but so far as anyone could remember, this was the first burning of a witch. The space was filled to overflowing with the curious, the cheering and the appalled.

The executioner made his first appearance a week before the execution. Gloriously outfitted, he rode in on the white stallion for which he was famous, and he was accompanied by his wife who arrived in a beautifully appointed carriage. So splendidly was the large woman attired (her saffron-colored bonnet, it was rumored, had been fashioned with silk from Italy) that when she stepped from the carriage, an audible sigh rose from the crowd.

Not everyone was so impressed. "Any fool can see she's the ignorant daughter of some ignorant plowman," said Klara to Katharina as they stood in the crowd. "Married she is to a sweaty smithy who happened to become an executioner of witches. And from the look of her backside she's been feeding on cakes and candies ever since. Her God-given posture, I tell you, is on her hands and knees scrubbing a floor and swinging that fat ass in the air. Which is probably how the man first saw her. Caught him in the wiggle, she did."

The executioner wore a pleated blue hat from which sprouted a fluffy gray feather. Above his skin-colored hose, he preferred garments made of blue cloth, linen above with damask-patterned pants below. Clothing that glittered in the light when he moved. And he had a grace-filled way of moving as he oversaw the construction of a tall platform where the execution would take place. The idea, as Johannes carefully explained to his uncle Sebastian, was to ensure that everyone in the crowd had a good view. The platform itself was built of stone, granting employment for a crew of masons. On the platform the executioner and his team installed a heavy metal base that he had personally designed and forged, and into which the stake would be fitted and around which the fuel would be stacked. If necessary, the wooden ladder giving access to the platform could be removed after the fire had been set.

"Clever, you see," said Johannes. "The witch burns, the stake burns, but the platform and the stake holder survive for another day. That this man knows his craft is apparent."

As the day of execution approached it became clear to the Helgen family how little they had to do with the witch. No one other than Irmele admitted to having actually paid for a consultation. Of course, everyone knew the woman and her enclosure by sight, and they knew others who had made use of her services, which in itself was not a wrong thing to have done. "Don't trouble yourself about it, child," Katherina said, patting Irmele's hand. "Isn't everyone sometimes curious about what the future holds?"

Klara had heard from Anna that the witch was particularly adept at predicting the sex of an unborn child, so it was not surprising that women went to her. According to Basil, some men claimed the witch could foresee a rainstorm four or more days away, a valuable knowledge to have. Ursula revealed what Elsebett had told her, that the witch complained of pain in her joints and that Elsebett had personally prepared a salve and had delivered it to her door.

"And where is that door exactly?" Jacob asked, rousing himself from slumber. Uncle Jacob had developed the admirable ability to marginally follow a conversation while also enjoying a nap.

She was not a landowner, that was agreed. And her home was little more than a shack that required repairs following every heavy storm. She had lived in the village for years, though as Klara pointed out, she was not born to a village family and had no real family here. Her husband had died that summer the plague swept through. No, not the time the eleven people were taken. The earlier one, the one decades before that had taken the life of Old Helgen, the grandfather, that is, of Basil, Jacob and Sebastian.

"She must have been little more than a girl back then," Ursula suggested. Everyone agreed. Her husband had to have been twenty or more years older than she was, a disgusting discrepancy that had caused finger wagging at the time. No one could picture the husband, but word in the village was that he had been a thief and a drunk who spent time in the stocks.

She had never remarried, and she had had no children. She was a decent enough worker. Katharina remembered that she did her part in the fields during harvest, and, according to Sebastian, she gleaned through the stubble after the harvest. It was known that at times she took relief from the church and from the village. And that yellowish enclosure she set up at the corner of the graveyard on market days had been a familiar sight for years, though in retrospect it seemed now a rather shabby one.

Irmele said: "Frau Mueller told us, me and Elsebett that is, that the old woman had never hurt a soul."

Irmele said this apologetically. She continued to feel a kindness toward the old Frau Grede though she was ashamed of the feelings she had. A witch! To have sympathies for her felt wrong somehow. Those warm hands—that is what she remembered—and that one dog who had just kept watching her with eyes so brown, eyes almost kind it had seemed at the time.

"That's the way it is with witches, Irmele," Ursula said, hoping to comfort her niece. "Sometimes you don't know. The Devil is a master of disguises, and what he can do for himself, he can do as well for those in his service, such as this woman."

"She tricked you, child," Katharina said. "She got you into that tent and she made you feel comfortable, and she filled your head with stories, but it was all a trick."

"What are you suggesting?" Klara bellowed. "Everything a trick? Not everything a witch does is evil."

"Not at all, sister Klara. But it is always a step toward evil," Katharina insisted, emphasizing her point with a raised finger. "She was preparing the girl, that's what I'm saying. Had she not been found out who knows where this might have led."

"But Frau Mueller…" Irmele began again, hoping to repeat what the midwife had told them.

"Frau Mueller, Frau Mueller," Katharina exclaimed. "You and Elsebett are the same. You both worship the ground that woman walks on. But Rachel Mueller is not a saint, young lady. And she does not know everything this witch has been doing. If she did, we would have to suspect her as well because only a witch can know fully what another witch is up to."

"Now, what are you saying?" Klara bellowed again. "The midwife a witch!"

"I am not saying that, sister, and you know it. What I am saying is what sister Ursula has just said. That a witch is a master of disguises and deceits. A normal person can never know just what a witch is up to, and if Rachel Mueller claims she knows, then she is talking nonsense and your daughter needs to know that. This witch has lived among us undetected for decades. Who knows what damage she has caused? New stories of betrayals and affronts perpetrated by this woman are coming available every day as people speak out. But until God himself steps forward to pull back the curtain, the full story will not be known. My own first husband's horrible death has always seemed suspicious to me. That man was as sure-footed as a tomcat and entirely sober at the time of his fall. You are a lucky girl, child, that this witch was exposed when she was. We can all give thanks to God and the Archbishop that she has been caught and has confessed and will soon receive the cruel punishment that is due her."

§

At the Feast of the Assumption two days after the burning, the market square was again crowded with people who had come to celebrate the holiday. The mound of ashes, the scattered teeth, the charred bones, had been swept up and tossed onto a dung heap, but the platform remained. Jutting from the blackened metal stand was the charred stump of the stake where the witch Grede had been bound and executed. The stub of flaky charcoal possessed an ominous blackness that seemed to draw attention to itself. Irmele, for one, could not resist staring at it. She felt only confusion about the witch, and about herself. Could it be that she had been taken in by those warm hands? Could she even now be possessed in some way she did not recognize?

Johannes had persuaded Irmele to witness the burning: "This is something that will be talked about for years," he told her. "You will be able to tell your grandchildren that you were there. Your father and mother are going, your aunts and uncles, your cousins as well."

Irmele in turn had begged Elsebett to accompany her, explaining how terrified she was. But when Elsebett spoke about it to Frau Mueller, she learned that her teacher would not be going to the square that day. "If Irmele needs you, I suppose you have to go," Rachel confided to Elsebett. "I feel as though I am abandoning you by staying away, but I do not want that vision to enter my head."

At the feast, the subject dominating the discussion was not the witch herself, or even the execution, but the executioner. It was said that early in the morning of the burning, a Jesuit priest had gone into the cell to hear the witch's final confession and to absolve her of all sin. But after he had left, the executioner himself had met privately with the woman. What she had said to him and he to her no one but God would ever know. But the way he treated her later in the market square astonished everyone. How attentive he was, how gracious even, taking her hand in his as he led the docile woman up the stairs to the stake. "It was as if he were leading a lady onto a dance floor," was the way Katharina had described it.

His attentive behavior stood in vivid contrast to the shouting crowd. "Death to the witch! Death to the witch!" The cry began with one solitary voice but soon spread through the square, a raucous chant expressing fury and callous joy. It would build in intensity, then fall off and build again as if it were the panting breath of some otherworldly monster.

A line of prominent men stood near the platform including the judge, the prosecutor, the bailiff and other members of the Archbishop's staff. Beside them were local dignitaries including the priest, the mayor, the village council and masters of the various guilds. And yet it appeared to many in the crowd that in the eyes of the executioner only two people existed in the square that morning: himself and the witch. Even as the chant rose and fell, even as his assistants stacked firewood around the woman, the executioner directed his attention and addressed his words only to her.

Then finally, when the witch had been secured to the stake, and the wood piled around her, a trembling hush had filled the packed square, and the executioner alone, his blue garments glittering in the sunlight, climbed the ladder. In his right hand he held a flaming torch. He held the torch aloft and stepped close to the witch. Those standing nearest to the platform could see that he was speaking some final words to the bound woman. What was he saying? Speculation spread back from the platform toward the edges of the crowd. He was obviously cursing her! No, he was offering her comfort. He was praying for her, one woman proposed. Or could it be, another voice speculated, that the man was apologizing to the witch for what he was about to do? Was he begging her forgiveness?

"Not a chance," hissed a hoarse voice. "Look at that man! That man is the executioner. That man does not apologize to anyone for anything."

Then, almost as if he were performing a dance pattern, the executioner moved gracefully along the edges of the platform and with flourishing sweeps of the torch, he set the wood aflame all around her. When he was satisfied that the fuel was strongly and evenly lit, he descended the ladder and handed the torch to an assistant. At that moment he turned and faced the platform.

And for the longest time he stood unmoving, looking directly into the face of the woman writhing in the flames. He watched as she screamed. Watched as she cooked and burned. It had been a remarkable, a most terrible sight. Of that everyone agreed.

But at the feast, seated at a long table with her back to the platform, Rachel Mueller had thoughts about things other than the execution or the executioner. She felt compelled to talk about the woman Grede, the way one desired to reminisce about the departed at a funeral. There would be no funeral for Grede. No body remained to bury, none to rise again at the final resurrection. What Rachel remembered, and what she described to Elsebett and Irmele, was the woman's susceptibility to painful inflammations in the ear.

"I met Grede soon after I arrived," she told the two young women. "Like her I was very young at the time, and like me, she too had only recently arrived, brought here by her beast of a husband. She came to us complaining about pain in her ear. It was the kind of ear problem you often see in children, and Grede, while no longer a child, was prone to it. My teacher, the old midwife, had a formula she used. It involved chamomile, marjoram, lavender and wormwood which she mixed together with wine and water. The idea was to pour this substance into the ear three or four times a day."

Rachel chuckled. "The problem was that Grede could not stand having the medicine poured into her ear. She just hated it, and she would push me away rather than submit to the treatment. What I discovered as a result of Grede's resistance, was that you really did not have to pour the formula into the ear for it to work. It is the vapor, not the fluid itself that contains the magic. I learned to heat the medicine, soak it up with a sponge and then place the sponge below the tilted ear so the vapors are taken in."

"That is just what you have taught me to do," Elsebett said. "Have the person tilt their head over the sponge."

"Yes. And it was because of Grede's resistance that I learned that important lesson. The lesson I have passed on to you. Our knowledge is fluid and changing. What I have taught you is different in some ways from what my teachers taught me, the one here and the ones in the convent. You are my book, Elsebett. Everything I have learned I have written into you."

Elsebett reached out and took her teacher's hand. The gesture caused Rachel to look away. She felt tears forming and rolling down her cheeks. Her tears were for herself, she realized, a reaction to the madness she felt around her. But they had to do with Grede as well. With how she still lived in the procedure that Rachel used to treat ear infections. And one day Elsebett might use it to treat the ears of children not yet born. In that way Grede lived on, and she, Rachel, would also still live. What she had passed to Elsebett, Elsebett would, she hoped, in time pass on to her students, having perhaps modified it in some way herself.

"I wish I had not gone to the burning," Irmele said looking around. "I tried not to look, but I could not help myself. They say they killed her dogs too. I heard that just this morning.

They thought she might have bewitched them. But I liked those dogs. They seemed so kind, so gentle."

"I never looked," Elsebett said, almost proudly. "Not once. I stood with my eyes closed. I heard the sounds, of course. That awful chanting. I fear my brother was one of those, I do…. And I smelled the smoke, the burning wood, the flesh, and I felt you beside me crying. I held your hand, didn't I? I remember that. But I never looked at the poor woman and I never watched that man, the executioner that everyone is talking about. That was the one thing I felt I could do. I could refuse to give my eyes to it. I just tried to think some good thoughts about old Frau Grede. I thought about her little shack, how cozy and snug and doggy it was. It was a dogs' house more than a person's house, really. And I thought about her knobby shoulders and her skinny arms. How warm her skin was, and how smooth it felt when I rubbed the salve onto her joints. She liked me to do that. She was always happy when I came."

"Her hands were very warm, too," Irmele said.

"That's awful about the dogs," Elsebett said. "I should have done something. I should have thought of them. I should have gone there and rescued them as soon as she was taken in."

SIXTY-THREE

With the burning of Frau Grede, there arose in the village a passion for finding and exposing witches. Though the contagion had begun elsewhere, it blossomed anew in the village, emerging now not so much from the Archbishop's men as from the people themselves. They felt a lust rise in them, a rage to avenge the injuries done to them. The mood had been souring for some time. The long drought the previous spring was remembered now as a cruel trick with its string of beautiful days that stretched into disaster. It had delayed the barley planting and had resulted in stunted grapes and meager rye and wheat harvests. Storehouses were near empty and accusations of hoarding were muttered in the streets. That the Helgens were named angered and worried Basil. Now, too, the master brewer complained to Zacharias that the inn should stop purchasing beer from Sebastian who belonged to no guild and had served no apprenticeship.

Famine was already at hand for a few and was a certain future for others. The church and the village relief budgets were under strain. For some, the food given out at the Feast of the Assumption of Mary had been the first good meal they had enjoyed in weeks. Bone-thin children were in the streets, sent out to sing and beg. During the long descent from what was remembered now as prosperity, the people had prayed fervently, made confession, done penance as directed. But be it God's anger or the Devil's mischief, their piety had done nothing to improve their condition. The burning of the witch Grede suggested a new way to make things right again.

Three elderly women were called out in the coming days. They were hauled in from the margins of the village and given over to the torturers. One of them was Frau Henn, a cottager, recently widowed, who had worked in the Helgen home during the years that passed between the death of Arved and Basil's marriage to Katharina. A long-time friend of Marsel, she was almost family to the Helgens, though a distant, unpopular member of the family in the eyes of some, unloved by Ursula and Klara and disliked by Katharina, who had encouraged Basil to dismiss her.

Basil was surprised by the news. That woman a witch? She was a mediocre worker, he agreed, a petty filcher, most certainly. A woman with a foul mouth, that too, but a witch?

The news alarmed Katharina. "That woman hates your guts and mine," she said to her husband.

"But is she a witch? I would never have thought that. She and my mother got along fine for years."

"Witch or no witch," Katharina continued, "that woman certainly is a bitch. And when she starts talking you know who she is going to complain against. Don't forget, her husband was a cousin, twice removed, to my late husband. The blood between us is foul and it goes back a long way. If she is a witch, if she has powers given her by the Devil, she might have been the one who pushed that poor man off the roof."

Basil took a deep breath to restrain himself. He was tired of hearing about his wife's first husband and his endless deadly falls from the roof. The fall killed the man, which was certainly unfortunate, but it seemed he would never stop falling.

"I do not see the woman being a witch," he persisted. "If they start dragging in all the foul-tempered old women in this village, claiming they are witches, they're going to need a lot of firewood down in the market square."

§

"Must be witches everywhere," Klara burst out at the Sunday table. "Three more dragged in just yesterday."

"And old Frau Henn, they tell me, was one of them," Ursula said. "Her breath was foul, but I would never have thought her a witch."

Irmele and Elsebett stopped whispering and giggling at the far end of the table. They looked toward their aunt. "Frau Henn?" they said in unison.

"Frau Henn?" Gabriel repeated across from them, his fingers in his bowl.

"Yes, girls, Frau Henn," Katharina said. "I was sorry to hear it myself. Not out of concern for her, mind you. A sack of yellow bile, that one. If ever a bitch deserved the stake, she does. But I worry that she is going to make trouble for this family. Your father, Elsebett, is the one who sent her away from this house. You might not remember that, but you can be sure she does. And she has no thoughts but ill ones for me. If she is a witch—and she must be if they arrested her—she probably had a hand in my man's terrible fall. The trouble between us goes back a long way."

"Her own husband died not long after we let her go," Ursula said. "The poor woman."

"Living off the crumbs the church gives out, that one is," Klara shouted, banging a heavy fist on the table. "A few roots from that tiny patch behind her house. I saw her out there, legs spread like on a horse, digging with a stick in the hard dirt. Nothing more, just that."

Irmele winced. "Legs spread like on a horse?" What does she mean? Whose legs are spread: the horse's, Frau Henn's, her mother's? Glancing across the table, she watched her brother Gabriel pull a length of pork from his bowl. Holding it in his fingers, he began to gnaw on it contentedly. Was she the only person in this family who could never understand just what their mother was saying?

"I was at Herr Henn's passing," Elsebett said. "And a slow and pitiful death, it was. A bad gash gotten on his foot when the axe slipped. Down to the bone, it was. Then gangrene set in and the flesh started to rot. They had no money so the physician stayed away. Herr Lochner, the barber-surgeon, came from the bathhouse to cut away the dead flesh, but it did no good. God was merciful to finally give the poor man his death. But this turn is awful. Frau Henn is not a witch!"

"They arrested her, sister," Johannes said. "They do not arrest for nothing. Something brought it about. Maybe the witch Grede denounced her."

"What I could never figure," Ursula said, "was the woman's scrubbing near the end. Floors, tables, pots, it made no matter. When she finished, the thing was little cleaner than when she started."

"Well, the woman grew blind in the eyes!" Klara yelled. "Perfectly clear to me. She saw a thing no better than Oma did. Oma would say, 'Clean this, polish that,' and she would scrub this and rub on that, and Oma would say, 'That's good.' But it wasn't good. Neither one could see past their noses. A perfect pair, those two. That's it in the shell of a nut!"

"Brother," Elsebett said. "How can you say that? You knew Frau Henn for years. We all did. You saw her most every day. Tell me one thing she did to show she was a witch. One thing."

"Witches do not show they are witches, Elsebett," Katharina said.

"She stole," Johannes said. "Our father caught her at it."

"Okay, she filched some flour, and she should not have done that. But that does not mean she is in league with the Devil. Her husband was feeble and could find no work. They had nothing but what we gave them. So, she took a bit of flour. And now we're going to let them burn her at the stake? This is not right."

"And the smell of her breath was worse than the privy," Johannes added, a half smile breaking on his face. "Like Aunt Ursula said."

"Bad breath does not make you a witch, brother! And a bit of fennel is all it takes to fix it. That old woman is not a witch and you know it. And they are going to torture and burn her."

Katharina shook her head back and forth, clucking like a hen. "You do not know the half of it, young lady. She and I go back a long way. She has had it in for me for years."

"Our grandmother loved her," Elsebett said to Katharina. Then looking at Irmele and Johannes, she added: "Oma would not want this to happen. She would have done what she could to stop it."

"And what might that be?" Johannes asked, laughing. "Are you planning to go see the Archbishop, sister? The Prince-Elector himself? You just go marching into his palace and tell him that some half-blind, foul-breathed old hag in one of his villages is not a witch and should be released. We'll see how far that takes you."

Elsebett jumped up from the table and began to pace back and forth. "You are mocking me, brother! Do not mock me! No, of course I'm not going to the Archbishop's palace, but I might just go to the inn and speak to the Archbishop's men there. And I want you to go with me."

The room got very quiet then. A stunned Klara looked wide-eyed at Ursula. Even Gabriel paused. Ready to dip a chunk of bread into his pottage, he held the bread in the air, looking first at Elsebett and then Johannes.

"Yes, you, brother. And Gabriel, too, if you want. You remember Oma. And you, Irmele. We should go to the inn together, all of us."

"Helgen!" Katharina shouted, pushing herself back from the table and getting to her feet. "Where are the men? Where are the men?"

SIXTY-FOUR

The sons of Johannes and Marsel Helgen were in the stable, crouched down beside the older of their two oxen. The old ox lay on his side, wild-eyed, breathing erratically, obviously in great distress.

For Basil the stricken animal confirmed what he had come more and more to realize: the Helgen luck had turned and ran now truly sour. Crops failed; the prudent, once admired, were now envied by the improvident and accused of hoarding. And now this. Without a team of healthy oxen you failed as a farmer. You did not plant, you did not harvest; you didn't pay your taxes or your rent; in the end you didn't eat or drink. Yes, you could borrow an ox, or better a team, but when you most needed to borrow, everyone needed their own. So, you planted early or late, you harvested in rain or sleet when the crop was not quite ripe or a little beyond ripe and blown to a frazzle. You did your work on those days when the better prepared could loan you an animal; and the animal the friend did loan you, he would have preferred to give a day of rest.

As he stared down on the stricken ox Basil knew he should have anticipated this. It was not bad luck. The animal was obviously past its prime, had been for a year or more. A more prudent farmer would have sold it, or the team, perhaps to a family with less land to till who might have gotten a few year's use from it. Then the Helgens could have purchased a new animal or a new team well in advance of the coming harvest. Now they had nothing to sell and would soon be stuck with a mass of dead flesh to bury.

More than that, oxen were a team. They needed to be trained, not just singly but together. You had to know them, and they you. And the team was composed not just of the oxen but also of the man, the plow, the wagon, the very earth. It all needed to fit together.

As Basil stared down on the distressed ox, he could feel Jacob and Sebastian turning to him as they always had for leadership. He felt himself a failure and their dependence a burden, a weight pressing down on his neck and shoulders. It was at this moment that Katharina burst into the stable, shouting that he needed to come immediately into the house. His daughter was acting in a crazy way.

"Helgen, you have to hear this! I insist you hear this, Helgen...your daughter..." Katharina almost pushed her husband into the house and then sat heavily back in her chair. "Tell your father, Elsebett. Just tell him what you plan to do."

Three men looked annoyed at having been so abruptly summoned by the aggravated Katharina, and yet they appeared oddly obedient as well, standing in an orderly line arranged by age. Marsel might have noticed, had she still been alive, that they resembled the three little boys they had once been, as if her man had returned to life and had ordered them inside to be threatened with the handle of his dreaded whip.

"Well, tell him. Go on, tell him!" Katharina insisted.

Elsebett looked at Irmele who, though deeply ashamed of herself, quickly looked away. Gabriel, his head down, focused on the bowl as he soaked up the remaining pottage with his bread. Johannes, she noticed, was gloating.

"Well," she began. "It is about Frau Henn, Father. Oma's friend. The woman who used to work here. She has been…"

"Yes, my wife has told me."

"That's not right, Father! Frau Henn is not a witch. She does not deserve to be tortured and put to death for stealing some flour."

"For stealing…?" Basil looked sharply at his wife.

"She has not been arrested for stealing flour, young lady, and you know it. She has been accused of witchcraft, of making congress with the Devil. And what does it mean to make congress with the Devil? It means you have denounced God and the Blessed Virgin and have pledged loyalty to the Evil One. Who knows what foul deeds she has performed with the Devil's help? So tell your father what you told us. Tell him what you plan to do."

Elsebett took a deep breath. "I want to go to the inn, Father. I want to tell the men there, the Archbishop's men. I want to tell them that I have—we have—we have known this woman for many years. I will tell them that she worked in our home with our grandmother, and that we have no reason to think she is a witch. That is all I want to do."

"That is not all. You want to drag your cousins with you!" Katharina shouted.

"Yes, that is correct. I would like us to go together. It would be stronger that way." Elsebett paused and looked around the room. "I would like all of us to go, every Helgen together."

"Every Helgen!" Katharina exploded, a look of amazement on her face. "Every Helgen she wants now!"

"They are going to torture this woman, Father. This woman who helped cook our food and clean our house. She sewed my apron, the old apron that had been Oma's, the one I still wear for work around the house. And after they have tortured her, they will drag her up on that terrible platform in front of the whole village. They will tie her to a stake like they did Frau Grede, and they will burn her to death. For what? The woman is not a witch!"

Elsebett's eyes were stinging; she was ashamed and embarrassed, furious and frightened. "I know that," she sputtered. "We all know that. Frau Henn does not deserve to die. She is not a witch!"

"Do you hear that, Helgen? Do you hear what your daughter is saying?" Katharina was struggling again to get to her feet. "Do you have any idea, young lady, of the damage you would bring to this family? We would all be at risk as a result of your rash behavior. And you want to drag poor Irmele along with you? Who already knew the witch Grede and did business with her? And young Gabriel here, and your own brother as well. This is madness, Helgen! This is your unmarried daughter speaking. She is your ward. Her behavior is your responsibility."

There followed a moment of tense silence, and then Katharina, unable to restrain herself, shouted, "This woman is your daughter, Helgen. She is your responsibility!"

"Wife! Silence yourself. I have heard your words. You need not keep repeating them."

There followed then another pause as Elsebett wiped her eyes with the hem of her apron.

"I know nothing of witches," Basil Helgen continued after the pause. "I am a simple farmer in this village, a plowman. I know land and animals and the husbandry of them. Of witches I know nothing. Nothing of who is and who is not; nothing of what they do, or what they do not do. But what you have said to us, daughter, has moved me deeply. Not for the woman, for whom I care little. But from what I hear in your voice. What I hear is the passion that I so loved in your dear, departed mother..."

That Basil was deeply moved became obvious. Brushing a hand across his eyes, he leaned back, bracing himself against the wall where he waited until his daughter had stopped sobbing.

"But I must forbid you, Elsebett, from speaking to the Archbishop's men. Frau Helgen is right. The only thing we have is this house and the land we Helgens own and manage. It is only this and the strength of our labors and the grace of God that keep us from famine and despair. The danger is very real, they tell me. There are those among the Archbishop's men who seek wealth more than witches. They use the rage building among the people to make accusation against those who have something with the goal of taking it away from them. That is what men have told me and I have no reason to doubt their words."

Elsebett wiped her eyes and nodded. "So, Frau Henn dies," she said as Irmele jumped to her feet and embraced her.

Her father nodded. "If the judge orders it so, then, yes, she surely will."

"After being placed on the rack and tortured to within an inch of her life."

"Yes, that too."

"Frau Henn, Oma's friend. The woman who worked in this house the whole time I was growing up. Who sewed my clothes and sometimes teased me about my hair."

"That is quite enough, Elsebett," Katharina said. "Your father has spoken."

'Yes, he has, Frau Helgen," Elsebett said, with a slight nod toward her stepmother. "And I will obey."

Then she turned and addressed her father. "But tell me, Father, because, as your obedient daughter I need to know. If it were Frau Mueller, my teacher, they took in, would you forbid me to speak for her?"

Basil Helgen slumped again against the wall, turning partially away.

"Elsebett!" Katharina shouted rushing toward her husband.

"Or if it were your wife?" Elsebett shouted. "Or my dear Irmele here? Would I be permitted to speak for her?"

"Stop!" Johannes shouted. He ran forward and gripped the shoulders of his sobbing sister.

But Elsebett, her eyes red, her nose dripping, pulled herself free of her brother and turned again toward her father.

"And if they come for me, Father? Would you speak? Would you or any Helgen step forward to speak on my behalf?" Wild eyed now, she looked around the room. "Anyone? Would anyone of you dare speak for me?"

At that moment, the flat of Basil Helgen's heavy right hand slapped hard against his daughter's face and knocked her to the floor.

"Finally!" Katharina shouted. "It's about time!"

Then a second blow sent Katharina to the floor as well, and Basil spun around and ran from the room.

SIXTY-FIVE

Basil Helgen had not felt such self-hatred since he stared down on the face of his dying Arved; the day he came to realize fully that his lust had brought death to the virtuous woman who had delivered only lilt and laugher into his life. He recognized himself now on a continuum: he and his father, the whip-wielding Johannes. To have brutally struck Elsebett who had spoken so earnestly, so passionately had only confirmed his ongoing failure.

Alone, he knelt in the stable. Even his brothers had not thought they could follow him out the door. He placed his still-stinging hand on the head of the dying ox and felt the coarse hair against his palm. In that moment, in a strange and narrow way, Basil felt closer to the old ox than he did to any other living creature. They were a team, truly wedded together, and they had been for fifteen years.

Arved, like Elsebett, might have wanted him to act to save the arrested woman, but they did not carry his responsibilities. He was the head of the Helgen family and he alone had to decide. Alone and imperfect, a failure in many ways, but he was right: the decision was obvious. Only one thing absolutely had to be saved and that was the Helgen holdings. What the family had acquired over generations and was now in his name, and would in time pass to the Helgen heirs. Telling no one, he had scratched his mark on a will. When he died the land and home would pass equally to those adult males in the family then alive. Not to Katharina's family, but to the heirs of Johannes and Marsel Helgen. Nothing else mattered but to protect that which he was charged to pass on.

As a boy, Basil's grandfather—Old Helgen as he was known in the family—had worked as the village shepherd. He had a saying he liked to repeat: The smart sheep stays in the center of the flock. Basil found that to be good advice in the present moment. To stand mute might reek of cowardice, but that was the way it had to be.

He pushed himself back to his feet. He and his brothers must to go now in search of a new team of oxen, a young strong team. And they would have to sell or borrow whatever they needed to accomplish that.

§

The next day, a Monday that began with a squall at dawn that included an intense downpour, swirling winds and streaks of lightning followed by thunder that boomed and echoed off the forested hill, the Archbishop's men, to the surprise of most everyone, packed their belongings and left the village. The torture ladder remained in the village hall, its wagon parked patiently below the clock tower. In the square, the executioner's metal stand that had secured Frau Grede's stake was removed by three men and loaded onto a cart. But the stone platform itself remained, thick and flat, looking somehow abandoned, as if it were the pedestal of an idol no longer worshiped. Boys scaled its sides and jumped off. One reckless lad positioned himself in the center and began to writhe and scream in feigned agony. Confined in their cell, Frau Henn and the two other recently-arrested women felt the thunder vibrate in their chest cavities and trembled. But by midmorning the storm had passed and the Archbishop's men were gone.

Where had they gone? And why? Rumors rushed from lips to ears along the muddy streets. Many felt betrayed, a few relieved. At the inn, Zacharias, calm as usual, explained to Johannes that the men had gone to the city but would return. When? They did not say, only that they would be back. They had reserved and continued to pay for the rooms. Why so suddenly? That too was not clear, though he had heard that some judge in the city had been convicted of witchcraft. A judge? Someone like that, Zacharias said. A man in a position of great importance. Of witchcraft? Yes, it was definitely witchcraft.

The blood of the great-grandfather who had died in the Peasant War still ran in the veins of Johannes Helgen. A judge! The idea that a judge had been pulled from his lofty perch possessed a visceral attraction for Johannes. "Imagine," he exclaimed to his cousin, "a judge convicted of witchcraft!"

In the home of Frau Rachel Mueller little notice was taken of the departure of the Archbishop's men. When Elsebett returned to the house after being knocked to the floor by her father, she had not been able to speak a word of it. So stunned was she, so shocked and shamed, so embattled and bewildered, so furious and betrayed, so humiliated, so bound and gagged and silenced. Silenced, even to the point that she was unable to speak to this woman whom she loved and admired, the one alone who might have brought her comfort.

Would Frau Mueller notice? Was her cheek as swollen and red as it was sore? Elsebett had no idea. She could drink beer and chew her bread. In a way that too infuriated her: as if the insult she had suffered demanded more injury than she had received.

Rachel Mueller, whose business it was to observe such things, did notice the swollen face, the discoloring that had begun to appear on the girl's left cheek. But though she ached to speak, there was something complete and distant about Elsebett that restrained her. She waited until her student rose to take the mugs to the wash pail.

"I can do that, Elsebett…"

"No," Elsebett said. Her voice was insistent, her manner deliberate as she rinsed the mugs and set them on the counter. Then she bowed slightly toward her teacher, her eyes filling with tears. "I'm sorry." And she turned and walked to her room. She needed to be silent and alone. Like an injured animal, she wanted to crawl into a dark and private place to suffer and cry, perhaps to heal, perhaps to die.

The following morning she was able to describe what had happened and to express her fears to her teacher. "It's not over. The injury is ongoing. Frau Henn is going to suffer and die; they will do nothing to stop it. And he forbids me as well."

"It has become fear," Frau Mueller said enigmatically.

"What? Is that it? I don't understand."

"The contagion is a living thing and it continues to transform itself. I used to think it was excitement, but now it has become rage and fear. It fills us. The contagion has become fear, and it has entered us all."

Elsebett scowled. The last thing she needed to hear was philosophy. "But why did he hit me?" She started to sniffle again. "My father! And her too? He struck her as hard as he struck me."

The two women threw their arms around each other, and for a time they had no need to speak. But then Rachel abruptly pushed herself back, her strong spiny fingers sinking into the flesh of Elsebett's shoulders. Her stare was so intense that Elsebett found it disconcerting.

"There is something I must say to you, Elsebett. It's about the future and I cannot delay speaking any longer."

Elsebett hardly heard her. Her neck ached; her cheek was tender to the touch, and she could not resist touching it. Her head was over-stuffed. She had no interest in the future; she was still reeling from the recent past.

"What I am about to tell you may be my fear talking, but I think not. If the Archbishop's men come for me, Elsebett…"

"What?" Elsebett shook her aching head. "No…"

She admitted to herself at that moment that she had mentioned to her family the possibility that Frau Mueller, even she herself, could be arrested, but she had not truly believed such a thing possible. She had been trying to make a point: Frau Henn was not a witch and failing to help her was a travesty. But Frau Henn was not Frau Mueller. Frau Henn was an elderly, unskilled cottager. Her teacher was the midwife. She was a skilled woman, essential to the community, recognized and paid as such by the village council. The idea that she could be arrested for witchcraft was the kind of horrific fantasy that one child whispered to another.

"Yes!" her teacher was insisting. "Listen to me, Elsebett. If they come it will mean that I have been denounced. And if they have denounced me, they will likely have denounced you as well. So, if they do come for me, you must promise…you must promise that you will flee the village."

Elsebett saw now that the so-called contagion had indeed captured her teacher. Frau Mueller's hands were squeezing her shoulders with a desperate intensity. Her eyes had the look of panic about them. The expression reminded her of what she had seen on the face of Herr Henn when he lay gashed and bleeding from that axe wound to his foot.

She took a deep breath and tried to steady herself. If her teacher was panicking it was very important that she not do the same.

"Frau Mueller, they are not going to arrest you."

"But if they do…"

"I'm sorry, but they won't."

"But if they do, you must go to your aunt Anna's."

"What?"

"Do not go home. If I am arrested, the Helgens will think you dangerous. They love you, Elsebett, but they are so afraid. I have spoken with your aunt about this. She remembers what we did for Agnes."

"Aunt Anna?"

"Yes! She will take you in. She has agreed; even hide you awhile if that is necessary. And then, if you go there, she has promised to speak with Zacharias. Or maybe Frans will help if he can be reached. The idea is to get you to Agnes in Cologne. Zacharias told us, remember, that this madness has not spread to Cologne. It is in another jurisdiction entirely; the writ of the Archbishop does not extend to Cologne. I pray you will be safe there."

Once—she must have been fifteen or sixteen—Elsebett had traveled with her family to Trier for a celebration at the cathedral. It was the time that Christ's robe was brought out and displayed, and lines of people came to see it. On a couple of other occasions, she, along with Irmele and the wild boys, had ridden to a neighboring village, laughing and bouncing in the back of her uncle Sebastian's cart. But those journeys marked the boundaries of Elsebett's world. Cologne was just a name to her. She had no real idea where it was, or what lay between there and the house where they now sat.

She shook her head as if she wanted to free herself from the very idea. To be a fugitive in a strange city. To not see Irmele or her family again. To not walk through the village. No. It would be like stepping outside of her own skin and trying to walk away from it. Besides, it was not going to happen. The Archbishop's men will not arrest her teacher.

"No, Frau Mueller, I will not go. I will not leave this village, or my family, or you. I cannot. They won't arrest you. But if they did, I would disobey my father. I would plead for you."

Rachel shook her violently. "No! That is exactly what you must not do!"

"I will," Elsebett insisted. "I will plead for you as my teacher. I will plead on behalf of all the women you have helped and those who need your help now. But I will not leave."

"No, you must flee!" Rachel loosened her grip and let her hands fall to her sides. She found herself shaking uncontrollably. Tears started to stream down her cheeks. Dread, terror, love. She had never experienced such emotion, such fear and love as at that moment she felt for Elsebett.

§

On a sunny afternoon a week later Frans arrived by cargo boat and came directly to the home of Frau Rachel Mueller. Elsebett, who had not seen or heard from him for several weeks, rushed to greet him. Rachel, too, was overjoyed to see the young man. Now she could speak to him about Elsebett. Perhaps he could persuade her to flee. He might even help her flee.

"The most surprising thing has happened," Frans exclaimed when he and the two women had settled in the study. "You will remember the sorry state I was in when I last left your home. I was so worried, so fearful. I had abandoned my place of work, as you will recall. And I felt only dread at the thought of going back. Then, when I finally got up the courage, I found on my desk a message from the Archbishop asking to see me."

"The Archbishop himself?" Elsebett was awestruck.

Frans nodded his head rapidly. "Yes! A note written and signed by the Archbishop! Do you know that he is only rarely in the city? He has a country house somewhere. And another palace beside this one. They tell me he is often in the company of the Jesuits. Anyway, I had never met him personally except the time he visited the manor and the lord introduced me. At that time I was little more than a boy. Then, the morning I left the city to come here…did I tell you this? I saw His Eminence in the cathedral. He was there with a large group of men and I had actually hidden my face at the time. I felt only shame that I had run and I feared he might recognize me. What a state I was in!"

"Yes, you told us," Elsebett said, laughing. She felt giddy that Frans was sitting a few feet away.

"And what a state I was in when I found the note. Can you imagine, finding a note written and signed by the Archbishop on my desk? At that moment I feared the worse. Perhaps His Grace had already informed the lord and my family of how I had abandoned him and my responsibilities. Now, he was going to dismiss me and send me home like a punished schoolboy."

"We understand," Rachel Mueller said, her tone hinting at the impatience she felt.

"Of course, I had to go. To his offices in the palace, that is. And there I sat for an hour or more, my anxiety ever increasing as important people entered and departed with sheaves of documents. Finally, I was admitted to his inner office. I found His Grace seated behind a desk, a huge gold chain and cross hanging on his chest. The only other persons in the room were his secretary, a short, abrupt Jesuit, and a large, bald man who stood silent and unmoving, his arms across his chest. This man I had also seen in the cathedral. He is, I assume, assigned to guard the physical security of His Eminence.

"I had never been in such a situation in my life. You cannot imagine the sense of power found in that room! There sat the Archbishop in person, slightly elevated of course. An elector, a counsellor to the Emperor. I was terrified. But I must tell you the Archbishop is not well. He gives the appearance of being crippled by some affliction that has pinched his face and tightened his extremities. His movements are careful as if he cannot quite trust his hands to faithfully carry out his intentions. I noticed a slight trembling as he reached for the message. He has deteriorated dramatically since the first time I met him."

"He reached for a message?" Elsebett asked, confused.

"Yes, I'm sorry. The note I had found on my desk. Fortunately, I had thought to bring it with me because it became obvious the Archbishop had no idea who I was or why I was there."

"Oh my!" Elsebett gushed.

"He looked at me and then at his secretary and the secretary asked me the purpose of my visit. I handed him the message. He read it. When he gave it to the Archbishop, the secretary whispered something in his ear. The Archbishop looked up. He studied me for a moment. Then he appeared to smile, not a real smile, just a pinched hint of a smile. 'From Fetterwalde?' he asked.

"I nodded. Fetterwalde is the name of the estate where I grew up. 'And you worked on the confession?' I nodded again, realizing that he was referring to the professor who had confessed and recanted. I had seen copies plastered all over town when I returned. 'We have heard good reports of your work,' the Archbishop said. I bowed, feeling at that moment a relief so sudden and complete that I thought my knees might buckle and I would end prostrate on the floor."

Frans laughed heartily at the memory, and Elsebett joined him, feeling an expanding sense of relief. But Frau Mueller could do no more than smile. And like the Archbishop's smile, hers was but the hint of a smile.

SIXTY-SIX

In the quiet of Frau Mueller's study, Frans described a mighty struggle that was taking place in the territory between God and the Devil. In this battle, the Archbishop himself along with the Governor of the city stood as God's representatives and the Evil One's arch-enemies. Some weeks before, he told them, his voice soft and conspiratorial, word had come to the palace of a fifteen-year-old boy in a small village. This boy had been beguiled by a confessed witch into attending several witches' sabbaths. According to the boy, he had ridden to the sabbaths on the back of a black goat, and the reason he was taken there, was to beat a drum to aid the witches and devils in their dancing. But while he was there, he saw and heard many things."

"This boy was fifteen years old?" Frau Mueller asked, her tone skeptical.

"He *is* fifteen years old, Frau Mueller. All of this has happened quite recently. When the Archbishop heard his pitiful story, he had the boy brought to the city, to the Electoral Palace itself, so he could be secluded and protected. And there, instructed by our priests, be freed from the bondage that the witches had placed him in."

"Have you met this youth?" Frau Mueller wanted to know.

"No, I have not met him. He is now being held in the Jesuit's college, I understand. This is because even while he was at the palace, he was badly tormented at night by devils who beat on him and threatened him with numerous woes. According to the man who told me this story, the boy was not safe even at the college until by the benedictions of the church, the room where he is kept had been purged by exorcisms and freed from all molestations of the Devil."

"I see."

"All of this was necessary," Frans continued, "because when the boy himself was being exorcised in the college's sanctuary in accordance with Catholic ritual, the priests noticed that he kept staring at the window-slit nearest the altar. Though at first he denied it, he later confessed that he was staring at the window-slit because he had seen Sambuco outside, looking in and threatening him."

"Sambuco?" Elsebett asked, glancing at her teacher. "Who is Sambuco?"

"I wanted to know the same, Elsebett. And here was what the Jesuit told me. When you have renounced God and the virgin Mother of God, and have made promises to the Devil, you are assigned to a master demon. This demon watches to make sure you keep the promises you have made to the Evil One. Apparently, this boy's demon is named Sambuco. And Sambuco was looking in through the window-slit, giving him the evil eye to make certain he did not waiver in his loyalty to the Devil. This in the very sanctuary of the Jesuit college!"

Rachel Mueller had been sitting quietly, listening with her eyes closed. Now she looked up and studied the young man. "Do you find this credible, Frans? A village boy of fifteen who has traveled by goat to a witches' sabbath and has a personal demon named Sambuco? Is it not probable that the boy you describe suffers some imbecility of the brain that causes him to speak in this strange manner?"

"I do absolutely believe the truth of what I am telling you, Frau Mueller. Much of what the boy has testified to has been confirmed by confessed witches who were also present at the sabbaths. Moreover, the man who told me of these events is himself a Jesuit at the college. He personally witnessed much of what I have described as having happened there. But there is more I must relate concerning this boy."

"Please continue then," Frau Mueller said.

"As I told you, the boy has been present at several witches' sabbaths. He has seen firsthand what goes on there and he has denounced a number of people he recognized as being present, people who would not have been there had they not been witches themselves.

"At one sabbath he witnessed a group of witches plotting to bewitch both the Archbishop and the Governor. At another he described an important man from the city who had arrived at the sabbath in a golden coach. In the presence of a number of witches including the boy, this man had boasted of how he had administered a deadly potion to the sleeping Archbishop."

"To the Archbishop?"

"Yes, and in the Electoral Palace! Later, the boy related all of this directly to the Archbishop himself. He described the man who had made the boast and the man he described was someone the Archbishop recognized. And he was a man who could have had access to his private chamber.

"Not only that, but the Archbishop told me personally that the boy had named the exact date the attack had supposedly occurred. And here is the amazing thing. The morning following that night, the Archbishop, though completely unaware of the attack, had woken very ill and had remained near death for several days. Not until a doctor prepared a healing draft for him to drink, did he recover. This is some indication of how serious matters have become."

"Yes," Frau Mueller said, glancing at Elsebett.

"The Archbishop, I must tell you, looked quite frightened as he told me this. He obviously believes, as do those around him, that he and the Governor are under attack by the Devil himself."

Frans then reached beneath his blouse and pulled out a waxen image suspended from a string. He held it forward so the two women could examine it. The pendent showed a lamb holding a flag and on the white flag was a red cross.

"An Agnus Dei," Frau Mueller said, studying the pendant. "I have been told that these pendants are consecrated by the Pope. Each one individually."

"Yes, Frau Mueller, that is correct. Mine was given me by the Archbishop himself. He and the men on his staff wear them day and night to protect themselves from the Devil's powers. When he gave me this, the Archbishop confessed that on the night of the attack he had carelessly removed the Agnus Dei from his neck before going to sleep. Because of this he was made vulnerable, and he urged me to never make the same mistake."

"I see," Rachel Mueller said. She looked at Elsebett and smiled. "Perhaps we should have a bit of cake. Would you, dear?"

SIXTY-SEVEN

As Elsebett left for the cakes, Rachel and Frans sat for a moment in what seemed to both of them, an uncomfortable silence. This young man felt so dear to her. He could be a son, a younger brother, a favored nephew. He was charming, innocent, well-intended, and her dear Elsebett was obviously in love with him.

But what had made Rachel feel particularly close to Frans, was that they had been co-conspirators. Here was an intelligent, educated young man who shared her doubts that the territory was infested with people who were in league with the Devil, witches who needed to be exposed and exterminated. But now he had returned to the fold; he had become a true lamb of the Archbishop.

Rachel Mueller felt deeply abandoned at that moment. Was there anyone? Did there exist in the territory a single individual other than that poor, tortured, recanting professor who believed as she did? It was clear from Frans's words that the palace and the Jesuit college were rife with true believers, terrified men who feared that a demon lurked in every shadow. Of course, among them there may be some who were duplicitous, cynical and calculating. Men who were familiar with the dense corridors of the palace and the courts who were utilizing the fervor of the contagion to destroy their enemies and fatten their purses. But that realization brought no comfort to Rachel. And perhaps even those men trembled, and in the dark of night pressed their waxen lambs to their chests.

She herself trembled. She herself wished she had a consecrated Agnus Dei to hang around her neck. That the Devil existed she had no doubt. That he was the enemy of mankind who sought to cause harm was obvious. But that women and men swore loyalty to him, that they flew through the night on brooms and caused hailstorms and met in sabbaths to worship him, seemed ridiculous to her. That torturing such people caused them to reveal the truth, that casting them to the flames purged the land of evil, these things she could not accept. Though, in a way, she wished she could. How much easier it would be to join the crowd, to raise her voice with the clamor.

When Elsebett returned with refreshments, Frans was eager to talk about the judge, the man who had tried witches, and who had now been convicted of being one himself.

"At the trial," he said between bites, "I was one of the two men who prepared the transcript. Think of it! The head of the civil court. A judge who had himself presided over the trials of witches. This man was a former rector of the university, the only non-cleric to ever hold that position. He was a personal advisor to the Archbishop, and a man of great wealth and distinction.

"You can understand why the Archbishop insisted that extreme care be taken with this trial. A high judge on trial for witchcraft! Word of it is on the lips of everyone. News of the trial has spread to every corner of the Empire. And beyond! To Amsterdam and France, to England, and of course to Rome itself. So, there were two us who kept precise records of every word said, and at night we compared them word by word to make sure there were no errors."

Elsebett was astounded. "How could this man be a witch? How could he have fallen to such low estate as to be himself on trial?"

"That is the marvel of it," Frans exclaimed. "It sounds impossible, but I was there. I saw it happen. The evidence against him is impossible to deny. The Governor and the head prosecutor have been collecting it for months. More than twenty confessed witches have testified that they saw him at a witches' sabbath. I told you that when His Grace heard the boy's testimony, he recognized the man who could have administered the deadly potion that nearly killed him. Well, that man was this judge! Not only did the Archbishop recognize him from the boy's description, but the boy himself, on seeing the judge, identified him as a regular at the sabbaths. Moreover, the judge tried to escape. He is an old man, and he was caught at the New Gate burdened with a large satchel weighted down with gold coins. The rabble in the street, you see, students most of them, had been hounding him. They had taken to following him everywhere and found him out. You must agree that nothing suggests guilt so much as an attempt to flee."

Rachel and Elsebett stared at each other, each seeming to hold her breath for a moment. Then Frau Mueller sighed loudly and began to speak:

"It does not sound unreasonable to me, Frans, that an innocent person might attempt to flee. Take this judge. He is being harassed by crowds in the street, as you say, and fearing torture from the courts, might he not seek to flee even though he were innocent of the charges made against him?"

"A common man, yes, Frau Mueller. I could accept that. But an esteemed judge? A man of such great wealth and position? I think it more reasonable that, were he innocent, he would use his wealth and position to defend himself rather than give them up for a life of exile."

"But why, in the first place, would such a man go to a witches' sabbath? Whatever such a thing is." Elsebett's expression suggested she was describing something that gave off a disgusting smell.

"More than twenty witches testified to it, Elsebett, both men and women from various parts of the territory. Among them were two priests who had themselves been convicted of witchcraft. The priests were brought before the judge personally and they denounced him to his face. The transcripts of the other witches were presented at the trial. They all saw him at one sabbath or another. Two testified that he created the snails that destroyed gardens. Others that he plotted the death of the Archbishop and the Governor. Still others that he helped to dig up the body of a recently buried child. This child's heart the witches cooked in a fritter and ate believing that to do so would keep them from confessing their loyalty to the Evil One. All of this and more they denounced him of."

"Confessed witches, Frans?"

"Yes, Frau Mueller. More than twenty of them."

"So, all these denunciations were gained through torture?"

"Of course. That is the method, Frau Mueller. I discussed this frankly with the Archbishop. I confessed to him my concerns about the use of torture and he kindly explained his position to me. Yes, people deny they are witches at the beginning, but after torture they admit that they are witches and they describe sabbaths and other strange events, sometimes in great detail. So it is legitimate to ask whether the torture forces them to tell the truth, or forces them to lie so to end the torture."

"Yes, Frans, that is exactly the question."

"And that is the question I dared to ask His Eminence, Frau Mueller. And the Archbishop told me that he has devised a method to ensure that the truth is known. After a witch has confessed and has denounced others, and after she has been sentenced to death, the Archbishop insists that another step be taken. The witch is then given a confessor and is allowed to meet with him, and after making confession she is absolved of all sins. After that a Mass is celebrated and she is permitted to take communion. So, you see, she now stands before God and the Church as free of sin."

"But she is still sentenced to die?"

"Yes, Elsebett, the sentence does not change. But her fate after death is much improved, you see, provided she does not sin again. So here is the final step as the Archbishop described it to me. The witch is now told to repeat her confession and her denunciations. You must agree there is every reason for her to now tell the truth, otherwise she would be lying and would place her soul in danger. And can you imagine? These confessed witches tell again the same story! They admit they are witches. They describe the same terrible things they have done and they denounce the same people. And in the case of more than twenty of them, the judge was one of those they denounced."

"And if they change their story?" Frau Mueller wanted to know. "If they go back to denying they are witches would they not again be submitted to torture?"

Frans looked flustered for a moment. Apparently, he had not considered that possibility. "So far I as I know, Frau Mueller, none of them has ever changed her story."

"And this judge? Was he, too, tortured?"

"He was, Elsebett. It had to be because in the beginning he denied everything. And it was my responsibility to be among those who witnessed it. My job keeping the records required that I be there, and I must admit it was a very difficult experience for me."

"You were there? As this man was being tortured?" Elsebett could hardly believe the words she was saying. Her Frans?

Frans looked pained. "You must understand, Elsebett, this work is not easy for anyone. Not for the Archbishop, certainly not for me. As you know, the last time I was here I was in serious doubt. Had I known then a safe way to leave, one that would not have damaged my reputation or those of my lord or my family, I would have done so."

"But…"

"But I did go back," he continued. "And His Grace welcomed me and gave me this pendant which I keep always near my heart. He has blessed me with more important work and has increased my renumeration. In this great battle, he knows that I am loyal to him, and that I will to the best of my ability do what I can to be of use to him."

"But…" Elsebett repeated one final time.

"No, I understand, Elsebett. And you as well, Frau Mueller. I can see the concern on your faces. For the two of you, being on the outside, seeing all of this only from the outside, it must be difficult to grasp—as it was for me. But once you have been inside as I have been. In the courtroom, hearing the testimony of confessed witches. Two ordained priests, think of it! Confessed witches, both of them, denouncing an esteemed judge to his face. Or once you have been, again as I have, inside the office of the Archbishop. Being face to face with His Eminence himself. Hearing first hand his heartfelt concerns for the people of his territory. Knowing the tremendous personal risk that this campaign has brought to him. Knowing how frightened he is, seeing how it has aged him. Once you have witnessed what I have witnessed, then you would know that this is not madness. The Devil is fighting back! But His Grace will not waiver. Nor will I. Do you understand? I do so hope you understand!"

Frau Mueller placed her hands on her lap. She looked at Elsebett and saw on the young woman's face an expression of absolute devastation.

"Yes, Frans," Frau Mueller said. "I understand what you are saying. I think we both understand. We understand perfectly."

SIXTY-EIGHT

From the moment Johannes heard that a judge had been convicted of witchcraft and would be publicly executed, he could think of little else. The death of the old ox, the arrest of Frau Henn, even the row between his sister and his father, paled in comparison to this great historic event. No wonder the Archbishop's men had left the village so quickly. They, too, did not wish to say to their grandchildren, years from now, that they had been elsewhere on the day the rich and esteemed judge was consigned to the flames.

How fortunate he was, then, to run into Frans in the village square. They found passage on a cargo boat that would carry them downriver to the city. He could even stay overnight in Frans's room. And Frans was equally happy to see Johannes. He was troubled that his meeting with Elsebett and Frau Mueller had not gone well. He had hoped that both of them, particularly Elsebett, would be excited by how his career had blossomed.

"But they seemed more disappointed than excited," Frans admitted to Johannes.

The two young men were standing on the river-side of the boat so as to not interfere with the tow and the crew. The river flowed gently: they could hear it lap against the creaking hull. The graceful hills across the water were green in the early autumn, though a few leaves on some of the trees had begun to turn. The tow rope scraped against the wooden boat; it bowed and flexed, stretching across to the bank to where the team of horses trotted along the path. The pull to the city was the easy part of the animals' day: it was the upstream pull where they earned what little grain they received.

"I admit, Johannes, that I take a certain pride in my ability to communicate my thoughts accurately and completely. My father teases me about my ceaseless talking, but it is only teasing. At the university I was not afraid to speak my mind to a professor or to a group of older students. The same is true now of my work. That a man has lived more years on this earth than I, or was born to a higher status, does not silence me, though I am careful to always show the proper respect.

"But on this occasion I failed. I thought Frau Mueller and Elsebett would be excited for me. Here I am, a son of servants, a descendent of serfs, and yet I now work with, indeed regularly speak with, the Archbishop himself, an elector to the Emperor."

Frans reached beneath his tunic and pulled out the Agnus Dei. "Look at this. Consecrated by the Pope himself and given to me personally by the Archbishop. It is a shield against the Devil's designs. I am now an important member of the Archbishop's campaign, and certainly a man hated by the Devil himself. The Evil One would love nothing more than to tempt me to betray the Archbishop and by so doing serve his diabolical wishes."

Johannes cupped the object in the palm of his hand and examined it closely. He could feel the warmth that the waxen image retained from Frans's body. The pendant felt magical to him, as if possessed of a mysterious power.

"Did you show this to my sister?" Johannes asked, handing back the pendant.

"Of course. And she was very impressed. Both were, perhaps Frau Mueller even more than Elsebett. Frau Mueller's admiration was, shall we say, the more sophisticated. She is better acquainted with such things. She has had greater exposure to the outside world. More, certainly, than our dear Elsebett…which, of course, is only proper, given the difference in their ages. But I can assure you both were rightfully and deeply impressed."

"And yet, you say they were disappointed by what you told them?"

Frans had looked away toward the far shore where a boy was trying with little success to herd three tan and brown cows away from the water.

"They were, Johannes, both of them," Frans said as he watched the child-herdsman. "They were surprised. Surprised and disappointed, I have to say."

"I don't understand," Johannes admitted.

Frans continued to grip the pendant against his chest. "I am very happy that I met you in the market today and that we are making this journey together. Not only because I enjoy your company but because I need someone I can speak my mind to."

"Of course," Johannes said. It was his turn now to look away. The young herdsman was yelling and swatting at the cows with a switch, but the three animals continued to stand knee-deep in the river and drink eagerly from the flowing water.

"The work I have been called by God to do," Frans said, "is very difficult, as I am sure you can understand. The more so as I have advanced in my responsibilities. Now, of course, I know better, but I confess there was a period of several months where I was deeply troubled. I came to accept Frau Mueller's interpretation of these events: that the fears of the people were exaggerated, that the accusation of witchcraft was often a disguised grievance against other, lesser wrongs, that torture caused the innocent to confess falsely and to denounce others who were innocent as well."

"I see."

The boatmen had noticed the boy and his cows. They were whooping and laughing and shouting out advice to the hapless lad.

"Much of this I confessed to your sister, both in person and by letter," Frans continued. "I was deeply troubled and she comforted me. She was wonderful, I have to say. They both were, both Elsebett and Frau Mueller. Now, of course, as I said, being on the inside I know better the truth of the matter. And I had hoped that I could convince them of the rightness of our cause. I made this journey for that sole purpose because I care so deeply about your sister, and Frau Mueller."

"I am not surprised that you failed," Johannes said. "And you should not judge yourself harshly. Nothing you could have said would have persuaded Elsebett. She has developed a fanaticism on the subject. Last Sunday she became almost hysterical in defense of an old hag recently arrested. So adamant was she, that our father found it necessary to strike her. I was astounded. Never, in my life had I seen my father strike my sister."

Having revealed this bit of family gossip, Johannes felt vaguely sordid. He remembered the instructions his dying grandmother had given him: "Look after your sister," Oma had said. "Someday she will need you and you must always protect her."

"Well," Frans continued, "I became very uncomfortable in their presence, I have to say. Their reserve was obvious. And so, as I was preparing to leave, it suddenly occurred to me that the letters I had written to Elsebett...well, were they to reach the office of my superiors, they could greatly damage my career."

"Yes?"

"I am telling you this, my friend, only because I love both you and your sister. I trust you completely, and, of course, I trust her completely as well. But who could know where those letters might end up?"

"Yes, I understand."

"So, as I was leaving, I asked to have the letters returned to me."

"I see. And did she return them?"

"Yes," Frans said. "She immediately went to her room and brought them to me. But I think it broke her heart, I do."

The two young men looked away from each other. The boat was arriving at a bend in the river and the crew had to forget the boy and his cows. The man on the rudder stood legs apart, both of his huge hands pushing against the long handle to keep the boat from running aground while his partners stood along the side with long poles to push the hull away from the bank should it float too close. Up on the towpath the man driving the horse team yelled and snapped his whip. Soon, the boat had made the bend, and the boy and his three reluctant cows were no longer visible.

SIXTY-NINE

Johannes returned from the city and the Archbishop's men came back as well. Over the next few days, the young man was a minor celebrity in the village. Because of his connection with Frans he had been in a favorable position to witness up close the final hours of the convicted judge. He even heard the presiding judge pronounce the death sentence on the man who only shortly before had sat where his judge now sat, who had been known and admired or at least envied by most everyone in the city.

Johannes was often called upon to repeat the judge's words as best he could remember them: "'That the accused now standing in the presence of this court, by reason of his crime, in that he denied God, devoted himself to the Evil One, served him and sinned with him, dealt with witchcraft and did despite the common weal, wrought injury to grain and herb, shall be punished with fire from life onto death.'" At this point, Johannes always paused to let the words sink in before adding the judge's final comment: "'As we hereby doom, sentence and condemn him, we commend his soul to Almighty God and his mercy.'"

Then Johannes would tell his audience that a surprising thing happened: the convicted man fell to his knees and begged the judge for mercy. At that point the judge leaned forward and gave a special instruction to the executioner. Because of the man's long service and his esteemed position, the judge said, the witch "'should be mercifully and Christianly strangled, and his body burned to ashes.' Here was an act of mercy indeed," Johannes added, "a quick strangulation in lieu of a slow burning. So, that is how it happened. Justice was in the end tempered by mercy.

"I should add that the old witch insisted on walking himself to the stake, and before he was strangled he spoke to the crowd in a strong voice. He confessed his many wrongs and urged those of us gathered to not succumb as he had to the Devil's temptations."

"Was it the same executioner doing the work there, as was here?" a man wanted to know.

"The one and the same Showman," Johannes said with a smile. "Elegant, efficient, a master at his craft. And this, beyond doubt, was his greatest performance. The crowd as you might imagine was tremendous."

"Can you tell us how he strangled this witch?"

"A good question. And from the moment I heard the sentence announced, I, too, was wondering how this act would be accomplished. It turned out the executioner had devised a special apparatus for the purpose. It amounted to a stool with a board running up the back. The witch was made to sit on the stool with his back and head against the board. An iron ring was then fitted over his head and the board and placed against his throat. The executioner took a position behind the board. He placed a length of iron rod between the board and the ring, and holding the board in one hand he gave a strong pull on the rod which worked as a lever, thus forcing the ring against the witch's throat and strangling him."

"Most efficient," the man said, expressing his admiration.

"Not so efficient as you might think, or as the witch might have hoped," Johannes admitted after a moment's pause. "It is not easy to strangle a man, even an old one."

The truth was, and he had seen this clearly, the executioner had blundered on his first try. He must have failed to position the rod correctly to maximize the needed leverage; though he pulled with all his strength and caused the witch great pain, the initial effort did not kill him. From Johannes's vantage point it looked as though the old judge had actually turned his head to speak to the executioner, perhaps to explain that the effort was not working, and this turning further protected the windpipe and denied him the death. The executioner appeared flustered for a few moments. Moving about the platform in an uncharacteristically hurried and graceless manner, he repositioned the witch and the ring and reinserted the rod. Then on the second effort he ended the man's life. None of this did Johannes explain to those listening. It seemed to him somehow inappropriate to speak words that would lessen the executioner's reputation.

"No, not an easy task," Johannes concluded. "But the truth remains, the man is clearly a master of his cruel craft."

The other Archbishop's men were also masters of their various crafts. They took Frau Henn and the two other accused women from their cell. They moved them into the room where the torture rack waited, and there they quite literally pulled confessions out of them. The judge and prosecutor then demanded names and to aid the witches' memories, the special accuser was brought in. Perhaps Severin gave the same names to the three women that he had suggested to Frau Grede, perhaps others.

§

Frau Rachel Mueller, a midwife and a wise woman, knew now that this contagion would be the death of her. It felt inevitable and unavoidable, as certain as an evening sky portends the coming night. On her better days she grew very present on the one hand, and somewhat detached on the other. She became what she touched and smelled, tasted and saw: this unique door with its rough wood and flaking green tinge, the squeak of its leather hinges, the smoke escaping the room as the door opened, the warm interior's disorienting dark, the voice of the pregnant woman welcoming her. These sensations had distinct separateness, a precise clarity.

But other days her wild thoughts and broiling energies could not be controlled. They insisted she pre-experience the coming horror. Worst was that the accusations against her would drag Elsebett along. That and the shame she felt as she imagined herself standing before everyone she knew, and there bound to a stake, confess to sins and denounce those of others, sins which at that point she might actually believe she had committed, and fellow conspirators she might by then recognize as guilty as herself. Who could say? No one who had ever been there could report back. And suicide was clearly a mortal sin to be avoided at all costs.

One thing she did know: the ordeal would have to be experienced not as an ending, but as a passage through, a kind of prayer that turned her inward and forward rather than away. As Gretel lay dying she had whispered to Rachel: "It's an awakening."

Thoughts of Elsebett brought Rachel only grief and guilt. Her every effort to convince the young woman to flee, had failed. Elsebett seemed to have entered into an extended trance. She ate, she slept, she visited the sick and the newly born; they spoke to each other of practicalities in quiet, tenuous voices. Elsebett went to the Helgen home on Sundays where everyone, herself included, acted as though the confrontation with her father had never happened. She seldom laughed; she never spoke of Frans. Passing through the village, she walked in silence, her eyes on the ground before her.

They burned Frau Henn and the other two women on three successive days, three days of fire, smoke and death. The day following the third death, Frau Rachel Mueller was gifted with a premonition: this would be the day they came to arrest her. It was a sunny crisp morning in late September, the kind of day Elsebett would love to spend wandering outside of the village: a day to walk along the river, to be among the trees and in the meadow.

"Do you remember the wild plum I showed you?" Rachel asked her student as they were having their porridge. "The one set in that sunny spot high above the river?"

"Along the tributary? I do, yes. It is a plum tree that my father had taken me to, back when I was still a child. Those plums have always been his favorite."

"I should think its fruit will be at their prime about now. And I know your father would appreciate having a few of them."

Elsebett frowned, looking down at the table. She recognized the gesture of reconciliation Frau Mueller was proposing but she was not certain she was ready to make it.

"It would be a fine gift," Rachel continued. "Gather some for us as well, and perhaps a few for your aunt Anna. Yes, you should take some to her as well," she added, still hoping that Elsebett would choose to flee.

"Will you come?" Elsebett asked, brightening.

"No, I have other tasks," Rachel said absently. "But I think you should make a day of it. It is a trek, as you know. And you might find other items we could use. That wild rose, for example. And some water from the spring. Yes, take the handled jug with you."

Perhaps Elsebett sensed something as well at that moment because she asked: "You will be all right, Frau Mueller?"

"Of course," her teacher said, gathering up the bowls.

§

Elsebett had never lost the desire to venture out from the village. She thanked her teacher, placed a light kiss on her cheek, and quickly gathered the items she would need. The moment she left the village she felt an intense lightening of spirit. Out here no one was plotting the deaths of witches. No one required that she justify herself or lower her eyes with feigned modesty.

The fields, the trees, the river possessed no malice, assumed no authority; they welcomed her as she was.

Elsebett had come to acknowledge a characteristic of plants that as a child she had intuited but had never consciously recognized: plants possessed a sense of pride. The word vanity even occurred to her. Plants were vain, but it was an innocent, earnest vanity, not a superior or arrogant one. How proud some noble trees were! They saw themselves as guardians, protectors. But all trees wanted to be appreciated, especially in the spring when the delicate new leaves appeared and again now in the fall when they colored. They wanted her to pause and admire them. Vines and branches, too, struck poses that asked to be examined and appreciated.

Among some whitish stones she saw a cluster of daisies; their white petals and egg-yellow centers seemed to quaver with enthusiasm. "Look at me!" they cried as she approached. "Look, look at me!"

An exchange was happening; she gave and she got something back; it had a way of extending her beyond the borders of her skin.

Water spoke to her as well, but in a deeper less insistent way. Water spoke in sound and movement, in eddies and curlicues that caught the light and disappeared. She recognized that the river was aware of her presence but had no desire for her admiration. It spoke of strength and accommodation, evoking a sensation somewhere between comforting and thrilling.

To reach the plum tree required that she climb some distance beside the tributary that rushed down from the hill behind the village. The water tumbled and frothed as it emerged from the forbidden forest where wolves lurked and bears were said to prowl. But Elsebett was familiar with this lower, more open stretch. It was here cousin Agnes had shown them the magical fish-birds that walked beneath the water, only to resurface untouched and dry.

Frau Mueller had been right. It had been a good year for the plum. Elsebett found the ground beneath it littered with the blue oblong fruits and many remained accessible in the lower branches. Her teacher had reservations about the plum. As a tree it was more hot than cold. It had a prickly nature and invited anger. The bark could be used for some medical purposes, especially the ashes that remain after the bark had been burned. The seed also had some value, but the fruit itself Frau Mueller ate but sparingly. A healthy person, she said, could eat the plum in moderation, but a weak or ill person would be injured by it. But Elsebett's father had scoffed at this. His own father had shown him the tree when he was a boy and he had been eating its plums all his life. "They do no harm to a Helgen," he liked to say.

Her pouch was heavy and nearly full when she started back. At the spring she filled the jug with water. In a tree that had lost most of its leaves, she saw two balls of mistletoe. She walked for a few yards along a strip of newly sprouted rye. How green and even it was! How joyous, exuberant, potent.

At the edge of the meadow, in sight now of Frau Mueller's house, she located the rosebush her teacher had spoken of. It was bursting with large reddish rosehips. A few of these would delight her teacher. About rosehips Frau Mueller had no reservations. They were very hot, she claimed. They signified affection and could be used to treat lung problems.

When she had packed all the space remaining in her pouch, she saw an eagle come into sight above the river. It was just a speck high in the sky, soaring on motionless wings. So still it was, so filled with grace it seemed to be.

When the eagle had disappeared, Elsebett picked up the jug of water. She adjusted the strap on her shoulder and turned toward the village. Across the meadow she saw three men. They stood on the road not far from Frau Mueller's house, near the old wall where the fragrant fennel grew and mounds of straw lay moldering. From the cut of their clothing she recognized who they were. They were men come from the Archbishop. Seeing Elsebett, they began to walk toward her.

A MOTHER REMEMBERS

SEVENTY

he place they put them was dark and reeking. An ill-kept stable, that's what if felt like. No beds, no chairs, not even a chamber pot. Just a scattering of straw on the ground. You could not step into that room and not believe you were guilty of something. I would find the three of them kneeling on the straw, holding hands and praying aloud. That's the way I still remember them.

I was the only Helgen who went to see them. Well, I was a Helgen back then. And once a Helgen, always a Helgen, I suppose. Something my Oma might have said.

She never forgave them for not standing up for her: her father, her brother, that boy she fancied. But they never dared to deliver a crust of bread. Johannes did run to the city to beg help from the boy but nothing came of it. The palace life agreed with Frans and he was not about to raise a ringed finger to save a peasant girl. He's one turned burning flesh into gold, or so I've always heard.

Her father died before you were born so you never knew him. But he was your Opa's older brother. The Katharina that I said burned the day after, she was his second wife and her stepmother. With his daughter and his wife locked in there, you'd think he might have done something. But he thought it was a plot to get the Helgen holdings, and that paralyzed him. The poor man died just like his father, walking home from church. God must have said, "I've seen enough of you," and struck him down in the street a few days after their bodies burned.

She was the middle one. First Frau Mueller, then her, then her stepmother, a three-day festival of death. It is hard to describe now how terrorized we were. Four already dead and the three of them locked in that stinking room, the torture rack waiting next door, the village alive with rumors of more.

What you need to know is they put an end to it: she, her teacher and her step-mother. They brought it to a stop in this village anyhow. They confessed to being witches. They confessed and they denounced each other and the already dead: Frau Grede, Frau Henn and the other two. But no one else. Not another name. All three told the same story, you see, told it over and over, each one the same. And that ended it.

She went to the stake bitter and terrified, but she was not defeated. "I won't be dying out there, Irmele. Remember that. My body yes, but not me. Hold that in your heart. We are preparing ourselves. We won't be dying, we'll be waking up!"

On the day she died even the executioner cried. That is well known, and many who were there would tell you this. When he climbed the ladder with the torch, his face was wet with tears.

Your namesake was my best friend in the world. Even now I can say that, my very best. And I was hers, that's what she always told me. So, I went to see them most every day until the end. I took my cakes, and I helped any way I could. Going there was the best thing I ever did, the bravest thing and the best.

POSTSCRIPT

In the sixteen century—which is now referred to as the first century of the Early Modern Period—the German-speaking people were part of a loose confederation of independent principalities and territories known as the Holy Roman Empire. Each territory had its own ruler. That ruler was also an elector, or a member of the body that chose the emperor. The diocese of Trier was an independent territory within the empire; its borders spread well beyond the walls of the city itself. The territory was governed by an archbishop.

From 1581 until 1599 Johann von Schönenburg was the Archbishop of Trier; he reigned under the title Johann VII. He was a man of noble birth and great distinction who was deeply influenced by the Jesuits. Today, in the Cathedral in Trier, one can visit a burial monument erected in his honor. It was a time of unsettled weather, part of the larger period some historians refer to as the "little ice age." It was reported that during the eighteen years Schönenburg was archbishop the territory produced only two tolerable harvests.

Between 1581 and 1593 under Schönenburg's direction more than 300 people were convicted of witchcraft in the territory and consigned to the flames. Most were women, many poor and elderly, but many others were women and men of distinction, some of noble birth, including judges, canons, burgomasters and priests. In a couple of villages only one woman remained alive to witness the departure of the Archbishop's men.

As Rachel predicted, the contagion did come to an end. A commentator at the time wrote: "At last, though the flames were still unsated, the people grew impoverished, rules were made and enforced restricting the fees and costs of examinations and examiners, and suddenly, as when in war funds fail, the zeal of the persecutors died out."

§

A word of context. In January of 1570, the month and year I give for Elsebett's birth, William Shakespeare was five years old. His fellow countryman Thomas Tallis was sixty-five and composing beautiful sacred music. In Venice Titian was at least eighty-five and still painting masterpieces. In Rome, Miquel de Cervantes, being twenty-two years of age, and having been exiled from his native Castile, was working in the home of a cardinal; perhaps he was already beginning to imagine his Don Quixote. In France Michel de Montagne turned thirty-seven that February. Inheriting his father's estate, he withdrew from public life, retired to the tower and began to write the essays for which he is famous. Four months before Elsebett's birth, the painter Pieter Bruegel, the Elder, died in Brussels. If we look at his work today, we can watch his peasants spring back to life. In 1570 Martin Luther had been dead for twenty-four years, but his powerful voice continued to reverberate across Europe.

SOURCES

In the early 1990's when the internet was first becoming popular, an acquaintance told me that he thought the World-Wide-Web—as it was then known—represented the greatest outpouring of generosity in human history. Every day, he said, more and more of that which had been private and proprietary was becoming public and available. As a writer who has spent many hours searching through reference stacks, I can only be grateful.

For most every question, Wikipedia became my starting point, and I would encourage everyone who visits that site to drop those good folks a few dollars now and then. Beyond Wikipedia it is astounding what is available out there. I read a wonderful description of village life in early modern Germany along with other items made available through the University of Warwick. I found English translations of ordinances, decisions of village councils, articles about pigs and oxen, churching, dress, farming, plagues, magic, etc.

The confession of Professor Cornelius Loos is available online for all to see, though the manuscript Frans's superior reads from remained hidden for hundreds of years. Perhaps the discovery that most excited me was an 1891 article by Professor George L. Burr of Cornell University titled "The Fate of Dietrich Flade" which is available at Internet Archive. Professor Burr, who seems to have been fluent in Latin and German as well as English, had access to the transcript of Judge Flade's trial and execution as well as other contemporary documents including reports from the Jesuits in Trier. It is a beautifully written, wonderfully footnoted piece of work. (Small confession: For purposes of my story I had the professor confess before the judge was tried while historically the reverse was true.)

Also online, of course, are many images. A copperplate print depicting the City of Trier made in 1572 by Georg Braun and Frans Hogenberg can be seen on Wikimedia Commons. I honored the two gentlemen by borrowing the last name of one and the first name of the other. The paintings of Pieter Bruegel, the Elder can be seen at The Web Gallery of Art. Also online are numerous contemporary depictions of witches' sabbaths, burnings, torture devices etc.

Among books that have proven particularly helpful:

Priscilla Throop has translated Hildegard von Bingen's *PHYSICA* from Latin to English (Healing Arts Press 1998). The original was written in the 12th century. From this beautifully constructed and illustrated book, came many of Rachel's thoughts about plants and stones.

Steven Ozment's, *Magdalena and Balthasar: An Intimate Portrait of Life in 16th-Century Europe Revealed in the Letters of a Nuremberg Husband and Wife*. Yale University Press, 1989. Mr. Ozment has translated the 16th century letters of this couple and provides commentary on the times in which they lived. I have allowed Frans to borrow a number of phrases and descriptions from the letters the Paumgartners wrote to each other.

The Little Ice Age, by Brian Fagan (Basic Books 2001) is a great source of information not only about climate and weather but their effects on life and farming during those difficult years.

www.ingramcontent.com/pod-product-compliance
Lightning Source LLC
Chambersburg PA
CBHW070736120726
47910CB00001B/123

* 9 7 8 0 9 9 7 3 5 1 3 1 6 *